PRAISE FOR *CREATION*

"Govier has crafted a novel of ideas, inseparably layering the ecological and personal. Redeeming both is that most human commodity, hope."
National Post

"Govier artfully conjures a brilliantly insightful and ravishingly sensuous tale of adventure and longing, and portrays a seer of epic spirit who knows that his beloved feathered creatures and their wild environs are as imperiled as they are spectacular." *Booklist*

"[Govier] spins in *Creation* an elegiac, entrancing web of fiction that sprawls across time and continents, bringing to life a fascinating time, and portraying a driven, fame-seeking Audubon who'll stop at nothing to fulfill his dream."
The Hamilton Spectator

"In *Creation,* novelist Katherine Govier imagines one summer in the life of John James Audubon. And what an imagination—if the famed bird artist was even half the man Govier paints, he was remarkable indeed. . . . It's an enthralling read right from the start. . . . Fascinating . . . an adventure-filled tale of a visionary whose revelations on this Canadian journey foretold a future that held destruction and extinction." *The Daily News* (Halifax)

"Rare is the work that transforms a reader so completely they are able to envision flight and attend to the imagined variations in birdsong. But this is *Creation,* the stunning seventh novel of Alberta-born author Katherine Govier. . . . Govier examines themes of preservation, exploration, progress and extinction. Hers is a serious and contemplative look at a world that has already been lost to us—species once captured on canvas now and forever gone. The challenge to readers is potent; and it is the natural world, creation itself, that hangs in the balance." *The Edmonton Journal*

Also by Katherine Govier

The Truth Teller

Angel Walk

The Immaculate Conception Photography Gallery

Without a Guide

Hearts of Flame

Before and After

Between Men

Fables of Brunswick Avenue

Going Through the Motions

Random Descent

CREATION

A NOVEL

—

Katherine Govier

VINTAGE CANADA

VINTAGE CANADA EDITION, 2003
Copyright © 2002 Katherine Govier

Vintage Canada and colophon are registered trademarks
of Random House of Canada Limited.

www.randomhouse.ca

National Library of Canada Cataloguing in Publication

Govier, Katherine, 1948–
Creation : a novel / Katherine Govier.

ISBN 0-679-31182-3

I. Title.

PS8563.O875C74 2003   C813'.54   C2003-902077-0
PR9199.3.G657C74 2003

Cover Design: CS Richardson
Text Design: Daniel Cullen

Printed and bound in Canada

10 9 8 7 6 5 4 3 2 1

For R., E., and N.

CONTENTS

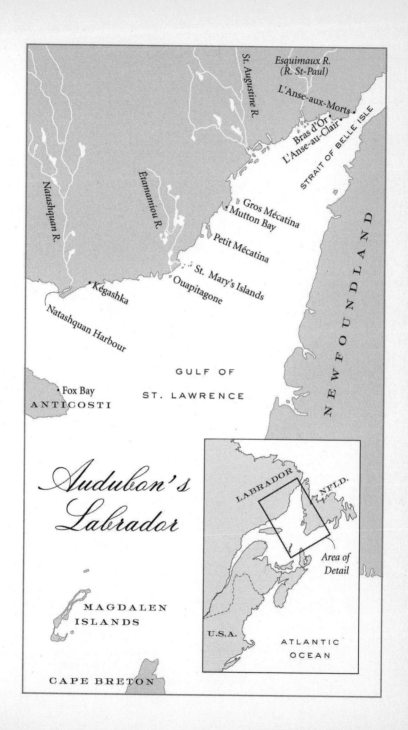

St. Augustine R.

Esquimaux R.
(R. St-Paul)

L'Anse-aux-Morts

Bras d'Or
L'Anse-au-Clair

STRAIT OF BELLE ISLE

Natashquan R.

Etamamiou R.

Gros Mécatina
Mutton Bay

Petit Mécatina

NEWFOUNDLAND

St. Mary's Islands
Ouapitagone

Kégashka

Natashquan Harbour

GULF OF
ST. LAWRENCE

Fox Bay
ANTICOSTI

*Audubon's
Labrador*

MAGDALEN
ISLANDS

CAPE BRETON

LABRADOR

NFLD.

Area of
Detail

U.S.A.

ATLANTIC
OCEAN

Goodbye
TO LAND

J ust suppose.

That it is a bright, cold May morning in the year 1833, and two men alight from the stagecoach in a little town on the Maine seacoast.

They are father and son, judging by their flowing chestnut locks, and aquiline features, by their matching one-handed swoop off the high step. The older man slings his gun over the shoulder of his fringed jacket; he must be a frontiersman, a hunter. But he has a certain vibrancy, as if his whole body were a violin freshly strung, and his deep, gentle eyes take everything in. The son, of more solid flesh, has a fine-looking pointer at his heels.

They send their luggage on and climb to a vantage point on the granite rocks of Eastport. There is birdsong: the Cardinal's whistle, the low warble of the Snow Bunting, the trill of the Pine Warbler. Side by side they look over Passamaquoddy Bay. Chunks of ice still float in the harbour among the muffin-shaped islands. They seem to listen to the air, to the wind; they scan the hills with eagle eyes, as if they might coax the spirits of the place out of hiding. At last, the father gestures below. They set off walking toward the harbour.

The schooner *Ripley* out of Baltimore is not there, but it will arrive any day, says the dray man they accost on the wharf. A certain gentleman has hired it for the season. He plans to sail west and north, around the tip of Nova Scotia, through the Cape of Canso and up into the Gulf of St. Lawrence, and from there up the wild north shore of Labrador where only the fishing boats go. He is a famous gentleman. That is to say the dray man himself has not heard of him, but the newspapers write about him.

What do they say, these newspapers? asks the older man.

Ah, they say that he is a great American and that we ought to be proud. He is a painter of birds. He is making a giant book that will have in it every bird in our land.

But that gentleman is me! exclaims the newcomer, and the three slap their knees and laugh.

THE TRAVELLERS HAVE come a month ahead of time. There is so much to do. The schooner, when it arrives, must be fitted with a wooden floor in the hold and a table nailed down for the artist to do his work. They find the captain.

Emery — spry, greying, moustached — invites them into his clapboard house at the edge of town. From the parlour he can look over the harbour. With the brass spyglass that sits on the mantle, he scans the port. He has been on the seas most of his life and was once captured by Spanish pirates off Puerto Rico. He eats tobacco as another man might eat a handful of nuts. He will hire the crew. There is a pilot from Newfoundland he knows, and a local boy, Coolidge, good on the water.

In the market, father and son and the three young gentlemen who have joined them from Boston buy oilskin jackets and trousers and white woollen toques with an oilskin awning that hangs down the back to keep the rain from sliding down their necks. They cavort in their outfits and flirt with the ladies who sell knitted goods. By the time a week has passed, they have charmed nearly everyone in town.

The gentlemen roar with laughter over their dinners in the public house. The artist has forsworn grog and snuff, but it does nothing to diminish his fun. He pulls out his flute and plays an air; his son plays fiddle, and the young gentlemen all sing and pull the barmaids from behind the counter to waltz around the room. Sometimes the artist takes out a piece of paper from his waistcoat and scribbles figures: *victualled for five months, $350 each month*. He checks his multiplication. He writes, *potatoes, rice, beans, beef, pork, butter, cheese*. Other times he falls silent and gazes, abstracted, at a wall. He goes to the harbour, under the moonlight, and looks to see if the ice is all gone.

His name — the name the world knows, two centuries later — is John James Audubon. He is here, with his great hopes and his desires and his premonitions of doom, preparing for his mid-life voyage. He is halfway through his masterpiece: a catalogue of every bird in North America, represented the same size as in life, and observed by him in nature. It has taken seven years thus far, and will take him six more to finish. He has done this without patrons, selling subscriptions to the book himself, collecting the dues, finding birds in the wild and sending his paintings across the sea to London to be engraved and printed, and then hand-painted.

The great man is as generous with his words as he is with his colours. He tells his stories in many places and in many different ways. He will leave, aside from his great book of pictures and the volumes of words that accompany it, his journals, and many letters.

In fact, in a life so well documented, these next few months form a rare gap. It is as if the dark cloud and fog he sails into transcend mere weather and become a state of mind. As if Labrador itself (or its weather) swallows the story. Strange.

Is it because he goes north and off the map?

Because he leaves the sacred ground of his own country and journeys to the least known part of the little-known continent?

Or is it because something happened there, an adventure so grisly the artist had no words to describe it? That he wrote about it and afterwards had second thoughts and destroyed his words?

Or — here we get to the nub of it — is there another reason, a reason to do with his human attachments? Those he loves and especially those who love him. With desire, possession, betrayal, the women and the children he leaves on shore? A reason rising out of old passions or new intimations? Has what happened on this voyage been ripped from the record because someone did not want history to know?

We do know, sitting as we do in their future, that the great man's son, young Johnny, the one so quick to learn the masts and ropes from the Yankee sailors, will have a wife a few years hence and that this wife will have a child. And that eventually, when the artist and his wife, and all their children are dead, this granddaughter, Maria, will come into possession of his letters and diaries. She will appoint herself keeper of secrets and protector of reputations. And what she reads about her famous grandfather's life, and particularly this summer of 1833, will displease her. She will excise huge portions of the journals. She will publish the bowdlerized version and destroy the original. Letters will be lost, burned, turned into dust.

Hence this hole, this gap.

A gap is an opening, a window, an opportunity.

JUST SUPPOSE WE CAN STEP IN. Let that gap become our present. Knowing future and past, we can live there suspended, masters in our little world of the now. The moment is our only dwelling and we create it with our own understanding. Audubon is a man but more than a man; he is a character, and as a character he becomes a vessel to fill with our imagination. This is, after all, how we understand the world, by investing ourselves in a creature moving through it. It is how he understands birds as well, with that intense subjectivity and identification that endures in his work.

Facts are deceiving. We may know them, but never all of them. Only the bits and pieces that survive the voyage. In real life, the story is never finished. Discoveries may be made to shed light on it; for instance, in some attic, some cellar, the lost pages of the diary may be discovered — Maria may have repented of her decision to destroy them.

Fiction is another story. We can be sure of it, for we make it up; it is complete and finished. We can embrace it, because it is what we know.

EVERY DAY THERE ARE letters in the mail at the hotel. It is by letter that he keeps himself tied to the world. Lucy admonishes him: "Do not sit in wet clothes. Watch out for Johnny. You know he is too wild."

The day before departure, he writes back to everyone.

"There are no post offices in the wilderness before me," he writes

Havell, his engraver in London. He writes to his older son, Victor, also in London, that in his absence, Victor must be vigilant to see that work continues, and subscriptions come in.

He writes to Lucy: "dearest best beloved Friend my own love and true consoler in every adversity. . . . the most agonizing day I ever felt —"

NOW IT IS THE VERY DAY: June 6. A festive atmosphere has taken hold of the town. The tailor, the publican and the knitting women, in fact most of the population of Eastport, have downed tools and filtered to the docks to see off the schooner and its crew. The Stars and Stripes are snapping in the wind. Girls in freshly ironed frocks present little baskets of warm bread, and their brothers run up and down the rocky incline of the shore in excitement. The battery of the garrison fires four reports. The cannon on the revenue cutter salutes. The shots echo from the cliffs.

On deck and holding the mast, John James Audubon lets the wind run through his hair. He has such hopes for this journey; will they be fulfilled? The birds — will they show themselves to him? He hopes to find new species, big ones to fill his pages, thirty inches wide by forty inches tall. Such ideas he has: winged creatures, huge and splendidly feathered. It will be a royal court of birds there; it will be the nursery of the entire world of water birds.

The anchor is shipped. The sails are set. The schooner moves gently out of the harbour. The boats that have rowed out to it turn back to the shore. The crowds on the wharf cheer. Then, all but the most loyal turn their backs, roll up their pennants and go about their business.

But not us. We can go with him to sea.

⁓

AND JUST SUPPOSE THAT ANOTHER MAN, in another port, is saying goodbye to land. Captain Henry Wolsey Bayfield is not famous, although as the highest ranking naval officer at the Quebec garrison, he is respected by all the British officers and French *noblesse*. He dines at the *table d'hôte* in the finest hotels, where the officer on his left may have a tattoo on his neck from his time living in Tahiti with the mutineers of the *Bounty*, and the lady on his right may be an opera singer from New York. He is such a favourite of the governor general's wife that he has to limit his acceptances to two a week because the parties interfere with his work.

Still, there is no one to bid farewell.

He does not mind. He does not like fanfare. He ducks into the little mariners' church at dockside, bows his head and prays. He recognizes, for an instant, that he is apprehensive, and then lets himself sink into the words of prayer he has known since before he could even say them.

On deck of the schooner *Gulnare,* he greets Lieutenant Augustus Bowen and Dr. Kelly, the navy surgeon he has requested for the voyage, because many accidents can befall a complement of thirty-four men chopping trees, dropping lead and scouting in wild water. He inspects the men and is not terribly pleased. This year it was harder than usual to ship them. Sailors are always in debt, and their creditors will not let them go until they pay. He was forced to give them a month's wages in advance. They got drunk and barely boarded on time. He and Kelly together inspect the chronometers, theodolite, sextants and sounding machine, and find all in order; he has already done this a dozen times.

He goes below into his cabin to enter the departure in the log. Neatly, he writes: "June 4, 1833. Departed Quebec seven hours, south east wind clear skies."

PAST THE ÎLE D'ORLÉANS. Past the Île-aux-Cordes.

He avoids the south channel and the lesser-known channel on the north side, and takes the middle, which was his own discovery.

Past the mouth of the Saguenay, where the water is half brine, half fresh, and hovers at the freezing point.

He can taste the salt in the air. The schooner leaps to the wind and it is like his own body. The cramped hours at the desk in the snow-bound garrison fall away. The smoky dinner tables and the forced conversations about the price of timber fall away, and the ladies with their fans fade out.

He feels the change coming over him as the river widens, and they face the immense force of the ocean. He is a man like the moon, with

SAILING DIRECTIONS

FOR THE

GULF AND RIVER

OF

ST. LAWRENCE;

BY

HENRY WOLSEY BAYFIELD,

CAPTAIN ROYAL NAVY, F.R.A.S.

BEING THE RESULT OF A SURVEY MADE BY ORDER OF THE
LORDS COMMISSIONERS OF THE ADMIRALTY.

LONDON:
PRINTED FOR THE HYDROGRAPHIC OFFICE.
MDCCCXXXVII.

*"He avoids the south channel and the
lesser-known channel on the north side, and takes
the middle, which was his own discovery."*

one side visible and the other hidden. Now, as always at this time of year, he enters the bright side of his year and the other half of himself. Every day is longer; the light continuing past twenty hours, twenty-one and twenty-two.

It is a stormy passage as they move toward the warmer but foggy waters of the Gulf, past Rimouski where he began this chart-making four years ago, and over the lip of the Gaspé. It is a relief to reach the little, low-lying Mingans: here, Bayfield permits himself an afternoon of dalliance.

The sea is calm and the sun is brilliant. These little islands, not far off the coast of the north shore of the Gulf, are of a peculiar limestone quite separate from that of the mainland. The shores have been pounded, worn to a fantasy of shapes. They are a little Egypt with their soft stone figures standing like bottles and whistling as the air moves through and around them. Standing trees that have died and dried in the sea wind rattle like white china. Even in rigor mortis, nothing has broken them.

THE IMMENSITY AND THE SHEER STRANGENESS of this place never fails to astonish him. The way it can become, suddenly, one mass of rock and water and sky, one colour, and one deadly hazard to sailing. The opposite mood can strike: sun exploding out of cloud, water turning to turquoise and lichen to flame.

And this is only the beginning.

From here he goes north and east, farther yet from home, to more desolate shores, colder and deeper. He goes to one of the last places on earth to fall under man's measurement, where only the whales, the birds and the codfish abound. He is the messenger of the future.

The *Gulnare* heads up the coast. The men cannot sleep, it is so rough. "We have no room to hang in cots or hammocks and therefore tossed about in standing bedplaces," he writes in his *Surveying Journals.*

～

THE *RIPLEY* ROUNDS THE SOUTHEAST COAST of Nova Scotia in a fresh northeast wind. She sails past Lower Argyle, a poor and inhospitable place, Audubon writes in his journal. Twenty miles offshore are Mud and Seal islands. They anchor and go ashore. Mud Island has spruce trees, purple iris, yellow silverweed and clotted mossy hummocks where gulls' eggs and chicks are tucked everywhere you would want to step.

From here they sail east to the Strait of Canso "in a horrid sea," he writes. On June 11, the weather clears and they sail through the strait with twenty other vessels, all fishing boats bound for Labrador. They pass Indians in a bark canoe. They pass Cape Porcupine, a high, round hill, and proceed northward up the western coast of Cape Breton. They land on Jestico Island and wander aimlessly for hours among swallowtail butterflies, picking wild strawberries. They are so tiny, so irresistibly sweet and pungent that it is impossible to build up even a handful. They pick and eat, pick and eat, with fingers stained red. They hate to tear themselves away but they do, as the wind sets fair for crossing the Gulf.

Flight

He has never seen this particular tern before. It is delicate, quick-silver, with lovely red feet and a sharp, curved red beak. It dives headlong, scoops up little fish from the sea, and then soars, playing the air as a fiddler plays his strings.

Earthbound, he walks the shore on a clean sand beach while others of his party climb to the top of the cliffs to see what lies ahead of them on the horizon to the north and west. The sand is sleek, the water falling over itself in clear, transparent folds at his feet. A piping plover runs and flies before him, chirping in mellow notes. The unfamiliar terns dip and soar overhead. There are dozens and dozens of them.

He wants to possess one.

He asks the boy to load the gun with mustard seed. When the boy hands the gun to him he takes aim and shoots into the diving, soaring congregation. Birds come whirling down, like seedpods out of a maple tree. He walks into the water, picks up a few and slings them into the leather bag over his shoulder. He is sorry to see the birds stilled, to see their flashing wings droop and carmine beaks slacken. They are never so beautiful, after. He notices that as a bird catches the bullet and begins to plummet, those near it also collapse. Like kites whose strings have snapped, these sympathetic others drop through the air as if stricken, coming alive only at the last possible second to rise up and away as the corpse of their fellow splashes into the water.

He ponders the sympathetic way the uninjured birds fell with the ones who were hit.

He has never seen this behaviour before. He wonders: are the mimic terns just playing? Are they so confused by the shot they think themselves hit as well? Or are they hoping to distract the predator? They might feel a creature loyalty to the fallen, much as one would expect to see in humans. It is not impossible. He has seen birds behave in ways he would be flattered to think of as human.

But perhaps it is merely the spring season tying them so fiercely to their chosen mate.

He tries an experiment. He shoots another tern and allows it to lie dead on the water. He retreats and watches as another, whom he takes to be its mate, lands beside it, and begins to caress it.

Does the bird imagine its mate is still alive? Or does he hope that his attentions will bring her back to life? It is an interesting question. He will mention it in his notes tonight.

He walks on as the uninjured terns escape along the beach. The frigid breeze off the water chills him and he beats himself about the ribs with his cold hands.

To fly.

To ride the air.

To be without heaviness, to have air in the middle of one's bones. To turn and roll and dive in the sky.

To see from above.

HE PAINTS THE ARCTIC TERN head down as it plunges. Like a white letter, a hieroglyph on blue sky. The crimson beak open, the crimson feet spread on either side of the split tail. Head down, as he saw it both diving and dying. Or feigning death, pretending to slip from its element, as if air itself had opened a passage downward.

He paints the bird that way. At first there was a background, perhaps the brooding plateau of Labrador in the distance. Sometime later, whether on this journey or after, he cuts the bird out of its background and pastes it on a painting of sky. That is how the bird seems, as if it were pasted on air. As if it has come from some other world altogether and only paused here before returning.

NAME

The Bird Rocks bear from each other NNW 1/2 W and SSE 1/2 E
and are 700 fathoms apart. Sunken rocks leave only a boat passage
between them. The south eastern-most is the largest and highest,
though scarcely 200 fathoms long, and not more than 140 feet above
the sea. The other is divided into two precipitous mounds joined
together by a low ledge. The lesser of these mounds resembles a
tower ... The two rocks are of coarse red sandstone, or conglomerate,
in strata dipping very slightly to the South West and are constantly
diminishing in size from the action of the sea. They present perpen-
dicular cliffs on every side; yet it is possible to ascend them, with great
difficulty, in one or two places, but there is no landing upon them
excepting in the calmest sea.

— *Sailing Directions for the Gulf and River of St. Lawrence,*
Henry Wolsey Bayfield, Captain, Royal Navy

He scans the northern horizon until he sees it: the rock with its
flat projecting shelves, the sea stack beside it, all white. The air
is so cold he assumes that the rock is covered with snow.

"No," says Godwin, the pilot. "That's birds. Like I told you."

He rubs his temples and looks again. The air over the rock seems to dim and the light to fade although it is midday. His eyes are failing. It is a fear, chief among many. He raises a fist and rubs one eye with it, like a boy.

He takes out his spyglass. The massive rock is crawling, heaving, white with birds. Thickly covered and veiled by multitudes, the rock is a living stone thrust up out of water to meet a cloud all its own.

He has seen multitudes before. Twenty years ago, he witnessed the flight of one billion passenger pigeons eclipse the sun for three full days. At New Orleans he watched while in a matter of hours two hundred market hunters shot fifty thousand migrating golden plovers. Multitudes, yet here are more.

He cries out. "Birds, birds. So many I cannot tell it. So many it is not to be believed!"

He has come with foreboding in his heart, parted from his wife with premonitions that he might never again clasp her to his chest. He hates the sea. In all his crossings, and there have been many, he has despised the tossing, the sickening depths, and the weight of deadly water, the transit over its uncertain surface. He would prefer flight, but men cannot fly.

"Wind's picking up fierce," says Godwin. It shakes the mast.

They are within a quarter-mile of the rocks. He sees them clearly now, through his spyglass. The two rocks are red sandstone, worn by waves to the smoothness of a fortress wall, rising straight up from the sea. The higher one is perhaps 150 feet, and the lower a little less; a line of breakers shows only a narrow passage in which to approach them.

He can see that the greyness of the air is caused by a torrent of birds, flying in a magnificent airborne mantle that stretches and thins, shrinks and darkens at will, as the birds which compose its every thread move through the air. It flutters as if blown alternately from above and below, so that here in this corner it shoots skyward and there it falls as if to drape the rock, and then divides in the centre, wafting low over the water. The birds are white with black pinions.

"Gannets!" He shouts again from sheer joy and skids across the deck for a better look. It is true, then. Birds in uncountable numbers are here. The perilous journey he is undertaking, where no one has ever come before to see the birds, will be worthwhile.

Lucy will see, if she ever doubted it, how right she was to support his dream. Lucy. He loves her so much when he is apart from her.

A FEW HUNDRED YARDS OFF THE ROCKS, gannets pinwheel overhead. The sky blackens further, the wind tosses the water up into spray, and the *Ripley* pitches sickeningly. He grips the mast, hangs on, rides as if he can tame the water. He and the young gentlemen stagger on the pitching deck as they step into their fishermen's boots, the soles of which are studded with nails so they can stand on seaweed-covered rocks.

"I can't land her," shouts Godwin into the tearing wind. "Can't even get close!"

"But you must! We've come all this way."

"Can't be done."

The pilot is a simple man; he attempts a simple command. "Land her! It is *imbécile* to be here and not land."

Godwin jerks his head at Captain Emery. "I can't put her in."

Emery, hired with his schooner, tugs first the right, then the left branch of his moustache. He is caught between two stubborn men. He does not wish to disappoint the painter. But he can't risk the ship.

"That pilot is an ignorant oaf," shouts the bird fancier, into the wind and so that his words are carried away from Godwin.

"I can go, Father," says John Woodhouse. "Tom Lincoln and I will do it. Let us go out in the whaleboat."

Johnny. The wild one. The one who he is meant to tame. Johnny and Tom are the strongest of the young gentlemen he has brought along to help him, his son and the sons of his friends Shattuck, Ingalls and Lincoln.

"We can."

Let him.

WITH THE WIND TEARING at the canvas, the *Ripley* furls her sails and lays to. Four sailors put down the little whaleboat. With Johnny and Tom they row around the northern point of the first Bird Rock in the driving rain, their boat heaving up, then nosing down on the crests of seawater. They disappear. Now the artist stands in the centre of the squall, braced on deck with his rain-spattered spyglass. Between sheets of rain, he can see the gannet nursery: the tall nests run north and south in rows, as straight as if they had been planted. He can imagine the eggs, one in each hollow, carefully guarded. He is bitterly disappointed not to be in the landing party, but to have his son there is almost as good.

"Have they landed?"

"They'll not land. Nobody lands here," says Godwin. "Not in weather like this. Nobody excepting the Eggers. And they're desperate men. Them you wouldn't want to see."

"Wouldn't I?" he says, talking to pass the time.

Godwin, stocky and taciturn, horks and spits before turning his head to give his employer a sour grin.

The artist is beginning to suspect he will dislike this pilot; two weeks' acquaintance has not given him warm feelings.

They stand, as the deck rises and drops beneath them, adjusting their weight and balance without remarking that they do so, watching for a sign of the little whaleboat at the foot of the Rocks. Watching for human figures on its steep red bird-spattered sides.

An hour passes. The man who came to see the birds stands on, now by himself, now with the pilot near him. The sky goes blacker and the sea becomes wilder. No young gentlemen appear on the rock. No whaleboat returns. His heart throbs in the base of his throat. His eyes burn. Feeling like an old man although an hour ago he felt in the bloom of youth — but that is what it is to be forty-eight — he stands sentinel with his glass until at last, as if he has willed it, the little boat appears around the point of the rock. The four sailors heave their weight back against the oars. They can barely move the barque through the water. John Woodhouse leans on a long oar at the front, with Tom Lincoln bailing and losing against the surf that flies over the gunwales. They are visible and then, in an instant, erased.

His son might be lost. Might, right before his eyes, be swept into the furious cold water to his death, so far from home. Might leave him to desolation and no doubt the failure of his life's work, along with the outrage of his wife. He and Lucy have lost two daughters already, a loss which has somehow been his fault, if only because he failed to make a good life for them.

The whaleboat makes progress, pulling ahead by what looks to him to be mere inches, while the wind and water thrust it back. After what must be an hour they are near enough. Godwin throws down a rope; the whaleboat is drawn in and up. Gasping for breath, faces whipped half white, half red, John and Tom clamber on board, with full baskets and a burlap bag that heaves and squawks.

BELOW DECKS, wrapped in rugs, Tom and John drink tea. Young John cups his hands around his steaming mug. Sweat drips off his forehead while his teeth chatter with cold. The father, worn out with the fear of losing him, watches his son warily. A man of twenty-one, Johnny has inherited his olive skin, brown eyes and chestnut hair from his father, but his stalwart courage must come from Lucy, that slightly-mad composure of the British under duress. He has enjoyed the risk, this wild one, this whippet. Johnny, who runs through the bogs, climbs the cliffs, captures the specimens, skins them. He shoots with a perfect aim, like his father. He is becoming an excellent painter. He sees the thing itself, sees through the surface.

"Tell me, son. I can see it as you speak."

Johnny gives his witness, while Tom is silent, nodding. "Father, they plummet from one hundred feet above your head. When they hit the water they're like cannonballs. Dropping all around the boat as you approach.

"As you come closer you smell them. You want to do anything but breathe it in, even in the sea wind. And there is an immense, rhythmic squawking filling the sky. There are birds moving every-where your eye lights; it's like an army massing. The nests are orderly in themselves. But the birds are raucous! We saw pairs together, one bird sitting on the nest, the other defending. They squawk and squabble and sometimes one takes to the air, only to return in half a minute. We would have fallen over laughing if we hadn't been so busy trying to stay upright.

"There is only one way to climb up but Tom and I found it. The birds occupy the rock in a hierarchy — lowest down are the guillemots, then the razorbills, and higher still the kittiwakes. The gannets are on top, the kings, and they lord it over the others, making such a din. We made our way almost to them. They are comical as they begin to worry — they jab their bills at the others' head; sometimes two will lock bills and each try to push the other off the edge. But they're also loving. They seem constantly to know where their mate is. I saw, when the one bird is sitting on the nest, and the other of the pair in the air, the sitting bird pointing skyward with her bill to call him back down."

"Aaaah," says his father. "Yes."

"The sailors were hollering for us to get back before the boat smashed on the rocks. I shot two pairs, both mature and young. On top of that we got half a dozen of the birds alive."

"You're a good boy," says his father. "And a great help to me."

"Look," says Johnny, reaching under the blanket into his pocket. "I brought you an egg too."

BY NIGHTFALL THE SQUALL is behind them and *Ripley* is on its way to the north shore of the Gulf of St. Lawrence and Labrador. The artist takes a turn on the deck, wrapping his buffalo robe around his shoulders to warm him as if it were love. He cups the gannet egg in his right hand. He turns the egg and taps the shell lightly with the tip of his forefinger, then places it against his cheek. He adores its oval smoothness, its weight, its hardness; above all, the way it takes warmth from his hand, and the sense he has that life is forming inside it.

The *Ripley* hides in the small bay of an island, beyond the reach of the surging water, inside a set of shoals. The sky is vast, reaching around the schooner in all directions, cradling it in its cold arm. The wind is foul, the fog malicious, the rocks studded beneath the waves like waiting tombstones. Clouds obscure the moon. And yet the night is white, somehow, padded, even benign. The nests are out there, the eggs tucked inside, emitting their strange light, visible perhaps only to him. There are millions and millions of laying birds, countless eggs — oval and marbled, or pure white dotted with red, eggs hidden on sea stacks, cliffs, in crevices and reeds of this immense nesting ground — a veritable Milky Way of egg-light.

He holds his gift from Johnny tighter, encircling it with his fingers. He wishes on it. That they all should return safely. That he should complete his master work. He has been a failure at everything else.

He fears, always, the bailiff who pursues him, the critics who have set out to ruin him and even the crowds who hail him, for it is them, more than anyone else, he has fooled. He fears losing his wits. Perhaps because he has lived so hard by them he senses their revenge coming on. He fears the loss of his eyesight. The loss of the strength in his legs. He prays to the god he scarcely believes in that his wits, his vision and his legs last a little longer. He has nothing else to lose, nothing of value in this world, save Lucy and the boys. He must finish.

He wishes that the Work will bring him wealth enough to provide for his family, and the respect of all those who have scorned him. Wishes that he, John James Audubon, will be known as the greatest living bird artist.

IT IS A SIMPLE THING, A NAME. We are given one, we grow into it, we bear it. Simple for the rest of creation, but not for him. He gives a name to each new bird he finds, but he hasn't one of his own, not a true name.

He has, instead, many names. Jean Rabin. Monsieur Newhouse. Jean Jacques. Fougère. John James.

To have many names is in fact to have none.

To seek a home is to be adrift.

To attempt great things is to be ridiculed.

To love one's country is to invite contempt.

A raucous voice rises, *crack, crack*, from the corner of the deck. It is the young raven he picked up in the Magdalen Islands. He has clipped its wings and decided that he will teach it to talk; ravens are said to have powers of divination. He has called the bird Anonyme after a French cousin he dislikes, but in fact he has begun to enjoy its company.

"Anonyme," he says. "Join me."

The bird, barely fledged, does not move. Audubon finds a seat on a barrel and takes the bird on his wrist. It is surprisingly heavy. The claws are long and hard as glass and threaten to puncture his skin. He strokes the raven's head. This tender act quiets the bird, as it quiets the man. He pictures the nesting gannet stretching her neck to call down her mate from the sky. They are loving to their mates, Johnny said. They caress each other's napes. It is strange that a tale of nesting birds can make him lonely.

The sailors are teaching the young gentlemen a shanty, the words floating back to him from the forecastle. Johnny's voice, braver and sweeter, rises above the others.

> *One night as we were sailing, we were off land a way*
> *I never shall forget it until my dying day —*
> *It was in our grand dog watches I felt a chilly dread*
> *Come over me as though I heard one calling from the dead.*

Godwin issues forth from a shadow, smoking. The pilot is a Newfoundlander. This had seemed a good thing back in Maine; the *Ripley* would be piloted by a man who knew the waters. Now Audubon is not so certain.

There is a silence as both men look out to sea. Anonyme pecks restlessly at the fold of skin between Audubon's thumb and forefinger.

"If you look long enough into the water," says Godwin suddenly, "you can see there's light down there."

"Not here. There's rocks. Maybe over a sand bottom you'd see light."

"Aye, here too."

"I doubt it. Where would the light come from?"

"Comes from below."

"And what gives off this light, pray tell?"

Godwin scowls, wary of being patronized. "Why, the living things that's there, I suppose."

The idea strikes a chord. Audubon has a private theory that the down on herons' bodies actually glows, allowing the birds to catch their prey in the dark. He has visions of night marshes illumined by the phosphorescent tails of herons. It is one of many scientific notions he has not had time to explore. Why shouldn't life at the bottom of the sea be like the life in the air itself, producing light?

He does not confide this to Godwin. "Do you know the eastern seaboard?" he asks.

"Clear down to New Orleans. I worked there once."

"I might have met you, then, when I embarked on the *Delos* for England?"

"Not in the port. I was a bodyguard then, for a man named Nolte."

"Vincent Nolte? The cotton merchant?"

"Is there any other? Cotton, to start. Then it was sugar, and then it was arms," says Godwin. "Used muskets. Bought them from the Prussians where they'd left them lying in the fields when they retreated in 1813. Sold them back to the French in '29, to fight off their own people. Most of 'em were useless. Some rough visitors he had."

Audubon steps away from Godwin, in the dark. It is bizarre that this pilot should bring up the name of Vincent Nolte. It strains even his credulity, he whose life has been shaped by chance encounters.

Of course it happens. This is the way life works in his adopted, his adored, country. People know people. Vincent Nolte more than most. He made a great fortune and lost it, and the last Audubon heard of him, he was on his way to making another.

There may be few roads in America but there is a skein of names connecting men to men. The high rub shoulders with the low. The famous make their way through crowds and wilderness alike, to fetch up at humble homesteads. Only this year Daniel Webster brought him a brace of ducks to be painted. He and Lucy encountered the great General Clark, who with Meriweather Lewis were the first Americans to make the crossing west to the Pacific, resting in his wheelchair on his sister's estate near Louisville. George Keats, brother of the poet John, came to Kentucky with money to invest — but Audubon does not like to think of it: Keats is another man whose debt he is in. Why, Lucy herself has links to the English intelligentsia; her family doctor in England was Erasmus, the grandfather of Charles Darwin the scientist. Everyone of significance has connections, and some people of no significance have them, and some, like himself, invent them.

He tells himself there should be no difficulty tonight, on shipboard, in an old acquaintance conjured. Yet he feels cornered and it seems as if the cold sinks deeper into his spine.

"We're a long way north of New Orleans. I do not know this Gulf. But you do, then."

"Aye. The Gulf, the Grand Banks, and all the way down north to the Labrador."

"Down north?"

"Down north. Up south. It's how we say it here. They say it's on account of the maps the Portugee had when they first come for the cod. They say north down's the way the ancients drew their maps. Or maybe not. Maybe it was just upside down."

Godwin moves away and is gone into darkness.

This is not inspiring Audubon's confidence.

THE MOONLIGHT DISAPPEARS and the night goes on and on, black and blacker. The singing is over. The sea briefly gives back a star's beam, and slops against the sides of the schooner. The mast creaks. The damp salt smell rises into his nostrils. It is quiet.

The bird's eye is open. Audubon's eyes are shut. He puts his thumb under the bird's neck and his forefinger on its crown, and strokes its feathers. It responds by cawing and jumping off his hand. Gone.

"Goodnight, Anonyme," he says.

He wants to sleep. But first he must speak to Lucy. He speaks to her each night before bed. He has done this in Edinburgh and Liverpool, in the Florida Everglades, wherever he has travelled. He will do it in Labrador as well. He speaks aloud as is his habit, and only the raven and the tar on the nightwatch hear.

"Lucy," he says. "My dearest friend and one true companion, my heart's solace, it is cold and I am afraid. Were I a bird I could escape this place and come to you. Instead I stretch my arms to reach you in the dark. But no. The *Ripley* is hundreds of miles from you, from anywhere. And I must tell you a strange thing: our pilot was a bodyguard for Nolte —"

The ship turns at her anchor. The stars reel in and out of cloud. The rocks, when struck by a bit of moonlight, glistern. There is a scuffle down below as the young gentlemen tumble into their hammocks. The mast creaks, and the ropes rub against the timbers. He will sleep on deck.

"Anonyme?"

A caw from a coil of ropes gives his whereabouts. Audubon gets to his feet, wrapped in his buffalo robe, and looks from shore to islands and back. Earth here looks as treacherous as water. When they want to go on shore, how will they walk?

Will he die here?

No. He cannot.

If he dies, would the Work then be completed by his helpers, his family — his rivals, even? No, he must finish.

On the northern horizon, he notices a great swipe of shimmering pale green, a curtain that seems almost to hum.

Is it some enormous migration of birds? He hugs the robe around his shoulders. Dear God, is it the future, written in wings? Can he read it? It is not so strange a thing, to read the future in what your eyes take in.

HE CAME TO LABRADOR ALMOST YOUNG. He will leave almost old.

He arrived here quite sane. When he leaves, madness will have taken root. He will live another decade and a half, at the end of which he will sit slack-jawed in his chair, a great man but still a poor man, and he will not know his own son.

He came here a hunter and a singer of birds and he will leave here a mourner of birds.

He came to Labrador an honest husband who loves his wife and two sons, though not above all, and he will leave — but this part is unknown. A blank. A darkness. The shining green curtain, as astonishing as the landscape out of which it sprang, is gone.

The
GULF

He wakes on the deck well before dawn, at three a.m. Usually he is ready for breakfast but today he awakes with a sense of injury; *mal de mer* has seized him although the sea is quiet. The air temperature is forty-three degrees.

He drags himself down to his berth and calls the captain. He reminds himself that Emery is a Yankee; Audubon believes the Yankees to be fine sailors.

"It was a tragedy we could not land on the Bird Rocks," Audubon begins.

Emery has already quelled the fears of the crew about the weather, which is even more foul than normal in these parts. His square face shows not a flicker of emotion yet one knows him to be benign. His moustache is stained coppery from tobacco. His eyes meet the artist's for a few seconds and then he says, "You had the next best thing, your son."

Audubon is not mollified. "Godwin puts caution above finding birds."

"In matters of safety, I will bow to his experience," says Emery. "You won't find birds if we're wrecked."

"No! But you must understand. The birds are the reason we've come. And I must find them before my rivals do."

"I fully understand, sir," Emery says gamely. "Obsession drives many a sea voyage." Were it not for the moustache, you would see a wry twist to his mouth.

Audubon is not amused by this perspective, and Emery continues.

"The seriousness of your mission was much impressed on me. It isn't for every sailing of the *Ripley* that the whole town turns out with a gun salute to send us off!"

Audubon, although feeling ill, grasps Emery's wrist, "My competitors have seen my *Birds of America* and they are rushing into print with imitations. One John Gould, for example, who has an excellent lithographer as a wife. But Gould stays at home and draws the birds from specimens. There are others — Edward Lear . . . but I am the only one who observes the birds in the wild."

Audubon lets his grip relax as he twists with his nausea.

Gently, Emery withdraws his hand. "There was one man. An Alexander Wilson. We have his book in our home."

"Wilson? He's been dead twenty years. I met him once, entirely by chance."

Wilson had come into the store Audubon owned for a time in Louisville, Kentucky, and tried to sell him a subscription to his book. He was a wizened, long-faced man with a sad look, the look of a peddlar who expected to be beaten back from the door. Audubon stood behind the counter, turning the pages of Wilson's portfolio. His partner stuck his head over Audubon's shoulder and said, "Yours are better!"

They spent a day or two together; he helped Wilson find birds. And then — how does the saying go? no good deed goes unpunished. Wilson passed on stories about him to all the important bird people in America. So, many other American ornithologists became Audubon's implacable enemies. A man named Ord, in particular, had staked his reputation on the wandering Scot. When Audubon began his own work, Ord teamed up with the Englishman Waterton to attempt to destroy his reputation. This is the worm in Andubon's belly; it has been there for years, and is clearly not to be escaped.

"Wilson did travel, I'll give him that," he tells the captain. "But he never went to Labrador."

THE *RIPLEY* MAKES SLOW PROGRESS through the Gulf. The following day is warmer and still calm. The ship sits at anchor. Audubon works at his table in the hold, rubbing his hands every few minutes to keep them nimble, stamping his feet, straining his eyes to see without sunlight. The young gentlemen fish for cod, and Johnny catches one that weighs twenty-one pounds. The cook fries it in butter and they dine on it. At six p.m. the wind springs up fair and they at last make sail to the northeast. Audubon sleeps, his sickness passing.

The next morning before dawn the sea is covered with foolish guillemots playing in the spray of the bow, and the air is filled with velvet ducks, thousands of them flying from the northwest to the southeast. The wind continues all day, and at five o'clock Audubon hears the cry of land. They think they see a mass of sails, but discover on closer examination that it is snow on the banks of Labrador. They pass the mouth of a wide river.

"What is that river called?"

"Natashquan, " says Godwin. "It means 'where the seals land' in Indian."

"It looks a good place for birds."

"We can't anchor there. That's the British trading post. No American boats are allowed. We'll have to go on." Audubon watches the river retreat behind them.

They come to the harbour the Americans use, known as Little Natashquan. As the *Ripley* nears the anchorage, seals rise to the surface, putting their heads and necks up in the air, sniffing it, and them, and then sinking back. From his position on deck, Audubon spots two large boats with canoes lashed to the sides, sailed by Montagnais Indians, all in European dress save for their moccasins.

He hails them to ask about the birds. The men are good looking with clear red skin and they speak French. They say they cross inland every year where there is not a single tree; they have to carry their tent poles. They hunt, though fur animals are scarce. He asks them to bring him grouse.

At last the *Ripley* makes anchor. He cannot wait to go ashore. He jumps into the whaleboat with Johnny and rows. Once landed, he finds a land bewitched, full of pygmy trees and bushes, velvet moss in which he sinks to his knees and not a patch of earth. The moschettoes swarm him as if they had not seen a red-blooded creature for a hundred years. He swats, and bleeds, and swats more until he finds the birds.

At the sight of wild geese, dusky ducks, scoters and red-breasted mergansers, he forgets his discomfort.

He encounters a solitary settler, a French-Canadian, who serves him good coffee in a bowl. The coffee warms his stiff and aching hands, as they sit inside his one-room log cabin.

"This land is a species of Eden," says the settler, "despite the seven feet of snow that fall in winter." He has an acre of potatoes planted in sand. The cod are enormous and plentiful, but there are fewer than half the fish there were when he first came here. The European boats are taking them.

"And birds' nests?"

"Back there," the settler says, pointing to the marshy bits near the river mouth.

On returning to the schooner, Audubon assails Captain Emery. This journey will cost him thousands of dollars; he has his son and the four young gentlemen to take care of, the provisioning, the hiring of crew. It is an outlay of money which must bring tangible results in the form of birds. "The best nesting grounds are back at the river's mouth."

Emery listens with his chin down. "The English keep the Americans out. Further on then, we'll find our own harbours."

Audubon stares at the captain. Emery is polite and immovable. By habit the captain's eyes scan the water. What he sees makes him smile. "Look."

There is another visitor to the harbour, a schooner that looks like a black man-of-war.

"What is that vessel?"

"We've just had a stroke of luck. It's the Quebec surveying vessel," says Emery. "If anyone knows these waters, it will be her captain."

"It's the Quebec surveying vessel."

The
SURVEYOR

LITTLE NATASHQUAN HARBOUR, *JUNE 22, 1833*

. . . We also found another American Schooner here, the *Ripley* of
Eastport, Maine, having Mr. Audubon on board, the Naturalist,
with several young men, two of them medical students of Boston.
Mr. Audubon has come principally for the purpose of studying the
habits of the water Fowl with which the Coast of Labrador abounds
and to make drawings of them for his splendid work upon the Birds
of America. He sent his card onb'd with a polite note and I received
him onb'd and we found him a very superior person indeed.

— *Surveying Journals*, Henry Wolsey Bayfield, Captain,
Royal Navy

Henry Bayfield stands on the foredeck of the *Gulnare*. He gazes
straight ahead, but from long practice he can sense her elongated
oval behind him. She is his world, a surveying ship made to his

specifications and chartered by the Royal Navy. He takes pleasure in her lines, her slender masts on which the flag now snaps in a fresh wind, and her gleaming black hull. Before him is the figurehead, the head and torso of a woman, gleaming too, in white with touches of blue and pink. He stands with feet apart, hands loosely gripped behind him, in full uniform, his cap on, prepared for any eventuality, even one as unexpected as this: that in this far-flung, rugged anchorage he should encounter an American painter of birds.

The whaleboat approaches, rowed by Yankee sailors, the same sailors who delivered a calling card only an hour previously. He has it now in his breast pocket. It is a most unusual card, bearing the stamp of a Wild Turkey and the motto "America my country." It has the name Audubon on it; the sailors will deliver the man himself, who stands in the bow in a rough wool jacket and fisherman's trousers baggy with damp, his head covered with a sou'wester, out of which streams a tangled mane of chestnut hair.

Augustus Bowen steps up to Bayfield's side; the lieutenant is a contained and dapper man, tall, lean, with pale lips. He and the captain have come through rough weather relying on one another. Bowen is perhaps less robust than his superior officer; he has had a cold since May. But it has not diminished his eagerness. This summer he expects a promotion.

"I've heard tell of the man in London," says Bowen. "Have you?"

"No, I'm afraid not." Bayfield has not been in London for many years. His work keeps him in the Gulf of St. Lawrence five months of every spring and summer, and he spends the winter at the garrison in Quebec.

"A colourful character, sir. He stalks through London like a Chinese coolie with his immense portfolio strapped to his back, smelling of bear grease."

"Bear grease? Has your godfather told you this?"

Bowen's godfather is the Duke of Sussex, a fact seldom forgotten by the young man.

"Yes, sir. You see, Audubon calls on the wealthy to raise money for his book on birds."

"I imagine that is what artists must do."

"There is much controversy about the merits of the birds he paints. Enormous, slatternly, violent creatures."

Bayfield removes his eyes for one instant from the approaching boat. "Is that intended to be a recommendation?"

"Opinion is divided, sir. Some call him a genius and are reminded of Byron. Others —"

"We shall put that aside while he is my guest onboard," says the captain. Byron indeed. The poet's work, despite or perhaps because of the scandal associated with his name, is a favourite with Captain Bayfield, although he is loath to declare his affection at the moment.

The artist swings himself onto the rope ladder, which has been lowered over the side. When he reaches the top rung, the captain steps forward, mild, tenacious, authoritative. As he holds out his hand in greeting, the three white stripes around his sleeve flash.

The artist sweeps off his sou'wester with the woollen flaps hanging down and performs a courtly bow.

"Good evening. This meeting is propitious."

"Welcome on board. What a coincidence that we should arrive at Little Natashquan on the same day!"

"I come to beg your assistance."

Bayfield is a good judge of men; he's had to be. Within seconds he has recognized the case. Here is one of God's blessed, gifted with elegance, charisma, and no small sense of theatre. The man before him is long-legged and still strong, although his waving shoulder-length hair greys at the temples. The eyes are soulful. The peaked face, with something of the child in it, beguiles. A restless energy manifests in his hands with their prominent knuckles, veins and sinews. He is brimful of himself and perhaps not to be trusted. But no, there is the gaze, full of candour; the handshake, sincere; the earnest spirit yearning to conquer a stranger.

Audubon meets the captain's eyes but withdraws his hand quickly, and, putting his own two together, rubs them. "I have been very cold," he says.

"The temperature is forty-one degrees. A little lower than normal, and somewhat difficult weather for surveying, with all the wind and rain," says Bayfield.

"Desperate for painting birds. My hands grow quite numb as I sit at my table. And it's no better for finding specimens; when the fog comes, as it has these last three weeks, you can rarely walk nor sail."

"On shore you will be driven mad by moschettoes and blackflies," says the captain. "The men working at the rigging smear themselves with paint, oil and tar. It helps a little. But — I suppose the weather suits the birds."

"The birds, but not those who pursue them."

"You count yourself amongst their predators?"

"I am afraid I must." The artist smiles. "But I prey on them out of love."

Bayfield remembers the presence at his elbow. "This is Lieutenant Bowen," he says. "The artist John James Audubon."

Bowen steps forward.

"I have heard talk of your birds," he drawls.

"Ah," says Audubon.

"Ah," says Bayfield. "Well. Well."

Bowen stares flatly at the visitor as Bayfield fingers his watch chain.

Audubon glances at the spotless deck, the gleaming timbers and neatly coiled ropes. He looks through the gloom towards the land, the morass of pitted rock, splash pools and deep mosses which he explored earlier.

"I have come to ask for your guidance. I am having grave doubts about our pilot," he says. "He would not take me to the river mouth."

"The English command the trading there, and American ships are banned," says Bayfield.

Audubon barely stops to hear him. "He cannot take us there, but neither will he take us near enough the mainland, insisting on sailing out in the open where we do not find the birds."

"I am sorry to say your pilot may be wise in staying offshore."

"I must find the nesting birds. It is why I have come."

"Would it not be easier to stay in your studio and have the birds brought to you?" asks Bowen.

"I observe them as they are in Nature," Audubon says. "Other artists may paint from specimens, but to me their work is useless. I follow my subjects to their nests. I watch their every move. It is why my paintings are superior to all others." He gazes boldly at Bowen.

"We are preparing new charts but have nothing to offer yet," Bayfield interjects. "As for those that exist, I am afraid that my predecessor, James Cook, did not distinguish himself in these parts. In fact he was called away to the Pacific, and his assistant did the measurements. We find they are not at all accurate."

"You give reason to my pilot, who refuses to use them," says Audubon, who begins to pace.

"He must use them but use caution also, I am afraid to say. It is my mission is to chart every inlet and shoal of the passage between the island of Newfoundland and the peninsula of Labrador. Seven summers, thus far, we've been working our way up the coast. And every year the demands of my Admiralty become more insistent with the increase of shipwrecks in the Gulf."

"You will encourage my fears," says Audubon.

"There is enough danger here without adding to it with your fears," says Bayfield kindly. "My ship and I will do all we can to assist you in your journey."

"I am grateful."

Bayfield reaches again for his watch chain. "Time is my obsession. I race to accomplish what I can before it, and weather, see me turn tail for home. How far do you plan to travel?"

"To the Strait of Belle Isle and, if we are lucky, round the point and farther north. Then overland to Quebec."

"Ah," says Bayfield. "If you are lucky."

THE HOLD IS VERY CLEAN and heated by the stove. The tools of the surveyor are here, the chains and lead plumbs, the theodolite with its gleaming half circle, various compasses and arcs. A chorus of ticks of disparate timbre — low, thin, glottal, whispery — echoes in the small space, a chorus composed of the voices of highly polished and intricate chronometers.

"How many clocks have you?" Audubon whispers.

"On this journey, we have thirteen on board."

Time is audible, each clock slicing the instants off the remaining day, their communal ticking an ode to time in its most precise configurations. The hold is a tomb for the present.

Sweat pops out on Audubon's brow.

Bayfield puts out his hand to give benediction to the row of clocks. "My chronometers are my most precious cargo. Without these I do not know where I am. I use them to calculate longitude between the Quebec Citadel and Greenwich. For latitude I use my sextant. I also make astronomical observations, principally by moon occultations, and eclipses of Jupiter's satellites, to 'fix' our location."

"I am astonished," Audubon says, "that you can see the moons of Jupiter. Even with those eyepieces of yours."

"From Quebec, it is easiest in the clarity of winter. But occasionally I see them from here, in the warmer seasons. The cloudless sky is a circumstance much to be looked for but rarely achieved, in Labrador. You can very well imagine how long we have to wait for good conditions and how rapidly we set to work when the weather is fair! I can give exact bearings of any point on water, determined by the stars, accurate to within five hundred feet. For instance, I know, at this moment, that we lie at 50° 12′ north, 23° east of Quebec and 61° 53′ west of Greenwich."

Audubon is short of breath.

"And when you cannot see the stars?"

"I still take great pride in my accuracy." Lifting a piece of chain, Bayfield explains how, on land, he measures small bases a quarter of a mile long or even less, every twenty or thirty miles. The chain is forged of narrow links, and is a little rusted, light as chains go, and folds into a neat pile at his feet as he lets it slip through his fingers.

AS THE DOOR SHUTS BEHIND THEM, the ticking of the chronometers is suddenly gone, and the rustling sea is again in their ears. The sailors below ready the whaleboat. The *Gulnare*'s figurehead looms as the ship rides at anchor. Her throat, her breasts, are magnificent and bare. "How strange to see a woman's form here, in this wretched place!" Audubon says.

"She is our spirit, Gulnare, named for the harem slave in Byron's poem *The Corsair*. Do you know it?"

Bayfield is eager for such conversation; he has been reading on shipboard since he first joined the navy at the age of eleven, and only rarely does he find a man with whom he can discuss his likes and dislikes. Too late he realizes he has used the name Byron: does his guest know he has been compared with the renegade? He blushes, and hopes it is too dim now for anyone to notice.

Bowen coughs ever so lightly.

"I am not a learned man. I travel with one book only. This." Audubon pulls a dog-eared copy of Linnaeus's *Systema Naturae* from his waistcoat. From the other inside pocket protrudes a flute. He tucks the flute back in and, bursting with impatience, says, "Never have I seen a coastline I liked so little! Wild, impassable, treacherous, with stunted plants that bloom and die in six weeks. No wood to make a shelter or a fire! Sir, I tell you truly, this country is a hard and angry place."

"She does not give herself up easily."

By way of accepting this judgment, Audubon makes his sweeping bow.

"I will not argue, but think of you, if I may, as my guide to this land."

On the point of saying farewell, he points upward. A little flock of a dozen small birds lands on the topyards of the *Gulnare*. Red with two white markings at the top of their black wings, they cling fiercely to the rigging in the gathering wind.

"These little ones led us here as we sailed across the Gulf," says the artist tenderly. "White-winged crossbills. They're heading to the pine forests. My gun —"

He gestures sideways, as if to his boy, never taking his eyes off the birds. "Do you see? Their crooked bills which look as if they could not get anything into their mouths? But they are perfectly made to cut pinecones. They can grip anything. If I were to shoot and kill one now, the corpse would cling to the rigging."

There is no boy and no gun. Bowen stares almost rudely at the painter's outstretched hand until it is withdrawn. As suddenly as they arrived, the birds take flight. They circle high above the schooner.

"Do you see? They wait for us to follow."

"I have often seen them thus," says Bayfield. Bowen slides away. The captain and the artist are alone now, looking up. "Why would they do that? Do they have an affection for man?"

"It is a mystery," says Audubon.

"I don't know birds. I prefer rocks. Those I can name."

In a parting gesture, the sun throws a beam under the low-hanging clouds and for a moment enlivens the deck. The faces of Bayfield and Audubon, their whiskers, their eyes, are suddenly lit.

The artist looks at the captain, and laughs. "Look how the sun fires the water to bronze. It has its wiles, this melancholy place, so far, so far from everywhere. Tell me Captain, what is your Greenwich time, if it is ten o'clock here? What is it in London now?"

Bayfield consults the timepiece in his palm.

"It is three o'clock tomorrow morning, Mr. Audubon."

"Three o'clock? Is that not a wonder! Imagine! You hold tomorrow in your hand."

The naval officer with his easy grasp of time and distance folds his fingers over the gold discus.

"Is it true then that if my eyes could penetrate that eastern horizon, I would be looking at London?"

"Well, you'd have to move Newfoundland, but in theory, yes —"

"I could see my engravers' studio on Oxford Street! In — what, only four hours time, at seven o'clock — I could see my son Victor approaching with his briefcase in his hand and figures in his head! The flame will be lit under the copper plate which hangs from the ceiling. Havell himself will hold the tapers underneath to warm it. And Blake will be putting his colourists to work with their brushes on the prints that were made yesterday. Thirty painters, at last count, seated in rows, reproducing, for all the world to see, the colours of my simple birds."

"I should like to see your pictures, if you would let me." Bayfield is taken with this strange intense figure who has risen up out of the mist.

"I have some drawings on board the *Ripley* I can show you, if we're forced to linger here at Little Natashquan."

"Whether we keep company will depend on what the wind and the skies have in store for us," the captain says as Audubon swings his long leg over the rail and puts his foot onto the rope ladder.

The
HOLD

There are light breezes SSW and the day — Sunday, 23 June 1833, Bayfield writes in his journal — is foggy but calm. He observes for latitude and records his findings. Then he decides to return Mr. Audubon's visit.

When he steps aboard the *Ripley,* he enters a different nautical world, neither shipshape, clean, nor tidy. Hip boots made of sealskin in the Esquimaux style are draped over the railings. Even in the fresh air, the ship smells of wet wool and leather, of unwashed men. The railings are unspeakable, caked with bird dung. He keeps away from them for fear of soiling his sleeves, although excrement is smeared along the deck so thickly that walking is hazardous.

Birds of various order are underfoot. There is a raven poking in the satchels for leftover food. One giant black-backed gull, hopping like a rabbit. A few huddling puffins. Some guillemots and several young gannets, awkward things with pale eyes. A sailor tosses mackerel in their direction and they catch it in their beaks. A small thickset man who Bayfield assumes to be the pilot lounges against a barrel. He does not stand up on seeing the captain in full uniform, but seems in fact to slouch in a more pronounced way.

"If it's Mr. Audubon you're after you'll find him down there." Godwin points.

It is not much of a welcome.

Bayfield finds the ladder down to the hold. The raven jeers in his direction and he slips on the ordure, nearly losing his balance. When he looks down the steps, his eyes fall directly upon the mahogany head, shot with silver, and the artist's hand slowly circling over the paper like a compass needle finding its direction. Audubon appears less like a man drawing, than like an instrument rendering its impressions.

Bayfield puts his foot on the step.

"Good day, sir. Do I disturb you?"

"Not at all," lies the artist.

So lies Bayfield himself when he is interrupted. "You are missing the chance to go on shore," he says.

"Captain Emery has gone with the young gentlemen to collect specimens around the harbour. He's taking a keen interest in my work."

"I have seen him," admits Bayfield. Nothing within the circumference of his gaze from his own deck escapes his attention. When he was taking his soundings, he watched the small black figures of Audubon's shipmates moving over the shapeless landscape, up to the top of the rocks and down on the shore. They were visible wherever they wandered, because there was nothing upright to hide them.

As his eyes begin to adjust to the dimness of the hold, he picks out hammocks slung at one end, and a stack of rifles in the corner. Bottles with candle stubs stuck in the neck are pushed to the edges of the long deal table where the painter sits, and plants hang upside down, drying.

On the table, two gannets are posing for the artist. The huge mature bird, over three feet long, is behind, his back and tail sloping downward to the left, his back wing tips crossed, his long beak raised diagonally upward, in quest of wind, perhaps. The immature bird, in front, and at cross purposes, twists his beak backward and down to preen his wing feathers, his eye hooded. They are extraordinarily still.

Bayfield peers, notices the wires that hold the raised beak, the spikes on which the birds are impaled. His heart thuds a little. "Good grief, are they dead?"

"Since this morning. We took several pair alive on the Bird Rocks five days ago; I sketched from the first and saved these for the colour," says Audubon. "They fade, so I have to work quickly."

Bayfield edges nearer the standing dead. They are self-conscious; they have died for a cause. They have a curious, sombre dignity, the paper reflecting back to them their flattened image.

Now he takes in the rest of the room. In large glass jars he can see the bodies of birds floating in oil. At the end of the table several deconstructed specimens lie on a tray, their stomachs and tracheae cut open, organs spilling out. Bayfield feels queasy, and trains his eyes directly on the models.

"Gannets," he says. "An elegant creature on the wing. One of the first you see when you have crossed the Atlantic. Sometimes as far out as three hundred miles from land, they are suddenly above the ship, high over the water, gliding silently, fishing. But when they travel in earnest, they fly low over the water. Then they overtake us. They flap their wings several dozen times, quickly, and then they sail the same distance, wings flat."

Audubon places his brush in a dish and his hands on the table, pushing himself upright and rolling his shoulders backward. He towers over Bayfield in the tiny space. His arms extend in imitation of the diver.

"You are right, they often travel low but they can fly high and even fish from that height. I saw one dive into a shoal of launces, from a hundred feet. He barely sank below the surface, but began to run on the water, striking out to right and left with his beak, eating fish after fish." He swings his own head, with its prominent, high-bridged nose, from left to right as he speaks. The birds are mute and frozen, as if all their animation has been transferred to Audubon.

Bayfield finally looks directly at the painting. He has no idea what to say. Bowen's words come back to him: Enormous, yes. Violent, no. There is violence in the room, but it is not the birds'. Slatternly? The schooner, but not the paintings. "It is — why, it is magnificent." He surprises himself with the strength of his response.

Audubon puts a drop of water on the back of the mature bird he has drawn and rubs it with his thumb, softening the colour. He sighs. "I've spent all day on it," he says with a degree of self-pity. "I haven't got the shade of it exactly right."

"Have you more?"

Audubon shows him the Arctic Tern, on which he is still working, and the completed Piping Plover.

"Very fine!" says Bayfield. "Exceedingly fine." But he now feels he is in the presence of an alchemist of sorts and is glad when they climb back to the deck.

There he is confronted by an indignant live gannet, its head thrown backward, its bill open. It is not the creature he knows from the air. It hobbles, using its outspread wings to keep itself erect. It throws its head back and howls wolfishly *kerew, karow.* It cannot fly; its wings are clipped.

Audubon nudges the bird out of the way with his toe. "Having lived the better part of a week with these, as well as more than a few corpses in various states of decomposition, I can say that I am tired of the gannet. It is not a clever bird, it may even be stupid: it certainly looks it. It does not sing but croaks, and the flesh is inedible. I prefer my raven. Come, Anonyme."

The raven jumps onto his wrist. The artist strokes its head with his right forefinger.

"I am teaching him to talk."

This does not seem to fit with the artist's reverence for the birds as they are in nature. "Why?" Bayfield asks.

The raven fixes him with its bead of an eye and caws.

Audubon's own moist and rather sorrowful eyes wrinkle up at the sides as he smiles. "Because I would like to hear what he has to say. The raven is said to have the powers of prediction."

"Is it not fanciful to think that once you give it words, the raven will confide its own thoughts? Do you expect Anonyme will tell you his purpose?"

"His purpose is to reproduce. That is what brings him here."

"I've often wondered how they navigate," says Bayfield.

"Like you, I imagine. By the stars."

"Could it be so? That they know the stars?"

"I believe it."

"Are they ever lost?"

"Rarely. I found a red-breasted nuthatch the other day; he seemed to be quite off track. A single bird may sometimes be found far off his range, and detached from his fellows, wounded or carried by a storm."

"As we may be, without our maps."

"I myself can think of nothing happier than to lose my maps, or your maps, as the case may be!"

Bayfield is taken aback. No one teases him. He is, after all, a captain with warior potential. He proved himself so while still a boy and his commendation is written into the navy records.

"You may say so, Mr. Audubon, but I do not wish it on you."

"No," Audubon concedes. His quicksilver mood appears to have changed. "Often, I seek to lose myself in the wilderness — not in this place. But you've come year after year to this comfortless land."

"On intimate acquaintance I have come to appreciate her inaccessibility. And so perhaps shall you."

Audubon looks skeptical.

"I wager it will change you. You will return to this place in dreams for the rest of your life."

"God help me," says the artist. He looks over the water, lit with the feeble rays of northern sun. "This land is too dark to monopolize my dreams. I long for sun and blossoms, for colour. It is so cold here, and lonely."

Bayfield is taken aback at the openness of this confession. Yet he rises to it. "It is the long hours away from shore that make you lonely. Are you married?"

"Yes, to my dearest friend. She waits for me in New York. I have two sons. One of them, John, you saw scrambling on shore. Victor, as I mentioned, manages my affairs in London. And you?"

"No, I have not had time to marry. We seafarers pay little mind to emotion; solitude is part of the venturing life. Then, too, we are obstinate creatures."

We.

The word hangs between them.

Bayfield, attuned to slight and gaffe by birthright, hears the other man's breath stop for a second and knows that he has erred. He sees a falling out of sympathy, a shutting of some door behind Audubon's eyes. But the chance encounter, the long grey hours of half sun, the way they are dwarfed in the vastness of the bowl of land and sea that holds them, his own restlessness, which has found a mirror in the artist, push him to go further.

"Certainly here on the water with my chains and my tripod, I dream of land. But I am at home in Quebec every winter, where I draw my charts and prepare for the next season on the water. There I dream in reverse. It is the sort of men we are."

The sort of men we are: again the captain has presumed.

Audubon's eyes narrow in what might be anger.

Bayfield grows more clumsy. Yet on he goes.

"I want to know how you came to be here, and how you came to paint birds," he says.

"If we meet again I will tell you my story," says Audubon. "And you perhaps will tell me yours."

"I have no story," he says. "I joined the navy at eleven years of age. When I came to Quebec in 1815, I was disappointed that there was no war. Surveying became my life's work." He could have added that he has made his name by labouring beyond the call of duty in places monumentally inhospitable to man, that he surveyed Lake Superior and the archipelago of Georgian Bay in two small rowing boats. But, being modest, he does not.

It is time to take his leave. Bayfield steps carefully over the slimy deck, toward the ladder over the side. "Thank you for showing me your drawings," he says in his formal way. "I did not imagine your Birds would be the same size as when alive, and so beautifully painted. I am delighted to have seen them."

The painter gives his queer bow again. Like a dancing master, Bayfield thinks.

"We'll be here in Natashquan at least another day. Perhaps, if lack of wind detains you too, you would come to dinner on the *Gulnare*."

"Another day? Why must we wait? The birds won't wait for me," says Audubon. But then he appears to resign himself. "I should like your escort up this perilous coast. If it is another day, we'll wait."

He glances at the sky again and, giving Bayfield a nod, turns to take the ladder down into the hold. "I must get back to my birds."

———

P.M. observed for Time and diff'e Longitude, also for true bearing. Variation & angles for the Survey of this small anchorage. At night the wind hauled more towards the SE with fog and drizzling rain.

— *Surveying Journals*, Henry Wolsey Bayfield, Captain, Royal Navy

Obstinate
CREATURES

The sort of men we are. What sort of man does Bayfield imagine Audubon to be? A sea-farer? A pedigreed hero? A warrior who spurns the passions and domestic life?

If so, the captain is quite mistaken.

He may be fantasist, a fabricator. He is even called a liar, with his grotesque, exaggerated wildfowl. He has told his English patrons that there are, in the New World, winged creatures as tall as grown men. His pictures must prove it. The flamingos and the wild turkeys, the cranes and the pelicans crowd the edges of his double elephant-size paper, bow and twist to fit the trim. But it is not his pictures that lie. He himself is too large for any frame. He was not built for the sea. His legs are made to leap over stiles; they slip and betray him on the rain-slick planks. He must not be contained in any way. His hair escapes its bindings and his enthusiasms exceed his ability to express them, so that even when he is deep in thought his hands and arms must be in motion. Speaking in English, he has a French accent and comical grammar, but the power of angels invests his tongue. He veers from glee to melancholy, each extreme mirrored in his dark brown eyes. He needs to take people by storm and he does.

Bayfield is entirely mistaken if he thinks Audubon is like him.

. . . how you came to be here, and how you came to paint birds.

I will tell you my story, Audubon promised.

Which story would that be?

Truth is discovered backwards, fact buried in the flow of impression, in the rubble of stories told then and now to suit a purpose. His friends and family guard his lies more jealously than he. Even the record, his own record, his tale of himself, is a story. But the impulse remains: find one story and make it true.

He was born Jean Rabin, in Santo Domingo. At three, he became Monsieur Newhouse, on the register of the ship that carried him to his father in France, in the care of strange men. Someone's idea of a joke, surely, to call him that, but it was a sign that he was leaving one life behind and going to another, that nothing remained behind for him to return to. To be cut loose like that, from land, from the women who cared for him and all he ever knew.

Over and over, he was cut loose. In his new house in Nantes, his father called him Jean Jacques. Later, when it became a crime to be Catholic, he became Fougère, "fern." When he was eighteen, his father sent Jean Jacques Fougère to manage his property of Mill Grove, in Pennsylvania. He hoped that the sale of the French colony of Louisiana to the United States might be the occasion for a questionable young Frenchman to get American citizenship.

In America, he became John James Audubon. And he fell in love, with Lucy Bakewell, daughter of his English neighbours on the property next to Mill Grove.

In summer he took her to watch the peewees nest. He placed a ring around the leg of the male peewee. He wanted to see if the same bird would come back the next spring. In April they went again, and sure enough, there was the bird with the ringed leg. When he held the peewee's little head to his chest, Lucy said, "You've wed the bird, instead of me."

And once he'd wed her, too, the bird was her rival. And every bird had a mate, and a home, while all she had was his protestations. It seemed he could only be faithful to himself by failing her. He was neither a domestic man, nor a wild one, but a man split by double yearnings: to be in the lap of his family, and to be off tramping. But, he told her often, wherever he was, he longed for her.

Pennsylvania, Ohio, Kentucky; mine operator, farm owner, storekeeper, mill owner. All his endeavours failed. He invested his father's money and his in-laws' money and he lost it. There, on the frontier of the still-wild continent, he did what he knew best: he followed the birds.

In fact, during these thirty years since he came to America, he has been apart from Lucy more than he has been with her. He has followed the birds and tried to know their world, his chosen continent. He has ridden its trails on horseback, tramped its frontiers, threaded its veins by riverboat and lake steamer, sleeping in its open air under his buffalo robe, alone and far from home. His daughters died. Lucy despaired of him and took a job as a governess. Her employer refused to have Audubon on the property. His enemies derided him as a ne'er-do-well who had abandoned his wife and children for a dream of twitterers in the bushes.

But he was not such a man. Even his father, for all his sins, did not abandon his children.

He found a job teaching painting at a girls' school in Pennsylvania. But he was not born to nurture the talents of others. As soon as he had money saved he headed up to Lake Ontario for the fall migration. He bought a little skiff and there, rowing alone, watching the flocks of birds muster and rumble up to wing southward, he understood at last the purpose of his existence: it was to create this giant book, a folio of every single bird of North America. The paintings would be engraved, and printed, and coloured. He would sell it by subscription. Fired with his idea, he sold his skiff for passage down the Ohio, sleeping on deck in his buckskins. At Cincinnati creditors chased him out of town. He begged fifteen dollars for a fare and wrote to Lucy. She sent him a message: if this is your life's work, be on your way. Mine must be to keep the rest of us alive. You have my faith, she said, but that is all you'll get from me, because my little savings are all I have left.

The artist's wife. Unsung and true as a sword.

He knew by the passion of her anger that the door was still open. He found his way to her and told her how the great book of his life and of the times they lived in and of the lives of birds needed only a dozen of his years, and her complete faith. When they parted he had the rest of her savings. He presented himself to Nolte and, armed with introductions, sailed for Europe.

From America to England, for the business of publishing, and back to America for the birds he has gone, stringing countries like beads on his life thread. Six crossings in as many years. But a seafaring man? Never. These crossings are his martyrdoms: on the sea there are wars and pirates, doldrums and tempests beyond his control.

What is his world then, if not ships and water?

It is a world of shores and arrivals. Of visions carried over water. Of a dream in a metal tube sent halfway across the globe. The sea is a gap to be spanned. It is the mother of his invention and the birth-place of his tales. In Europe he hobnobs with princes, while in America he is known as a bankrupt and a charlatan. He plays the two worlds against each other, acting the frontiersman in Europe, and the aristocrat on the fringes of civilization. He turns up in his fox-tailed fur hat at the Louvre, but in the wilds of America, he hints that he is the lost dauphin.

But he wearies of stories now, especially his own.

AND ONE MORE THING the captain said. *Dream in reverse.*

Here he is not mistaken.

Yes. Dreams of heat and sun, dreams of tenderness. Of the scent of roses. And a small woman's heart-shaped face. What would the captain say if Audubon were to tell him: I love a woman not my wife.

The sort of men we are.

THE YOUNG GENTLEMEN RETURN. They clatter down the ladder with their baskets.

"Look! Six little horned shore larks, two living, four shot."

"We watched them fly," cries Johnny. "They spiral up in the air hundreds of feet, and tumble back down. Then up they go again, for the joy of it, as if in their own glass chimney, singing as they rise. Over and over, they did it."

"I wish I'd seen it!" says Audubon. "How did you get them?"

"We found two young in a burrow under a bush; the male was nearby and Tom got him."

"Were they sitting right in the bush, nesting there?"

"They were all on the ground, hiding."

The male is horned and masked with a black bib. The female is dun brown all over, and shows less white. The young are plump and downy.

The deal table becomes a surgery. Shattuck and Ingalls take the little larks apart, searching for clues to the mystery of their flight. They pull out the minuscule livers and intestines and hearts, even their tongues, with tweezers and drop them into bottles of alcohol, writing their notes in spidery black ink. They examine the muscles, the way they are attached across the bird's tiny chest, the hollow bones of the wings. When they cannot identify what makes them fly, they leave the bones and go to bed.

STILL LATER, Audubon sits alone with his gannets. The last few moments before the light dies are the best to check light and shade. They stand reproachless, slowly disappearing as darkness comes on. The young bird is good, the speckled grey of its plumage nearly exactly as he saw it. He narrows his eyes critically on the adult bird. Its white feathers no longer give back light. The white is not right. He has not made it *resplendent*. He would like some chalk from the rocks, or perhaps the white inside of a mussel shell, but there is nothing at all of the pure whiteness that he needs. Nothing in nature is that white except the feathers of the bird itself.

He looks again at his rendering. The two are a pair of opposites — one dark, one light, one contemplating the air, the other the self. Their shapes gash open the great horizontal emptiness in which they live. In the background the Bird Rocks sit in blue-grey water. He is rather pleased with the composition. But the birds are still. They are dead. He sees in his mind's eye their flight. The wide, peaked pinions. The thrust of those strong wings, and the easy glide forward that follows it.

He has not captured the life of them. When he is tired like this, he wonders if he ever will. He wipes his brushes wearily and goes on deck to say goodnight to Anonyme. He calls the raven and when it comes he absently strokes its head with his thumb and forefinger.

"*. . . a chaos of upstart ragged black rocks.*"

The sky is dark, lined with cloud, the stars occluded, the moon a suggestion of silver, the only visible landfall a chaos of upstart ragged black rocks. There is snow to the west, on the hills, and something resembling rain in his face. The air presses at Audubon's cheeks; it is as if he stands in a moist element stretching from fathoms below his feet to yards above it, the air merely a less dense, floating version of the sea. He feels, beneath him, the secret flurry of cloud after cloud of fish, and around him the reek and teem of winged life.

He thinks of Bayfield, on the deck of his own, nearby ship, measuring the stars. Of the *Gulnare* herself, all curves in this jagged land, silently riding out the night.

"Lucy," he says, "Captain Bayfield came onboard today. He is an eminent man, the best surveyor in the entire Royal Navy, says Captain Emery. And he liked my pictures." He tries to think of more to tell his wife, but he cannot. He pictures the wooden figurehead of the *Gulnare*, her conical breasts and slender neck. Once Lucy looked like that, but no more. No, it is the shape of Maria.

THE STORY OF MARIA, the fact of Maria, began in the fall of 1831 when he was walking the streets of Charleston with his assistant, looking for a room to rent. He planned to stay until he could connect with a revenue cutter that would take him to the Floridas. Into his line of sight rolled a buggy loaded with baskets of artichokes, carrots and beans, bunches of tall chrysanthemums and roses sticking out of cones of paper, and, laid one over the other, braces of game, partridge, wild turkey, woodcock. It was a vision of plenty.

As he gazed the driver hailed him. He was John Bachman, pastor of St. John's Lutheran church, a writer of books on nature himself, and a hunter. Bachman had a guileless bright blue eye and his enthusiasm was as generous as his buggy load of produce, gifts for his parishioners.

There were greetings, introductions, and warm exclamations — Painting the birds! I must be of assistance! — and the pastor insisted he could not let them go.

The artist and his boy climbed aboard and rode the rounds, eventually coming back with empty cart to Bachman's house. It was a great square mansion with balconies on two levels, set in brilliant gardens and fanned by a breeze off the sea. As they entered, a frail woman came briefly to greet them. This was his wife, Harriet, Bachman explained. Withdrawing, she called her younger sister to entertain. After she had faded down the hall he explained: the granddaughter of a Revolutionary hero, she had seven living children, two daughters and five sons. Five other children had died of tuberculosis. The exertions of producing this dozen, the combination of their living and their dying, had sent her almost permanently to her couch.

Into the parlour walked Miss Maria Martin, as quick as her sister was languid. She was tiny, like a child, but her face brought the light of day into the shuttered drawing room. She greeted Audubon in French, the language which was dear to him. As she put the two girls through their curtsies, and gave instructions to the slaves to accommodate their guests, he could not stop looking at her. She was not beautiful. Or not what he had ever thought of as beautiful. She was like a little brown sparrow. He was fascinated by the bright receptivity of each part of her face and figure to every voice, every nuance, each glance.

After dinner the men repaired to the low-ceilinged study on the ground floor. There, under the eye of the great stuffed horned owl, between the two giant globes, one of the earth and one of the stars, amid the leather-bound books, the bottled reptiles and freaks of nature, the caged screech-owl and the pet muskrat, they worked. Audubon and his new friend exchanged notes on birds while the boy assistant sat down to paint some backgrounds.

Later that night Audubon wrote Lucy, elated, of his good fortune in this friendly town, of his new friend John Bachman, the house full of children, and the sister-in-law, who he had been told was a promising artist.

How was it that Maria ended up in the library den working with the men? It must have been that she offered to help, and they found within hours that they could not do without her. Already she had been drawing flowers for Bachman's books. She wanted to learn. Still, Audubon cannot claim his pleasure in teaching her to draw was free of the enjoyment he had in merely sitting across from her and looking at her face. The down-turned eyes with their full lids, the tiny mouth set carefully, lips softly together but never pressed, the pointed chin and nose, the width of her forehead showing intelligence, the modesty disguising much strength. He drank it in.

Maria. He practised her name. It seemed too ordinary for her. But that was its magic, and hers, to be hidden in this modesty.

To feel this way was not new, to him.

There were women like her everywhere he landed. Intelligent, accomplished and lovely. They offered him their sympathies and he offered them his ardent admiration.

Maria tried inordinately to please; she would work for hours correcting a mistake. That, and all the household tasks that were hers — to teach the children French, to oversee the laundry and the cooking — ought to have tired her. But she could match his energy, and give it back to him. When all the others at last gave up trying to meet his demands, there she was, patient, calm, perfect. Attentive. And soon, affectionate.

They rose at dawn, before the children were up, to walk in the garden. He watched the birds and she named the flowers for him while the air was cool, and the household at bay, as the scent of the roses came on. They sat together; she sketched botanical specimens while he painted. She wanted to draw the birds, but he kept her busy with the cane vine, the loblolly bay. In the evenings the three of them, Maria, John Bachman and he, sat in the study and were happy, working.

In this way two months went by while he waited for that revenue cutter. The good reverend's hospitality did not fail. The boy assistant had to be let go, as he quarrelled with Maria. She was Audubon's companion throughout the day, his confidant, his pet.

This much had happened before.

But another part was new, and unfamiliar. There were three of them. The third was the Reverend Bachman, who rapidly became Audubon's dear friend. The reverend called Maria his sweetheart. Audubon followed his lead, daringly. The three of them were always laughing. I am not your sweetheart nor yours either, she would say to the men. But then she would be alone with Audubon, and they would laugh and tease and kiss close against the back of her brother-in-law's house, where they could not be seen from the window. He prayed that the revenue cutter would be delayed.

One day a caller came to Rutledge Avenue, a man by the name of Martin. Audubon did not connect the caller with his sweetheart; he was hardly aware of Maria as having another name. A servant announced him. The women scattered. Harriet shut her door and could not be roused. Maria for once lost her composure. She came to Audubon in the study. "Jean Jacques" — she spoke to him in French — "you must tell him to go away. Tell him there is no one at home who can see him. The Reverend Bachman is out on calls."

Audubon went to the parlour, where the man waited. He was small, with a waistcoat that fairly bulged with entitlement. He wanted to see Maria. "You may not," said Audubon. "The Reverend Bachman is out on calls."

"It is not the Reverend Bachman I have come to see." The man Martin laid his hand on his belly, over his watch chain.

Audubon was forced to insist that the man leave. When Martin said he would come back with a letter, Audubon determined that this letter would not make its way into Maria's hands.

The next morning at dawn they walked in the garden. She told him that the man was her father. He had left his family when he fell in love with another woman. He had moved a hundred miles away and had a bastard child, perhaps more than one. Her mother had died of the shame and Maria was left dependent on Reverend Bachman's kindness.

"You could have married?" breathed Audubon.

"It set me against marriage," said Maria.

"Did you have a suitor?"

"I never met a man I could love," she said. "I have my work. I will paint. I will learn with your help. If you do not think me too bold, I will come with you into the wild."

The revenue cutter arrived, and Audubon had to go.

———

The fogs which accompany Easterly Gales extend high up into the atmosphere and cannot be looked over from any part of the rigging of a ship. They, however, are not so thick as those which occur in calms after a strong wind. These are frequently so dense as to conceal a vessel within hail. The former often, but not always, admit the land, or other objects, to be distinguished at the distance of half a mile, or more, in the day time. The Dense Fogs, which occur in calms, often extend only to small elevations above the sea. It sometimes happens that when objects are hidden at the distance of 50 yards from the deck they can be plainly seen by a person 50 or 60 feet up the rigging.

— *Sailing Directions for the Gulf and River of St. Lawrence,* Henry Wolsey Bayfield, Captain, Royal Navy

———

The *Gulnare* is trapped in fog. Captain Bayfield can do nothing else and therefore he tries to take the dimension, the measure of this fog.

The sea is perfectly calm. Captain Bayfield, or Henry, as he thinks sometimes thinks of himself (someone has to), has climbed to the very top of the *Gulnare*'s rigging. He loves to scale her heights, to top her, even now, when she is listless, her sails loose against the mast. In her "dishabills," as the Irish seamen say.

Fog has its comforts; it affords a little privacy in the constricted quarters of a schooner. From here, he cannot see her deck below. Which means, of course, that no one on deck can see him above.

Hanging by one arm, with both feet tucked into rope loops, he can see the masts of the *Ripley*. Only a few hundred feet away, they protrude like tiny spires from the white billows. There is no one up the rigging of the other schooner; he alone is above and in a position to see over the fog. Like a bird, in fact. Where do the birds go in this fog? Can they fly without seeing? He wishes he could sail blind.

He swings out a little way, and gently back again, testing the strength of his arm. He feels playful though it has been years since he played like a boy. In fact, he does not remember ever playing like a boy. At Bayfield Hall there was the governess, the marshalled walks across the soggy fields, the forced silences for chapel. Then, the navy, and always, work. But today, there is a lightness in him. Despite his annoyance at being held hostage by fog, his impatience to get on with work, he is happy. He enjoys Mr. Audubon. His conversation is stimulating, something rare on shipboard. The man challenges his ideas. A captain of a schooner in the Royal Navy is not often challenged.

He changes arms and swings out farther, attempting a circle around the mast.

When he was packed off straight from Bayfield Hall to the *Pompée* as supernumerary volunteer, the nearest thing to play was the fighting action with the French privateer six hours after leaving port. He was slashed across the shoulder by a cutlass and would have lost his arm or worse if he, unarmed, hadn't had the quickness of wit to dart under the man's thrusts, staying so close to his feet that he couldn't cut him, find a rope coiled in the lifeboat and whip it at his attacker's knees. Then, when the man stumbled, to lash him in the face so that he could not see, and when the cutlass clattered to the deck, to steal it.

His arm was cut deeply at the shoulder. The same arm by which he now hangs. He cannot remember the pain of the cut. But he enjoyed the attention it gave him. In fact, in the rough company of men he keeps, it is the only time he can remember being tenderly treated.

The boy! The boy! the men called out when he was injured. For those few moments he became a boy, although he was an officer and in charge of grown men. They defeated the French pirates. The prisoners, in chains, were sent off to prison. The sailors wrapped Bayfield in warm blankets, and held a cup to his lips. He remembers the feel of the metal. He enjoyed being injured. Imagine that. No, if he is honest, he would say he enjoyed being tended to.

If one was married, one would be tended to whenever one liked. And when one didn't like.

He swings himself around the mast one more time, lazily.

Mr. Audubon is married.

God knows the Quebec matrons have tried to marry Bayfield off. Invitations to parties at the castle fall through his door too often. But those winters in the garrison are his working times. He has to admit that, when forced to be in society, he has noticed some attractive young ladies. There is one called Miss Fanny Wright. She is very young, not even twenty. She is white-skinned and black-haired and has a look of robust merriment. But what would a wife do but divide his emotions while he is away for five months of the year, then want his company when he is at home?

Mr. Audubon has lain with his wife night after night. Engendered two sons. His mind veers away. Family life is a mystery to him. He looks all around the horizon, or what would be the horizon if he could see it. In patches, mainland is visible. Mounds of rock here, penetrating the grey fuzz with their own grey, black and reddish brown, aged lichen and twisted trees that have seen ships like his come and go for centuries.

It is important work, the hydrographical survey. He had said this to the same young lady at Castle St. Lewis in Quebec. Crucial, defining work, to verify the boundary of this country and the United States.

It is a difficult boundary because so much of it is water. Water is a most unreliable surface. Beyond that, the survey marks the channels that are safe for navigating. The Admiralty wants our charts quickly now, as the number of shipwrecks in the Gulf is rising, he had explained, even as he spoke, feeling a rising urgency to be off.

Briefly, Collins's head appears out of the mist covering the deck. His voice rises and falls, saying what, Bayfield cannot quite grasp. He thinks of the time they were both young assistants under William FitzWilliam Owen in 1814. He, Bayfield, had expected to fight a war and had been selected not for valour but for the neatness of his handwriting. Collins, a midshipman at the time, was relieved to have steady occupation that did not involve the use of violence. They cut their teeth on the Thousand Islands, verifying the American boundary from Montreal to Kingston in anticipation of another war with the United States. In fact, there are more than one thousand islands. There are 1,768 between Brockville and Kingston, ranging from a size of one acre to twenty-two square miles, to be precise. Owen drove them to exhaustion, day and night, even in winter, until even he had to concede it was too difficult to pierce the ice and handle the frozen lines.

And the islands! So many that the naming of them became a delirium. They began with groups: the Old Friends, the Hydrographers (half a dozen named after each other), the Statesmen, the Admiralty (all the British Lords), the Navy Isles, and the Lake Fleet (including nineteen vessels or types of vessels including the Punts, the Cutters, Gig and so on). But soon they ran out of words. It is a solemn act to confer a name; it gave one the feeling of being a god.

That has been his story.

Come for a war and found a boundary.

Come to survey a boundary and found nothing so simple as a line through water: found land smashed up and broken to bits, humped and rising out of water, shallow and sometimes disappearing. Irrational, useless and obstructing land, needing to be made sense of.

With Collins's help, he finished in August 1816 and presented his masterpiece, "A Chart of Lake Ontario, Scale 0.835 Inches to a Mile of Longitude, or about 1.65432. Particular Places on a Scale of 1.12,000"

*"Bayfield had been selected not for
valour but for the neatness of his handwriting."*

to the Lords of the Admiralty. But the Lords were fickle; the survey was no longer essential, as peace had been achieved, and the longest undefended border in the world had been established by the Treaty of Ghent. The Lords sent Owen off to Africa and suggested abandoning the Great Lakes survey, "unless you want to leave Bayfield to do it."

So Bayfield became lieutenant and almost by default went on to complete the survey himself. Lakes Erie, Ontario, Superior and Huron with its enormous sidecar, "la mer douce," Georgian Bay, followed. He did it all in two small boats, with only Collins to help. The waters were capricious, festering with granite teeth both above and below the waterline. In the early 1820s, they were granted chronometers to determine longitude. Now he had the means to make his survey perfect, and he was determined to. There were more islands, including a long archipelago in Georgian Bay.

He arrived in London in 1825 with the product of their immense labour: the completed surveys of Lakes Huron, Erie and Superior, including charts of no fewer than twenty thousand islands. He thought perhaps he would be sent to Africa, where Owen was, or the Indian Ocean, or the Pacific, where Cook was. But no.

Instead he was promptly put on half pay. Half pay meant ten shillings and sixpence a day. What was worse was that he had nothing to do. He took up residence in his brother's Chelsea house, and paced the banks of the Thames. His mother wrote from Bayfield Hall that she feared he was wearing himself out in "the fleshpots of London." He could not visualize a fleshpot, but he would not tell his mother that. He read and watched the traffic on the Thames. This went on for an interminable year and a half until Owen returned from Africa, found him languishing and promptly made an appointment with Lord Melville.

The Canadian survey had given the Admiralty ideas. The survey was mammoth; it made a claim; it gave glory to Pax Britannica. They had done such a fine job with their chronometers that the Admiralty now made chronometers available for all His Majesty's ships.

Through Owen's intervention, Bayfield was promoted to captain. He took on the task that, he imagines, will occupy the rest of his working life — the survey of the St. Lawrence to the sea, and the entire eastern seaboard of Canada including the Gulf of the St. Lawrence, and the islands of Anticosti, Prince Edward and Cape Breton, and Nova Scotia. This summer he will proceed into the most dangerous part of it all, the isolated and treacherous coast of Labrador, as far as the Strait of Belle Isle.

Thousands, tens of thousands, more islands.

He will spend his life amongst these ropes and sails. That was determined when he was a lad. He did not question it. Boys are the best warriors, unfettered by conscience, by remorse, by compassion. Or at least boys raised as he was, to be leaders of men. It was his duty to take charge of others, and, if necessary, to lay down his life on their behalf. He seemed to recall the moment when he was told this. He sat in a large chair and his feet did not touch the floor.

Henry sits now, legs wrapped around the mast, and looks over the top of the fog into the other direction. Though grey cloud clogs the foreground, such is the perversity of this fog that he can see the shore a hundred yards away. Speaking of the devil, he spots the painter walking on shore. His posture, the eagerness and set of his step, put Bayfield in mind of Captain John Franklin, whom he met at Fort William on Lake Superior. Franklin and his party of thirty-three were on their way to the Arctic coast. It was in May of 1825. It strikes Bayfield that these men share a fiendish determination that separates them from others. Where does it come from? Is it all these hours alone in the weather and the wild? Or is it from setting oneself a near-impossible task that tempts God? Perhaps he, Henry Wolsey Bayfield, might appear fiendish himself. He prays not.

Audubon is likely doomed, too, Henry thinks. Then he wonders why he should think that. Was it the joy and relief on his face as he thought of returning to his birds last evening?

The *Gulnare*'s figurehead emerges for a moment from the fog beneath him. Her wooden shoulders and back make Bayfield smile. If he were alone and out of sight of Bowen and all of the crew, a highly unlikely possibility in the close quarters of the schooner, he would go and stroke her shoulders. What would if be like to feel love? No doubt pleasant enough, but troublesome. Lust is that way.

The painter climbs up on a rock and disappears into a billow of fog.

Henry takes one last look around. The coast is out there, unmeasured, unknown, untamed. He climbs down the mast.

"Impenetrable in all directions, save for from a distance of fifty feet up!" he announces to Bowen. "We shan't go anywhere today. Have the men swab the deck. And scrape the boards clean in the hold."

"Why don't you take a walk onshore and look at the rocks?"

"Thank you, Bowen, for your suggestion. I'll give it due consideration," Bayfield says dryly.

His lieutenant flushes.

When Bayfield enters his cabin, the ticking assails him. It is as if the moments up in the rigging above the fog erased time for a stretch. Now that it is back, it finds an easy way to his nerves. Time pressing implacably on is not what he wishes to hear. He takes a length of chain, some lead weights and his leather book, and heads for the *Owen*. At least he can take a sounding.

KILLING

I n the way of footing, the harbour offers two extremes: uneven erup-
tions of rock and an evil-smelling mixture of drowned grasses and
black mulch.

Audubon tries the muck. It is deeper than he thinks. The instant
he steps in it, it swallows his leg up to and above the rim of his hob-
nailed boot. Dragging it out (suck suck suck pop), then placing it
ahead, where it sinks again (with a sound like a fart), he feels he walks
with ball and chain. As he would in debtor's prison. He drags up his
foot, nearly losing the boot, and wades toward the rock, which seems
to shoot up at him as if with intent to injure. Once out of the muck,
he springs light-footed from jagged head to jagged head. Rejoicing in
his nimbleness he leaps onward until his foot slides into a crevice and
the boot is caught. The same boot that sank in the mud. This is the
land that eats boots.

He sits and pulls. His muck-slippered foot pops out but the boot
remains firmly wedged three feet down. Below it, the fissure opens to
a window of red sand over which the sea sucks and foams, then disappears with a hollow thump. He contemplates abandoning the boot
but he needs it. He has no other footwear except thigh-high moccasins
made of sealskin, and their soles are not hard enough for this punish-
ing surface.

He lies on his stomach, exposing his gut to a rough fist of rock.
He reaches down with a long arm. Long but not long enough. The
boot beckons another six inches below. A surge of sea comes up to
ruffle its sole.

He shifts to his side, the aggressive fist pushing now into his kidney. He grasps the upper of the boot. He pulls. Nothing happens.

He rolls on his back. The clouds are scudding quickly; the fog may blow off. It is three o'clock in the afternoon and he already put in ten hours at the deal table in the hold. His eyes ache. His back is tired. His brain is fevered. The stuck boot seems an insurmountable problem.

The black rock on which he lies is rough and porous. Under its carapace the sea expands and retreats with hollow, percussive sighs. He closes his eyes. Peace, he admonishes himself, peace. He thinks of Maria. Bachman's last letter reverberates in his mind, the one he received in Boston just before he left. "Our sweetheart . . . willing as ever to do backgrounds. To gratify you will always afford her pleasure."

The man does not know what he is saying.

He sees an eagle above him, soaring. It plunges from the sky. He turns his head to watch as it emerges from the water triumphant with a fish in its claws. It rises into the blanket of fog, then reappears like a ghost gliding in circles. How does the eye of the eagle penetrate this grey mist? Does the eagle see him, a little X on the rock?

He realizes with a shock that he has painted himself from an eagle's-eye view. It was the last painting he finished before coming to Labrador. He was a little X then too, insignificant, and caught straddling a log over a chasm.

That golden eagle was magnificent, a male that had been caught in a fox trap in the White Mountains. A man from the Boston Museum came to Audubon's rooms with the cage in his arms. "This is an emperor of birds," said the man. "There is a story that it seized a human child in its bunting and flew off with it to its aerie. The mother of the child ran after it and climbed where no man had dared to climb before, found the nest, and took back the child unharmed. Then the people trapped it."

"That is not a story about an eagle," said Lucy. "It is a story about a mother."

"That it should even come into my house is a sad thing," said Audubon to the donor, "for this bird more than any is meant to soar."

But he took it anyway.

The eagle was majestic, even when caged. His talons gleamed and his black eye glinted. He knew there was no escape, and was too dignified to beat his wings against the bars.

Audubon sank into a chair opposite the cage. Eye to eye and beak to beak they sat for hours. He did not know whether to kill it or keep it.

He stood and paced and his eyes filled with tears. The bird sat, hunched, eyes glittering.

"Fougère," Lucy said. "You want to paint it."

"I must. And if I kill it, I do not damage it, only stop it, fix it in its perfection, to make the painting."

And there began the drama.

As hard as he fought to snuff its existence, so did the eagle strive to remain alive. ("I warrant that the rest of us have not put up half the fight against being overtaken by my husband's conviction," Lucy would say after it was all over.)

First he decided that, in order not to mark the creature in any way, he would asphyxiate it. He put it in an empty closet, stopped the doors with cloth, lit a charcoal brazier alight. He stayed in the closet alongside the bird. It seemed the respectful thing to do. After some time he lifted the cloth: the bird's eye gleamed in the sooty air and he stood just as magnificently as before on his humble perch.

Startled, Audubon dropped the cloth.

"I think the bird does not wish to die," said Lucy through the door.

"Go away, Lucy! I do not need your tongue!"

Adding sulphur to the fire, he bowed the way he had been taught, as a gentleman would in a ballroom, or a parlour. The bird failed to acknowledge this courtesy. The eagle had become, through Audubon's murderous intent and low violence toward it, superior to his jailer. He backed out the door.

He waited more hours and then opened the door again. The sulphur on the charcoal had made a terrible stench and had turned the air brown but it had made no impression on the eagle. Audubon was divided between his will to kill it and his admiration for its will to stay alive.

Lucy hovered. "You've met your match. You'll do yourself in, Fougère, if you're not careful."

"Away with you!"

Again he stepped into the closet with the eagle. He hovered over the cage, fanning the poisonous smoke towards the bird. But before long he began to feel faint, though the eagle glittered with regal hostility, his talons firm on the perch. Prompted by Lucy, John Woodhouse poked his head in and pleaded that his father come out.

"I will not: I will honour the creature as it breathes its last."

"Father, it has not breathed its last nor does it show any sign that it will. In a contest, you will succumb first."

"Go away and shut the door!"

Audubon sat with the bird in silence until his eyes ran with tears and he could not see, until his throat burned and the breath backed up in his chest. Finally he opened the door and demanded a large sewing pin. Lucy found one in her basket. Locked again in the closet and out of sight of other humans he loomed over the cage. He felt faint. There was a fog in that closet, yes, a fog thick as today's but yellow. He must have laid his hands on the bird somehow, though how he did without being torn by the beak he does not understand. He does not remember. He only knows that when it was done the bird was stabbed through the heart.

Lucy opened the door to find him wavering with the enormous fallen bird in his arms, tears from smoke, rage and grief striping his soot-stained cheeks.

But there was no time to mourn. Within twenty-four hours the plumage would fade by one quarter from its colour in life, he knew. He took the still-warm corpse and wired the wings up and back. He placed the bird in the position he knew so well from having seen eagles in the wild; he raised the throat and opened the beak to the air as if, triumphant, the bird were rising up from a kill, its talons buried in the flesh of its victim.

And he set about to paint, although he clearly was ill. He spent the whole night outlining it and then began to work. For two weeks he worked sixteen hours a day. He was too tired to sleep and too agitated to stop. The portrait was as grand as the creature that inspired it, the eagle in flight, the prey a rabbit whose black eye, like the eye of the bird itself, was accusing and pitying and pierced directly in its centre by the frightful talon. When the painting was done, he found he had added his small self as a hunter with his gun, astride a log which bridged a chasm. The little human hunter was miniaturized by the great bird, on a perch himself.

When he was finished, he collapsed. A strange spell came over him; his heart palpitated, and he could not move his limbs. For three days he lay swooning. Lucy called the doctors from Harvard, who gave him medicine and told him not to tire himself. He went back to work, which was all he wanted, setting up his trip to Labrador.

Now, HE LIES ON his back staring at an eagle in the sky, his boot stuck in a hole, confused and breathless, cold to the bone. Has he had another spell? Is he dreaming or merely numb?

The sea slaps the underside of his crust of rock and sends up a frigid spray, which wets his backside. The tide is coming in. How long has he lain here? He does not know. There is no sun to track across the sky. He must retrieve the boot. It may be floating now. He tries to force himself to move and cannot. And then there is a flash of dark blue above him.

"Good afternoon, Mr. Audubon."

A hand slides under his back, and two legs brace him as he is lifted to his feet. One foot is bare, the sock gone with the boot. The naval officer reaches down and without effort, it seems, retrieves the trapped boot.

"I seem to have lost track of the time, Captain."

"I've never succeeded in that myself. How did you manage?"

"By watching the eagle."

"You saw how many clocks I have on the *Gulnare*," says Bayfield ruefully. "In the fog they oppress me." He hands the painter his boot.

"Clocks always oppress me," says Audubon with as much vehemence as he can muster in his undignified posture. "It reminds me that practical tasks await when I only want to follow the birds."

"But surely time is neutral. It simply exists, and we pass through it. I measure it to find my location. It is another scale, if you like."

"It does not feel neutral when you wonder every day if you will die here!"

"Ah!" says Bayfield. "Then it is death that oppresses you, not time."

Audubon scowls. He is not sure he wants to be understood so quickly.

But now he is righted, and booted, and solid on his feet. They make their way back to a smooth rock where the surveying launch is pulled up on shore, beside Audubon's skiff.

"The *Owen*," says Bayfield. "It is named after my superior and my teacher, Captain William FitzWilliam Owen. I revere him, although he worked us far too late into the night." A thought occurs to the naval officer. "I suppose you too, Mr. Audubon, had a teacher or a guide?"

"I did not," says Audubon. "It is said I studied with David, the king of France's own drawing master but —" he pauses. "My system is my own."

Tired of stories, especially his own.

He never studied with David. And now, today, faint, cold, in the company of a sympathetic stranger, he is ready to abandon the pretence.

"Shall we sit in this rare sun, and talk a while? I will tell you something of how, since I was a child, the birds have beguiled me."

IT WAS SIMPLE, at first. Birds were easy to find. Free for the taking. He was never happier than when watching for the rustle in the leaves overhead, listening to the song, and following a flying creature deeper into the forest.

They drew him to wild places, away from soldiers.

HE WAS JUST NINE YEARS OLD. It was 1794, the Reign of Terror. He was living in Nantes with his father and stepmother. The soldiers of the French Republic came. They emptied the jails of all the people the Commune had put there, men and women and children, clerks and priests and teachers, people who had been named as enemies. The soldiers didn't shoot them. They had neither enough guns nor enough bullets. Instead, they herded these people into wire cages on barges in the Loire. They took the barges out to the centre of the river and pushed the laden cages over the sides, so they sank in the freezing water. But the river was not deep. The cages were there, just under its surface. Jean Jacques, who had been renamed Fougère, thought he could see them, the drowned bodies floating up against the roofs of the cages, the water running carelessly and always over the heads of the dead.

His parents moved outside of Nantes, to a house by the marshes in Coueron. Now he did not want to be Fougère, either. He called himself LaForest, which was where the birds lived.

In Coueron there was a neighbour, a doctor, D'Orbigny. He saw the boy without a name running in the woods and called him Fifi, nature lover. D'Orbigny had a little laboratory at the back of his garden. There he and the boy examined the birds. D'Orbigny impressed on Fifi that if he was to appreciate the birds he must know what is inside them. Fifi had no thought yet of becoming an artist. He was simply obsessed with birds, because they flew. In the makeshift and amateur lab, they took the birds apart. Sliced their breasts, opened their rib cages. Examined the tiny bones, the structures inside, excised what would perish and tried to preserve it.

When he was eleven his father, who was an admiral —

"An admiral?" exclaims Bayfield.

— an admiral — tried to make him a naval man, but he was sent home from the school, hopeless at geometry. He returned to his birds, and the woods.

THE FOG IS closing in again.

Bayfield pushes the *Owen* back into the water. Audubon stays behind. His young gentlemen are coming for him.

NOW THEY ARE WAITING FOR WIND; they cannot sail. The whole of Audubon's party sets out in the whaleboat to search for specimens. Godwin has his eye on a high, cliffed island that is a breeding place for foolish guillemots. They approach from the lee side in the whaleboat; the male birds with their white breasts stand about in throngs. The females are on the nests in the grey, monumental rock.

"If we land there they'll all fly off their nests," says Audubon, and points the way to a smaller island nearby, where there is a set of rock ledges over the waves and the colony is smaller.

When they climb ashore, hundreds of birds come to their feet, walking erect with their legs apart, waving their short, paddle-like wings. They try to sense the men's intent, and, finding no violence there, push each other out of the way with human-sounding complaints, to let the big boots pass. Audubon leads the party gingerly up from the shore, careful not to trample the clustering birds.

The guillemots try to run with him. They fall over and flap their wings; they sprawl head-first down the rocks. Their white shirtfronts are stained with the muck of the cormorant's nests that are mingled with their own. Speaking soothingly, Audubon walks to the end of the point to look at the breeding island. Its cliffs appear deserted.

But Godwin has seen the shallop anchored behind some rocks by the nesting island. It is a poor excuse for a ship, with patched sails and unpainted sides themselves patched with seal skin on the seams.

"What on earth is that?" says Audubon.

"Eggers," says Godwin grimly. "They've claimed it." He points to a party of men skulling a skiff toward it. "We'll go elsewhere. We don't want to get in their way."

"They'll disturb the nests! I'll warn them off," says Audubon.

"You'll stay back, if you have half a brain," says Godwin. "I've seen honest fishermen killed for getting in the way of their take."

"You know far too much about these Eggers," Audubon says.

"I've been amongst them."

"And a bodyguard too! A man of wide experience."

"Gentlemen," says Captain Emery.

"That I am not," says Godwin. "But I'm bound to see that the one who is does not get shot."

Johnny prevents Audubon from launching himself across the Eggers' path.

"Listen to him, Father," says Johnny. "Stay and watch from here."

As the Eggers' skiff approaches the rocks of the breeding island,

Godwin turns his back on the scene. "You'll see for yourselves. They won't hesitate to use their muskets."

The party waits to watch the Eggers land, Audubon with his spy-glass. He sees the ruffians clamber out of their boat and, shouting, march up the rock. Clouds of guillemots rise in the air but thousands more remain standing over their nests, each, Audubon knows, with its single egg. When the first birds fall dead on the rock, the rest of the flock rises up and hovers over the killers. This gives the men free reign over the nests, and on they plunge.

Johnny holds his father back as the men continue firing into the air to frighten off the birds. Some fly away, but thousands are forced downward by the wings of their fellows, and the men wade into heaps of them, beating them with clubs. The birds are thick on the ground, battered, broken-winged, easy prey. From where they stand, Audubon and the young gentlemen can hear shooting, shouting and the screams of birds. It takes only thirty minutes, and then, with baskets loaded with eggs, the bloodstained men climb back in their skiff.

By this time Audubon has turned his back on the grisly scene. His face has gone white; his voice is rough.

"Six men have destroyed hundreds of birds and their futures," he says. As if he might add, "Are you satisfied?"

"Aye," says Godwin.

"What will they do with them?"

"They'll stash the eggs and rest now, and rip the feathered skin off the birds and cut the breast for bait. They'll eat what they can and get drunk on the grog they keep in the hold and fall asleep in their dirt. Next day they'll go to the next place, for they know them all, and begin again. There isn't much left after the Eggers have been. They don't care, for every year, there's more where that came from. Makes a nasty scene though," says Godwin, "all that waste. It smells frightful too."

The instant they return to the *Ripley,* Audubon goes to his deal table. He paints the Foolish Guillemots on guard, large, stark, with a funereal dignity. A pair, their white breasts lined up to the left of picture, and their bills identically angled above the horizon. Black, blue and white, male with a white tearline from its eye, female without. The female opens her bill to reveal a startling yellow mouth lining. But the picture is mute. The birds have presence without depth, their animation temporary and without meaning.

It is the night they have promised to dine on the *Gulnare*.

"I must dress for dinner? Quite a bore on the coast of Labrador," Audubon quips.

There is no light below; he has to make his toilet on a barrel on deck. The sun that has threatened to emerge for the latter part of the afternoon is now beaming above the narrow band of dwarf trees on the mainland to the west. He splashes his face with the fresh water a sailor has carried from the stream that flows into the harbour. Brushes his hair with the ivory-handled brush Lucy gave him when they married. Johnny offers him a small, cloudy-looking glass in which he notices, with surprise, that the sheen of grey growing over his locks merges with the silver backing of the glass.

"Why have you brought this, Son?"

"So that you can see yourself to shave."

"I am to shave as well?"

"You are."

Audubon raises the glass. It catches the sun and sends a white beam across the deck. He turns the mirror in his hand, playing with the beam, flashing it on the floor, at his son's feet, at his own feet. The beam cuts the air and can be seen, flickering, knifelike, at long distance. He sets it, a white circle, an interrogation, on the back of his hand. It reveals a delta lined and wrinkled, with raised sinews. An old hand. What is forty-eight? Far more than half a life, he thinks. And the Work is only half done. He still hears the birds screaming over their murdered eggs. There will be, tonight on the surveying ship, the implacable ticking of Captain Bayfield's chronometers.

He flicks the beam to the back of Johnny's hand. Johnny poses, keeping his hand exactly where it was. He knows to do this.

The same delta. *My son.* But the skin is plump, without the tiny diagonal puckers or the thin staves of sinews. He flicks the circle back to his own hand. In the intense reflected light, every line and hair of his own skin is suddenly sharp, separately defined. Lifted out of reality. "Do you see?" Audubon says, sharply. "This is how I paint a bird's feather. With that light, that beam."

He lets the beam escape across the deck, skipping, where it catches the raven's eye. The raven hops to its master's feet. He props the mirror behind the basin, from where, as the ship turns and tilts slightly on the lambent sea, the beam plays recklessly with sunlight. His razor is sharp, unused these three weeks. It cuts through the suds and stubble and, when it is pulled away, reveals the contour of his cheek. The flesh is a little sunken; he is thin beneath the cheekbone and his teeth are mostly memories.

"I grow old at the pace of light."

"No, Father, you do not."

And there he goes again trying to read the future. "What is in store for me? Will that god I pretend to worship allow me to see the Work through?"

Johnny, daredevil though he is, has the fear of God. "You mustn't pretend."

"I do. My only religion, as I have told you, son, is the Golden Rule."

"Of course, Father. Do unto others . . ."

"As you would have them do unto you."

Audubon is not through. "But if your god, Johnny, your mother's god, does not permit me to live, you and Victor will ensure the *Birds* is finished?"

"There will be no need for that. You are vital. Look at your eyes."

His eyes are peat brown, almond shaped, knowing and childlike.

Johnny's eyes are opaque, those of a caged wild thing.

WHEN AUDUBON ARRIVES on the *Gulnare*, Bayfield is busy with his theodolite. The device commands the centre of the foredeck, an altar around which he, the priest, in his blue uniform, moves with stately grace. Its brass wheels and dials with their intricate markings, their reflecting surfaces, are another kind of mirror into which the captain stares with no trace of vanity.

"Don't hurry; I shall wait," says Audubon. A silent Johnny beside him, the artist turns and looks out to sea. Again, as when he first saw her, he is pleased by the female shape of the figurehead. Gulnare herself.

Beneath her narrow throat, her bare breasts ride high over the calm and silvered surface of the harbour. She gives her presence to the waves and to what remains, to him, a shapeless landmass. Her proud shoulders are wide but her back flutes inward at the waist to the sweet triangle above her tailbone. "Good evening," he says to the figurehead.

A long, slow swell comes from nowhere and the woman bows back.

"Do you see what beauty does," he says to his son. "It presides."

Audubon is its captive. Powerless in its face, whether bird or woman.

"GOOD EVENING MR. AUDUBON. And young Mr. Audubon?" It is Augustus Bowen. His smile is not kind. With him he has a rotund little man with an eager, genial face. "This is Dr. Kelly, a naturalist who travels with us. You will enjoy one another's company."

Bowen withdraws, and Kelly begins to talk of today's discovery: the burrows of the *Mormon arcticus*, which they call sea parrots, or puffins. "They are dug in loam," he says, "in all directions under the surface, in some cases connected. When you find the end of the burrow there is the pure white egg. I would love to go collecting with you. But it is my job to run to the hold to keep the chronometers from being damaged when the sea is rough. Since the sea is always rough, I am scarcely seen above decks!"

When Bayfield completes his measurements he comes to stand at Audubon's side. "Now that I have seen your paintings, it is only fair that you should see my charts."

Audubon is unresponsive, staring at the water. His son can do the talking.

"I would like that very much," says Johnny firmly and loudly, taking his father's elbow.

The charts themselves are rolled and tucked into crevices in the captain's cabin. Some are flat and held together as the pages of a book, while others are loose and bound with black tape. Bayfield unrolls a large one, backed with pale blue linen.

"These are my letters to the pilots and the captains who come after us. Like your portraits they represent three dimensions settled into two. They tell us where we are on the globe. We delineate the coasts, locate and describe aids to navigation such as lighthouses, buoys, identifiable land structures — if there are any. Here, of course, there are almost none. We describe the characteristics of the bottom and add tidal data."

Audubon recognizes a line drawing of the shape of the water's edge at Little Natashquan, with indentations of shoreline and shoals. The depth of the water is marked; the hazardous hidden rocks are drawn in as if they were visible. Audubon traces with his eye the delicate, frenzied line that outlines the coast, that chaotic mess of rock and water rendered onto graph paper.

Johnny leans with curiosity over the chart.

"That shoal nearly stopped us," he says, pointing to the low reef that protected the harbour from winds from the southwest. "It will be of great help to those who follow to know exactly where it lies and at what depth. Although of course the depth changes with the tide."

Bowen materializes behind them; his courtesy belies the faint sneer that lingers on his face. His mock-solemn blue eyes hang on the painter as the captain lifts the sheet of paper and reveals a second beneath it.

"This is the passage we have travelled thus far. You see here I have used a much larger scale. But I am having difficulty with the Admiralty secretary. I need the largest scale where the sailing is most difficult, and the smallest when it is easier. Their Lordships want me to limit my use of scales to five only. But I maintain that I must be limited only by my own judgment. Their Lordships are concerned merely with the practicalities of printing."

Audubon smiles. "With this I can sympathize! I have sworn to reduce nothing. The birds will not shrink. But they overflow my pages!"

"Indeed. A bird may be rendered life-size. But this landscape must be reduced to be contemplated."

Audubon traces the line of the coast with his finger. Then he steps back. "How easy it appears to sail there! On your charts there is no fog, no cold, no tearing winds. You proceed by simple logic."

"The fog, the wind — these are moods, if you like. The map is free of these emotions."

Audubon looks more closely into Bayfield's calm visage.

"And the mapper? Is he also free?"

The question takes Bayfield aback.

"The only emotion we have during our computations," he says, "is the desire to save lives."

WHEN THEY STEP BACK ON DECK the sky is filled with scudding white clouds; new weather has arrived. The *Gulnare* faces a streaming wind and foam on the sea.

"This is a force four wind on the Beaufort scale," says Bayfield, almost automatically. "Do you see the foam? We shall be off at daybreak."

"Force four, climbing to five," Bowen says, happily.

But Audubon misses the good news. "You measure everything against a system," he persists.

Bayfield nods politely. "I do. My 'system,' or rather Admiral Beaufort's system, is science. Like your Linnaeus."

"No, no, no," says Audubon testily. "I am ahead of science. Science lives in books and dark laboratories. Mine is a new kind of truth, drawn from nature. People who see my book will never see the birds in the wilderness. They must be made to believe. I sit for hours within feet of the bird. I get my hands on the bird and in its blood. I must be accurate, or I am called a liar."

At this word, Bowen finds his opportunity. "I must ask you this. Your bird portraits may be beautiful to look at; I have not seen them, but the captain says so. But — 'accurate,' 'truthful'? You cannot paint a fact. I have seen the birds, and I doubt I would see them as you see them."

The painter is glad to have an opponent, a man on whom to train his anger. Johnny shifts as if to back him up.

"There are men, like you, Mr. Bowen, who say that my birds are deformed, or even creatures of fantasy. There are those who call me a fraud and a man of no talent. Who do not recognize nature when it is laid out on paper before them. They are not my concern. They have not sat three feet from the nest and beheld the duck who nourishes her young from food she first digests and then regurgitates. Nor have they watched the females form teams to protect fledglings, or sink themselves in water to allow their young to rest on their backs, and watch over them with what appears to be devotion," says Audubon. "I feel the birds in my heart."

Bowen smiles. "I have no doubt you do. But do you not wonder if your feelings mislead?" he presses.

"No. Feeling is my compass and my sextant," says Audubon. "It is all I have to judge by."

"You say 'simple' measurement," Bayfield says, "and you say we 'measure against a system' any distance from point A to point B. But that is not so. The distance is too large for us to measure. We *calculate* it. I measure a length, put this on a triangle, read an angle, multiply by a number. Only then do I have the distance, and it is arrived at by faith."

"By *faith?*"

"Yes. Faith in my mathematics. But faith requires imagination, don't you agree? Triangulation is an act of the imagination. There are three points — the base which is my eye, the distant station and the immutable star."

"Another sea captain once taught me something of this," says Audubon, warming just perceptibly. "On the *Delos.*"

"Three points. Where you stand, where you strive to be and the unreachable star by which you measure."

"I like that very much. He did not teach me that. You have laid down the coordinates of my life."

"Of mine as well. Where I stand, where I strive to be and the fixed point which defines both. Between these three is a relation. Once you know it, it can be used to discover any distance you have not yet travelled."

"I would like to know that prophetic relation," says Audubon gently.

The two men join in a smile that excludes Augustus Bowen. Johnny, relieved to have gotten this far without an explosion, places his hand on the small of his father's back.

THEY SIT AT THE ROUND TABLE in the captain's cabin, Bayfield and Audubon, Lieutenant Bowen, John Woodhouse and Dr. Kelly. There is an oil lamp and the smell of smoke. The soup slants in its bowls as the *Gulnare* strains against her anchor in the wind.

"Have you, in your rounds of potential subscribers in London, encountered my godfather, the Duke of Sussex?" Bowen enquires. "If not, I could arrange an introduction. I should think he might be useful in persuading the library of Parliament to subscribe."

It is a mischievous remark, as he is certain his godfather would send Audubon packing.

"I am not above knocking on strange doors, Mr. Bowen. God knows I have done it. But the doors of English lords, I have generally found, are not worth the trouble. In fact, English lords in my experience are worse than English rogues."

Bowen flushes red, while Kelly hides a smile: he has suffered far too many references to the duke on this journey.

"Take the Marchioness of Hereford," says Audubon. "An ignorant woman. I am told she papered her walls with the prints from my first volume. And the British Museum, which subscribed from the beginning, is so far behind on its payments that we are going to suspend delivery. I have no time to deal with these matters. My son Victor does it."

"And Mr. John Audubon Junior?" says Bowen, emphasizing the American way of naming. He has not yet relinquished his attack. He can only be a few years older than Johnny, who is intimidated into silence.

"Johnny is my right hand. A very fine shot and a fine painter too," says his father.

Bayfield takes charge. "A toast. To Labrador. To the birds that brought you here, Mr. Audubon. Shall we say grace? There is much to thank God for."

"May I?" says Audubon.

Johnny hides a smile.

On the table is a basket of eggs. Audubon lifts one and holds it to the lamplight. The egg is an oval perhaps three inches by two inches, its shell a cloudy blue green with pale green crusting and reddish blotches which are closer together toward the narrow end.

"Let us give thanks for this. Do you know what this is?" Audubon asks.

"The egg of a large waterfowl, I warrant. A Foolish Guillemot?" says Bowen.

"Yes, it is. A miraculous sort of egg. This guillemot, which is not foolish at all, mind you, nests high on the cliffs, on narrow ledges. Its egg, as you see, would be in danger of rolling and falling off into the sea, were it nudged, or blown by the wind. But the clever bird has adapted the shape. One end is more narrow than the other. See how it moves when pushed?" He pushes the egg. It rolls around its narrow end in a circle.

"Look," says Bayfield, delighted. "It is a compass."

Kelly murmurs in appreciation.

"You speak of grace and God. To the bird, indeed to me, the egg is god."

"You are bold, sir," chokes Bowen.

"Bold? Of course I am. And yet what I say is absolutely true. The egg before it is laid — that is, the instinct for the egg — brings the bird here. It forces these delicate sojourners made of cartilage and feather to fly thousands and thousands of miles, guided by we know not what, to this lonely place, in order that their lives should be renewed. Do you not think it is miraculous?"

"Yes," says Bayfield, "I do."

"This is our grace." Audubon puts the egg up against his eye. "This is the moon and the stars and the wind. It is the compass, the sextant if you like, and the calendar."

"Amen."

Bowen nudges Kelly. His godfather had said the painter was a showman.

A SAILOR WAITS ON THE TABLE, starting them out with glasses of grog. After the soup they eat cod, pan-fried, and then the flesh of four eider ducks, which have been skinned and torn apart and put on a fire. When they finish they are all heavy with food. The fat of the duck has congealed on the heavy white china plates and the juice has stained their chins. The men wipe their beards on napkins that are washed only when there is sun to dry them.

Now Bowen begins.

"I've been told that three hundred fishing vessels work this coast, averaging seventy-five tons each, and manned by fifty men to each six vessels," he says. "If you do the mathematics, that equals two thousand five hundred men. About one half of them are French and the other two quarters British and American. Each vessel when it leaves carries fifteen hundred quintals of codfish. Using the equivalent of one hundred twelve pounds per quintal, I get the figure of sixty million and four hundred thousand pounds of fish per season. Of course the fish are small on this coast, and weigh an average of four pounds each — we are talking of somewhere in the neighbourhood of twelve millions of fish." He smiles as he arrives at his figure. "It is a fine harvest."

"A great deal too fine," says Audubon. "When you understand that it has been going on for at least two hundred years and probably more. It cannot go on forever. They may just as well make a clean sweep of it and rid the seas of all fish forever!"

"But that would not be possible. Not by any chance at all. The fish are so numerous."

"On the contrary, it is entirely possible. And that is to say nothing of what these Eggers are doing to the wild birds! It is a war of extermination."

"Father," says Johnny.

"Have you seen Eggers?" asks Bayfield. "They generally try to stay out of our way."

"Oh yes, only today, just outside the harbour."

"They are a rough bunch, it is true. But, surely the birds abound in so many millions as to be beyond harm."

"I wonder that we all believe so. There are instances where the depredations of man have created scarcity in animals. In fact, where a species disappears altogether."

"I know of none such," says Bayfield, as the sailor brings pudding. "What sort is it?" he asks the sailor in the same breath. It is an acceptable vice, a love of sweets.

"Bread, sir," the sailor apologizes.

"I had them ask for berries on shore today," says Kelly. "But as I suspected, it is too early in the season."

"Later on, the native women will come selling cloudberries, as they did last year," says Bayfield with hope.

"If the smallpox or starvation hasn't taken them," murmurs Kelly.

"You say a species may disappear altogether? Of what example are you thinking, Mr. Audubon?"

"The Dodo is one. *Disparu.*"

"It is a French word," sniffs Bowen. "We don't have it in English."

"The key to it is flight. The birds could not fly, you see, and man simply killed them until there were no more."

"We do not see the Dodo today. But we cannot prove that the Dodo has *disparu*," says Bowen.

"In English we do have a word. Extinct." Kelly bestows his smile on the table.

"Surely God would not permit such a thing," says Bowen.

"I doubt that God has much to do with it," says Audubon. "It is man's doing."

Bayfield rises and lifts his Bible off the nearest shelf. "I keep this to hand," he explains. "God has entered our conversation twice tonight. Shall we look at his own words? Genesis 1, verses 27 and 28."

And there they sit, five men, full of dinner, under the light of an oil lamp, in the farthest reach of the charted territory of the New World. The wind is up and the ship's timbers creak and sometimes there is the snap of a bit of canvas; the coffee tilts in their cups. The captain reads from his favourite book and the others listen obediently. His voice deepens, betraying the pleasure he takes in the words.

"So God created man in his own image, in the image of God created he him; male and female created he them. And God blessed them, and God said unto them, Be fruitful, and multiply, and replenish the earth, and subdue it: and have dominion over the fish of the sea, and over the fowl of the air, and over every living thing that moveth upon the earth."

Audubon has listened with drooping eyes. He has never liked long meals.

"'Have dominion over the fish of the sea, and over the fowl of the air, and over every living thing that moveth,'" Bayfield repeats. "That would seem clear."

There is no response.

"Have dominion over," repeats Bayfield.

"Replenish the earth," rebuts the painter.

"And subdue it. *Subdue*," insists Bowen. "Perfectly clear."

Audubon is suddenly weary of the English. They are too sharp. They smile but do not mean it. "All that is clear is that the Bible was not written by a bird or a fish!"

"I find that a sacrilegious remark," huffs Bowen.

"Ah no, but to the contrary! It is an expression of one of your facts."

Johnny knees his father under the table.

"Perhaps I do not say it well," says Audubon. "I mean to say, it shows that the Bible was written by men."

"The word of our Lord is that the creatures of the earth are for us to make use of."

"It does not say that after we are finished there ought to be nothing left moving!"

This is a strenuous remark and for a moment the men sit stunned. Then Bowen speaks.

"Surely you exaggerate. The birds and the fish exist in such pro-fusion!"

Now there is a longer silence. Audubon reaches, as if for reassur-ance, for the eggs, which still sit in their basket in the middle of the table. He takes one between thumb and forefinger and holds it before his face.

"This egg," Audubon says, "is the future."

The other men push back their chairs.

There is a silence in which they hear the creaking of the mast, a sound which brings Bayfield peace, but only increases the artist's anx-iety.

"Nature is unbounded," says Bayfield gently. "It is our duty to contain it."

Audubon's face registers his scorn. "Once contained, it is no longer nature!"

"I am not certain I will grant you that, sir," says Bayfield. "It is nature but nature brought under man's influence."

"It cannot be both," announces Audubon savagely.

Bayfield subsides. He is a little in awe of this strange man.

DINNER IS OVER. The five men stand on deck. The ship rolls. The demoiselle Gulnare arches into the gloom. And at this moment, because it is their moment, the cusp of day and night, the birds pass. There is the sound of an urgent whirring of wings as a long line of eider ducks heads majestically out to sea. The artist looks up, exultant.

"There is one final hour of daylight," he says. "I must get back to my birds."

Song

No sooner does he put his foot on the red and grey shore rocks than he hears the magical song. A little like that of a canary and resembling a wood lark. But more beautiful than either. Perhaps a finch, but more vigorous than any finch he knows. He hears it and then it is gone. He stops and stands silent to hear the song again, and when he does, it is coming from another bush, a farther grove; he moves toward it stealthily and as fast as his legs can take him.

The bird's song draws him around the shore. Odd, to be chasing a song. It strikes the ear and gives pleasure and then it dies away. The singing bird flies from one tree to another as he walks underneath.

The song is unknown to him, and beautiful. The song is louder, stronger and more wild than that of the canary. It is the most beautiful song he has heard on this continent.

Following the song, looking upward, he loses his way. This happened when he was a boy, in France. But he always got the bird in the end. Wanting to know what was inside it, where the song came from, he took it back to D'Orbigny, and they took it apart. That is how he learned what a bird is.

If he ever learned.

There is tame song and there is wild song. Tame song is beautiful, but wild song is haunting.

The bird, alone amongst creatures, has song within its being.

Song has been given to the bird to attract its mate, and perhaps to remind man of what lies beyond. The song can be a warning, or a call, but sometimes, Audubon believes, the song is play. A bird may sing for the joy of it.

Bachman has accused him of having a poor ear for birdsong.

His English, too, retains its odd French accent and rhythms. Yet he is musical; he can play the flageolet. What does it mean to have no ear for birdsong? Perhaps only that he cannot remember it. He can never recreate the song, later. He cannot imitate the birds' song.

The bird is singing out its essence.

What does the bird's song mean?

Perhaps it means nothing except this: that the singer and the listener come to each other with need and hunger in the joy of being made of flesh and air.

And then it is over.

The end of the song is present in its beginning and all through it, and this too is its beauty. There was no other possibility than this, and hence no blame, no hurt.

He shoots. The song stops. A tiny feathered dart falls from the treetop to the ground.

He searches the spot but cannot find the bird.

At Last
THE WIND

The *Ripley* slides beyond the shoals. Godwin and Audubon are on deck. The wind from the open water slaps both men across the back as they stand beneath the crossbeam, the painter looking back at Little Natashquan and the pilot looking to where they are going, and back again, to be certain of their progress through the gap. They have left the *Gulnare* behind. Bayfield's schooner trembles within reach of the lethal black arm of granite lying in the passage.

"He's taking the west channel out."

"He can't get through there. He ought to know," says Godwin. "He surveyed the damn thing yesterday."

The naval schooner tacks, hangs, swings about and appears to be turning back.

"You see? She can't get out," says Godwin with satisfaction. "Even the damn Royal Navy surveyors can't get out. You're bloody lucky we're still afloat."

"Where's Captain Emery?" Audubon scans the deck, casts his eyes up the rigging and sees Emery's reassuring legs descending. The Yankee captain jumps the last two yards to land beside Audubon; Emery is grinning in his confident way.

"That's done it," he says.

Godwin turns his back. "I'll be heading out to sea. I'll try to manage this rotten coastline no more."

"I asked him to stay close to shore, Captain Emery. But it seems our pilot would prefer to take his instructions from you."

"Gentlemen," says Emery mildly.

"Plenty a' birds on the islands," interjects the pilot. "The painter can see 'em."

Each man now having become third party, they speak to and through Emery, who turns his head politely first one way then the other.

"On the islands? There's gulls and gannets. That's about it."

"Perroquets too. It'll have to do 'im. I'm not bringin' this ship to ruin."

"This man said he knew the coast."

"No one knows this coast," says Emery gently.

"I'll tell you what I know," says Godwin, growing louder and more pugnacious. "This coast is bloody black hell on the water. And haunted into the bargain. You hear that howling at night?" His obdurate stance on the foredeck reminds the painter that, for the moment, the pilot has the upper hand.

"That howling is wolves," says Audubon with asperity. He doesn't like the sound much himself; he'd prefer the gentle hooting of a barred owl, for instance, such as he heard near Charleston.

"That's another good thing about staying out at sea. We won't hear the wolves."

"Can it be that the one-time bodyguard of a New Orleans cotton speculator, a fighter of duels and trader in used muskets, is afraid of a wolf? You have charts," he persists.

"Charts! You mean those rolls of paper? It's no good pretending they can help. You can't read 'em and sail too! Damn rocks lurking under the water popping up wherever. And that's to say nothing of the fogs that choke a man and wind that tears at you 'til you're mad. Charts don't tell you about sailin' blind. And who's to know whether the depths was taken at low tide or high? Anyways," he says with finality, "they're all wrong."

He gestures to the harbour they've just come from. The *Gulnare* has retreated. "Look at that! Just about hit, they did. You can bet the new charts your Royal Navy friends are making aren't going to be any better than the old. Look! They can't even get their ship out!"

"We've an advantage," the captain puts in. "The *Ripley* can manoeuvre in less space. The *Gulnare*'s too big for that harbour. She's

140 tons to our one hundred and she draws much more water. They know it. But they've got a job to do. As do we."

"I'm just telling you that I won't be getting us in to shore, not until we get to Ouapitagone," asserts Godwin.

"Let it drop, then, Godwin," says Captain Emery, genially. "You've won your battle, don't you see?"

The wind has caught them fair now and, as if it subscribed to Godwin's views, whisks the *Ripley* out toward the open. Audubon eyes the pilot with fury and then retreats to where Anonyme is chained. He takes the raven on his wrist.

"Godwin is making us sail in the open sea all the way up the coast to the next harbour," he confides. "It is dangerous in the open, and we'll miss the birds. There will be storms. We could be wrecked, out so far from land. This bodes ill." He exaggerates the movement of his lips: "Bodes ill, bodes ill, bodes ill."

Anonyme cocks his head; the black beads that are his eyes glisten.

"Bad luck! Bad luck! Bad luck!" Audubon's visions of fire at sea, of flailing until he sinks under the frigid grey water, of his drawings washed out and flung on the winds, all these are conjured by the pilot. The knowledge that he is in Godwin's power is enraging.

He paces.

The raven paces, too, on Audubon's wrist, lifting and placing his feet as if kneading the man's flesh. He caws gently, craning his neck. Only when Audubon talks does the tame bird become silent.

"You are still young," the artist murmurs to the bird. "But when you are my age you will notice how strange are the circles of life, that I should encounter a man who worked for Vincent Nolte here, in this place. It is strange but it is not meaningless. I fear some evil pursues me."

Anonyme stretches his head, nudging the artist's finger from underneath. Audubon lifts and turns the bird's head so that its black eyes are directed toward his lips and about six inches away. "Bodes ill," he says again.

"Bodes," says the raven.

Audubon smiles and rewards the bird with a piece of bread. "The globe is a smaller place today than it was a decade ago. The man who is disconcerted by the closing of these distances is he who resists capture. The man whose truth is out there, in the wild."

The bird rests his beak on the very edge of the man's lips. "Anonyme," says Audubon. "You have been taken from your element."

He feels a sudden, intense pity for the raven. Its name suits it much more than it had his poor cousin, long ignored in France. But he regrets bringing the bird, and the name, on this journey.

He likes the past to stay behind him, not to loop forward and menace him from the front. Nolte's reappearance threatens him: but why should it? He tries to see this coincidence as other than a bad omen. It was Nolte's kind introduction, after all, that had led him to the Rathbones, in Liverpool, and the Rathbones to his first success in England. It was pure luck that he came upon Nolte in the first place, and better luck that he approached him for aid before the cotton market collapsed. If he is frightened by the spectre of Vincent Nolte it is because the merchant personifies the slings and arrows of outrageous fortune. And most tellingly, the man saw through him. Recognized him as kin. Saw through to his inferiority. And appeared to like Audubon nonetheless. It puzzles him and it shames him.

WITH THE WEST WIND IN ITS SAILS, the *Ripley* flies up the coast. Audubon is young again and riding hard on that little Indian pony, Barro, that he bought for Lucy for twenty dollars. Racing on a trail along a high ridge in the Allegheny Mountains, he came upon another rider. The man wore beautiful oxblood leather boots and sat on a tall, glossy stallion. They were going the same way. The stranger suggested a race to a little inn in Laurel Hill. Whoever got there first would buy dinner. Audubon arrived and saw nothing of the man so he went to bed, certain that he'd won.

He was having breakfast the next morning when the landlady asked could a gentleman join his table: it was very cold and he was by the fire. The tall man with the oxblood boots entered the room, hearty, handsome and wearing a topcoat. He realized how rich Nolte was when he said he'd had to bail out Congress, which had promised Lafayette two hundred thousand dollars but had no money to give him. When he asked Audubon about his nationality, the artist said he was an Englishman. After all, he had married Lucy.

"You are no more English than you are American," roared Nolte into the stillness of the breakfast room. "You are French and not a regular Frenchman at that!"

Audubon admitted it. It turned out the merchant had his own confused background, Italian and German and Swedish all mixed together and descended from an Austrian deserter to France. He too had become an American through the Louisiana Purchase. But Nolte had succeeded in business where Audubon failed; Nolte had connections with everyone from Napoleon on down. Encouraged by the other man's bluster to tell his own tales, Audubon made his father an admiral, and his painting teacher, David, the king's drawing master.

"David. He's the clever one, changing horses midstream," said Nolte, peering at Audubon. "First the king's painter, then Napoleon's."

Audubon had to admit he was out of touch.

"When were you born?"

"The year 1785. The same year," he smiled exquisitely and sadly, "as the little lost dauphin."

"Where?"

"In Paris, of course." It was easy to plant the hint; he'd done it before. The son of the beheaded king and queen was just his age. "But I was taken away by the family members who survived. For a time I was imprisoned. That's how I came to love the birds. My keeper made me an aviary so that I could watch them. They were free, and I was not."

But he had told this story to the wrong man; he often did.

He and Nolte rode together all the way to Lexington. Audubon showed him the few bird portraits he carried. Nolte squinted at them and asked why he didn't paint classical subjects. "You'd find more ready buyers than with birds. Or go around to the military camps and paint the generals and heroes of the day. There's a market there." Nolte confessed that he had wanted to be an artist, but his father discouraged him. "You will have to feed on crusts," the old man said.

When they parted, Nolte revealed he was no ordinary victim of Audubon's charm.

"There are men who cannot tell the truth," Nolte had said as they shook hands. "There are men who, if they tell you they are lying, are still lying, so that only a fool would believe them. It is a mark of genius, and I would never accuse such a man of chicanery. I believe scarcely a thing you say, but you have entertained me well. I wish you good luck with your paintings. You will need an iron will and much perseverance, but I suspect you know that already. Good day to you, sir."

Audubon had stood awash, first with a kind of delight in being seen through, and then with regret that pride would likely prevent him ever seeing the man again.

But that pride had deserted him when he was desperate.

When Lucy was a governess at Bayou Sarah and Audubon was living on crusts, he went to New Orleans. He knew Nolte was in the town. He even saw him in the streets, so tall, so charged with energy, followed by this one and that to do his bidding. We met as equals once, thought Audubon, fading into the shadow of the public house where he stayed. He was ashamed to look him up.

Later, armed with his dream and Lucy's savings, he humbled himself before Nolte. He told him that the Americans mocked him, and that he must launch himself in Europe to make his book.

Nolte was no less amused than he had been the first time they met. He offered an introduction to his partner Richard Rathbone, a Quaker cotton merchant in Liverpool. "Please do all you can to help this fine artist," he wrote, "of European birth and well connected."

Audubon wonders now if Godwin had been there at that meeting, lurking in the background, out of the candlelight? Did he watch the rough frontiersman; did he wonder if he was a danger to the rich?

WITH HIS PORTFOLIO and his box of watercolours, a fugitive from debt and a disappointment to his family, he boarded the *Delos*, bound from New Orleans to Liverpool, on the 27th of May, 1827. He carried Nolte's letter to prove that he was a man of consequence. There were other letters, but now, looking back, they did not matter at all.

Boarding, he was fired as if from a cannon into his future, the one he must invent. Then the wind failed and the *Delos* sat, becalmed, just out of the harbour. He was frightened of what he would find in Europe; he had been schooled by the scorn of the Americans, who smelled something suspect in him. He read Byron's *The Corsair* and identified with the hero. "Feared, shunned, belied, ere youth had lost her force."

He watched dolphins leap around the ship. The sailors caught a shark that had ten live sharks inside, only one of which made its slippery way out into the sea and away. He took this as an omen and conjured the multiplication of his successes.

He drew terns, warblers, green herons. He wrote in his diary. Sat, sat, sat, with no wind and a heart that was sad, excited, torn and set. He fretted for Lucy and his children: he imagined what disasters might befall them without his protection. He was occasionally stricken with horror that he should be so bold as to try to conquer England, grand England, whose language he butchered daily.

WHEN AT LAST THERE WAS WIND and the *Delos* began to fly, it was as if the sails had filled with his own fear. The wind carried them south and across the equator. "Why south?" he asked the Captain.

"To catch the favourable trade winds."

To go east, to Europe, he had to go south, to the world of his past, of his island birthplace. In his diary he alluded to this southern place as his home, to this mixing of dark and brilliant sun, to the remembered yellow, red and turquoise. To his name: Jean Rabin, Creole of Santo Domingo. *Obscene child, born of whoredom*: that is the language of the law. He was created by heedless behaviour, and kept by connivance. A man such as he made his way in the world only by a constant application of will.

The captain of the *Delos* taught him a little navigation. What were Bayfield's words? Where I stand, where I strive to be and the fixed point which defines the two.

THE WIND CARRIED him eastward. When it dropped, he was set down. At British customs his drawings were passed from hand to hand

and examined with dull prurience; his work was declared American (little did they know!), and payment of fourteen pence per pound exacted. Beyond the customs house he was free.

Liverpool delighted him, viewed from the water. But when he stepped on land he discovered that the air was black with coal smoke. It was a black that stayed on every window, and soon filled his own throat. He hoisted his portfolio to his shoulders, and strode from door to door. Many of the people he had letters to, including Lucy's relatives, snubbed him. He forgot their names. They were insignificant. None of it mattered — not the waiting, the cold-eyed servants, the quizzical matrons — because Nolte's letter to the Rathbones bore fruit. The Rathbones took him to their bosom overnight; the children clustered at his knee and pulled his long coiled locks, the women fanned themselves and extended to him the clever little tendrils of conversation that only ladies can invent.

And praise! They exclaimed over his drawings. The mother was called the Queen Bee. The daughter was Hannah Mary. A sense came on him the instant they met: she was his kin; she saw into his heart. When he showed his drawings, when he made the sounds of the wild birds, and told his tales of adventures in the wilderness, Hannah Mary was stirred. She giggled when he leapt a gate rather than open it. She called him spider legs. His strength, gained from days on horseback and week-long walks, could be tamed for a cotillion and his touch was delicate enough for a cup of fine china, his eye sophisticated enough to see the beauty in old books. Her too-frank brown eyes could not hide her feelings, could not leave his. In her presence he knew himself to be a conquering hero. And he was comforted. The shore was not so strange.

It was, of course, the world of Lucy's past he was seeing. He wrote to her, describing the delights of Hannah's person, her slowness and grace, the low and musical constancy of her voice. He told Lucy she would love Hannah, and the Queen Bee, and described to her the musical evenings and the games of cards. His joy flowed back to him, joy in the shapes, sounds of English hills and English houses, English birds and English talk. He saw himself in Hannah's eyes, and the vision gave him courage.

He drank up his hosts' affection like a man who has been lost in a desert and suddenly finds water. In America, there had been a pressing sense of familiarity, a dangerous tendency to bring him down to the level of others, to bring in information from his history. But here in England he had none. The behaviour of ten years before, or twenty, was of no interest. He was remaking himself; all that mattered was what he would be.

He lied, although it did not feel like lying. His father was that admiral. He himself studied with David. He did not calculate these lies, he merely applied them. He told the story that the moment required. There was no way to stop. He had no control over his lies, if that is what they were; they were impulses.

And yet he did not always lie. He told the truth one night to Hodgson, Rathbone's partner. Hodgson, who also had a letter of introduction from Nolte, had invited Audubon to his country house; the painter spent a night. He watched the children say their prayers, and played French lullabies on his flageolet for them. Before bed, he confided to his host that he was Haitian: Jean Rabin, Creole of Santo Domingo.

A secret is a seed; it lies in darkness until it meets its season. Scattered carelessly, it most often dies. But rarely, it finds a hospitable place where it swells and sets down roots. Hodgson was surprised but not concerned by the news; he noted it in his diary and went to sleep. When the artist began to attract admiring notices in the press, Hodgson might have denounced him as a liar. He did not. Instead he left this puzzling contradiction of nativity to lie in his leather notebook, where it might have turned to dust but where, instead, it came to light a century and a half later. Perhaps he understood. Audubon lied but he sometimes told the truth and that was the trouble. Perhaps Hodgson saw that Audubon was doomed to a lifetime of arriving, of using every fibre of his considerable will to win over the stranger.

THE NEXT DAY AUDUBON was gone before dawn to walk through the fields to the seashore, and finally home to Rathbones. He returned to Hannah Rathbone's loving eyes, her hands laid in his open palms and he, facing her, square-shouldered and almost of a size. He did not tell Hannah his secret. He could not risk the loss of her good opinion. One can never have too much love.

August, September, October, and Audubon stayed on with the Rathbones. He could not leave. He listened to advice on how he should proceed with his birds. He basked in home and family. He wooed Hannah when he might have been courting fame. But he had no choice: he must be loved.

To arrive in a new land. To step off a ship into unknown territories, meet strange faces, find warmth and shelter and food. This was his task over and over. As the birds find mates and nest at the end of each journey, so he must win his due, time and again.

His life he now recast; it became the Work whose birth he had come here to shepherd. He took Nolte's introduction to the naturalist Thomas Traill. Thomas Traill introduced him to the bookseller Henry Bohn.

"The birds must be life size," he said to Bohn.

Bohn replied that a large book was possible. "It is the taste of persons who entertain company these days to have a book laid out on a table as entertainment for visitors. But," he said, "it cannot be so big that it makes the others look the worse, or clutter the table."

These were not factors Audubon had considered.

"A book as large as you want would be beyond the means of ordinary people. You could hope for sales only of one hundred copies, for large public institutions."

"There is so much competition," said the bookseller. "You will need to find attention for yourself. But you are charismatic. Your tales are fascinating. And the birds, of course, are good. I believe you have the seeds of success." Bohn said that if he wanted to know more he should go to London immediately to consult naturalists on the subjects of engravers, printers and papermakers.

But he did not go to London.

There followed a lost pocket of time. Two months when all the world was held off. Just as he courted Lucy in the caves where the phoebes nested, so he courted Hannah on the hillsides near Matlock.

All day they rambled through reddening leaves and flocks of migrating birds. Out of sight of houses and passersby they spread a blanket, and sat. While he sketched she fell asleep and when he was finished he lay alongside her, so still that the birds forgot them. In the evenings he wrote in his diary and to Lucy. To Lucy he did not lie. He shared all his passions with his wife, and Hannah was one of them.

Holding Hannah in his arms, as the imagined and now conceivable future took form in his head, he pondered Bohn's advice. Finally in October he tore himself away and travelled to Edinburgh, again with his portfolio and dozens of letters of introduction. But something of Hannah's love made an aura around him. When he walked into the tall, steep city with its enveloping fogs and soft grey stones, it was as a conquering woodsman. And Edinburgh too had to open its heart to him.

BAFFLED

———

LITTLE NATASHQUAN HARBOUR, *JUNE 28, 1833*

The *Ripley* barely weathered the East Pt and got out. We were less fortunate for the wind headed us just as we came to the Pt and obliged us to tack within 10 fathoms of it. The western channel appeared the widest and Mr. Owen thought he had found all the rocks in it but we soon added to his knowledge for on the second board to the Westw'd in the narrowest part of the channel we struck.

. . . I ordered the after sails to be taken in, the headyards thrown aback & head sheets over to windward keeping the foresail set to assist in paying her off more rapidly. Had this not been done she would have no sooner floated than she would have run stem on to the rocky Islet. As it was a man might have leaped from our flying jib boom to end upon the rocks. Having enough of it for one trial I ran back and moored again. No injury was done even to the rates of the Chronometers for Kelly instantly ran down to them & took them in his hands 'till we were afloat. I thought it proper to remain for the night.

— *Surveying Journals*, Henry Wolsey Bayfield, Captain, Royal Navy

———

Having failed to make his exit, Bayfield has no choice but to remain at Little Natashquan throughout the next day.

He searches out Kelly in the hold of the ship. The near grounding on the shoal at the harbour's entrance made the doctor fly below to the chronometers. Each of the thirteen is swaddled in cotton and cradled in some niche he has found. One is in his arms. He is pink-faced as a nursery maid. Bayfield wants to talk about Audubon.

"Last night our dinner guest was vehement on the subject of killing birds. But he is a hunter."

"I believe it is not killing but plundering that angers him," says Kelly in his gently correcting voice.

"You used a word last night. I have consulted the dictionary." Bayfield pulls a piece of paper from his pocket. On it is written:

Extinct: *middle English from Latin* exstinctus *past participle of* exstinguere *(fifteenth century) a) no longer burning b) no longer active c) no longer existing.*

"Is this what Audubon meant by '*disparu*'? The Dodo is extinct, can we say?"

"It has been proven with the Dodo, and other examples both before, and since. Species can disappear, never to return." Kelly moves from clock to clock at a rather rough toss of the ship, tucking the padding around the ticking metal instruments.

Bayfield trails behind, wanting his attention.

"What is this 'never'?" he challenges. "How do we know it will 'never' return?"

Kelly has the number 761 chronometer in his hands, careful not to tilt it. He bends his ear to listen for any irregularity of its ticking. "When there are no living individuals left, not a male, not a female, we assume the species cannot return," he says.

"But then is it not ordained? Can we not say this is a result of natural violence — savagery, if you will? Could we see the natural world as ruling itself, if not God ruling nature?"

The doctor has an authority that comes from a sense of quiet goodness. And he is the only one on shipboard not under Bayfield's direct command. "Animals never kill enough to extinguish a species.

Man may do so. If I understood the artist correctly, what he meant was that the greater danger we face is in man's encroaching on the wild lands, which these birds and animals need to prosper."

"So he means *I* am a danger?" Bayfield is not so much incredulous as fascinated by the idea of himself as villain, of his enterprise as being in any way sinister. "Because we open the frontier for people we close it for the wild creature?" That he is a danger has never before occurred to him. He is Bayfield of Bayfield Hall. He has taken the benevolence of his service to God and King for granted.

"Not you, yourself, Captain. Not personally." Kelly keeps his eyes on number 761. There is definitely a tremor in the minute hand.

"And why not? If this is the truth then I must consider my part in it."

Bayfield climbs the ladder to the deck and looks out at Labrador. Green and rocky wastes rise to distant plateaus, all empty save for the itinerant Montagnais, all shapeless, unknown country. He loves it, he knows that. But how does he love it? As a territory to be possessed? Claimed for a country? Yes. But he is dimly aware of another way he loves it, as a refuge to himself, a place apart. He has given no thought to the loss of that. And he will give no thought to it now. He reviews his mission: to chart the unknown. That Audubon would refute its value astonishes him.

An artist must allow his mind to run contrary to the thoughts of the day; otherwise, what news would he bring back to tempt his audience? And yet, in having these thoughts, in stepping beyond the conventions of his society, he risks offending. Audubon did offend, last evening, charming as he was; he offended perhaps as much by his ideas as by the strength of his passions.

THE *GULNARE* PASSES one last night at Little Natashquan. The harbour feels empty without the *Ripley*. At daylight on the thirtieth the wind is moderate from the southwest and the sky cloudy, with not enough sun to make observations. The captain has every sail set, fore and aft, and the jibs half up, ready. Conditions are not ideal but he decides to risk it. He sends Bowen in the second gig to sit on the lee side of the central reef to keep the *Gulnare* off it. The instant the men lift anchor they hove away and in a minute are standing out under full sail. They pass Bowen and get to the end of the reef, but the wind suddenly heads at them there, just as they are crossing into unsheltered water. He feels the swell under the bow pushing them for the shoal. Bowen prepares to fend off, though how to do so without crushing the gig, he does not know. Kelly dives for the hold, where he can be heard speaking in soothing tones to his clocks.

They stall. It looks, again, as if they won't make it out. Bayfield nearly gives orders to tack to avoid hitting, but just at that moment the wind gives them a compass point, and there is no choice. Ten yards off the bow the surf is running up on the end of the point when they swing around and out into the wind. The sails are useless, baffled by the wind. The swell shakes the wind out of the sails, so that she moves more slowly than can be believed, but with several tacks they inch their way past and are suddenly clear of the reefs, into deep water.

The wind continues light all day. The tars put out their lines and jig for cod. They catch one that is three foot, six inches long and weighs twenty-one pounds. When, at seven in the evening, the *Gulnare* finally gets around Natashquan Point, Bayfield stays on deck. By one in the morning they only have eight or nine miles to go to Kégashka, where they moored the year before and where they have left a beacon. Bayfield goes below and sleeps three hours. At four Bowen calls him: they can see the beacon. At six, on a calm, cloudy morning, they pull into their old Kégashka berth. This was where he ended last summer and turned back.

Bayfield goes out to a little island in the harbour. The gulls retreat with raucous protests to the waves. There has been no sign of the *Ripley*. He wonders where the Americans are. Godwin will have them out beyond the islands. With good reason: the sailing near the shore is even trickier than Bayfield recalled. There are few harbours deep enough for a schooner. Ahead now is all uncharted territory. He wonders how he ought to proceed, himself. The only way is to use the smaller boats and leave the *Gulnare* moored. His plan is to stay with the ship and take his measurements, and at the same time to outfit the

Owen, provision it for ten days and send Bowen in it up the coast to Ouapitagone.

Thinking with every step of Audubon's prohibitions, he takes only one egg from every second or third nest. These will go well with breakfast.

TUESDAY DAWNS A RARE, marvellous, sunny day. The *Ripley* has anchored beside a large island miraculously clear of shoals on the leeward side. Audubon goes on land with the young gentlemen.

He makes it past rocks and around swamp and climbs over a ridge, finding himself in a small valley out of sight of the sea and out of reach of the wind. The country becomes an arbour of green of an alchemical vigour that he has never before seen, the closest being the slime of a North Carolina swamp. But this is crisp underfoot, with a close ground-cover in which berries and tiny unknown flowers grow. He stoops to examine them. White, yellow, blue, none taller than a few inches, each flower is exquisite. He puts several in his specimen basket for the flower press. He will send them to Maria. He commits to memory the exact blend of coral, red and pale green, and the gleam of each fine hair on the underside of the petals, the small black dot that stands out from the tip.

He hears a set of sweet, magical notes. He stops, captivated, the tiny flower and its root between his thumb and forefinger. He does not even expel his breath. If the bird sang once, it will sing again.

He hears it. *Jew-jew-jew-jew-je-eeeeeeee-do-je-e-e-e-to*.

It is the song of that new bird, but what is it? A wood lark? They are only known in Europe. It must be a new bird, a bird with an angel's song.

He hears it again, to his far right. He glides silently to the place where his ears tell him the bird lurks. But he can see nothing. There are no trees; the largest vegetation is bushes perhaps eight feet tall. In one of these, the bird must perch. His ear strains for sound. There is a stream, a thin rush of water under the sound of the moschettoes and the occasional *burr-up* of a frog.

The song comes again. It is the most superb birdsong he has heard on this continent. *Jew-jew-jew-jew-je-eeeeeeee-do-je-e-e-e-to.*

The songster repeats his notes. Audubon's eye follows his ear and there, just before the last note sounds, he sees, in a bush, the telltale flicker of a wing.

He whistles low. And then in pursuit raises his voice. "Come, John, Tom — over here!"

Tom Lincoln and his son are on top of the ridge. But they hear him, or perhaps only see his beckoning arm.

The bird dives off the branch to the ground under the thicket, where it vanishes.

The three spread like a net over the green-clad rock. The little bird is wild, so wild. They follow its every move for an hour. It flits from bush to bush, then to the ground, and each time it alights it sings so sweetly. Strange that, although it is pursued, it sings for its mate. The notes are either a warning or a mating call that the bird cannot restrain.

Tom goes far out to one side and up on the ridge. The little warbler alights on a bush within shot. He raises his gun and, with his usual accuracy, hits it.

The body is there, in the moss. In a moment Audubon is holding it in his hand, its wings spread open in his palm. He strokes its feathers. He can feel the life ebbing, the heartbeat diminish.

It is lovely. It was even lovelier when it sang, and now the air is lonely without it.

When the young gentlemen catch up with him, he is still gazing into the palm of his hand.

"A new species!" he says.

It was what he wanted, more than anything. It is what he must do here: find new species, to keep ahead of his rivals. To prove his worth, not just as a painter, but as a new kind of bird artist: an ornithologist who observes in the wild.

"I'll name it for you, Tom. Tom Lincoln's Finch. *Fringilla lincolnii*."

In that instant the bird grows cooler and lighter in Audubon's hand.

"There must be another. And a nest as well."

The two young men are off to prowl the thickets, squatting, reaching with their guns. He tucks the little creature into his basket and races back to the *Ripley*. He tries to remember the song but he cannot, exactly. Bachman is right when he tells him he needs bird-song lessons.

DOWN THE LADDER to the hatch he goes, out of the sunlight to the dark, damp hold. It is filling up with specimen jars and hanging skins, like the tomb of some primitive king.

The bird is tiny, but he succeeds in wiring it on the plank into the position he wants, perched on a twig, one leg extended backward, its head lightly tipped away from the viewer so that the fine stripes of blue could be seen along its top of its head, and also the pale yellow of its breast. Without its song, the bird seems insignificant. He begins to draw, and for hours he is lost.

Johnny and Tom return. They are without the mate of the finch.

"There was only one, Father."

"It cannot be," says his father. "There is never only one."

"Perhaps the female heard the shot and flew off. We could not find the nest."

Audubon's temper flares in the dank close space. "We cannot lose this! Do you know what depends on this bird? All, all. How can you fail me? Do you not love me?" Johnny's head dangles on its stalk, his chin on his chest. Tom Lincoln is flushed red and staring at the wall.

On Audubon rages, sometimes in French, sometimes in English. How can they say there was only one bird? Do they not know anything? They are stupid, they are lazy, they are not fit for this mission, they do not understand his fatigue, they do not understand the pressures, the necessities. Has it all been wasted on Johnny, all these years of work?

Johnny does not fight back. He knows better. He understands that his father's anger is too great. He even guesses that it has little to do with the lost mate of *Fringilla lincolnii*, the undiscovered nest, his own or his friend's supposed inefficiency and laziness. What it has to do with, he does not know. But a clear sense of the otherness of this mood and this voice saves him from the despair he would feel if he believed that his father's accusations were true.

"Tomorrow we'll go back," he says.

It is night. The meal has been served, the grog opened and the storytelling begun. The painter, having darkened the atmosphere with his mood, has retreated in to his Whatman paper, his circle of light on the deal table. The other end of the hold resounds with laughter. The ship's cargo of young gentlemen, and Emery, all dedicated to his mission, tell their stories.

"The thing led us a merry chase!" he hears Johnny exclaiming. "But Tom, Tom climbed the ridge and saw it land on the uppermost branch of a bush, not twenty yards away. He got it in his sights —"

"That cut short its career!"

Above, in the forecastle, the sailors sing their ballads. The words echo down the ladder to where he sits.

I had a dream the other night, I dreamt that I was home.
I dreamt that me and my true love were in old Marylebone,
That we were on old England's shore with a jug of ale in hand,
But when I woke my heart was broke, on the banks of Newfoundland.

But Audubon's ear is tuned to that other melody, the song of an untutored, untamed bird. To open one's throat and to have that music pour forth, what is it like? He wonders where, exactly, the song lived in this throat. How does the throat of a bird produce such affecting notes? He longs to take apart the throat but he has no other specimen so he must keep this one intact.

It is why he is so angry at Johnny.

He remembers being back in Coueron with D'Orbigny in his little laboratory behind the house, how the good doctor taught him to take the birds apart. Audubon was then a young gentleman himself, younger than Johnny now. At first his fingers were clumsy with the sharp instruments, and he cut himself. He dropped the tiny hearts and livers, lost them in the tangle of intestines. He and the doctor were butchers together, but it seemed harmless, their victims were so tiny. "You must understand the science of the bird," D'Orbigny told his young friend. "You must know how the thing works."

Fifi told the doctor of his dream: He will be an American. And the good doctor, his apron messed with bird entrails, promised to help. So that, when the documents came, D'Orbigny signed them, as he had signed Audubon's birth certificate before. And in that flourish of the pen, Jean Rabin was dissolved. He was created anew, and his past was an empty shell.

He left for America on a sailing boat. He was off to make his way.

The light is gone. Audubon puts down his pencil, lifts the drawing and places it on a pile. The finch is perched, throat open, silent as the dusk that rolls at last over its enormous country.

He leans back in his chair and covers his aching eyes. He tries to hear the song of the finch.

He hears instead the songs of his loved ones. Of his family, whom he calls the Holy Alliance. His wife and his sons. They all have their songs. He knows the notes and even the words that rise from the heart but are never spoken.

We are the unknown relations of a famous man, they sing. He owns us, by virtue of his obsession. Or believes he does, and we have come to accept this. We remain tied to him and to each other, for no one else understands us. We love and hate one another, in the same way that we love and hate Himself.

Johnny sings louder than the others. He is the wild one; his submission will be defiance one day. The second born, but first in love: John Woodhouse, best of his young men, the one who gets the bird.

My father need only say he wants one, and I have its little neck between my thumb and forefinger. I can feel the double pulse in my thumb, my own and that of the bird. I may fail him today, but not in future. I too shall be an artist. It is me who will capture him, in the end. Trap the colour of his vivid cheek, the heat of his beating heart, trap him in the full bloom of his existence. Capture him with his own tricks, by watching, taking careful note of the way he holds his gun, his wariness, the glimmer in his eyes, which is sometimes good and sometimes fearsome.

Victor's song comes from far away, across the sea. It is an angry song, a puzzled song.

I am the elder son, why am I sent away? First to my uncle's counting house, then here to manage his business. When I was younger, I hated him for the hardships he visited on my mother. For his selfishness: his birds, his book, his fame. Whatever else he may profess to love, those things are what he wants.

He wrongs my mother with his flirtations. I have seen her cry.

I am the one who refused to be part of this Work. He promised to send me to school. Yet here I am, in London, with the printer, nagging for payment of subscriptions.

When is a son no longer a son? I am not a boy, but a man, with the needs of a man. On what day does my own life begin?

My father left his own parents behind in France. On his father's death he did not heed his mother's call. When letters came begging him to visit, he never replied. I know, because my mother told me. He did not help his half-sisters or any of his family. His family began with John James Audubon.

Why must we be different? Who is this man, who thinks he owns us? Shall we all be broken on the wheel of his ambition?

Lucy's song is happier. His dear old girl, his best friend. His heart swells to hear her.

I am married to John Audubon, and he is married to his birds. All over my girlhood he danced like a dream. He won me, but the birds won his heart. His bird passion cannot be reasoned with and cannot be bargained with. I am not jealous: his sweethearts believe they can trap him by painting little branches for his birds to sit upon. But they cannot.

Sometimes Lucy complains, but she is loyal always. He knows he must hear her out.

I wanted an ordinary life. Comfort, respite after a day's work, society. To feed my children, to be above humiliation and reproach. But I got this! A husband once despised and now revered. A man who must have his dream. A man who depends on me utterly and on whom I cannot depend.

She comes around now; she always comes around in the end.

Still, I would not trade what I have. I am chief of the Holy

Alliance. My sons and I promote his cause, for it is ours. The world has misunderstood him, and treated him shabbily. Do you blame Fougère for preferring the wild creatures? To see him fail and see him triumph is to learn much of man. I will stand by him against his enemies, and I will endure hardships and count myself blessed to be his wife. I would like only a little security.

Audubon twists on his chair, his eyes shut, while the songs bedevil him. The Holy Alliance sings in harmony. He is as familiar with their singing as they are, and he sympathizes with each one. But nothing can be changed. They must be together; it is the only way he can succeed.

There is one more voice. Unbidden, Maria's song comes to his ears. Discordant and beguiling.

I am the desired one. I am the beloved. He holds me as tenderly in his heart as he does his wife. He told me so. I give him kisses and I understand him. I ask for nothing. It is our secret: no one knows.

I am humble, as befits a single woman. I am grateful that I have come to the Bachman house, where I can work with a famous man. I am useful. I am clever too. Both the reverend and Mr. Audubon tell me sweet things and we all laugh together as we bend our heads over our work.

I am an artist too. I call myself that because the great Jean Jacques Audubon tells me so. I am good enough to paint flowers and butterflies for him. When Audubon leaves me I am sad but he writes to me and I to him. I do not go out in the world, I may not, for I have no means. Instead I remain in the parlour, dipping my paintbrush oh so lightly in the most intense colours I can find.

If I could, I would be with him. Wander free as he does. Wade in the marsh with a gun. Meet the learned and the royal. Feel the open air. He desires me and I —

Audubon stands, abruptly. Her voice disturbs him.

"No, Maria," he says.

"He's talking to himself, Johnny," whispers Tom Lincoln.

"Father?"

Audubon ignores him.

"He's very tired," says Johnny. "He's working so hard."

Audubon stares at his paper. He admonishes Maria. "I told you this when last we saw one another. I explained it all to you. I am a man. I follow the wild creatures. There is no place for you here."

Yours is the world; mine is the parlour? Yours is the frontier and mine the garden? Yours is the bird and mine the bud?

"That is right, Maria."

Beware, Jean Jacques, beware. I know I am a woman. A single woman without means. But my flame in this confined space burns as brightly as yours does in the open.

At Godwin's insistence, Audubon and his party are consigned to a sea world as they beat their way northeastward up the coast. The mainland broods an unbreachable gap away, sometimes visible as a dark-reddish rim of hills, sometimes veiled by layers of shifting fog. The islands they drift among are of iron-red rock with green moss hillsides and plateaus trimmed with stunted, ancient and twisted trees.

When Godwin can find an anchorage, he takes it; the young gentlemen get out in the whaleboats to scramble over the low rocky ridges that stand only feet above the water and are smoothed by the constant action of the waves. Some islands are so zealously defended by incubating birds that the men are attacked from overhead with wings and bills and beaten off. At other spots the frightened birds rise in a flock and abandon their nests.

Audubon wakes before dawn, seats himself at the deal table, and draws for hours.

He finishes Tom Lincoln's Finch. He cannot remember its song at all. Johnny and Tom Lincoln never found the mate of the little bird they shot, and now the mating season is over: it will not sing again this summer.

In a rainstorm, he watches as a black-backed gull takes a young duckling from a nest, flies to a high point, and drops it on the rocks below. Not satisfied with his kill, the gull seizes the duckling, flies up and drops it again.

Audubon is tired of waiting. He has no time, no time to waste. Wind and water seem designed to hold him back. They do not see the *Gulnare* again.

Then Johnny shoots a white-winged crossbill on a bunch of grass growing out of the fissure of a rock on a small island.

He knows the bird when Johnny brings it in, a beautiful male, its red back, head and chest gleaming against the white patches on its wings, and its sharp curved beak giving it the look of a Renaissance cleric. He recognizes it as the little creature that rode for a time on the rigging like a herald the night he first met Captain Bayfield.

"Ah, you," he says to the almost weightless mystery in his hand, "we've caught up with you at last." He remembers the dry, rattling *chuck chuck* of the entire flock as it settled in the masts of the *Gulnare*. And the solitary *trreeeee-ker-treeee-ker-treeee* that it makes on its own, a rising trill when it is on its way.

How small the bird is! Yet its migrations are enormous. In this tiny body is the strength to cover one quarter the globe. It is clearly at home here, a true northerly creature. It can lay its eggs and raise its young even in January.

He begins to work. The red darkens into the shade of dried blood the second his back is turned. He wires it, quickly, in profile, with wings down and half outspread to best show the lovely egg-shaped white patch on the top of the wings. This white has a sickle of black across it, a curve that is echoed in its beak. He portrays the curious beak open, in profile. The upper bill crosses over the lower when closed and is razor sharp, this strange twisted bill slate grey with a blue tinge. Beside the beak are bristles of yellow. The iris of the bird's eye is hazel and weirdly human. The back feathers are that lovely pinkish red and sometimes crimson, with black tips. The white spot is absolutely pure, such a whiteness he cannot replicate. The feet again are different, the golden brown of pine sap.

In fact the bird is nearly a rainbow. And the female, which Johnny brings in later, is entirely different, dark yellow with grey and white bands, her feet more brown than red, and her bill the same. The young male is yellow like the female but will grow redder and redder as it matures.

He makes notes in the margins, notes which are directions for Havell. And he paints, mixing the watercolours he has brought with local tinctures from berries, which are never quite true, and coats them with egg white to make them shine. He has never been able to make paint do what he wants it to do.

Hours pass: he notes them only by the way the light moves across his paper. Drawing is a meditation to him. His hand imitates every line of the posture in which he has arranged the bird's wings, tarsis, bill and feet; he outlines each feather fastidiously. This very absorption allows his mind to rise freely to another plane, to the place where there are no lines. His hand moves without his conscious guiding. The force with which he applies the paint is the same force that joins him to the bird. He feels the bird's joy and terror. He knows its sufferings and its obedience to waters and heavens. He wills his bird beauty. And it is good, this one.

At noon, he rises from his chair, one hand on the small of his back, the other on the back of his neck. He climbs the ladder out into the day and takes the food the cook brings him. He can see the young gentlemen resting on a bit of flat rock not far from the schooner, catching the sun while it is high, and eating their dinner. He rests his plate atop a barrel, but he does not sit. He chews with little awareness of what he is eating, taking in fuel because he knows he needs it to keep warm, to keep alert, to work.

Anonyme struts and preens, making it clear that he must be dealt a large measure of deference by the rest of the menagerie. The greedy gannets make their awkward quarrelsome way in the wake of the cook, who walks the deck dropping kitchen refuse behind him. For these handouts, they now compete with the young of the black-backed gulls. These junior predators are growing every day, their feathers darkening to take on the sinister aspect of their elders. One of them has begun to chase Johnny's pointer. The bemused dog backs across the deck while the bird, still walking clumsily, menaces with its bill.

These pets seem suddenly oppressive to the painter. He recalls a series of them, birds that have been taken from the wilds and come to live amongst men, birds with names and even characters, amusing, tolerated, subjects of study, objects of affection. Come to think of it, they all met with a bad end. The Canada goose the boys called Google that lived in the dooryard of the log cabin in Kentucky. And the wild turkey cock they took in, which came to its name and was known to all the neighbours. Lucy tied a red ribbon around its neck, so that any man who got the bird in his sights would know it was theirs. But the ribbon only postponed its inevitable end, and someone other than themselves ate it.

The charm of his shipboard menagerie is utterly lost to him. He cannot abide the waddling, quacking, peering, preening, ordure-dropping presence of the fowl. It is as if he is being watched, judged and even, perversely, captured by their presence.

He finishes his lunch quickly and, although reluctant to leave the deck when the sun is high, descends again to the hold and takes up his pencil and his brushes.

AFTER HE SAID GOODBYE to Maria and boarded the revenue cutter *Agnes* for Florida, he found himself on a dreadful trip. Florida was hot and dry and sandy; the birds were wily, and the ship's captain hostile. He returned to Charleston with only a few drawings and no new species. He'd been gone two months and he hadn't shaved. He had been thinking the whole while of her.

"You look like a bear," she said.

They walked in the garden, accompanied by the dawn chorus. The voices of the birds wove in and out of their own, which were heavy with feeling. Two rows of balcony windows from the back of the house looked down on them. Any of the children, the slaves, or John Bachman himself could look down on them. He overflowed with words, and the wonders that until this moment had been lost on him.

"I must tell you something. Up the Halifax River the unearthly Roseate Spoonbill sits high in a tree like some giant hothouse flower bending the branches. Or feeds in the shallows, its wide green bill swinging from side to side. Then there is the little Green Heron with its neck pulled aggressively into its burgundy chest. Best of all is the Yellow-crowned Night Heron with its jaunty striped cap, who flew ahead of the boat from branch to branch."

Maria was so small she reached only to his middle chest. She smelled of roses. She always did. He bent over her so he could speak softly and so, when she answered, he might not miss a word. And she listened, listened, watching his eyes and his throat where the words came out. She did not look at his lips. To him, they felt electric, they were so aware of her nearness.

"The pink of the Roseate Spoonbill," he murmured, "is like the roses over the arbour where I first sat with you; the yellow of the Yellow-crowned Night-Heron is as lemony and pure as the sound of your voice; and the plump chest of the Green Heron, where its soft plumage blends into a sumptuous wine colour, is like that other breast on which I would die to lay my head. At the end of the day the Mangrove Swallows go mad, swooping over the surface of the river. As I thought I would go mad until I saw you. Then a rainstorm broke, a downpour, without wind, simply splashing out of the heavens, and it was as if I had given in to my longing for you. Then, magically, in the clouds on the horizon appeared two rainbows one overlapping the other. I thought we might by a miracle be together."

"Good morning, Audubon!" The call came from the second storey of the house. The painter straightened without haste, and turned back to hail his host.

"And good morning to you!"

The preacher was in his bathrobe.

"Are you just wakening? I have been up for hours."

"And my sister too? Are you tiring her?"

Maria looked up at her brother-in-law impishly, too modest to call up to the second floor of the house.

"We are here in the garden!"

Had he spoken too plainly? Of course they were in the garden. Where else would they be? It is obvious they were in the garden; Bachman was looking right down on them. "We are looking at the myrtle tree to copy it."

"You are teaching my sister then? You know she's most willing!"

HE FOLLOWED HER into the brick outbuilding that housed the kitchen, overflowing with the fall produce from the garden. Rows and rows of tomatoes on the sideboards were waiting to be put up, and the cook, whose name was Venus, was sweeping the stems and leaves from the floor. Venus's brother, Adonis, poured water, brought in a barrow from the garden well, into the great stone sink. They sang as they worked, in a language he did not understand. He stood awhile, watching; Maria moved so quickly and with purpose.

She was absorbed in washing the giant French artichokes. The beautiful swelling leaves with their nib-like points turned and turned in her hands. She pulled off the crêpey, purple blossoms and set them aside. She pulled off the outside leaves, continually turning the bulb itself. The vegetable was a flower, its centre unrolling in her hand, like the inside of a rose. He grew dizzy looking at it. He tried to tell her what he had been thinking.

"Maria," he said, "I am mated, like the birds. That is nature, as it must be. Lucy is my dearest friend, my partner in life. She is part of me, and part of my work. I need her; I have a right to her. She is my wife, but part of me still longs."

She took the purple blossoms and put them in a thin muslin bag. Their curves and points showed through the fine white net.

"What is longing?" she said.

"I may still fall in love with another woman. I may woo her with my words, with my art, with my dreams. Do you understand? I have a passion for you."

"If you had, you would come to me."

"No, Maria, you did not say that."

"You are right. I did not."

"We are what we are. You are a spinster. I am a married man with a family. I look after them. They are my life and they help me with my work."

"And I?"

"You help me too."

"Is that all?"

"I desire you."

Venus placed a large saucepan of milk on the stove to heat. Maria pulled a cloth from her waist and placed it over her head. She slid it backwards to secure her hair. As she tightened the cloth into a knot, the slanted bones of her cheeks and the hollows beneath them stood out starkly. Her head was an elegant skull. She retrieved the translucent sack. The purple of the blossoms was darker — he could see it palely through the sack. She crossed on her small feet to the stove, holding the sack high over the saucepan, and then began to let it down. The pile of artichokes with their endless folding intricate centres sat beside the sink. He felt himself sink under the surface.

"And why are you drowning the blossoms in the milk?"

"To turn the milk sour."

"Why would you want to sour the milk?"

"It is what I must do. It is my work."

"But why? I don't understand."

"To make the slip for dessert," she said, turning to him and laughing.

ANOTHER DAY THEY SAT in the rain under the giant magnolia tree, on the bench that encircled its trunk.

"Desire," she said. "That intense wanting that seizes the body."

"You know of that?"

"I suppose you think that I, a spinster, should be ignorant of it?"

He bent his head, to hide the proof that she was right. "Tell me what you know of desire."

"Desire burns through the frames within which we live. Desire is the defence of the sinner and the redemption of the prodigal."

He looked up at her again.

"And something more. Desire makes a place in the world for people who have not got one."

"We all deserve a place in life."

"Yes. Even the spinster sister."

Even John James. Fougère. Jean Jacques. Monsieur Newhouse. Jean Rabin. Even the motherless boy.

SHE SAT, trim in her brown bodice, across from him at the study table where they worked. The sun fell through the casement windows onto his back. It illuminated her face, which was not beautiful but clean and fine. She was painting the trumpet-creeper, which she had picked earlier that morning in the garden. Her yellows and reds, her pinks, were sharp and full blown. She had spent hours mixing the colour exactly, but she used it sparingly. The blooms were imperfect, different, richly curved, the flowers lush, lolling, wide open.

The trumpet-creeper was a love letter from Maria to Jean Jacques. It was exquisite. And bold. He could not speak.

He took the watercolour from her and began to place his Black-throated Mango Hummingbirds on the vine. He positioned the birds in and about her blooms, playful, ecstatic, hot, tropical. The birds were large, they seemed larger than life. Dizzily, they approached the flowers from all directions; one was upside down in the top left-hand corner, another had his entire head buried in a flower. A third flew in from the side to touch the outer curled lip of flower with his long narrow beak; still another rode triumphant on top of a pink fully opened blossom.

"Do you see, Maria?" He placed females upright and half hidden. The males were more exuberant and fully stretched out. The wings, the body, were stopped as if for a fraction of a second in their constant, tremulous flying. The flight of the birds was as true to life as he could make it. The blossoms and the birds were perfectly balanced; one knew the birds were weightless in their excitement. The flushed insides of the trumpet flowers matched the fuchsia of the birds' underparts. It was rapture, this collaboration of bird and blossom.

"You have known this before," she said, in French. "How long does it last?"

Did she mean the feeling, or the picture?

"The sun has risen so high," he said, "that I cannot see you."

"Then come closer."

LATER, IT WAS COOL in the room with the deep-set windows under the presiding stuffed owl and the great globe. He could feel her breath on his face, sweetened by the scent of the rose petals that tumbled off the blooms that stood in vases on the window ledge.

"Mr. Audubon," she said, "do the birds feel desire?"

"Oh yes," he answered without ceasing the sure and careful movements of his pencil. "Oh yes, they do. Can you not see it in their flight? Hear it in their song? Feel it in their colour? Birds are the very embodiment of desire."

"I can see that what you say is true," she said. "Birds *embody* desire. But what I asked was different. Do they feel desire?"

He looked at her hard. She has checked him; it is as if she has quarrelled with him. She has not done that in all the time he has known her.

The Country
SO WILD AND GRAND

———

OUAPITAGONE, *JULY 2, 1833*

Went on shore and was most pleased with what I saw. The country
so wild and grand. Its mossy grey-clothed rocks heaped and thrown
together as if by chance in the most fantastical groups imaginable,
huge masses hanging on minor ones . . . bays without end sprinkled
with rocky islands of all shapes and sizes where in every fissure a
guillemot, a cormorant or some other wild bird retreats to secure its
egg. The peculiar cast of the sky which never seems to be certain,
butterflies flitting over snow banks probing beautiful dwarf flower-
lets of many hues . . .

— *Journals*, J. J. Audubon

———

On a small island he discovers, half hidden by short grass, several
dozen nests of the Eider Duck. The females are sitting; they
pay no attention to him. They let him get to within ten feet of their
nests and settle himself down on a damp patch of moss. He leans

against a granite boulder and watches the birds; alone with them, he is at peace.

But, too curious, he soon stands again, leaving his gun and satchel on the rock. He chooses one of the ducks and manages to get within two yards of her before she takes flight. Then he glides the last few feet and looks down inside the nest. It is deep, and tightly packed inside with mud, twigs, seaweed. Puffs of down cushion five eggs. Five! Beautiful oval eggs, of a pale olive green, perhaps three inches long and two inches wide.

He is tempted to take one for the cook. They are delicious. But he knows if he does, the duck may not return. He retreats to his seat.

The duck, which was sitting on the water a hundred yards away, flaps herself into the air. She lands a few feet from the nest; she has clearly decided that he is not dangerous. She walks directly to it and, backing, swiveling her tail, tipping forward and back, arranges herself on the eggs. He can almost feel under himself the hard, cooling shells. She plucks down from her hindquarters and tucks her eggs in.

Other females are near, on their nests, but the ducks sit without mates. He has seen the mature males out on the water, lines of a hundred or more of them flying a few feet above the waves, imitating the rise and fall of the water. These drakes accompanied their mates here, flying in great flocks of pairs, but since the eggs have been laid, appear to have no thought of the mates they courted so passionately a month ago. Even immature males forsake the nest, spending their time with the barren females. The female alone bears the responsibility of incubating and raising the young. Why? Simply because she can? Her down, which warms and hides her eggs when she needs to fly in search of food, makes it possible.

The duck sits on. Of what does she dream? Of her young, soon to hatch, their nestling bodies under her own? Or of the mate who, short weeks ago, she encouraged? And the drake, of what does he dream, now that his task, which was only to fertilize the egg, is complete? Of sea islands, and diving eight fathoms to capture small fish in the clear, cold water? Perhaps he rehearses his eventual migration southward, which he will undertake before his mate.

*"He discovers, half hidden by short grass,
several dozen nests of the Eider Duck."*

Audubon tries, as he has tried before, to have the mind of a bird. He puts all thought away; the dream is in the body, not the head. His blood cools and his flesh livens to the air and the earth. He is alert but held in check, poised. He stays that way for a long time. Until his duck, or rather the duck that has either forgotten him or included him in her idea of security, gives signs that she must leave the nest. No doubt she has to feed herself. She cranes her neck backward. She lifts her body to expose the eggs. Down nearly covers them. But she pulls more and more soft fuzz until her tail is quite bare and she is satisfied that the eggs are under cover. Then she tips herself forward and waddles off the nest. She walks a little, and then takes to the wing, leaving him there, with her unborn.

As if to prove himself worthy of her extraordinary trust, he watches the nest for her. The duck is Lucy, the eggs his children. He himself is not away over the sea, but nearby. He is lulled by the sun. Suddenly the sky goes dark, and there is a great commotion in the air, a shrieking sound in his ears. Dark wings flap in his face, and a huge black-backed gull is hunched over the eggs, its sharp bill drilling downward.

"No!" he cries and scrambles to his feet, rifle up, shooting first high above the nest, and then down toward it. The gull continues its work.

Audubon leaps forward and jabs his rifle butt at the giant, its wingspan easily five and a half feet. Crushing the other eggs with its curved feet, the gull screams and flaps in his face. Then with a deep, hoarse *gawp gawp gawp* and a massive shudder, it departs upward.

The nest is destroyed. The artist retreats in horror. He sees his duck swimming in tight distraught circles at the shore. Her nest is defiled, and her brood, or dream of brood, is gone.

He watches her display of grief with fascination and guilt. He has not caused it, but then neither has he been able to prevent it, and it is as if he promised her. She turns, twists and pecks at the water. She opens her wings as if to fly and collapses. She watches her nest and she watches him. She hops a short distance off, and then hurries back, as if with hope that she might find the nest restored, the attack never to have occurred. He sits in agonies; he can do nothing. He waits half an hour, an hour. She appears calmer and finally she rests.

And here is the miracle. He knows that nature will give the duck a new set of instructions. She will not mourn for long. This evening she will go to where the sterile females and the drakes roost, and find a new mate. She will draw him away from his fellows for a week or ten days. They will preen one another, swim together. The drake will do his job and when she is sitting on a new nest of eggs, he will leave her to fend for herself.

Audubon's mind clears. It is neither that of a bird nor that of a man. It is not really a mind at all but an eye, greedy, seizing the image. There is the nest, a mass of gluey yolk and broken shell, drying in the sun. There is the duck. Preening. Drawing her wing feathers one by one through her beak. After witnessing the destruction of all her hope, she has retreated from the future, the demolished future, to the moment.

IT IS EVENING IN THE HOLD. The young gentlemen have shot half a dozen eider ducks and as many drakes. They sling the bodies out of the bag and onto the table. Tom Lincoln sets out to skin them. The medical students take a carcass to dissect, talking in the candlelight about the bird's esophagus, its fishy smell. Audubon takes three, a duck and two drakes and choreographs his scenario with wire. The duck has been roused from her nest, which is hidden in a clump of grasses. There is an intruder, a second drake to the left, threatening the nest. The mate of the duck lunges at him, defending.

He begins to paint. The birds are rendered from eye level: it is as if the painter lay in the grass three feet away, watching the drama. The pair of eiders, though opposites in colour and markings, are identically posed, identically angled, and on the offensive — wings back, tails tipped up, bills open. She is that gold red-brown, finely marked with darker brown and white. The snow-white back of the drake who is her mate fills the centre-right of the picture. Behind their tails the greenish-brown eggs are just visible, open and uncovered. The intruder has spread his wings, exposing his black underbody and the yellow patch at the neck. His black raccoon mask is displayed to advantage.

There is fury in the great swatches of white on the males, the fine lines of light and dark brown of the female's feathers. Intimacy is being defended here, the treasures of the nest protected. Audubon is writing a new story for the duck. The predator is successfully driven off; the nest and the eggs are saved. Instead of portraying the drake flying with the other drakes, and the duck left to fend for the family herself, he has turned the eider drake into a model husband.

This is what he means by "drawn from nature."

THEY SAIL beyond the islands, in the safe, deep water. Audubon feels let loose, untied. He hates to be away from land as much as he hates to be away from his loved ones. And this time is worse than others, because he cannot send letters.

He paints while there is light to do so, and if his eyes allow, he writes episodes for his letter press, stories which, like the paintings, have grown more theatrical with each year. When that is done he writes letters, letters that he will hold until he is home again, or until the *Ripley* encounters a ship that can take the letters back to civilization.

He writes to Robert Havell. "I must tell you your last engravings, the Whip-Poor-Will and the Screech-Owl, are superb."

He writes to Victor. "You must keep an eye on Havell. You must ask him what is wrong with Blake. Carelessly coloured portraits sent to Selby and Jardine have them threatening to cancel. But do not be too rough with him."

He writes to Lucy. "I have done six paintings so far in Labrador. Some of them will please thee, I think, dearest best beloved Friend, my own love and true consoler. Are you certain that you have soldered and insured the tins of drawings? I am worried about the bindings of the folios."

He writes to John Bachman. Bachman, who has counselled him to quiet his enemies by stepping out of the debate on whether the vulture has a nose for his carrion or hunts by sight, and whether the rattlesnake climbs trees. "I cannot step away from scientific fights," he tells John Bachman. "Because I am right. I know more about birds in the wild than any man alive. I have watched them for all the days of my life. Who are these parlour scientists to tell me how the creatures behave? Besides, although I have enemies, I also have friends. Did not Baron Cuvier call my bird portraits 'the greatest monument yet erected by Art to Nature'? And did the Duc d'Orléans not get down on his knees to call me king of bird painters? Even my compatriots are coming around, and may one day love me. The *Baltimore Courier* has written about the great Audubon: 'his exploits as great as his genius.' Did not the great actress Fanny Kemble say of me that I am 'like all first-rate people, radiating simplicity and total lack of pretension'? I pray you do not think me boastful if I tell you this. Your friendship is the most important of all. Yours, and that of your sister-in-law. How is our sweetheart?"

Then, at last, he writes to Maria. "There are millions of tiny flowers, which in their multitudes stain entire rocky plateaus with colour. But when I reach my hand down to pick them, I discover they are smaller than the nail of your own tiny, baby finger. They are all I have here to remind me of your kind self." (Oh my darling, how I wish we could go on one of our dawn garden walks. I walk here, but the very earth is treacherous, and I am alone.) "I had expected exotic birds, bizarre unknown species. But north, I discover, offers not variety but multitudes. There are *huge* flocks of birds, hundreds of thousands of birds, but few species. Can it be that extremes of climate limit the birds' variety but increase their numbers? I am not finding the new species I dreamed of. I am not even finding the species I know exist. Where is the Great Auk? And where the Labrador Duck?"

IN THE DOG WATCH, at six o'clock in the evening, the sailors are on deck. A few try to arrange foot races for the birds with their clipped wings, but the half-fledged gannets and puffins, the guillemots and Anonyme himself are not co-operative in starting off at the whistle. On the foredeck, a sailor is singing the ballad of Captain Kidd. The young gentlemen come up to listen, and Johnny pulls out his flute to join the fiddling.

> *My name was Robert Kidd, and God's laws I did forbid,*
> *and so wickedly I did as I sailed, as I sailed,*
> *And so wickedly I did as I sailed.*

Godwin is half standing, half seated, on a barrel and has in his hand the backbone of a shark. He is working at it with a knife. Audubon finds himself elbow to elbow with the pilot.

"What would you be crafting?"

"A fine walking stick."

The music goes on, a tune both witty and mournful and wrung from the sailors' hearts, the tale of the pirate who was hung in London.

> *I'd ninety bars of gold, and dollars manifold,*
> *with riches uncontrolled, as I sailed, as I sailed, as I sailed,*
> *With riches uncontrolled as I sailed.*

A long file of razor-billed auks flies toward them, only a few yards above the surface of the sea. The song ends — *lest you come to hell with me, for I must die* — just in time. As the silence falls, the men hear the beat of the wings. The lead bird seems to head toward the schooner, as if he intended to land his troops there. The line curves off only a hundred feet from the ship, the birds aiming for the rocky cliff of a nearby island. For a moment they are exactly synchronized. Their bodies tip, their wings beat up together, and down together; first the bellies flash white and then the backs jet-black.

"Pretty sight, that," says Godwin.

Audubon had not taken him for one who could be impressed by beauty.

THEY SAIL ON, and wait, becalmed, before sailing on again. At last they come within sight of the great cannon-shaped rock that marks the entrance to the mainland harbour at Ouapitagone. Audubon is ecstatic, though they sit for the time being before an immense wall of rock. No one but Captain Emery would have guessed there was an entrance there, but he finds it, a slip of a passage around the cliffs.

Inside is a harbour such as Audubon has never seen. The entire Spanish Armada could anchor there with ease. And beyond it is land, the solid mainland Audubon longs for. There are beds of moss and piping larks! Young codfish skip along the surface of the deep cove as if the water cannot contain them.

Shortly after their arrival, they see a British flag flapping behind a rocky ledge. It is Bowen, the lieutenant of the *Gulnare*, in his launch. Hailing him, they discover that he has scouted the route and is expecting the *Gulnare* to arrive this very day.

———

OUAPITAGONE HARBOUR, *JULY 1, 1833*

At 5 rounded the rocks which lie off Lake Island (Île du Lac) passing between them & the Southmakers' ledge in very deep water, stood in sounding for the entrance of Ouapitagone harb'r where Mr. Bowen had just arrived and hoisted a flag. He however had not had time to examine the place and we should have had some difficulty in getting in had it not been for the kindness of the Captain of the *Ripley*, who came off to us and piloted the *Gulnare* into the Harbour. We were moored in Ouapitagone near the Ripley at 7 p.m.

Fine night, an Eclipse of the Moon, she rose eclipsed and we missed observing the termination of it by accident.

— *Surveying Journals*, Henry Wolsey Bayfield, Captain, Royal Navy

———

OFF THE STERN, Bayfield sees a kafuffle in the water. The back fin of a large fish chips the grey glass. The tailfin slices it, in circles, then shatters the glass with a flap, and circles again, like a knife wielded clumsily, with increasing panic. The fish — it is a dogfish, a small shark — slaps the water hard with its tail and lifts itself out of the water. It seems that it would fly before it would sink. It does not go below the surface. He looks up and there on the deck is Molloy watching the commotion in the water with malicious amusement.

Bayfield had been about to descend into the pilot boat but he stops. The shark's circles are growing smaller; every third or fourth time it makes an enormous effort to dive and seems to nearly succeed, but then subsides in exhaustion.

"Molloy!"

"Sir?"

"You've done it again, haven't you?"

The sailor grins insolently. Bayfield's pale complexion turns a mottled pink.

"You have been expressly forbidden to spritsail the sharks!"

"Useless ugly thing," says the sailor. He ducks his head and is gone.

Molloy has threaded a piece of wood through the creature's gills so that it cannot dive, and he can amuse himself by watching its agonies. Bayfield looks after him, contained fury steeling his glance. He will discipline the man. But he is distracted by Audubon, whose whaleboat approaches. The artist stands in the bow, as if in stirrups, his hair flying in a brisk wind.

Bayfield paces, agitated, on the deck, and then, folding his two hands together at his waist, makes an effort to put aside his anger. He calls for the ladder. He finds that he is glad to see Audubon.

"We had great difficulty entering the harbour. The *Gulnare* is large for these bays; I am grateful to your captain for guiding us in."

"It has not been easy then, my friend."

"This coast is never easy. How has it gone for you?"

"Whatever the harbour I'm glad to be in it. I thought we'd parted from land for the rest of our days."

Out of the corner of his eye, Bayfield notices the dogfish give up his fight to live. It makes him feel ill. And, strangely, it calls to mind his last conversation with the man who stands before him. "I have been thinking about what you said about our carelessness with regards to the creatures of this world. Mr. Audubon, I think you are at least partially correct," he says.

"How do you come to that?"

Bayfield tells Audubon about Molloy, and how he has warned this man before. "I sometimes think sailors hate all creatures — the fish and the birds. They are, it seems, infected with a deep antipathy for nature. That or, if nothing so deep, only ignorance, and grog.

"Now that he has offended again," says Bayfield, "I will put him ashore at the Ouapitagone trading post, be rid of him. I will put him ashore and leave him to fend for himself."

AT LAST NIGHT BEGINS TO FALL. The clouds stay at the rim of the horizon and the stars are shaken out of their sleep into white swaths across it. Audubon remains on the *Gulnare* to observe the eclipse of the moon. Dr. Kelly has set up the telescope and the theodolite on deck. He cradles a chronometer against his stomach.

Audubon aligns his eye to the pinhole. He sees nothing, and then, as he moves the scope around the skies, the painful blue-white beam of moon. A small bite has been taken out of one side of it.

"Did you know that, to early navigators, the moon was a clock hand as it moved through the stars?" says Bayfield.

"More clocks!" says the artist.

"They took its angular distance from certain bright stars to calculate Greenwich time. But it was not accurate. With our chronometers we find that our calculations over a length of sixty miles may differ by only half a second of time."

"I see," says Audubon. "I do not much care to know that it is exactly 9:41 and thirty-five seconds, or 9:41 and forty-five seconds. Even as I observe the time, it changes."

Bayfield next demonstrates the use of a quadrant. "We hold it vertical, like this, and tilt it to where the sun's — or, in this case, the moon's — rays penetrate the sights. Then we can read by the thread on the plummet the altitude of that sun or moon. This simple instrument is poetry to me. Galileo was born in the same year as Shakespeare, did you know?"

"Shakespeare," muses Audubon. "I suppose he is your great English genius. I would like to be like him."

Bayfield is shocked. "He knew all there is to know of life. No one yet has or ever will surpass him."

"But I too know so much that I must tell. Perhaps no one will know the birds again as I do. I have a vision of my paintings being looked at by people of a long-distant future."

A commotion breaks out below. One man is roaring and there is the sound of splintering wood. Other men take up the shout, and sailors' cursing is suddenly louder than the sound of water and birds. This eruption is violent, obscene, under the stars. Bayfield is gone, a blur of blue serge, and now the voice of authority slices the sounds of the fight. "Men! Who is that? Molloy!"

"Sailor Molloy's in the grog, Captain."

"All hands! Attention!"

Men stop their work. Stop their hauling on ropes, swinging on hammocks. There is no movement then, only the heave and stagger of one man bumping into the mast, the doors, the railings.

"Bring him here!"

The surly sailor is propped up between Collins and Bowen, in front of the captain. Bayfield's charm is now cold, the will that rules other men.

"Molloy. I told you not to touch the dogfish again."

The sailor's mouth is twisted so far to the right it closes one eye, whether deliberately, or because he has been struck, Audubon cannot tell. "I say you're nothing better than a tyrant. I tell you now, you'll all die on this duty, mind my words. You can't find your way along this coast, not on any man's life. It only gets worse with the rocks and the wild weather. What's in this for us? Bloody maps, we can't take a share of that, can we?"

Bowen wears a tight smile, though he struggles to hold the man. "He's been stealing grog, sir. We found his stash in one of the boats."

Bayfield's eyes have hardened at the corners. "I was going to put you off in the morning," he says to Molloy. "I shan't wait. Tie his hands. We'll take him in to shore tonight."

"What'll he do 'til morning, sir?" asks Collins. "The moschettoes will drive him mad." He is an easygoing, soft-hearted Irishman.

There is no answer.

Molloy is hustled away.

"If he's lucky, the trading post will have a porch he can sleep on," Bayfield says, but not to Collins. "He'll find work on another ship, perhaps even tomorrow. But he shall no longer be mine to contend with."

Bayfield returns to Audubon's side as gentle as ever.

"The eclipse," says Kelly. "I'm afraid you've missed the height of it."

A shadow has removed a part of the moon. The three men exclaim over it, taking turns at the telescope. They forget, for a time, matters on the earth and on the water. It grows later. As he turns to leave, Audubon bows. The wooden bust of *Gulnare*, protruding straight forward, seems to bow with him.

"We shall be celebrating the Fourth of July on shore and invite you and Mr. Bowen and Dr. Kelly to join us," he says.

"How very kind of you. We shall be delighted."

"Come when you are ready. The night will be long and you'll hear our fiddles playing. You may bring your lady," he says impishly, gesturing to the *Gulnare*. "We are short on feminine inspiration."

"Thank you," says Bayfield, the glimmer of a smile on his taut lips. "But she is mine and remains always in her place."

"A pity."

"Perhaps you require an effigy of your own."

MARIA. And in his mind, he sees Maria. The delicacy of her tipped chin as she looks up from her sewing to his face. It is a tiny face, wide about the eyes narrowing to a pointed chin. Her jaw is beautiful, almost prominent, a lovely curve leading from its widest place at the hinge to the narrow tip of her chin; he can see the bone, shaped like a wishbone, beneath her translucent skin.

He longs more than anything to put his hand there, on the soft whiteness of her upper throat, which is hidden, for she does not throw her head back to show that unprotected place. It would be unseemly for her to do so. But when she sings, which she does, *Fait do-do*, a little French lullaby, seated at the pianoforte with the children around her, this part of her throat moves with the notes in it.

He imagines she is here with him on the *Ripley*, drawing. He watches the light purchase of her hand on the pencil, the calm that suffuses her face as the fingers trace out a blossom, as if by some inter-vention. As the curve of the petal is set down on paper it is no longer dark, cold and late in the day. It is morning and sunlight lies in squares on the floor.

He observes her behaviour now in his mind's eye the way he observed the eider duck. In the carefulness of Maria's movements can be read her situation. There is no man here. She has no protector. She is barren, circling her sister's nest.

He wants to take her into his arms. He wants to trace her skin with his fingers. It is so strong a desire that now, as more rain runs over the tipped glass skylight of the ship's hold off the coast of Labrador, he can feel her.

BAYFIELD, on deck alone, watches the moon slide free of the shadow which has hidden it, earth's shadow, his own shadow. The moment awes him, evidence of the habits of celestial bodies that are to him almost gods. Suddenly the freed, reflected light falls on the *Gulnare* and lights the slave girl herself. She *is* his. He is duty-bound to ensure that on the ship she leads nothing less than honour will prevail. He walks to stand under her, placing his hand on the curved wood. He strokes her side. Mammoth solid woman that she is, it steadies him to feel her there, her lines so different, her curves extended, not predictable, not coming back to themselves, but lengthening, extending outward.

There is much expressed in her lines that he could not put into words.

America

MY COUNTRY

To discourage the moschettoes from attending the evening's revelry, the tars set fire to the grass growing in the crevices on shore. The flame races back and forth along the narrow cracks, consuming the lines of pale yellow plumes. When there is no more grass to be seen, smoke continues to issue from the cracks between the rocks, as if the fire has sunk deep into the earth itself. When that smoke screen dies, the sailors burn the little spruce meadow next to the beach. The flames shoot up fifty feet in the air.

Godwin has been climbing the hill with his shark-spine walking stick. He watches the flames from apart. "Is this how you celebrate your country's birthday?" he asks. "You burn the place down?"

Audubon too has been apart, drawing in the hold. He has finished the Eider Duck, the White-winged Crossbill, *Fringilla lincolnii* and, to show Maria, three plants of the country, all new to him and probably never before drawn. He is loath to befriend the pilot, but they share age, if nothing else; the others are so young.

"The idea was to defeat the moschettoes coming from inland but I see we have only drawn more from the other side of the harbour. Not only that, the sailors have consumed a good deal of our fuel."

The young gentlemen go foraging for more wood. By evening the pyre stands on the bare rocks at the head of the harbour. The British arrive in their launch, fresh from their measuring and calculating. They are in uniform, the three white stripes on Bayfield's sleeve gleaming. There is navy grog, in a barrel taken from the *Gulnare*'s hold.

Emery welcomes Bayfield. "Every Saturday night, like other sea-farers, we salute our wives and sweethearts. But tonight, we celebrate our motherland."

Bayfield has been apart from womankind since he was nine. On Saturday nights he takes a daguerreotype of his mother from his trunk, sets it up on his bunk, and walks back and forth in her presence for an hour.

His motherland is a fact, like his name and his status. It is dear to him but he is not given to demonstration. Besides, his real country, the place where he lives, is his ship.

"It serves, this day, as a kind of midsummer," he offers. "And your 'America' is a midsummer of countries, is it not? Bursting with life, but with a long season of ripening ahead?"

As they sing the anthem, Audubon has tears in his eyes. The British stand respectfully at attention.

"How have you come to be a citizen of America?" asks Bayfield in a rare display of curiosity. His host's French accent is so strong.

"My father sent me away from France, to avoid conscription for Napoleon's war."

Jean Jacques Audubon, an evader of the draft? Albeit the draft of France, his enemy. Even so, it seems a dishonourable act.

"You are right," says Audubon, catching the distaste. "I ran away."

Bayfield suddenly sees the humour in their situations. "You came to escape a war. I came to find a war but was disappointed. Buried alive I thought I would be, without one. Now, I am content to conquer coastlines."

Audubon raises his glass. "Buried is what I'd have been, without my country. Drink to the Labrador wilderness! And to our loved ones at home!"

The men toss a torch into the pyre. It burns merrily as the sailors and the young gentlemen cheer and sing. There is the sound of drumming from the trading post across the harbour.

"What is that?" Audubon asks.

"The Esquimaux people are doing their circle dance. Have you seen them? It is a fine sight."

"It is an occasion for them?"

"Not, I think, America's birthday," laughs Bayfield. "They have their own gods." Even as he says this, he is conscious of an absence, of what he has never known, or thought to ask, of the natives' gods.

Fires in the night and drumbeats. Audubon slips again from this landscape and become little Jean Rabin, on sad dry paths through canefields.

All around him others are running in the dark. A large fleshy hand has grasped his and, as invisible legs pump, lifts him off his feet. The canefields are burning. The slaves are coming out of the night, with machetes. They will kill everyone in their way. A woman has him by the hand. Her fingers are black, her palms pink.

Bayfield drinks slowly, methodically, tasting the liquid on his tongue. Audubon takes another swig. "You said you dream in reverse. What do you mean?"

"That here I dream of land, but when I am away, I dream of this."

"My dreams," says Audubon, "take me to a tropical place. To heat and sand, not rock and water." He sees it all: the light sharp as teeth, the palm fronds that cut your hands. The deep rustle of leaves, the sea water lapping his feet, warm as mother's milk.

Bayfield inclines his head.

"I believe they take me to my birthplace in the Antilles."

Truth, not lies. Why does he tell the truth this time? Because he is afraid he'll die on this journey and leave it unsaid? Because to tell Lucy (dearest best beloved Friend), or even write it in the diary which has become a letter to her, has become impossible? Because as he goes on he has a need for newer, stranger hiding places for his secret? Or a need not to hide it at all, but to plant it where it will grow, come forth into the light, on this journey which feels like no journey he has ever taken, a journey with no return, no shape to it, unless it is a loop where he continues to encounter himself, just as he did when Godwin said he knew Nolte?

It does not matter why he tells the truth. He has told it before. He has lied, to be sure, but he has never lied enough, never consistently enough. It is in telling the truth that his troubles begin.

"There is a secret burning inside me which I would like to tell you."

"I don't like secrets," says Bayfield.

"I must tell you. And when I do, you will look at me in astonishment."

"I shall?" says Bayfield, looking at him in astonishment. No Englishman and not even a proper Frenchman would engage in so unwanted an intimacy. "I cannot imagine what you could tell me that I should know. I am sure there is no need."

"But there is a need. For thirty years in America I have kept secrets. Now the secrecy and the lying is heavy on me. It divides me from my name, my past, and my children."

Bayfield shifts his feet. He would very much like to be off this rock but escape is not so easy. Reluctantly he tips his face to the taller man's, adopting a listening position.

"I have told you I am European but it is not so. I was born in Santo Domingo. My mother was a maid my father met on ship as he journeyed to his plantation there. He did not marry her, for he was married already. Therefore I am, I have been, all my life, without a true name or a true country."

"Ah," says Bayfield.

"An illegitimate son, while he cannot be a citizen or inherit, is not exempt from being cannon fodder. This is why I felt no duty to fight Napoleon's war."

"I see," says Bayfield, who is beginning to.

"Hence my flight to America. My good father and his wife reasoned that in Louisiana, the French part of the continent which America purchased, a questionable Frenchman might, with a forged document or two, become an American citizen."

"I see," says Bayfield again. He tries to imagine the man's predicament. He casts his mind back to the society he left at eleven. "'Stampt in nature's mint of exstasy,'" he says. It comes from some recess of memory.

"What did you say?"

"The Bastard. That was he: *Stampt in nature's mint of exstacy*. A line of poetry. From a poem I read in school, by a man called Savage.

It was not assigned to me of course, but I came across it and remembered it. 'No tenth transmitter of a foolish face,'" he continues. "That line would come back to me when I looked in a mirror; that was me, a *tenth transmitter of a foolish face*. I think I rather admired the Bastard."

Audubon laughs, an odd, barking cough of a laugh. He has disrobed, and been foiled in his disrobing at the same time, because he has not succeeded in shocking Bayfield. "That may be, Captain. But there is more to me which you must not admire. I am mated, as the birds are. But my wife occupies only a part of my heart."

Bayfield rebels. "Why do you tell me this?"

"Every day I face the chance that I might not see my home again. And I may not see you again. Soon you will turn back where you came from, while we go northward."

Bayfield subsides.

"I love a woman not my wife."

"I know nothing of these matters. Though I believe you have mentioned the woman."

"Maria. I long for her, for soft, clever, tender Maria. Long to hold her, but I cannot. Do you see my trouble?"

"I am beginning to see it," Bayfield says testily. "Although I see no reason why I should." The wild coast that has been his comfort and his haunt for seven years begins to feel like a Quebec levee on New Year's Day: one is expected to be festive when one longs only to be closeted with charts. One is forced to remain in the hail of unsavoury confession when silence would suit. "You must be happy here. Nature does not judge."

The shriven Audubon looks for a blessing in this and finds none.

"Nature is uninterested in man's pleasure. Would you agree?"

Audubon agrees. "Marriage belongs to society."

"It has its purpose."

"Like the birds'. To reproduce."

They hear a loon's cry. It goes on and on, rippling into its own echo.

"Storm tomorrow," says Bayfield. "It is a portent."

"That is a sailors' myth," says Audubon. "The loon is merely calling his mate."

"You see? A married man is fortunate," says Bayfield.

"So is a bachelor," says Audubon, and laughs.

THE SAILORS are teaching Johnny a hornpipe. Before long, the irrepressible artist pulls out his flute and joins the music making.

"Dance!" he commands.

He has them off their haunches now, Shattuck and Ingalls and Emery. Bayfield and Bowen stand stifled in serge but that won't do. He gives his flute to Johnny, who takes up the air without missing a beat.

> *Her cheeks were like the rosebuds and her sidelocks all in curl.*
> *The sailors often smiled and said he looks just like a girl.*

Audubon places himself amongst the rest and begins to dance, his locks bobbing on his shoulders, his entire body a song. Bayfield now knows why the artist's bow had reminded him of a dancing master's: Audubon could have been one. It is clear that what he does is what dancing *is*: all the other men only imitate it. Except for Johnny, who in the grace he shares with his father is suddenly not like him at all, but his own elegant creature.

"A fine reel, save that we are men without women," says Audubon when the air ends.

"It is the seafarers' lot."

"Not always," Audubon laughs. "My father had a wife at each end of his journey. And one on shipboard if he could. Had three women, in fact." He is roaring, now, with the grog in his belly. There was Anne in Nantes, the sensible, hardworking widow his father married, who died asking for her adopted son every day, the boy she'd entangled in a snare of false names and lost forever. Sanitte, the mulatto mistress he kept in Santo Domingo. She bore Audubon's older brother, his father's first born, that taller, shadowy half-memory pressed behind her as she sent Monsieur Newhouse off on the ship. The boy died in the slave uprisings, his father told him. She bore too the half-sister called Rose who followed him to France.

And Jeanne Rabin. The girl conjured by his father nearly ten years later. Audubon remembers the inn, the day and the confession, as unwanted as his own. A French girl, from a town near to Nantes. Illiterate, bound to become a maid in Santo Domingo. Not a Negro, his father repeated. It would have been easier had she been.

The inn was near the port in Nantes. His father sat Fougère at the notched table in the dim early-winter afternoon. And unburdened himself of his story as if it were a romance, a fairy tale, as the English say.

She was beautiful, his father said again and again, as if it were a reason, as if he could explain it that way. But all he could see was the moment she was dragged away from him on the landing in Les Cayes, Santo Domingo, that port of human misery, in front of the slaves in their chains and under the whine of the lash. The French officer not looking back, the young woman tugged by the hand to the other plantation where she had been promised.

She must have been like me, thought young Audubon. (No, I am like her.) No wonder I hate partings! Like me, she felt love that strongly, the burning in all her limbs.

She went where she was told, but not for long. Six months later she ran away and came to her lover's plantation, begging to be taken in. And his father took her in, although he already had Sanitte there. What could he do? She was a white girl, a French girl. She must have been pregnant already. It meant that he had been conceived on a ship, one explanation for his constant *mal de mer*. She gave birth to her son, and six months later she died. Perhaps she was ill already, his father said. Perhaps she died in the violence. I've never known.

There is a moment when a boy's eyes are rinsed clean of childhood's sleep. When they understand adult error, and adult grief. His father that day gave him the acid bath. He has sworn never to give such moments to his own sons. He spent the next few years trying to remember his mother, but he never could conjure a face. He told himself that she was not sick and that she was not murdered, but that she ran away. It was better that way. Jeanne is to him *she who escaped*, not *she who died*.

Johnny is innocent of it all. Audubon has made certain of that. He remembers that first sea voyage. Some cabin boy, assigned to make sure he did not fall overboard, who enjoyed teasing Monsieur

Newhouse when he cried. The hideous and endless rocking, his sickness. He will not have his son burdened by the duplicities of the past, as he has been. He came to America to forget the sins of his father. He has not gone home.

The dancing master is on his feet again, swirling through the polonaise with Tom Lincoln, the mazurka with his son. Audubon is certain it is Jeanne's ghost that animates Johnny's feet, just as she animates his own. He wonders if Johnny, like poor Jeanne Rabin, will throw himself away for something he calls love.

The dancing master dances, chest high, chin up, neck long, back perfectly straight, arms out at the elbow, the breath which flows into him seeming to lift the weight off his feet. His clever feet remember the waltz, the cotillion, the gallop. The English society ladies in their red turbans, the eyes that followed him flat, slightly red-rimmed, the eyes of animals intent on their needs.

There's a long tongue of flat rock just right for a gallop so he gets them all to stand in lines. The place hasn't heard such song before and maybe won't for a hundred or two hundred years more. The man who steps up to put more of their hard-found wood on the fire is doing a clog dance himself.

"Some of us will have to be ladies," Audubon announces, putting half the men down one side and half down the other. The young gentlemen grumble but goodnaturedly change their bows into curtseys. There is another dance and another. Bayfield taps toes and sways a little but does not join until Audubon hooks his elbow and swings him, letting him loose squarely in the midst of the men and he is helpless, caught by this one on his left and that on his right in the allemande. He is embarrassed, a little, and he feels himself thoroughly Bayfield of Bayfield Hall — *tenth transmitter of a foolish face* — but at least he is dancing.

Finally they have burnt every bit of trunk and root of tuckamore that touches the shore. Audubon kicks the embers together but there is little left to burn. The dark has still not fallen but Bayfield's stars are in the ascendant. The naval officer makes for his skiff. He will not let a clear night go to waste.

The schooners stand in the great harbour of Ouapitagone, their shrouds limp against the masts. Candlelight glows from inside the *Gulnare* and the *Ripley*. Wanting perfect blackness, Bayfield rows out under the bare breasts of the figurehead. He lingers there a moment, taking pleasure in his schooner, the dark curves of her hull, the slenderness of her masts. Then he makes his way beyond the harbour wall and through the cleft in the rock into the open where this lost arm of the Atlantic Ocean claps against the red granite cliffs, the locked iron gates of Castle North America.

Pitch black greets him as he rounds the point. He hears water for miles, sea smoothing and circling the shoals. It had been wild, earlier, but now it rests. He rides the swells as peacefully as he did his nursery horse long ago. On those solitary night rides he dreamed of adventuring, and now here he is. Why was he out of bed in the middle of the night at six years old? Why not asleep? Preparing for a lifetime when he would not sleep a night through?

The answer comes as a muffled, intimate blow, delivered by himself to himself, and hence the more shocking. He, the boy warrior, had been afraid. His thoughts are reduced to nothing by this insight and he sits idle in the launch for he does not know how long.

But of what was he afraid?

Of Bayfield Hall, so many rooms, so cold, as busy as a ship with all the servants?

The dark, which is now his domain?

The quiet, which he loves more than any living soul?

Being alone, which he has chosen?

He does not know.

AT LENGTH THE MOON emerges and silvers the crests of certain swells around the rocks. Luminous ruffles unfurl against a shoal. The rest is black water and lethally frigid. But tonight, in the calm, and this little boat, he is in no danger. He rows and lets the boat drift, rows and drifts until he is precisely over a shoal and then, with an ominous scrape, precisely on it. Caught.

Standing, he is careful to brace his feet on either side of the floorboard. He takes the sextant in his hand and directs it toward the horizon, now just visible as the darkness divides itself into depths for him. He looks through the eyepiece at Altair, in the eastern sky. Keeping his eye on the star, he moves the index arm of the sextant back and forth. Altair seems to swing back and forth along a short arc. He catches it at the lowest point and tightens the screw. He can feel with his fingers the tiny engraved lines giving the angle at this precise instant. He presses the stop button on his chronometer.

The air rising from the water has chilled him to the bone. He knows the water temperature; out here, it will be about thirty-nine degrees. He measures it nearly every day. He knows that were he to fall into it, he would have less than a minute to live.

But he would love to walk on the shoal.

It is a foolish idea. What if he lost his footing? If he tipped the boat with his instruments in it, even worse.

But he likes the idea of standing on the rock, which is just inches above the surface.

No.

Yes.

He places his hands on the thwarts and steadies the boat. He inches the hull forward so that the boat is more secure. He gets one foot on the shoal, and balances with the other in the boat. He slowly shifts his weight. The boat rises under him and slides a little on the shoal. He holds his breath. Then, quickly, he pulls out the other foot and stands. The water swills around the mound of granite, only a few feet across.

He has done it. He feels as if he is walking on water. He wishes he could stay all night. He could fool the fishermen as they went past in the morning. They would think he was the Almighty. He laughs out loud, picturing it. He is becoming profane.

THE NEXT DAY Bayfield seeks out Audubon in his dark and damp hold and invites him for a walk. He has a question for the artist, but he scarcely knows how to formulate it.

Bayfield peers at the rocks with ferocity, picking up this one and that, looking for ammonites. Looking down is rare for him; he looks up constantly when he is at sea. Audubon is staring into the distance when suddenly he whistles quietly and motions to Bayfield to be still.

His sharp eye has seen a flash of colour. A woman enters the clearing, unaware that they are there. She is clad in white man's clothing; her skin is a deep mahogany red. Her cap, which has little points that droop above her ears, is of cloth woven in black and red stripes as if she got it from a Frenchman on the side of liberty. She wears a multi-coloured skirt and a neckerchief of bright red, blue and white. There are embroidered bands about her bodice and her hat.

She comes closer. She has two huge silver crucifixes on her breast. And her legs, which move in and out of the blue-green leaves, the pale laurel bushes, the sun-shrivelled leaves of tiny blueberry plants, are in stockings knit with the colours of the rainbow. On her feet are low moccasins.

Bayfield rises. Audubon puts out a hand to stop him.

"She'll fly!"

"You'll frighten her," Bayfield says. He presents himself to the woman. "Good evening, miss," he says.

She stands still while first the one then the other man materializes from the berry bushes. She reaches up and removes her hat in respect. She looks on either side for an escape route but in the end bravely stands her ground. Her hair is knotted above her ears, in glistening, braided ovoids.

Audubon is enchanted. He would have lain hidden for hours; he would have stalked her.

Bayfield steps closer. She shakes her head *Not understand English*. She giggles. In only a few minutes Bayfield, who listens to Kelly the botanist, has her giving the names of the tiny flowers he pulls from the tangles of moss.

"*Vie toujours*," she says.

"We call it lungwort," says Bayfield.

Audubon, competing, points to the rocks below where the birds come and go. "Foolish guillemot," he says.

"*Murres*," she replies.

"Cormorant," he points to the black ones with the neck like snakes.

"*Ouapitagone*."

"Ah, that is the name. And the sailors think the name denotes the shape of the rock, which resembles a cannon."

Audubon speaks to her in French, attempting to explain this, pointing to the gun which is always at his side. Her eyes widen. He asks her about more birds. She does not speak back but she gestures them to follow. They walk inland over the clumsy piles of rock and across the open spaces, where the terrain is dry. They come to a rim of trees and, inside of it, a pond. They make out the shape, in the gloaming, the beaked periscope of the red-throated loon. They hear the cry.

"*Whabby*," she says.

"An ancient bird," says Bayfield, "and lonely as the rocks."

"Not at all, not at all," Audubon says. "That cry in which you hear loneliness is in fact the sound of devotion. They have a devoted family life."

"Oh, they too," says Bayfield, dryly.

"They do! They fly here in pairs, the male taking the lead. Sometimes they are so high that you cannot pick out their shape, only, if it is calm, hear their wings beating the air. Whenever the bird alights it dives, as if to taste the water. When it surfaces it shakes its wings and makes that cry to reassure its mate."

The Montagnais girl comes to the edge of the pond. The loon pops to the surface of the water in front of her, its young behind. On seeing the people, she begins to run on top of the water, racing along the surface with her tail digging a little furrow behind her. Her young dive.

They all laugh.

They stand, marvelling as the birds gather at the shore. Bayfield finds the moment for his question. "Mr. Audubon," he says. "I have a strange question. Do the birds play?"

Audubon does not answer directly.

"Do you want to see how we toll a loon? I tried this with Johnny and Tom Lincoln."

"What is tolling a loon?"

Audubon undoes the kerchief at his neck. And, imitating its cries, runs at the birds. They become confused and fly at him rather than away. It is a contest to see who veers first.

"No other species of waterfowl is deceived so completely by this game," says Audubon. "They become very easy to kill."

"Ah," says Bayfield. "Perhaps it is only you who are playing."

The Montagnais girl has flown. Her red stripes can be seen ascending the hill.

"Ravens, on the other hand, play. Anonyme, my pet, whom you met when you came to see my paintings, will roll a stone along the deck of the ship. He will drop it from a height to watch it bounce."

Bayfield laughs at the image. "Is he talking to you yet?"

"Sometimes," says Audubon. "At least, he will say what I tell him. He has not predicted the future."

"Perhaps you have not given him the words."

The two men climb the rocky hillside. The terrain is very rough. They walk a long way and come to a petrified forest less than three feet tall. Audubon dodges through the spiked, silvery, barkless branches, which are hard as glass. The forest appears to have died long ago, and to have been under a spell ever since. He sits on a rocky ledge.

"Time is your business," he says to Bayfield. "Am I correct?"

"You might say."

"For me, time, which you measure so carefully, has begun to move at a most awkward gait. It is neither slow nor quick. It is willful. It speeds, and then it stops. It toys with me, quite suddenly driving me backward to a place I have long deserted. But what is worse is that now

I fear it will drive me forward. When time drives me forward then surely I shall rebel. I am aging too fast."

Bayfield is ten years younger, and smiles. "What form will your rebellion take?"

"My life moved with painful slowness until I was forty-one. And then, when I realized what I was born to do, my days began to race. That was seven years ago.

"I had come to Europe from the backwoods, unknown, and in Edinburgh the cultivated classes embraced me. I *became famous*," he says, so baldly it embarrasses Bayfield. "I understood that I would have the chance to create the great Work I dreamed of. But to do it I would be torn away from my life as it was, and would spend years at a time apart from my loved ones."

THE COACH ENTERED SCOTLAND at ten in the morning on a fine October day in 1826: as soon as they crossed the border from England, the country became beautiful. Audubon hung out the window as they passed the seat of Sir Walter Scott.

"That man has given me such intense pleasure, I want to thank him," he announced, but the other travellers, scandalized by his suggestion, offered him only a drink of Scotch whiskey.

Edinburgh delighted him, with its spires and steep hills, with the mountain, the sea and the castle. He found a room for a guinea a week: from its window he could see the boats on the Firth. He was not in the city half a day before he walked out to call on five notables to whom he had introductions from Thomas Traill, leaving his new card, given to him by the women of the Rathbone family.

"It is the same card I presented to you," he tells Bayfield.

Back in his room he unpacked his portfolio and lay his favourite birds around on chairs and tables. He stood a long time in front of his Carolina Parakeets. They winked in full colour, green, orange, yellow, cocking their heads at him and at each other, bills open to strip the cocklebur on which they sat. They were themselves, they were his own, and yet they made him afraid. Abruptly he took them off their tabletops and chairs and packed them away again.

He went for a long walk alongside the public gardens, the poor women in the street reminding him of Shawnee squaws, with their burdens laced to their back by a band across their foreheads. He heard himself discussed. "That man must be a German physician," or "There goes a French nobleman." He became aware — or had he always known this, and rather liked it? — that he was extraordinary.

When he returned to his rooms he looked at himself, not his birds. A mirror in a rented room in an unknown city speaks frankly to the question of one's face. He was forty-one, and he saw, for the first time, a great resemblance to his father, husband of Jeanne, of Sanitte, of Anne. *Hungry* was the word for what he saw. A man gnawed at by hunger, beset by hunger. Hunger for comforts, hunger for acknowledgement, hunger to make a place in the world for his birds, his wife, his boys. *To make the boys better than myself.* He swore to himself that they, Victor and Johnny, would never stand alone and unknown across the wide ocean from loved ones, and know they must conquer the town.

People do not know this face, but they will.

"FROM THAT DAY," Audubon tells Bayfield, "Fame coasted down on its great wide wings and seized me in its talons. There I was, helplessly lofted."

He notices Bayfield's discomfort. "Am I not famous?" he challenges. He recites again the accolades: that Baron Cuvier of France called his bird portraits 'the greatest monument yet erected by Art to Nature.' That the Duc d'Orléans got down on his knees and called him king of bird painters. That the *Baltimore Courier* wrote, 'His exploits as great as his genius.'"

"Excellent," says Bayfield. "I am very impressed."

"Of course I am inclined to agree with the laurels. Yet there are those who call me a fraud and a conniver. My detractors will hold that I am mad until I have proven myself and then they will say they always knew. This is human nature and troubles me little. It is merely the relative proportions of humankind in each camp that concerns me."

Bayfield could scarcely imagine living with notoriety. "What was it to be seized by this raptor then, Mr. Audubon? I have no desire to be so."

"What do you seek, then?"

"The approval of my superiors."

A look of amusement crosses Audubon's face: this captain is a bit of a prig. "Renown may come to a quiet man," he says, "and that is a pleasure, I suppose — to be known by your fellows, and respected amongst your peers. Fame is vulgar, to be pointed at in the street, to hear your name on the lips of strangers. To hear stories, both miraculous and vile, circulating about yourself. It is to be mortified and aggrandized in equal measure. You may disdain it, but I courted fame. I acted a grand figure of a man, I told stories of the wild, I gave red Indian calls. I *needed* fame to win my cause. It was a way to make my book of birds a reality. I wanted not just to be the greatest bird artist of my time, but to be known in the world as such. I am. But there is a hollowness now. Fame has consumed my entrails, and played upon the falseness that was in me. Fame may have won, in the end."

"It is not the end," says Bayfield, distressed. "You said to me yourself you have only come halfway."

Lizars, the engraver, was the first to be astonished by the Birds. The others followed with dizzying speed. Within a week, one hundred drawings were hung and displayed. The newspapers published such glowing accounts of Audubon that he was embarrassed to walk on Prince's Street. His evenings were given over to long dinner parties and meetings with men of such achievement that he was abashed in their presence. It was their wives, so often great beauties, and intelligent too, beside whom he was seated. He made certain the wives were entranced. But even when they were, he was certain they noticed the inferiority in him. When he went home to his rooms at night, he wrote to tell Lucy. It was the only way he could be sure that it was truly happening.

The invitations fell through his landlady's door. Somehow during this time he painted the Wild Turkey with nine young. Lizars made it his first engraving. Audubon was amazed in his own turn. How adroit he was to form all the lines exactly the opposite to

Audubon's drawing, using it only to copy! Audubon's work astounded the rest of society. Artists and naturalists like Selby and Jardine came to his rooms for lessons.

"I came to understand that *big* was necessary," says Audubon to Bayfield. "To be large as life. Myself and the birds. Nothing reduced. Nothing to limit the grandeur. I determined, in calm moments during Edinburgh's romance with me, that I would publish the *Birds* at my own expense with a list of three hundred good names. That the Birds must be life-sized. The pages double elephant portfolio. It went against the advice of my friends. But I wanted it that way. I made a pledge to myself. I would give over my life to this endeavour no matter what I had to sacrifice — even those who loved me."

Through all this he was alone: his letters took a month or more to reach Lucy and he had not heard from her at all. He went to parties where a great many glittering ladies and gentlemen grazed. He would stand as motionless as a heron and, when he dared to, look around himself, and often, as he was Mr. Audubon, the great artist from the frontier, no one would come near. Then a lady would float to his side and, by speaking to him, ease his shyness.

"I came to understand myself as I understood a bird. Now *I* was the creature from the wilds never before seen. *I* the subject of fascination, and others making a replica of me. There was the portraitist, making me stand for dull hours as if shot, stuffed and wired."

The snow had fallen on the hills of Edinburgh by then and his new friends insisted that he wear his wolf-skin coat for the portrait. And he did. If the head were not a strong likeness, he joked, perhaps the coat would be! He saw it when it was done and was horrified; his eyes looked not at all human but like the eyes of an enraged eagle.

The strangest was the man who studied heads. George Combe showed up in Audubon's rooms early in his weeks in Edinburgh, and chatted with the men of learning who gathered there. He said little about the birds, but offered that Monsieur Audubon had a most particular head, and that he would like to make a cast of his skull. Audubon was pleased; the shape of his head must be of interest even to himself, now that he was becoming famous.

A week later, at the end of a tiresome dinner at a country house, Combe came upon Audubon as he sat apart from the company on a chair in the corner. Combe wore spectacles over large, ice-blue eyes. His hair had vacated his head in order to make his own skull available for examination. It was a large, high, domed head, and his eyebrows, which were black and furred, sat a long way down from the top; more than half of his face was forehead, a frank, wide forehead with three even lines across it like the lines on a musical score. Combe enunciated his theory; a head of a certain shape implied particular strengths or talents in the owner. "Your head," he said, pacing in a circle around Audubon's chair, "is unique. But so I would expect it to be." His long, knobby fingers seemed to twitch. He asked if Audubon might come to the next meeting of the phrenologists' society, and Audubon agreed.

On the night of the meeting, which was a chill, foggy evening in November, he mounted the steps of an elegant Georgian mansion to be greeted by a phalanx of men, with one lady amongst them, wringing their hands and bobbing at the sight of him. He was not introduced, for he was a subject, Exhibit A.

He sat on a stage on a wooden chair with his back to the audience, a huge white bib tied around his shoulders, no part of him visible but his head. Audubon wore his hair long; sometimes he tied it back, sometimes he allowed it to flow. He'd never in fact liked to bare his head, considering it a little small for his height. George Combe begged his pardon before lifting his hair off his neck and tying it out of the way. There was a circle of candles around him. He felt he was posing for an oil of the head of John the Baptist on a plate.

The master phrenologist emerged from the wings, to restrained applause. He wore a black university gown. His skin was an unhealthy grey, and his eyes flickered half shut as if the candlelight was too bright for him. Standing centre stage, he could reach out and touch Audubon's head.

Combe made the introduction.

"Our master here has no knowledge of our kind volunteer tonight. Only shall I say that he has a particular calling and an unusual way of life. He is, in his field, eminent."

"That the Birds must be life-sized.
The pages double elephant portfolio."

The phrenologist stretched his arms high, letting his sleeves fall away from his wrists. His hands were large, fleshy, insistent. He first pressed the flats of his palms slowly over the whole of Audubon's head and face. He dug the rounded ends of his fingers into Audubon's skull. He turned and lifted Audubon's head on his neck, describing in a toneless voice his discoveries: a flat nape, hollows behind his ears, a certain ridge across the back of his head that ran between his ears. He measured the cranium over the top, from ear tip to ear tip. All the while his fingers prodded and pushed, and in their pushing, shook with excitement. Audubon understood all too well the shaky fingers. He was the bird in the hand, snatched from its habitat. He was to be proof of a theory. As the fingers roved and probed his skull, a chill worked its way up his spine. He shivered under the white draping; he felt his captivity.

The phrenologist spoke.

"It is in fact a small head. But the muscles of the neck tell me that the man himself is tall and strong. He is a little primitive: his head slopes back quickly from the eyebrows. His forehead flows backward, rising to the height of the crown, which tells me he is unlearned, close to the animals. He is not a parlour creature, not an intellectual."

Audubon began to feel quite separate from his head. He could see it, floating in the air ahead of him. The phrenologist took his chin in one hand, the back of his head in the other, and measured, describing a particular arc here, a nodule there.

"One is reminded of certain African mammals — the gorilla, yes? But in direct contrast to that is the aquiline nose, evidence of the high born, of a fascination with detail, or a Mediterranean antecedent. A very mixed parentage. The deep eye sockets suggest restlessness and passion. He is genial on the whole but quick tempered. Here, just here, the line, which should be smooth from temple to temple, is oddly uneven. It meanders, in fact, showing a great inconsistency of character."

The man's hands roamed more urgently over the territory of Audubon's head, and seemed now to be expressing irritation with what they found. Devoted but faithless. A dangerous split in his personality . . . "There is one other man alive whose head has these characteristics. I am reminded now of, I am reminded of the great poet, of Byron."

The audience gasped.

Audubon was flattered. Byron, indeed!

"BYRON," says Bayfield. It has been said before. And now he can see why. Both men show what ordinary mortals might consider a triple insolence; they had beauty, talent, and a ferocity of spirit. It is bound to raise hackles.

"I am frightened," says Audubon, suddenly. "Do you see? Not by Fame but by the strange coils of life. Do you know, I had been reading Byron's *Corsair* on the *Delos*, as I approached Europe that year. I still remember his words, because they struck such chords in me: 'Fear'd, shunned denied 'ere youth had lost its force.' 'Warp'd by the world in Disappointment's school': it was exactly how I felt, then. Now, short months later, it seemed the opposite was to be my lot. You treat Time as if it were a predictable force, as if it could be trapped. But to me, Time is a sea monster. Do you not see the beguiling loops and coils? It is a shapeless coastline along which we journey in the fog.

"And don't you think it strange," he remarks in Labrador's nearly empty theatre, to his audience of one seated in tiers and tiers of rock, to Captain Henry Bayfield at Ouapitagone, "that you sail with the figure-head of Byron's heroine?"

Bayfield remembers distinctly that, on first meeting, Audubon had said he did not read. It unsettles him: a needless lie. Why does the man tell it? In an effort to escape what he called "the shape of life?"

THAT NIGHT in Edinburgh, Audubon found, cloaked in white, anonymously famous, that he enjoyed the danger; to be at risk of exposure was thrilling. He flirted with the credulous public. There is a beauty in lying. A freedom in lying. An art in lying.

He was safe in the fact that he was not who they thought he was. The phrenologist might take his skull between his palms and prod, but he did not know what was hidden within. J. J. Audubon, son of a French nobleman, possibly possessing royal blood, was nowhere to be found. Within was Jean Rabin, Creole of Santo Domingo. An adoring public would never hold him in its hands, nor, if they turned on him, could they wound him.

"This man is a fraud," announced the phrenologist.

Combe nervously came to stand at Audubon's feet. "When you hear the name you shall be highly amused that you have made so categorical a claim."

But the phrenologist's hands did not give way, nor did his opinion. With the man's fingers pressing into his head, Audubon felt his brain shrink away in self-protection.

"What sort of fraud?" said Audubon, his French accent sounding very strong to him.

"A fraud who delights in crossing borders, leaving mystery in his wake. A seller of patent medicine, perhaps? Or an artist."

The phrenologist's voice suddenly sank in a hush. "Oh, feel the knobs here behind the ears. Yes, the man's métier is either art or medicine. Art, most likely, for there are more frauds in that world than in the other."

He tapped the top of Audubon's skull, twice, three times, as if knocking on a door. And he took himself away from the light.

Then Audubon was introduced as the greatest bird artist of his day, to much applause.

The next candidate was a musician, and, under the fingers a short time later, was pronounced to be exactly that. Hence, the theory of head shape was proven. Afterward there was a bit of Scottish music, airs and glees and madrigals.

"IT MAKES A GOOD STORY," says Bayfield.

"Yes it does, but this one is true. Can you believe that still Mr. Combe was not finished with me?

"I had to sit for the plaster cast of my head. My face and hair were covered over with plaster of Paris, my nose as well; I had a greased quill in each nostril so that I could breathe, and worst of all, I had to keep my eyes closed for an entire hour. A miserable ordeal, and when it was finished I hardly knew my head."

Bayfield sits with his face turned up toward the sky. He is waiting for day to end so that his friends and guides, the planets and suns so unimaginably distant, will show their light.

"You dissemble," he says.

"I do," laughs Audubon.

"You neglect to tell me of the great satisfactions fame has brought you. The rewards of a great name. You pretend, in fact — yes, pretend — that it is of no import, and yet everything about you speaks of a man who must impress himself upon the world, who must be larger, in his deeds, than others."

"A-ha!" cries Audubon, leaping to his feet. He stands over the naval officer, legs apart, fists on his hips. "We return to the question of scale. How big must I be? Or you? Do you accuse your new friend of seeking attention? While you, a modest chartmaker, are content to labour in obscurity with only your excellent reputation and the truth of your renderings to warm your heart at night? You think that I lie even when I tell the truth."

THEY WALK ON through the light, which is silvered and blue with the slowly approaching night. The rock is cleft; from here a green bed of moss spreads. Their feet sink, but bounce up again. Audubon stops to examine a nest. Bayfield trudges, staring at the rock so intensely that he does not see where he is going. He kicks the rocks at his feet, making automatic notes. Granite as at Sept-Îles. Grey feldspar. Augite as well as hornblende, traversed by large dykes of basaltic greenstone. The direction of these dykes is northeast and west, he notes. Also traversed by dykes of an unknown red rock, like fine-grained granite. He wishes he knew its name.

Audubon finds a soft patch of moss and lies in it. His mass of curly hair confuses itself with the tendrils of moss. Bayfield steps a little closer and sees that the artist's eyes are closed.

"Try it. It is soft. And dry, to a point." His eyes do not open.

The captain looks over his shoulder. It would not do for his crew to see him in so undignified an action. But there is nothing and no one, not a path, not a dwelling, not a viewpoint. He pokes at the moss with his toes. He bends over and presses it with a hand. Softer than the softest eiderdown mattress in Quebec. He bends a knee and his knee sinks deep and hits first cold water and then rock.

"Ugh," he says and lifts his knee.

"All at once. Let yourself down all at once. Along the length of your leg with your weight on your arm. As if you were to lie down on thin ice."

Bayfield does as he is told.

"Ah," he says.

"Have you ever felt anything so wonderful?"

"Not in a long while," admits Bayfield.

"Anything. Ever?"

"It does feel very comfortable. Compared to a hammock."

"Of course there are things better. Lying with my wife feels better than this."

Bayfield has no reply.

Audubon laughs softly. Then, loudly. "Here is what a woman must aspire to: to be a better mattress than moss."

Bayfield is offended. "It is very rude to think of a lady that way."

"You are not married."

"I am not."

"Therefore you must respect women. It is only right. However, I am married. With my actions I respect them. Pray God my words may find some humour in the situation. You must find a wife, captain."

Bayfield is finding this intrusive. "I am at sea from April through October. A wife would be left alone." (And Fanny Wright is far too young.)

Audubon rolls on his side, gets up on an elbow and looks at his friend. His elbow and hip sink in the moss. "And from October to April? A wife would give you comfort. If it's comfort you want."

"Has yours given you comfort?"

"Oh, yes indeed. Certainly a lot more comfort than I have given her." A soft groan of repentant laughter rises from the bearlike man. "She is my most loyal friend and my partner in this huge endeavour. Do you know what love is, my friend? If I may call you that." He does not wait for an answer. "You have to place yourself entirely in the hands of the beloved. You have to trust your lover or you cannot feel the pleasures. If the trust is there, it is perfect. But it begins to die, of course, it dies as, little by little, we disappoint one another. Each breach is punished by a diminution of joy. Being imperfect beings, we break trust with one another."

"I see," says Bayfield.

"I doubt that you do."

Bayfield closes his eyes, as an experiment. It feels wonderful. But as he drifts, Audubon summons him.

"What are you thinking?"

"That it is a relief not to see."

"I feel the same."

"But still I see."

"Of course. One cannot help it."

"What do you see?"

"The rocks. Blue where they are wet from the sea. The trees on the sides of the long peninsulas, black when the sun has gone off them."

"Which is most of the time."

"Aye."

They lie in silence a little bit more.

"And I am thinking," says Bayfield, "that it is a miracle the flies have not found us."

The men laugh aloud.

"Now you've jinxed it. Here they come!"

A battalion of blackflies bombs their bodies. First one then the other jumps to his feet. In so doing, Bayfield staggers and flings out a hand, accidentally hitting Audubon in the leg. The artist retaliates with a pretend punch to the captain's shoulder. Their feet sinking unevenly in the foot and a half of moss, they dance apart, then Audubon dodges in again and lands a blow to Bayfield's stomach. The younger man has fighting reflexes and, before he realizes it, has blocked Audubon's arm hard and landed a blow on his chin. Still they are laughing. They fight like that until, breathing hard, Audubon backs off, suddenly short of breath.

The
LAUGHING SONG

On the next day, July 6, Audubon walks with Johnny and the other young men. The geese, which honk and glide away from the water, tell him there are marshes inland. Amongst the naked rocks and open quagmires he sees the Red-necked Partridge, or willow grouse, as it is sometimes known. He had suspected it could be found here, for he knows it to have been shot in Maine. It counts, he supposes, as a new bird for Labrador.

These partridge are silent, familial birds that creep around at the roots of bushes, scuttling over the bare rocks if startled. When Johnny pokes about with his gun, he scares up a family. The adults fly into his face so that he is forced to beat them off, even killing one.

Their behaviour excites Audubon. It is different from that of the grouse he knows in the south. Among other grouse the males leave the incubating females; both sexes and the young fly from man.

He stirs up and follows a pair that has no young. These birds do not attempt to intimidate him, but fly ahead, from hillock to rise of rock. He sees them standing, watching, until he gets to within two hundred yards. Then they run from the bare rock to the silver green moss, where they are invisible, only to reappear ahead on a rise, looking back. *Dyow*, they bark, *cluck cluck cluck*. Then they laugh, smoothly, and the laugh grows and speeds up. Again he has the feeling of enchantment, which has come over him before in this country. It is as if these birds are mortals, under a spell, as if they must draw him onward, as if they have a message for him.

He follows the two willow grouse and before long arrives at a great black quagmire. On it is floating some tangled green vine; pitcher plants with their leathery red cups stand on thin stalks. The grouse fly over top of the quagmire and land in its centre. They laugh: *heh heh heh heh*. He steps in. The black is a mix of all colour, all matter. The mud sucks at his feet and at the feet of Johnny, who has stepped in after him. It is not very deep and he decides to carry on.

He takes a few more steps into the quagmire. The surface ahead seems to move, as if the bog were a being, awakening to his presence.

Now he tries to lift one foot but as he transfers his weight the other foot sinks further. He staggers. The first leg buckles at the knee, sending him down to his calf. With an immense effort he lifts his standing leg. The mud makes a loud pop. The other leg sinks to the hip, and he falls forward, the queasy matter working itself into his wool trousers.

"Johnny," he calls, over his shoulder, "take care how you tread on this surface." Johnny is not two steps behind him and in the same difficulty. He strikes the surface with the butt of his gun, breaking the tension; his feet begin to sink. The bog has a gloss like fat on gravy. When it is cracked, the whole mass quivers.

"Do not try to run, whatever you do," Audubon warns him. He is now, himself, fully immersed to his waist. The partridges are lightly perched on the green leaves that dot the surface. *Dyow, cluck cluck cluck. Heh heh heh heh heh.*

Johnny's struggles make vibrations travel across the bog.

Audubon breathes heavily in and out. In such a place do pirates throw their victims to perish, he thinks. Do horses plunge to their deaths, drowning in mud, do murder victims sink to oblivion. In such a place do the bizarrely preserved corpses of animals that existed before history occasionally burp to the surface. Audubon imagines himself in aspic on a table at Baron Cuvier's laboratory:

ORNITHOLOGIST, 19th century. The long-legged behemoth of Santo Domingo and other parts.

Or, all flesh consumed, his skeleton pressed farther and farther down under the weight of rotting matter, himself as a mere sketch on rock, obsidian, a fossil. The man who chased the birds once too often.

"I'm going down, Father," Johnny is saying, puzzled.

Carefully, Audubon turns his head. Johnny's knees are disappearing, both at the same time. Behind him and off to the right is Tom Lincoln, balanced on the quivering surface. Wise fellow that he is, Lincoln has taken the measure of their enemy and stands on the green matter. He stoops, arms out, knees bent, motionless.

"How far down does it go, Father?"

"I don't feel the bottom." Audubon has now sunk to his hips but goes no farther. His legs are split apart; the saddle of his body supports him. The ripples from Johnny's struggles are making slurping noises against his thighs.

"Do not come any closer!"

"I'm trying to reach you."

"You mustn't!"

Their voices rise in fear and anger.

The bog, as it makes to swallow Johnny, emits gaseous odours and strange gasps; bubbles break on the surface. Audubon stands in fragile equilibrium, mud hugging his hips. His waistcoat is soaked, its pockets of pencil and paper, snuff, knife, heavy. The collecting basket with the dead grouse that rode on a belt around his middle is now a mass of wet humus. It settles on him that he can go no farther and that he is in an element utterly indifferent to, in fact malignly affected by, his efforts.

"I may die here! It will be the land, and not the dreadful sea that finally swallows me."

Johnny stops flailing and stands observing himself disappearing by inches.

Tom Lincoln still has not broken the surface. He wears, instead of the moccasins preferred by the Audubons, his fishermen's rubber boots. They have huge soles as wide as snowshoes, and let him remain on top. "What I need is a plank," he says, quietly.

The others snort. There is no plank within a mile. Johnny's pointer stands whining at the grassy edge of the bog. No one dares look his way in case he should decide to follow.

And now Time plays one of its tricks. Audubon remembers the skating parties of his youth, how he skimmed over the ice on the Schuylkill River.

One night he nearly flew. He was the brave young Frenchman newly arrived in Pennsylvania, next door to Lucy Bakewell, who put on blades for the first time and outskated them all on the frozen Schuylkill.

The girls want to hear his French, and his English, which is even funnier. They laugh, this night, whenever he speaks. They drink warm cider and clap their hands to warm them over the bonfire. Then comes the race. You are to circle the pond once and when you return to the bonfire, leap over a barrel which is laid on its side. He remembers the tour in the darkness, unseen, his cheeks and ears flaming from wine, his hair lifting in the wind. He flies toward the crowd of people, toward the firelight, skimming faster and faster, trusting his legs and trusting the ice. He gathers his legs under him and without slowing springs into the air, tucking them sideways. He enters the yellow light of the fire; he clears the obstacle. One barrel is easy; he lands on his blades on the far side without slowing. Then there are two barrels and another circuit of the pond, another entry into the fire's glow. Then there are three, and the set of young men skating is now smaller. Somehow there are now five barrels and one rival, who hitches up his pants as a farmer would and advises: Fougère, drop out before you hurt yourself! The swaggerer loses courage and clatters ignominiously into the side of the first barrel, knocking the whole line askew. He waits for the barrels to be realigned and then does his triumphant tour of the pond, all eyes on him in the darkness, no eyes burning more brightly than Lucy's. He clears all five easily. He is launched.

Lucy waits by the fire to hand him a towel to wipe his brow. He has his flute, as always, and when he does not skate he plays for Lucy, watching her out of the corner of his eye.

Once, while skating, he went through a thin patch and plunged into water. The shock of cold felt, curiously, like its opposite, like fire running through his clothing. But he was young then and that wild zeal surged through his arms and legs. He gave an enormous kick and pushed with his arms and shot forward over the ragged edges of the ice and found himself lying on his stomach several feet away, the wet of his clothing instantly gluing him to the surface.

His friends built a fire and massaged his limbs, undressed and dressed him again in pieces of clothing each one could do without — here an undershirt, there socks, extra trousers from the man who had prudently worn two pair, a muffler, a shirt, a topcoat. The sun shone and they laughed, bundling his cold wet clothing, the French shirt and jacket, which Anne Moynet had sewn for him a world away, and they all skated on down the river, laughing still.

He hears the song of the partridge.

Here too are young men, but not he. He imagines kicking forward onto the surface, crawling on his belly without breaking it: not possible. The heavy mould of mud works its chill right into his heart. He wonders if it is not easier to give in. He has had many setbacks. Might it be forgiven a man of forty-eight, when sinking in a bog, to merely continue to sink?

The partridges chuckle, luring him to his death or signalling for his rescue.

He watches Johnny now with a detached admiration: his son has devised a way to slowly withdraw himself from the sinking mass. He has lain back, arms out, with his gun in one hand lying alongside him to take some of the weight. He is wriggling slowly backward, toward his dog in the weeds. One belch of the quagmire could take his head under the surface. Meanwhile, Tom Lincoln approaches as stealthily as a hunter, speaking softly.

"Be calm — I am coming."

But Johnny is out, out but not erect, lying on the surface. He tries to roll toward his father. The waves begin again.

"Do not come near me!" commands Audubon. He does not want to be disturbed from his reverie of giving in, giving up the struggle against the lack of light, the confinement, the rancid butter, the frigid fingers, the difficulty of creating a perfect bird in paint on paper.

Johnny, obedient, stops. His pointer is frantic, foaming, snapping on the edge of the bog.

"Stay!" commands Tom Lincoln. It is not clear to whom he is speaking.

Johnny slowly works himself, on his stomach, back toward the shore. Tom Lincoln waits, eyeing the distance between himself and Audubon, which is still long.

The dog ceases to bark and begins to moan. They cautiously turn their heads, all of them, so concentrated, each in his own predicament; two Montagnais men are speaking in their soft language to the dog.

Where did they come from?

Audubon knows. They have come from the land of enchantment. They wear the same red-and-black cap that was worn by the beautiful young woman of the day before. They bear the heavy silver crucifixes on their breast. And behind them they pull a toboggan. It is made out of planks, curved planks, and is pulled on a rope; they use it to carry their goods over deep snow. They shout something to Tom Lincoln, who does not understand. Then, bending, they take a few steps into the bog and push the toboggan, curled front first, toward Johnny. Johnny reaches out and catches it alongside himself; leaning on it, he moves the few remaining feet and manages to stand. Then he pushes the toboggan to Tom.

The curious wooden contrivance glides over the greenery that festoons the surface. In one patch it slows, and seems about to stop, but there is enough momentum for it to go farther. Tom Lincoln, nearly bent double, reaches out, careful not to disturb his footing, and catches it.

The rest is easy.

Except this.

Now, now that he is about to be saved, Audubon gives in to his fear; he begins to struggle against his suspension in the stinking mass. His acquiescence of minutes before is gone. The idea of letting go of his burdens suddenly loses all its attractions. Not yet! Not this time! He manages to raise himself six inches but the effort is rewarded only by his sinking a foot. He is terrified of going down now, of feeling his mouth and eyes fill with the greasy grey-black ooze, he is terrified he will not live to complete his Work, he is terrified of failure. He begins to thrash with his arms.

The young men approach him now, both on the surface, between them the toboggan. The red-necked partridges rise from the surface and offer their soft condolences: *Dyow. Cluck cluck cluck heh heh heh heh heh.*

ONE MORE EVENT makes the day miraculous. They are back at the shore, wanting to be near the ship's stove, laughing over their near catastrophe, Audubon wrapped in Johnny's coat. It was Godwin who rowed them to shore, and Godwin who waits to take them back. He says nothing while they climb into the boat, makes no intervention as they talk of the killing bog, the horror of its maw, the strange grace of the Montagnais appearing with the toboggan and disappearing again, so quickly, before they could be rewarded. They sit in the boat while Godwin and a sailor row them back to the *Ripley.* The soft chucking of the partridges comes maddeningly to Audubon's ears. "What is that?" he says several times, listening. "Stop, please."

The men obligingly halt the oars in the oarlocks. There is the sound. *GoBEK goBEK goBEK poDAYdo poDAYdo. Cluck cluck cluck.* Audubon cannot see the partridges but he is certain they are following him home.

When they row up against the sides of the *Ripley*, Godwin pulls out his basket. He lifts the lid on the basket and shows what he has caught, a fine pair of willow grouse. There is much laughter all around.

Even bloody Godwin is helping him now.

Colour

Audubon heard the sweet trill of a prothonotary warbler; he spied the bird in a flash of yellow, green, white and blue. "The colours, Maria!"

He and Maria were walking on Reverend Drayton's plantation outside Charleston; John Bachman was far behind them with his gun. The forest floor was lit with azaleas and occasional purple iris. Deadwood crossed all the paths. He helped her step across the tree trunks. Her feet were impossibly small.

The path wound to the edge of the swamp, a patch of black water surrounded by trees. Grey and bearded, the trees stood like a thin drizzle. Their bases were bulbs half-planted in motionless green slime; the water itself was a flat surface mottled like marble. Amidst the trees were stumps drilled through by ivory-billed woodpeckers. The colour was layered from green, to grey, to the blue of the sky above. Audubon rehearsed the names of the trees: tupelo, loblolly pines, lodgepole pines, gum trees, red maple, red cedar, American holly.

He blinked and the birds emerged from their camouflage. A Lesser Yellowlegs pecked at the ground near the edge of the swamp, its long legs like stalks of grass. On the water, their presence betrayed by their bright red bills, were several wood ducks — the *Anas sponsa*, or Betrothed Duck. They went in pairs, the spectacular drake and his soft brown mate, gliding soundlessly, moving neither the water nor any visible part of themselves.

One dove and made the water boil for a moment.

He and Maria took seats on a dry clump of grass at the edge of the swamp, his gun at his side, their backs against the base of a tree.

They watched the gregarious turtles sunning on dead logs that slanted up to catch the beams, their necks lifted as if to test the wind. Occasionally a grackle seemed to fall out of a live oak, flapping like paper.

At first the alligators did not seem to be there at all. On the water were floating islands of vegetation next to which were grey logs, half sunk. But once the eye saw one log as an alligator, it saw every log as an alligator. The swamp was transformed into a waystation of sleeping alligators. He blinked again to make them recede.

The wood ibis stood breast-deep in the slime. Patient. Focused. The yellowlegs lowered his beak and took a stab with it. He missed and returned to his watch.

Just beyond Audubon's foot was a lizard with a big pink fin under its chin, which it blew up, and then allowed to shrivel. The lizard wore its scarlet half-moon painfully, a brand. A diffident little blue heron stepped from the reeds, its long thin beak darting to stab the lizard. The heron was a deep blue, the blue of a clear sky at early dark lit by stars. It shone and shimmered, a dense, serene majesty. Audubon matched his stillness to the bird's, memorizing its essence.

"I have painted this bird," he whispered to Maria. "But I am not satisfied with my work. I tried to get that blue but I failed."

After a few stabs the heron got the lizard. He swallowed it, conveniently in profile to Audubon; the prey was large enough so that the heron's neck was distended.

The sun rose a notch overhead and vanished into the arms of a live oak. Woman, bird and man were in shadow. The little heron turned to face Maria and Audubon, thereby nearly disappearing; the blue of its plumage became a deep, absorbent black, like a blotter. Only the fine, drooping crest on top of its head remained blue: a little bit of the sky, perhaps, reflected.

"Do you not see?" said Maria. "The colour comes from the sky, from the sun. It is nothing but light seen through the feathers."

Could this be possible? Or does he already know this? It seemed to him he did.

"Of course, Maria. I know that. The feathers act as an elaborate prism. That blue is not to be caught."

"It is fugitive." Maria looked at him and her eyes seemed to be laughing. "That is what I asked you once: can you make it last?"

The heron stretched its wings and flew. It sailed, breastbone like the keel of a little boat, across their line of vision and alighted not far away.

The word remained behind. Fugitive. Which meant it flies. It escaped, it was not real. He could not capture it, that blue. He could not replicate it with brush and paint.

As he had been fugitive, possibly all his life. He thought of explaining this to Maria, but it seemed an impossible task. He felt the pressure of tears in his throat and behind his eyes.

The birds themselves are not to be captured, which is why I love them.

He reached out to touch her. She was silent and still beside him, leaning on the tree. It seemed terrible to Audubon that Maria was his dear friend, as dear to him as his beloved wife, and yet he had never told her his secret. Lucy knew, once. But now Lucy kept the secret more closely than he did, and spoke as if the lies were true. Secrets keep a man apart from other people, make him a fugitive. And lies make him afraid of love.

The heron, indifferent, lifted one foot out of the water.

Here came the wood drake, gliding around a clump of lilies. It waddled to a stand on the slanting mud bank, proudly flamboyant. Nothing was spared in the coloration of this bird. The red bill had white outlines, and there were white markings like a curlicue under each eye. Its luminous green crest-feathers were slicked back over its head and fanned out at the nape. There was a white diagonal stripe on its flank and under its tail, and white curling lines under its crest, over its beak. It was this white that made the colour profound. The wing feathers were green and teal. It had a brown cowl around its neck, below which was a white necklace.

The bird wandered into shadow. And Maria said, "See how the red of the bill is a solid colour and does not vanish?" Yet the green on top and the teal were snuffed. So it was only the plumage that took its colour from the sun.

They stood, and walked, passing the soft brown female wood duck upended so that her tail feathers looked like the splintered ends of stumps. There were lily pads curling and blowing up. There were queues of turtles craning their necks, oval backs on an inclining log. There were scattered yellow daffodils. The blue-black male grackle flew low over the surface of the swamp. A host of graceful wood ibises with their long hooked bills alighted in the upper branches of a tree, and the branches heaved.

At the approach of night outside the harbour at Ouapitagone, the great cormorants return from the fishing grounds. The barren birds spend the night apart from the rest, standing erect on low rocks in the water, in lines, hundreds of them. Their necks make a graceful curve and their backs are straight. Sometimes they shake their wings open and stretch them out, in the shape of a Celtic cross.

The nesting birds fly to the highest shelves of the huge south-facing cliffs, over the water. It is to these cliffs Audubon goes at dawn, with Captain Emery, who has become a good specimen hunter. Audubon lies flat on the edge of the precipice, hundreds of feet above the turbulent water, directly above a nest. Emery is behind him, holding the end of the rope which is tied around the painter's waist. The waves crash so violently that the birds do not know Audubon is there.

He looks down to see two parents asleep, erect, on their nests. He could have angled down a pole with a loop on the end, placed the loop right over one head, tightened it, and pulled up either bird. But he has no pole. He shifts his elbow and a rock scrapes. The male takes to the air, cawing. The mother bird looks upward and her light blue-green eye meets his in a way that is quite human. She too croaks in alarm, unfolds her giant wings, and rises into the air, the brood which was hidden under her feathers abandoned.

He scales down the rocks and takes the young.

NOW HE WATCHES them crawl sluggishly on the deck. They are dark purple with huge feet. As he approaches them, they open their bills and stretch their necks so that the skin is taut as a rattle; they somehow pass their breath through it to make a snake-like hiss. They will take a bit of cake or a potato peel, a piece of the rind of a ham, and swallow it whole. They eat more than their weight, which is three pounds, in a day.

He scoops up the unfledged birds and tosses them overboard, to see what they will do. They swim off underwater quickly, beating their wings in the sea, just as their parents would, but they soon tire. He sends Tom Lincoln down in the boat to rescue them.

The young gentlemen go back to the cormorant roost the next morning to get a nest and some adults. This time Johnny has a pole. It is a difficult bird to strangle, with its long, sinewy neck, but he manages to do it, holding it out from his body to prevent its breaking its wings on him. The nests are pasted to the rocks with excrement, Johnny reports; each one weighs fifteen pounds. They reek. There seems to be nothing attractive about this bird: even the locals never eat its flesh or eggs.

Audubon measures the adult male, which more than covers his table; from bill tip to the end of its tail, it is the size of his double elephant page. The wings, open, are sixty inches — five feet across. The bill is about the length of the head, rather slender, somewhat compressed, straight, with a curved tip. The head is oblong. The feet are short, and placed far behind.

But it is the colour that fascinates him. All the silky plumage is black, glossed with deep greenish blue. The upper mandible is greyish black and yellowish white along the edges, but dusky toward the end. The iris is a sea green that seems to reflect the warm shallows. The space around the eye is dull olive above, and bright red below. The gular sac is yellow. At the base of the gular sac is a broad gorgelet of white, and the feathers over the head and upper neck are white; there is also a large clump of long white feathers on the side of the thigh. For a bird that appears black to a casual glance, it is a feast of hues.

The female is almost the same, only missing the white crest and thigh feathers. The piece under the eye is bright red in the male but bright yellow in the female.

The head and upper neck of the young unfledged bird are bare, but over the body there are small downy tufts of purple. The ears are tiny and the eyes very small as well, with a grey iris.

SHE SAT OVER HER PAINTBOX. She used colour sparingly. She had a perfect memory for it.

"Was it like this, the Roseate Spoonbill? That is the depth of the pink in the myrtle."

"No, perhaps a little deeper. A little less orange, more white. No, that is very good, such a soft, soft pink. It is uneven, deeper where the feathers are closer to the body; it lightens as it goes outward in swirls."

She made the centre of her spot of colour more intense and softened the colour toward the edges. He watched her dab lightly with the brush. Watched as she dipped it once more into a little water. A bead of moisture from its end dropped onto the cake of colour. She put the brush tip in it and swirled it. He felt himself growing dizzy.

"Like the pink of lips? No, not that, lips are not really pink — it is more livid than that; the lip is a purple, really."

"This pink, where else does it exist, other than in the flower?"

"Perhaps inside my mouth," she murmured.

He was quite short of breath. "You are a tease, Maria!"

"I beg your pardon! Who is it who calls me his sweetheart? You and my brother-in-law both. Between you two old men I don't know how I shall ever get my work done."

"Us both?" he cried, pained. "You would not make a difference between us? But surely Maria, you are *my* sweetheart, not his."

"Let me make the yellow of the crest of the night heron, too. So soft you said it seems to be a new leaf, yet yellowish, too, creamy almost, like skin."

"Maria."

"Let me make that scarlet of the tanager," she said. Just a flash, on the wing, like a throb in the clearing, like a heart suddenly exposed.

HE TAKES UP his instruments to investigate further the immature cormorant. The aperture of the posterior is smooth and half an inch long. He introduces a probe into it, which passes right through the body, and out by the nostril. He observes that the tongue is extremely small, four-twelfths of an inch long, and elliptical. He is able to dilate the esophagus by blowing into it.

The heart he finds within the tiny chest seems large indeed, triangular, and two and a half inches long.

He thinks of Maria. He cannot help it. He cannot look at the heart of the bird without looking at his own heart. He cannot look into his own heart without coming face to face with Maria. He is sick of her, sick to death of longing, but the anatomy of birds has become the study of his longing.

He imagines that, rather than the fragile cormorant, he holds the cradle of Maria's bones within his hands. He tests the soundness of it, pressing here and there on the curved ribs, sensing, exploring the strange, magical construction of this creature.

He frightens himself.

He cannot think any more of what he is doing.

THE SPELL IS BROKEN.

Before he was famous, his painting was a private act of homage. He drew the bird for the bird's sake, and for himself, because to make it right filled some need in him. But he is no longer alone with the birds. He is not Anonyme but John James Audubon with an audience of detractors and admirers. A veritable crowd sits at this deal table. His family. His friends. Bachman. Maria. Havell. Agents, suppliers of bird skins, critics. They help him. Yet it feels today as if they hinder him. They depend on him. They need to be guided; they need to be provided for. They offer advice. They want acknowledgement, or simply pay.

Havell, for instance. Several subscribers have found fault with the last two prints, saying they look too much like lithography for the line is too strong. If it were not that they were behind in paying his wages by fifty pounds, Audubon would dress Havell down. But he does not want to lose him. If he is to become discouraged, and quit? If he is to die? Perhaps — there has been no word for months — he is already dead? Then what?

Now, in the event that Havell is dead and word has not yet reached him, Audubon thinks, his hand still vainly attempting to draw the heart of the immature cormorant, perhaps Blake can continue.

No, Havell must not die. The man's understanding of the Work grows with each plate he makes. So that now, with nearly two hundred birds rendered in copper, printed onto elephant folio paper and hand-coloured, Havell Junior, or simply Havell, as he has called himself since the death of his father, inhabits Audubon's brain.

There he must be, even now, labouring under the dreary London skylights that, like the hatch above the artist, let in only a thin gruel of insipid daylight. And even now, Victor will be on the job. The last letter he sent, before leaving for Labrador, gave his son instructions to chide Havell about the lines on the last etching, and some blotting on the colour. Also, he is grossly behind in the water birds.

To soften the blow, Victor will take Havell for a pint at the end of the day. The two men, both sons of famous men, will complain, Audubon realizes with a smile as his fingers continue to examine the cormorant. Havell will say that the family has been engravers for two generations and that his father, Robert Senior, had been determined his son should not make the third.

This has been his song ever since Audubon met the family. Eight years ago the artist arrived at the door of Havell Senior's shop by the Natural History Museum. It was frequented by naturalists, full of stuffed dead animals and arcane maps. There was the smell of the chemicals that snuffed the animals, the resonant deadness of taxidermy, of relics, of old men. Here in this temple to embalming appeared the Wild Man, as they have since called him in the family, and he would not be sent away. Since then Audubon has been admitted to the drawing rooms of rulers and rich men, and Havell Senior, could he speak from the grave, would say he never doubted it for a minute.

But then, Audubon had a terrible job to persuade him. Havell Senior was taken with the work, but he was fifty and doubted he could see it through: a double-elephant-folio-sized book of etchings of every bird in North America! But Audubon would not take no. Havell

Senior agreed to supervise the job of producing the pages, if they could find a younger artist to do the work.

They went down the street to the next shop, a publisher of engravings; the owner showed them an etching, unsigned, and said: this man is the best of the young engravers working today. Audubon did not need to be told: he could see it was the best. He said, Let us find him then. But the shop owner demurred, with a curious look at Havell Senior. "Don't you know where he is? He is your son."

At this time the son was estranged from his father, as the elder man had adamantly insisted his son take up a profession, and not be an artist. Robert Junior had taken himself off for a sketching tour in Monmouthshire. Now the son will say, "Our progenitor was yeoman of the Tower of London. Think on it. I do. He would maintain order through torture and chaining, and be deaf to the terrible cries of those condemned to death, and see them dragged to their execution. Yet my father called being an artist the worst possible life!"

And over the pints, Victor will concur in his sad way, saying that Havell's engraving tools are like instruments of torture — the torch, the acid, the resin, the burnisher, the anvil, the hammer. He will remark that what a father does and does not do makes a son, and perhaps there is no other way.

And the two men will walk out into the yellow-orange glimmer of the London summer twilight.

Audubon pictures his son with a helpless, angry love. Victor has begun to walk with a stoop, as if burdened. Is it because I did not send him to that school he wanted? It had been Audubon's ambition to give the boys the education he never had. But there was never enough to spare from the *Birds*.

Or is it because Victor wanted to paint, and was not allowed?

Audubon understood Havell Senior. He had imagined himself as the last of the Havell engravers. He wished an easier life for his son. Or he did not wish to be outshone. Either. Audubon does not know which is true in his own case; it depends on the day, on how well or how badly the drawing is going at that moment.

Lucy told him once, "A man does not own the lives of his off-spring, or that of his wife."

In his urgency Audubon has acted as if he does. And, they have colluded; they have given their lives to him. The family needs each member; the giant book calls them all into service. Even friends must be press-ganged. There is so much to be done. It does not do to con-jure enemies. His critics jabber in his mind, repeating malicious judg-ments. Then Bachman arises, insisting he ignore them. It is not worth taking up your noble mind with their pronouncements, he chides.

But the noble mind is by now thoroughly distracted by friend and foe.

There are men who have been to Audubon both friend and foe, a combination he is too simple to understand. Charles Napoleon Bonaparte, a nephew of Napoleon himself, at first a great supporter, but now mysteriously taken with his rival Alexander Wilson's work. His letters arrive steeped in vinegar as a way to destroy the germs from plague-ridden Italy, where he stays. Audubon remembers drawing the pungent page out of the envelope. The stink went up his nose, bringing tears to his eyes. The writing was elongated, the text unclear. I have soaked the page in vinegar to destroy the germs, Bonaparte explained. We cannot pass on the infection. Then he asked for information on a bird.

"Don't tell him!" commanded Lucy. "He does not have your best wishes at heart."

"But he says, dear heart —"

"You are too easy! Don't read his writing, just look at this," she warned, holding the page between finger and thumb. It was a message all by itself, sour and sterile.

Poor Lucy hates his enemies with more passion than he does.

To think of Bonaparte is to think of the Philadelphia group, who laugh at Audubon's exuberant creatures and call them "wretched." To subdue the Americans he must conjure the Europeans, who love him: there is Swainson, whose ecstatic review in his magazine soothed the painter's hurt feelings in London at a time when it mattered. And there are signs that the Americans are warming to his work. He sold new subscriptions before he left for Maine. And there is the heartening *Baltimore Courier* that denounced his "own country's neglect of the *Birds* . . ."

NOW AUDUBON is in the final stages of his distraction; his gaze has floated to some far dark corner of the hold, where he stares as if at a shadow play. He is not in Labrador in a forty-degree chill at all. It is a summer day.

THEY WERE IN THE GARDEN of the house on Rutledge Avenue, walking through the piazza where the vines of Cloth of Gold roses hung, and the white star jessamine. The garden was formal there, and they had to follow the intricate stonework that made a path amongst the beds. There were flowering pomegranates, and a huge quince tree, espaliers with the *Mannetia* vine from Brazil, and the yucca with its towering cloud of snowy bells, which the children called Adam and Eve's Needle and Thread because they used the spikes and the threads to sew. The orange wallflowers filled the air with their sweet scent.

They passed from the formal area to the arbour covered with the little yellow Lady Banksia roses. It was their spot. They sat on the bench. Surrounding them were the wild plants that Bachman brought from the woods — azaleas, woodbine, dogwood and Cherokee roses. The well was there. Beside it was the green water cart, into which Adonis, the gardener, pumped water for the plants and for the kitchen.

Audubon exhaled the harsh, salty and cold air of Labrador and inhaled the rose-drenched oxygen of Charleston. Maria stepped away to admire the small pink Zephyr lily, the white callas, the deep crimson amaryllis.

"Come, child," he said, taking her by the hand and drawing her toward him.

"Child?" she said. "I am not your child." Of course they were laughing. They were always laughing. "I am not your sweetheart, nor his either," she said.

"Come," whispered Audubon. He and his friend the pastor divided her kisses between them, as many as she could spare. Yet he saw her this way: child. How was it he loved in a carnal way one who he also loved like a child? Here was a thought he could not follow, and he dropped it.

"No," she said. "I cannot come to you. I have work to do."

"What work? You have given the children their lessons. You have given instructions to the cook."

"I must work on my painting."

"What painting do you mean? I am your instructor. I give you the painting work. You have painted the little shrubby tree, which I will use in my Scarlet Tanager. And now I say to you to stop."

"But I am drawing a bird."

"Why are you drawing a bird, Maria? I have not asked you to."

"I am copying your Snowy Egret. I do it because I want to learn. Here, let me go. I say no, Mr. Audubon. I must work. When I finish I want to do the Little Blue Heron. No."

He did not understand this no. She was always there; she was warm; she was open; he could go to her when he needed her. He did not understand this refusal to be to him whatever it was he wanted to make her, call it a child, call it a lover, call it a friend or a helper or an angel. Maria was whatever he made of her. She must be.

"What do you mean no? How have you learned to say no to me?"

She pulled away from him, and she was gone.

FOR THE FIRST TIME since he met her, he contemplates the loss of Maria. That she should refuse him her kisses, her soft attentions, her aid, her affection. It would be dreadful, fatal. He sees her again, rising from the bench under the magnolia tree, nodding her smart, efficient little nod, dulling the spark in her eyes so that he can no longer see into her, and turning on her heel.

His eyes come back to the bird before him, and he sees not the great cormorant, immature, pinned down and eviscerated. He sees his finished watercolour of the Black-throated Mango Hummingbird. Maria has painted the trumpet-creeper on which the birds cluster. The flowers are wide open, the throats of the blossoms matching the fuchsia of the bird's tail.

The birds approach dizzily from all directions: one is upside down in top left-hand corner; another has its entire head ecstatically buried in a flower; a third dives in from forty-five degrees, touching the outer curled lip of flower with its long narrow beak; another rides triumphant on top of a pink, fully opened blossom. Seeing his work in his mind, he finds it difficult to believe that birds and flowers have been done by a separate person — they are a whole. If two people have created this, it is two people who are entranced, enraptured, as entangled as the birds and the vines are entangled.

He is happy with what he has done. He sees that it is beautiful. If he can produce these works — and even now, knowing Maria's part in it, he thinks of himself as the sole creator — if he can continue, it will not matter if subscribers are cancelling, reneging on their payments, complaining of the quality. It will not signify that Victor cannot pay Havell his fifty pounds, that Audubon is constantly in need of defending against the scientific establishment. He himself will not, finally, matter. He is only a vehicle. What matters is the bird and his rendering of the bird.

At last the people who haunt him desert, and the little corpse comes into focus before him. It seems a poor thing. Yet he knows that from these little agonies, the greatness is born. The bird in his hands is a form, a foreign being, a message only he can decipher.

He draws his instruments closer to himself.

He removes the intestine of this young cormorant, two weeks old, and stretches it out on the table. He measures the intestine: it is an incredible five feet, two inches long. He discovers in the stomach fragments of fish (with bones) and a small pebble. When he is finished he writes out a tag and ties it around the feet of the bird, and drops the specimen into a jar of spirits. It sinks into the alcohol in its dark container.

Bayfield is in the launch at dawn. The wind has turned from north to west, to blow offshore. The locals call this the flat wind, because it makes the waves drop.

He spends the day surveying the protected passage between Ouapitagone on the north and the outer islands on the south and east. The tide is out. He has to work quickly. He measures, makes notations, measures again. He must record the shoals as high in the water as they ever get, four or five feet above where they lie in low water. In the existing charts this difference is not accounted for, creating great danger for a vessel.

By late afternoon he has all the vagaries of the channel and its entrance. But the offshore wind is stronger. He decides to wait until it drops before rowing back into the harbour.

He beaches his boat. The shore is a narrow curl of sand, which a temporary sun turns into a dressy gold braid. He climbs the height of the big island, through grey, black and white rocks that he is careful to call by name — feldspar, granite, gneiss. When he gains the top he sees a wide-open horizon to the south and east. There is a haze on it, which is not a good sign for tomorrow.

He turns to the west. The horizon is a circumference, his rock a small dome in the centre; he is a fleck, his eyes, as he rotates, a measuring clock hand. Last night a god, today a speck. This is what he loves about life at sea.

By now he has accepted islands as his fate. The sense comes over him each time he circles another, measures it, names it, the sense of creating a world. He thinks how as a younger man he wanted an enemy to test himself against. Instead he got earth before it was ordered, land masses floating in water, islands upon islands. Is-land. The land of is. The land of "to be." Sum. I am. In this lonely, potent way he has gone from youth to middle age, for he is thirty-eight and has been at his work for eighteen years. He has developed an affection for rocks and learned their names too. There were moments among those islands, moments of perfect stillness, heat, sunglint, with nothing around except the horizon like the dial of a compass, and he the pin that held the needle in place.

The horizon is flat, constant, *there* even when it cannot be seen, his immutable, but ever-retreating goal. It is, in its way, perfect, a kind of justice, a reduction to terms. A sea horizon is imaginary, he knows. An idea. Yet he has sailed over it more than once. He has believed perfection to be attainable.

He turns north. Here the horizon is interrupted by land, bulky and stubborn, rocks piled up and tumbling down. It is the wildest shore he has ever seen; it has the most bizarre topography, and the foggiest, windiest, rainiest weather he has encountered. Impossible weather.

Doubt has entered his mind.

His goal this summer is to survey to the Strait of Belle Isle. He knows now he cannot do it in the *Gulnare*. At 140 tons, she is too big. She draws too deep, and though she handles well she can't manoeuvre in the narrow channels. She was built for him, for his work, but she cannot do this part of it.

He struggles with his doubt. Four years he has been at this survey, beginning at Rimouski. It is slow work. It will not be completed this year, or the next. But it is not impossible. He will not admit that. He must devise a new plan. It was one thing to send Bowen forward to Ouapitagone in the open boat and have him come back again: that was a relatively short and protected passage. It would be extremely hazardous to venture in an open boat as far as the next stop. He isn't even sure what that next stop might be. And to be truthful, he is not entirely positive that Bowen, who this summer seems delicate and somehow difficult, could manage. Bayfield would not send a lieutenant on a mission too risky for himself. No, he must go.

He is the captain of the *Gulnare*. When Admiral William FitzWilliam Owen asked for him as assistant surveyor, young Bayfield was not pleased. But the wild shore won him; he has served and will serve until he dies. There has been hardship enough. Danger enough. Opportunity for heroism of the unsung variety. He knows his charts save lives. He makes the wild less wild; he brings it onto his graph, into his scope, and he lays it down on the scrolls of the Royal Navy. He will not be stopped by geography or weather.

The plan begins to form. He will leave the *Gulnare* where she is, safe, at anchor. He'll take two open boats forward, the launch victualled for Collins and seven men, the *Owen* provisioned for three weeks with himself, Bowen and eight more men in it. They will scout the next leg and, if they make it safely, return for the surveying ship.

It is a risky plan. It is what Owen and he did in Georgian Bay, the inland sea, which was rough and wild enough, and they lived to tell the tale. Can this task be tougher? The men will be vulnerable in the small boats. The weather will be foul, the coast its indecipherable worst. Sometimes he imagines it to be on Mr. Audubon's side, wilderness with an active desire to remain just that.

SURE ENOUGH the east wind picks up next morning, bringing its constant companion, fog. Nevertheless Bayfield, Bowen, Collins, and the sailors say their goodbyes to Dr. Kelly, who will remain with the *Gulnare* to guard the chronometers in their absence. Bayfield says goodbye also to the men of the *Ripley,* and shakes with surprising emotion the bloodstained hand of Mr. Audubon, whom he doubts he will see again.

On July 7, in the morning, Bayfield and seventeen men set off in two open boats to survey north and east to Mécatina. What follows threatens to be disastrous.

Once underway, they are among rocks and islets, shoals and inlets so confusing they soon lose sight of what is mainland and what is an island masking the mainland, a kind of screen, or foil. There are thunder squalls all afternoon; some they row on through, but during others they stop alongside a high point, if only to avoid being a magnet for lightning. There is no hope of staying dry. There is no dry wood either, and that night the fire is barely hot enough to boil water.

The next day is the same. Learning from the previous day, they search for an overnight spot with wood from the very outset. They find one, pitch their tents and gather anything they can find that will burn. They smoke the clouds of moschettoes — and themselves, to the point of staggering blindness. Two of the men shoot a brace of ptarmigan for dinner, which, soaked, cold and swollen with bites, they eat.

For the next four days Bayfield takes no observations. At night the wind attempts to tear their tents off the ground; by day the fog closes in, uniting water, land and air in one impenetrable mass. Blasting wind is followed by soaking rains with no sun between to dry anything. In a fit of temper, Morgan, the *Owen*'s coxswain, swings an axe at a piece of driftwood and nearly severs the toes from his right foot. He howls with pain as Collins pours rum down his throat and wraps the toes tightly in bandages. Toes can reattach, grow back, says Bayfield. He's seen such things happen. He chides himself for leaving the doctor behind. The men are sullen; one or two grumble out loud that this survey shall be the end of them.

On the fifth day, July 11, the sailors take to the boats at dawn only to find both injured and uninjured coxswains drunk in the hulls on stolen grog. Bayfield orders Collins to keep the grog keg in his tent. Collins sets off in the launch toward the islands, and Bayfield in the *Owen* to the mainland shore.

On July 12, the morning is fine. Bayfield is up at four, observing altitudes with his altazimuth. Collins has not yet come back and Bayfield is concerned. No sooner has the sun got up twenty degrees over the horizon than fresh gales come in from the east. The minute the men get out of their tents they are soaked. But before long Collins returns and they have measurements to put in the books.

On July 13, the weather is at least dry. Collins this time sets off to the St. Mary's Islands and Bayfield returns to sketch the mainland. Here he spies, grey and soft-cornered and seemingly ready to slide into the granite, a cedar cabin. Approaching it, he sees a man seated on a rock scraping the flesh from a sealskin in the way of the Esquimaux

"The men will be vulnerable in the small boats."

women. This man stands and greets him as if it were normal to
encounter a British officer rising from the mist. He is named Joshua
Bussière, and is a hunter and seal fisher who trades with the Indians
who come by. Bayfield opens his sketchbook to show his approxima-
tion of the nearby coast. Bussière extends a finger to indicate what is
the mainland and what is island. Even better, he lends Bayfield his dry
hut and a table on which to make his notations.

Bussière has brought good luck; the next day they have fine
weather for only the second day since leaving the *Gulnare,* and manage
to cover thirteen miles from Watagheistic Island past the Étamamiou
River. The scenery is magnificent; there are falls above the mouth of
the river, and a sand beach with long spits running half a mile on
either side. Beyond that is a forest of tiny dead, silvered spruce trees
preserved like glass ornaments. They camp on a high, barren granite
island — *red feldspar with quartz and black mica, no hornblende,* he notes
— with a dangerous reef to the south. It has been their best day since
leaving the *Gulnare.* But as night falls Bayfield looks apprehensively to
the north and east: the view is crammed with rocky islets and sinister,
half-sunk rocks.

On Monday, July 15, the wind, the rain, the cold, and the fogs
descend again. They have no wood and no protection. Their attempt
to cross to the northeast is baffled by the weather. Both boats retreat
to a small cove of a smaller island of the group they are in. The men
collect driftwood. They make camp but cannot make the wood burn.
The rain is falling so heavily that Bayfield can neither write nor calculate without risking an ague from sitting still.

There is nothing to be accomplished. Augustus Bowen, stalwart
that he has been, has a deep, sore cough. Bayfield commands him to
have the men run races on the rocks to keep from freezing, all but the
lame Morgan, who sits nursing his toes. Bowen takes his orders with a
smart nod, but, as he stands, chronometer in hand, presiding over the
sullen ragtag relays, there is a new distance in his manner. It is as if he
were not really here, but only looking in on the adventure.

"If my godfather could see a lieutenant of the Royal Navy thus
employed!" he says.

"Would he be amused?" asks Bayfield, who is not. "A little play will distract and lighten us."

Bowen gives him a look not of the sort one gives a superior officer, but because it is without words, Bayfield decides to ignore it. They have been together for six years and have seen things no man should see; it is a bond. The man is simply not feeling well.

Only Collins gets into the spirit of the races. At length Bayfield allows Bowen to step away, and Collins, stopwatch in hand, soon has the others tied in pairs for three-legged races and, improbably, cheering and laughing.

For the next five days the weather is unspeakable.

Morgan's foot is swollen red up to the ankle. Bayfield chews stolidly in the mess under canvas with Bowen, who appears to be waiting for him to act. The men refuse to eat breakfast. Even Collins cannot make them pleasant.

"You cannot make a man eat who will not," he observes. The eggs, coffee and biscuits go to waste. Aided by an ever more saturnine Bowen, Bayfield takes what observations he can. The men watch hungrily for any sign of weakness in him. There are no such signs. At night, under the stars, when the men are in their tents, Bowen speaks.

"The men feel there is no reason to risk their lives. This coast is so bad, they say, no one will ever sail it."

"That is not for us to judge. We have our task."

"Of course we do, sir. I merely report what the men are saying."

July 18 is a useless day sunk in dense fog. Bayfield sits with the measurements he has made, trying to the best of his ability to plot a future course for the *Gulnare*, assuring himself they have not left out any of the rocks in the channel. On July 19 he orders the provisions enumerated; they have enough for nine more days. He sets the men to catching puffins and young gulls and collecting mussels to supplement their rations. Egged on to disobedience by the limping Morgan, they simply refuse to catch anything.

"You cannot make a man hunt who will not," observes Bowen.

"Indeed you cannot."

"Perhaps they believe that if they don't hunt, you will let them return to the *Gulnare*."

"I shall dispel that notion."

Bayfield announces to the men that, if they are short, they will go on half rations. He goes out to hunt and by sheer luck finds and shoots three partridge. The men are not too proud to eat them. After dinner he sits in his tent and writes in his journal. *Description of the coast from Petit Mécatina to this camp: labyrinth.*

At one o'clock the next morning Bowen enters Bayfield's tent to report talk of mutiny.

VOLUPTUARY

Audubon tarries longer in Ouapitagone. He and the young gentlemen return to the inland lake. Fresh blades of grass of a pure pale
green have sprung up at its edge; here, summer is only now beginning
even though it must end in a few weeks. The Montagnais woman does
not reappear. Perhaps she was never there at all. She might have been a
spirit, a creature of the wilderness, were it not for the crucifix at her neck.
It is a mark of the white man, and to his mind it makes her vulnerable.

The loon is there, her beak like a periscope aimed over the surface
of the lake.

He settles himself in the reeds. The loon is a bird he loves to
watch. She appears to be alone but is never so. Before long the male
speeds into view, his neck curved downward, acknowledging her.
Some distance away he glides down to the surface of the lake.
Waterborne, but well apart, they call gently back and forth. Then they
beat the water with their pinions, dive and rise side by side.

Audubon searches for nests at the water's edge, and finds several.
He observes that, contrary to the assertions of both Wilson and
Bonaparte, the loon does not cover its eggs with down, and that not
only the female but the male sits on the nest. He sees young birds,
downy and new, one day out of the egg. They already swim like fish.
The little ones dive under the water, wriggling into the mud. Johnny
catches several on the bottom by placing his gun rod in their way.

But the adult birds are not easy to kill. Audubon shoots one on
the wing. It falls to the water, but then dives and swims a long way
under the surface before bobbing up at last, breast skyward.

The loon is no easier a bird to paint. He sets up a male, nailing its feet to the wooden stand; it has a tendency to fall face forward, its feet being so far backward under its body. He threads wires upward through the cavity of the bird, into the neck and through the breathing passages. He arranges a pair in summer plumage as if they are floating on water by impaling them on several stiff wires that run through their bellies. He draws their long graceful feet and webbed toes fanning beneath them through the water. He gives passing thought to how Havell will manage to replicate this transparency, but is confident that he can.

He sketches a downy fledgling half hidden in grasses, with a pitcher plant to the left. The male's beak tends to the sky, slightly opened. The back of his head is to the viewer; the bulge of his eyes shows on either side. Are his eyes really that big? Audubon sees them that way. He draws their long webbed feet scale by scale, using, for this task, the quill of a trumpeter swan, which, he has discovered, is sharper and more flexible than any steel nib he could buy. He then returns to the centre of the picture. He creates with delicacy the profile of the female's sharp, straight, definitive bill, shut tight. But there is great sensuousness in the necks of the pair, which answer each other curve to curve.

He moves on to colour: with blue-black and chalk-white he spends hours dappling the bird's backs. He uses a fine, soft brush for these teardrop dashes of white. The young bird, in contrast, is mossy brown, shadowed by rock. He paints the respectable grey of the adult heads, the shameless nude beige-white of their breasts. Red eyes. Red throat. Claret for the petals of the pitcher plant.

He remembers, as he uses a shade of red that the gloom of the day hardly allows him to see, the afternoon he spent with Bayfield. He remembers tolling the birds, running at them with handkerchiefs waving, and the birds taking the challenge, running head on to meet them. A game, he called it, but Bayfield was not so sure. He considered the loon a valiant bird, almost British. But in Audubon's hands the loon becomes a voluptuary.

In the hold of the *Ripley*, dabbing with his red paint, Audubon is maddened to be reminded of Maria again. He could draw the

shape of her now although his fingers are numb. The upright car-
riage, the small breasts — a girl's breasts that never suckled a baby.
He pictures her neck tilted and inclined lightly over her drawing:
she does not tighten over it, as poor students do, but rises to the
paper. The shapes rise with her breath and make themselves on the
paper. Her lips are shut but lightly so, ready to change at a word of
affection or a criticism.

"Why are you drawing that Snowy Owl? Have I asked you to?"

The lower lip drops a fraction of an inch, wobbles a little even
while her eyes grow huge and wet and a small flush makes itself visible
above the tight lace at her neck.

Perhaps it is Maria's responsiveness he loves. Certainly it is long
past the day when he had such power over Lucy, who no longer blushes
or nearly faints with his attentions. Lucy is not tender. She is not beautiful. Or at least, he says, castigating himself, he cannot see beauty in
what she is now. It is his fault. But he cannot change this. Would not
change it if he could. What is he, if not a lover of beauty? Maria tells
him he is an ungrateful child. Maybe so. But ungrateful children are
full of passion and passion itself is the stuff of life.

Who is this woman who haunts him from south to north, she
who waits in hot Charleston painting butterflies and flowers? A spinster engaged in a spinster's work, weighing no more than a hundred
pounds. A magnet to his eyes; a new enchantment to be discovered
every day. Only two weeks after meeting her he wrote Lucy about the
Ground Dove: he had drawn five of them on a wild orange branch. *It
is one of the sweetest birds I have ever seen*, he told her. He did not tell
her that the pastor's unmarried sister-in-law was at his side, or that he
gave Maria a piece of the precious Whatman paper to work on. That
she was inspired by his example to paint a Ground Dove herself. Hers
had a certain charm but lacked finesse.

But Lucy would know, without him telling her. And what she did
not divine, she heard from Bachman, who wrote to Lucy that her
husband taught Maria to draw birds. "She now has such a passion for
it that whilst I am writing she is drawing a Bittern he put up for her
at daylight."

Bachman has played a curious role in this flirtation. First he offered his sister-in-law to Audubon. "Drawing is an amusement to her, and to gratify you will always afford her pleasure," he said. He gushed her praises. "My sister Maria is all enthusiasm and I need not say to you that she is one of your warmest admirers. The admiration of such a person is a very high compliment."

Now he seems to want her back. He has little possessive fits; he acts as if he owns Maria Martin in the same way he owns his wife. Bachman liked to tell the story of the six months he and Maria spent together in upstate New York, years before Audubon met the family. He had fallen ill and could not travel home. Maria nursed him. For weeks he lingered near death. When he could walk she took him to Thornburn's Establishment for Rare Plants. There, in the greenhouse, the glass bubble, the world within the world, they saw orchids and African grasses, bizarre meat-eating plants, giant roses and shy water lilies.

Maria told the same story, of her sick, diminished brother-in-law and how together they roamed the world in miniature. Only Harriet did not mention it. Audubon is shot through with rage when he thinks of this time. Bachman must have held her arm, he must have leaned on her, so much younger, so tiny but so strong.

But he can do nothing but house this rage, hold himself still when it shakes him. When she painted the Snowy Egret, he allowed himself to become angry with her. Such a relief it was to give in to his temper, to shout and swing his arms, to let his words flay that ivory complexion, to see the lines of scarlet rise in her throat, to flush hot with his own sense of rightness. In response, her flowers became more sumptuous. He used her *Gordonia* for the Fork-tailed Flycatcher. He copied her watercolours of the male and female sylvia onto the sheet of *Franklinia* she painted the previous summer. Then came her incomparable trumpet-creeper.

Once the jar of that feeling was opened, they could not keep it closed. Again and again there were words. She was spirited; she did not give in; she only appeared to, and then defied him again, clever and staunch and ready to go as far as he did while still, somehow, remaining in that tight bodice, with that perfect little chin held high. How he longed to disturb her! He was spellbound by the beauty of her person and her work, and he could not allow her to have this power over him.

So, he has vanished into the Labrador wilderness, leaving her to Bachman.

HE WORKS IN DRIVING RAIN under the slanted glass roof that lets light into the hold. His neck aching, he is driven on deck to search the sky. There are birds in their millions, but only familiar ones. Where are the new species? He still hopes to see an Ivory Gull, the dainty, all-white bird that is reported to dye itself red with the blood of murdered seals. He has yet to lay eyes on a Labrador Duck. He must find the Great Auk.

"You want to see that bird, you should go to the Funks," Godwin offers. The pilot spends his time astern, near the rudder, chewing tobacco, and the artist is still not used to his habit of materializing out of shadow.

"So I have heard. At this rate I doubt we'll make it."

"'Tis a barren spot."

"You've been there, then?"

"Used to go with my Da round thirty year back," he says. "You know why they're called that? From the stinking smell that greets your nose when you land. Astonishing quantities of birds. You wouldna believe it. Unless," he adds modestly, "of course, you've seen something similar in your peregrinations." This nod to Audubon's experience is in the nature of a peace offering.

"I don't know that I have. Tell me."

"Ah," says Godwin, his voice saddening with the memory of it. "I were only a lad. Still, I knew there were a sin in it. Watching me Da and his friend, I'd feel right ill. You couldna step on the shore, the thousands of birds just stood so lazy there was no place for your feet and they wouldna move off. The men just tramped on them little pinguins, you know. Can't fly. What did you call it?"

"The Great Auk," says Audubon.

"Them days, if you came for their feathers you did not give yourself the trouble of killing them, but laid hold of one and pluck off all his best. You then turn the poor bird adrift, with his skin half naked and torn off, to perish at his leisure."

Audubon listens intently. "Do you take the eggs as well?"

"Oh, for sure you do. Still do. You go to the Funks for eggs. That's one main reason you go. But you have to be certain to get them fresh. Here's exactly how they do it. They drive, knock and shove the poor pinguins into heaps. Then they scrape all the eggs in tumps, in the same manner you would a heap of apples from an orchard down in New England, eh?

"Numbers of these eggs, from being laid days ago, are stale and useless. So you leave those and clear a space of ground about as big as the pile of eggs you want."

Godwin has moved out of his corner into the centre space of the deck, stretching his arms and circling his feet to show the size of the circle in which the birds would lay.

"Then you retire for a day or two behind some rock. Drink your grog. Sing your songs and sleep it off. At the end of that time your circle will be full of eggs freshly laid."

Audubon shakes his head at the strange connivance of creatures in their own destruction.

"These men," Godwin says, "while they abide on the Funks, are in the constant practice of horrid cruelties. They not only skin the pinguins alive, but they burn them alive also, to cook their bodies with. You take a kettle with you into which you put a pinguin or two, you kindle a fire under it, and this fire is absolutely made of the unfortunate pinguins themselves. Their bodies, being oily, soon produce a flame: there is no wood on the island, you see."

Dark dark dark. Tales of savagery. Audubon wraps his arms around his chest and thumps himself on the back to warm up. "What a land it is, what a land."

"We have to stay alive," says Godwin. "I suppose from the start it were a contest, us or them. Question I always asked myself, do the little birds feel the pain?"

"Ah," says Audubon. "And what did you answer?"

There is a quiet moment while Godwin gets more tobacco out of his pouch. "We can't afford to know," he says.

"I'd like to find 'pinguins,'" Audubon says.

"We'd be lucky to find any now."

"Why is that?" says Audubon.

"Ah, there's not so many, are there? Not any more, not since them days. Stands to reason, don't it? Well, they made it unlawful, taking the birds for feathers, didn't they? I seen men whipped in the stocks in St. John's for the crime of it. It's only if you're going to use them for bait they say you can kill the birds. But the Funks are a long way off, and who's to know when the pirates and robbers come? It was still going on when I was a lad. I saw two fellows flogged at a Cart's Tail in St. John's for gettin' caught," he repeats.

Too late, too late, thinks Audubon, is he going to be too late for the birds?

"Think we're a hard people, don't you sir," Godwin persists, coming closer in and proffering his tobacco tin.

"It's a hard land."

"Harder even than that." Godwin laughs. "God made it, I suppose, and put us here."

AUDUBON TAKES HIS SEARCH for new species to the inland marshes. He collects half a dozen boreal chickadees and draws them. But there is nothing more to be found. He speaks to Emery; together they decide to leave Ouapitagone and head up the coast to Petit Mécatina. Godwin insists on taking the outside route. The wind blasts like a November gale, and reluctantly Audubon agrees.

The *Ripley* sails up through the open water, away from the coast. Fourteen days. Fifty miles of islands. Audubon is frustrated, and both his anger and his curiosity return him to Godwin.

"Did you ever see a Labrador Duck?" he asks. "What about the large birds of prey? The White Gyrfalcon?"

Godwin has no answers. At length, questions about birds become questions about the past.

"What took you to New Orleans?"

"Sailing ships," says Godwin. "One place leads to another."

"And how did you come across Nolte?"

"Nolte?" says Godwin. "He come across me. He decided he needed a bodyguard after two gentlemen tried to take his life in a gaming club. That's how I understood it. And he picked me for the job. He was walking in the port one night when I dragged on a sailor who was crazy drunk and would have missed our sailing. I just held the fellow still. He was lucky somebody didn't kill 'em. He was asking for it."

"So Nolte has enemies?"

"That time he had a lot of money. Got a lot of money, you got a lot of friends and some of them you'd just as soon not have. Later he didn't have the money or the friends. Still, when the generals come to the country it's him they want to see. He knew them all, the lords and ladies from France, and the ones who'd had their eye gouged out on the frontier, and the ones with the brand they put on you in prison. He has the knack, does Nolte, for walking through the filth and the glory. He keeps his own path."

"He and I understood each other," Audubon says. "We've both been high and low in society. And learned to prefer our own company."

AUDUBON BURIES HIMSELF in the birds close to hand. He takes some white-crowned buntings and a black-capped warbler. He picks flowers for Maria, and discovers them to be Labrador tea, wild peas, and a catchfly called silene. One day he and the young gentlemen set out to row miles in the small boats to the mainland. He sees a flock of titmice. But the water becomes too rough for the whaleboats and they turn back. It is two days before Audubon sees the little birds again. He follows them into a clump of dwarf coniferous trees. They disappear but he discovers where they hide. The bird has dug its nest out of a rotten stump, leaving only a tiny round opening barely big enough to admit his thumb. The inside of its den is like a fur purse, of a softness he can only dream of on these days.

This bird has never been drawn before and Audubon is intrigued. He calls it a Hudson's Bay Titmouse, a buff-coloured, round-bodied little bird with a black throat and yellow lining of the mouth. They cling to the underside of branches and show no fear of him. He paces slowly, closer and closer to a trio, holding out his hand and murmuring. Curious and chatty, one little creature takes up a perch on his extended finger. Its claws cannot encircle his finger and nearly puncture his skin. But the creature is no heavier than breath.

Saturday, July 20, 1833, is the finest day Bayfield and his men have had since leaving the *Gulnare*. It is also four years to the day since the captain began to survey this coast, at Rimouski. He marks the day with the observation in his journals that crisis has been averted; his hopes and even the spirits of the men are high. With good weather and feverish work, they advance the survey through a labyrinth of islands to within three miles of Gros Mécatina Point. When they make camp for the evening, they can see its magnificent cliffs, which soar a thousand feet above the sea.

On Sunday they set off early, five men at the oars with the officers in front in their caps, hoping for another day of such progress. They head to the third islet southwest off Gros Mécatina, but as Bayfield and Bowen observe for latitude, a fog descends, placing clammy hands up against their mouths: They can neither bat it away nor see through it.

The mood reverses quickly. The men see their hopes of finishing and getting back to the ship diminish. They lean over their oars to this side and that, spitting and muttering. The lame coxswain Morgan wears a new, ugly face of power, having gained three or four sympathizers. Collins gamely sings Irish songs to cheer the sailors. When a blow with heavy rain attacks them from the slant, they strike a camp. The sailors refuse to eat, and lie listless in their tents. They all hear Bowen's cough in the night.

Bayfield paces. Paces in the rain, his gear leaking everywhere, his cheeks so cold he cannot feel the water running down them. But he will not let himself sit. If he does he too might be frozen into defeat.

"Bad weather, sir," says Collins. "But it is only weather, and all weather must change."

Bayfield is surprised to feel cheered by the simple man. He is full of doubt once more, and Bowen's company does not satisfy his need.

Then the fog does lift. And, better still, a schooner arrives.

"Sails!" cries Collins, only seconds after Bayfield has spied them himself.

Bayfield and Collins watch from the pilot boat. The *Ripley* hauls in around the islands.

"Where is she going?" says Collins.

"Looks like she's intending to anchor in Gros Mécatina but, not knowing the place, has run into Portage Bay instead."

Bayfield is uncommonly glad to see the schooner.

Then fresh gales come on and the sails are hidden in darkness.

THE *RIPLEY* IS RUNNING FOR COVER. After one fine day when Audubon found a white-throated sparrow and heard the beautiful song of a ruby-crowned wren over and over, the horrid weather has descended again.

"This is Petit Mécatina," says Godwin.

"It is not. There is a settlement there. It might be Mutton Bay," says Emery peering at the charts.

"No, it's Petit Mécatina."

They're both wrong, but they are lucky; the water is fair and they pass. Inside the shoals, they slide past the point of a barren granite outcrop to find a tent and two launches hunkered down.

"What do you know? The Royal Navy's come to grief. No other men would be fool enough to be out in two open boats," growls Godwin.

Audubon clambers up the mizzen. A thinning of the fog allows him to glimpse his friend Bayfield and entourage. But he is nearly blown off by a gust. The *Ripley* retreats to anchor. Hours later the gale gives way a little. The *Ripley* is still sheltering when the surveying boat puts up a double-reefed sail and heads toward them. Lieutenant Bowen hails the Americans, his voice croaking so that he cannot be haughty.

"Marooned for five days! Injured coxswain! Impossible weather!"

Captain Emery produces a ham and some potatoes; Johnny and the young gentlemen set out after the surveying boat to deliver the rations to the *Gulnare's* crew. They return with the offer of a cache of wood for a bonfire.

THAT NIGHT, they camp side by side on the shore. The British have made the best of miserable conditions. Their camp looks almost snug, covered with canvas, tea things laid out on an iron-bound bed, with trunks serving as seats and sailcloth clothes bags as cushions. Audubon is quite envious of the domesticity it conveys. His own camp is haphazardly struck; every night ashore is a trial for the Americans.

Under a large tarred cloth rigged to keep out the rain, the sailors feast on the ham and potatoes. On the windward side of the fire, eyes streaming red from the smoke, but at least undisturbed by the moschet-toes, the men shake hands and clap backs.

"My friend. I expected I would not see you again," says Audubon.

"I too had that thought. This meeting is a pleasure."

In truth, Bayfield is embarrassed. To be caught marooned on a granite island and running out of food! To discover the Audubon expedition sailing prettily in a little cove, albeit mistaken about which cove it is, with ham and potatoes to spare!

Pacing back and forth, they concur: it has been the most miser-able stretch imaginable; how will they ever finish?

"The birds are nowhere to be found. I have discovered no new species."

"I don't understand you. We see flocks and flocks of birds."

"But not the species I need. I need the Labrador Duck, the Great Auk, the Gyrfalcon. And summer, such as it is, will soon begin to turn. The birds will leave."

"Summer is short. You've said it yourself. You must not take it personally."

"It is not only the season, I fear. There are fewer birds and fish all up the coast. The natives say so, and the settlers. Our pilot tells me more tales of Eggers."

Bayfield gives his slow nod.

"It is as if the birds are abandoning me. As if Nature herself were perishing. You may think this a strange thing to say but I have thought it in the last two weeks — it is as if I were being punished."

"Punished? For what?" says Bayfield.

"My deeds," says Audubon woefully. "What I have done and not done."

"I am only an Englishman," says Bayfield. "You must explain your troubles." This time he is eager to listen. It lets him forget his own for the moment.

"I was in Paris, Captain. Looking for subscriptions for the *Birds*, of course."

HE CARRIED HIS PORTFOLIO on his back through the city, the same one he carried through London, the wide leather case weighing one hundred pounds. The ladies in England scolded him for it; a gentleman would not bear such a burden in public; a gentleman would not arrive at his destination in a sweat; he ought to have a man to carry it for him. But Audubon would not put it down. His entire life was inside. He had lost his work more than once. One hundred sketches went when the rats ate into his wooden case. Another three dozen disappeared when a porter forgot to put his portfolio onboard a riverboat. What did he care if people objected? He took no chances.

In Paris, his height helped. Dodging messengers scurried under the case, but plump businessmen were clipped in the head, or had to swerve, and cursed him. Young women stared at him from behind their hands and giggled.

Perhaps he even *wanted* the burghers of Paris to stare: he was still wearing his fox-fur hat. When the guardians of the Louvre judged him unfit to enter, he strode away defiant with the tail prickling his neck. He kept his eyes high because he did not like what he saw down low. On the pavement were one-legged old soldiers, missing ears and fingers, veterans of Napoleon's Moscow campaign. Had his father not had the bright idea to send him to America, he would have been amongst them. Or worse, dead, with snow for a winding sheet.

"Would they judge me, Captain, for not wanting to fight a war for a country I never thought my own? A country in which, because of my birth, I could neither vote nor inherit?"

He had not been home for fifteen years. Anne Moynet wrote all those letters begging him to come see her, letters that made their laborious way across the sea, following him wherever he went, letters like burrs, this complex family a curse, dragging him back to Coueron.

She was not his real mother, but his father's wife. Did that make the difference? But she loved him, Anne Moynet. Why did he neglect her? He is guilty, guilty, and now the birds hide from him.

"I have written it, Captain. It is all in my journal. That some day people will know. But what do you suppose happened? I went to meet the Duc d'Orléans. The king in waiting, he was. A handsome man, who himself had lived in exile. He opened the wide black covers of my portfolio. He fell to his knees, Captain. I remember what he said exactly: he said, 'Now I understand why Redouté praises you so highly.'"

AUDUBON BOWED. There were important men to be met. There were connections. And to each important person Audubon must be introduced. But how was he to be introduced? As whom was he to be introduced? This was France. Here, most certainly, he could not be the lost dauphin. Here he could not risk claiming to be the son of a French admiral. The highest rank Jean Audubon ever achieved was that of lieutenant. He could not say he studied with David. So who might he be, in France, his homeland which was never his homeland?

An American. Anyone could be an American. He could be born in Louisiana.

Introductions led to introductions and one day in October he stood in a salon with many elegant men and women. The host was a man named Gérard. This Gérard was a painter of portraits. He took Audubon's hand and kissed it and called him a genius. And insisted on introducing him to a zoologist.

The zoologist was born in Rochefort. Too close to home. He ought to have run. But drawn by danger, or perhaps confused, or perhaps simply wishing that it would be simple, Audubon said that he spent childhood summers not far away at Coueron.

Coueron!

There was a stir in the salon. The zoologist jumped up in pleasure and said, "I must bring you someone from your home village." He disappeared for a minute, long enough for Audubon's heart to pump and for him to reach, instinctively, for his gun, which he had left behind. Into the room the zoologist hurried with a young medical student. And here it happened, this encounter which Audubon had been dreading. He thinks now he even felt this moment approaching, with a dread and a delight, the doubled pain and joy of being unmasked, shamed, reduced for once and for all, and perhaps recognized, forgiven, heralded, made into one man.

"May I present Charles-Henri D'Orbigny. This is Monsieur Jean Jacques Audubon, who has travelled here from America."

The face, the name, loomed up. Time was diving and looping over the artist's head again. That narrow lip and the pointed chin, under the high, domed forehead, the penetrating eye of the scholar. D'Orbigny! Could it be his old neighbour and teacher?

"I believe we are already acquainted," said Monsieur D'Orbigny.

"Indeed we are," said Audubon.

"CAPTAIN BAYFIELD," says Audubon, "through our journeys and our decades, we travel great distances and meet people in the thousands. And yet, our lives are determined by a very small cast of characters, some half a dozen I think, who we meet by chance and then meet again, either by themselves or through another. Do you agree?"

"My life has a simpler trajectory." Bayfield is thinking of his own meeting with Audubon. That it has force, that it will make a shape in his own life.

AUDUBON DOUBTED this could be the father. Too much time had passed, and this D'Orbigny was young. He must be the son. Could this one be his godson, another obligation left behind? No. It must be the other son, the younger one.

"Indeed we are," he repeated, confused, trembling. "Your father was my dear friend when I was a youth."

"He named you Fifi. I have heard speak of you. But you have been gone, I believe, since I was a small child."

To meet the son of D'Orbigny, who knew him to be Jean Rabin, Creole of Santo Domingo, who aided the falsified baptisms so long ago now. And taught him taxidermy in the barn. To be introduced as an American!

He swayed in the embarrassment of his lies. In the zoologist's parlour, he sank to his knees on the stone floor, but no faster than he, this D'Orbigny.

Andubon remembered the plaintive letters from his father, and from his half-sister, and from his cousin Anonyme, asking for help. Remembered then the widowed Anne, who mothered him, with her many bills to pay and no money to pay them with. The cousins wishing to enlist Audubon in their attempts to claim his father's estate. The debts. The quarrels. It had been like a terrible odour following him, like a trap, a trick, an awful reminder that he was fraudulent.

The complications of his father's estate had spread like a contagion. There was Sanitte, and the half-sisters of colour, quadroons and octoroons who were his relations. He had cast the letters away from him. He did not have enough money to feed his own children. He could not help.

"I knew my own lies had caught up with me, Captain Bayfield. But I had not accounted for the lies of others. There was money owing. For this man's father, old Dr. D'Orbigny, had fallen out with my father. The doctor borrowed a sum which he never repaid. When my father died his widow needed the money. But D'Orbigny could not or would not pay.

"That was what held back this long-lost neighbour of mine, what gave him the mysterious downward glance. He could not unmask me — his shame was as great as mine."

Charles-Henri said nothing tear away the disguise that made it possible for Jean Rabin, Creole, to stand before a king-in-waiting. He merely stepped forward and clasped him about the shoulders. Tears stood in both men's eyes.

"And how is Anne Moynet?" Audubon said.

"You don't know? Madame Audubon is dead. These past seven years. Can it be you have not been told?"

BAYFIELD IS PALE with indignation. "I must say that story reflects ill on you," he manages. "It is a poor fellow who will abandon his parents in their age and their need. You must have a weight on your conscience."

"She was not my real mother. And I was saved, as a matter of fact, by her death, by the way it had shamed D'Orbigny: he was as bad as I was."

"There are no mitigating factors," says Bayfield. "You have put your own selfish interests ahead of the very people to whom you owe everything. I am afraid it is unforgiveable."

"You don't understand," Audubon shouts. His face has purpled. His hands are drawn up, his long fingers curled into a fist. "In this matter, as in others, you are a virgin!"

Bayfield is aware of himself as straitlaced. He knows he suffers a lack of imagination. He is humbled by the quality of intimacy that Audubon gives to him, which he cannot return. He is prepared to listen to almost anything. But this is too much. He is most definitely not a virgin.

"Be careful what you say."

"You see, I am right," taunts Audubon.

Bayfield has eaten better and drunk more than he has in weeks. Perhaps he is inebriated. Or coming down with Bowen's cold. His men are threatening mutiny. The tilting rocks give him vertigo. He feels light-headed. His discipline fails him. He moves into the chest of the taller man, takes his arm and twists it behind his back. Pins him over his knees. Force-marches him to a four-foot boulder. He pushes the artist back against it, and then stands over him, one foot propped on his chest.

"Take that word back."

Audubon's chest heaves. He waves a hand in front of his face to dispel smoke, flies. "What word?"

"You know the word I mean."

Bayfield puts a little pressure on the artist's chest. He does not know why he does this. He does not know where his outrage comes from. He does not understand why in this moment it is crucial to him that the artist retract. He does know that, in the real world, so many hundreds of miles of fog and rock away, none of this matters. No one will hear of it.

"Take back that offensive word."

"I do not see why it offends you."

"Don't ask questions. Do as I say."

"You fear the word 'virgin'?" Audubon says, carefully, laughingly. Bayfield lessens the pressure of his foot and then almost stomps on Audubon's chest again.

Audubon rolls away, leaps to his feet and seizes the captain's forearms. But Bayfield easily throws him off, turns, reaches around and has him in a headlock. The sailors stand back in the gloaming, as if they are not listening. Johnny starts forward as if to intervene but his father signals him away.

Audubon, no longer laughing, takes the navy sleeve with its three white stripes between his teeth. He spits it out, gagging.

"If you let me breathe I will find another word for what I mean."

There is a slight release of pressure. Audubon draws breath.

"You are not — dirtied."

"By what?"

"By what dirties the rest of us. And you don't even see it. That is your difficulty. What was that about the tenth transmitter?"

"I have no idea what you are talking about," says Bayfield. But he loosens his grip.

"You have your king. You are high born. The yoke is not on you."

Bayfield drops his hold and walks away. He stands ten feet off, his arms behind his back. "What yoke?" he says.

"The yoke of man. The harness that makes a man an ox."

Bayfield is charged with what? Being different than others, more free, above it, somehow, less human. He does not like it. It seems to him unfair. He moves farther, drawing Audubon after him, away from the other men. He lowers his voice.

He makes a confession he has never made before. It is easier than he would have imagined.

"I have a yoke. It weighs on me every day. My yoke is fear."

"Fear?" Audubon is contemptuous.

"Not of pain, or death, not anything like that. My fear is . . . I fear that — I cannot find my way through this frenzy of rock and water. I cannot make a perfect chart. It would take me a dozen summers. And in those seasons more ships will go aground. More lives will be lost. My men will strike against me, as they nearly have done already."

He loosens his hands and lifts them in a gesture almost of supplication, then drops them.

"And even if I do produce the absolutely correct chart, no sea captain can read it. In the fog, no one can tell one island from the next. I will not turn in a sham chart as my predecessors have done. But I must be reasonable although it wounds my pride. I will tell the Admiralty it is impossible. That is the heart of it, I fear the negation of all my efforts."

"*Impossible,*" says Audubon in French. It is a word he discussed with Nolte, those many years ago, in the inn in the Allegheny range. "'The word impossible is not in my vocabulary.' Napoleon said that."

"Nor has it been in mine," says Bayfield. "But I fear it may be about to enter." He looks to the east at the maze of islands.

"It is a word to dream but not to say."

"Will it be my secret then, that I fear I cannot succeed?"

"If it is your secret, you have told me, and we are even."

"I may be forced to give up."

"I cannot believe it."

"I may choose to give up."

"Then I shall think you are a coward," says Audubon pleasantly.

Bayfield is on him in a second. Easily, with the advantage of surprise, he forces the artist onto his back on the ground. He places his foot on his friend's chest, heavily, again. Audubon goes completely still. Bayfield, too, freezes. Then he removes his foot and helps the artist to his feet.

"So behaves the Wild Turkey in mating season," says Audubon, dusting himself off.

"Pardon me?"

"The cock will attack and kill his rival. Yet the moment the vanquished is dead the conqueror treads it underfoot with all the movements usually employed to caress a female."

Bayfield has no more words.

HOPE

It is much later. A front of drier air has blown through. Two men —
Godwin and Collins — stand around the fire in the long pale night
holding their clothes to the flame in hopes of reducing the damp. A
full moon like a cool blue sun hovers above the horizon.

Johnny is stretched out on the rocks, where a suspicion of warmth
lingers. His eyes are closed. Audubon and the captain talk on. They
have covered many subjects, the Church of England, and the hatching
of eggs by steam. Their voices rise again.

"We kill too much, Captain Bayfield. We kill for sport. Do you
never fear, Captain, that we are destroying nature?"

"There is so much of it you cannot make a dint."

Audubon seems not to hear. "We do make a 'dint.' We are trapped
into doing so by the circumstances of our lives. Do you see? I, above
all. I set myself to make this Work; I set my wife and children and my
friends to aid me. The wheels are in motion. I must find the birds.
The book must be printed to satisfy the subscribers. The printer must
be paid, the dues — the 'Trash,' I call it — collected. It is not only my
art, but my means of survival. The birds — the wilderness — are at
my mercy."

"You see yourself as very powerful in this enormous wild,"
soothes Bayfield.

"I have seen the Eggers. I cannot forget the spectacle. They have
no right to be here," says Audubon. He points his long finger at
Bayfield. "Do you see what you do with your maps? Bring all manner
of ruffians and murderers to these shores."

Bayfield smiles. "Piracy was never started, nor will it be ended, by Navy charts."

"You and your government are wrong!"

The insult brings Johnny to a sitting position. "Father. The captain is not wrong. Just not of your view. You know how a man hates to be called wrong."

"If my government is wrong, then I am wrong, my friend, if I may call you that," says Bayfield.

"You are my friend. Yet, though your mission lives as strongly in you as my own in me, if you failed I would rejoice!" Audubon is so agitated that he steps away, swinging his arms.

Johnny stands. "Captain Bayfield, forgive my father. He is frustrated."

But Bayfield appears unruffled. "Imagine that from my charts will come more ships. Not the thieves you describe, but trading vessels, shiploads of immigrants seeking a better life."

"You would see this shore settled?" Audubon speaks out of the darkness, incredulous.

Godwin interjects. "These settlers must come from a bad place indeed to prefer this."

"Aye," says Collins in his gentle way. "There are such places, made ill by man, not by God."

"You would see this shore settled?" repeats Audubon. "Where will I go then, and visit nature undisturbed?"

"Is that what you expect then, that Labrador's curtains of fog should close at your back, and no man follow you here?"

"Why would any man want to?" That was Bowen.

Collins speaks in the weak firelight. "I could make a little cabin here and bring my bride. Put potatoes in the sand. They'll grow. A happier life I cannot hope for."

Bayfield tries another tack. "Man has ventured out since time began. He will not stay home for lack of instructions. Are you happy to hit a rock or lose your way at sea? The number of shipwrecks is increasing and with it a terrible toll in human life. You speak of your dark vision. I wonder if you have seen the darkest of it."

It is a question that does not want an answer. There is silence, and Bayfield continues. "I know you love the birds, Mr. Audubon. It is most passionately your cause and I commend you for that. But, with all due respect, I must tell you I have seen worse than Eggers."

He throws this challenge across the glowering coals. Audubon is silent, staring into the fire.

"May I counter your testimony with a story of my own? A harrowing story which may explain what moves me onward on what you call a worthless task.

"It was four years ago on the island of Anticosti. Lieutenant Bowen was with me."

Bowen's low cough punctuates the telling.

"We arrived at Fox Bay and heard from the local people of the ill fate of the *Granicus*. She sailed from Quebec on the 29 October, the previous winter, bound for Cork. Have you heard of the ship? It had disappeared and until that moment had gone unaccounted for."

"Aye," says Collins. "Taking the poor Irish settlers who'd failed in America back to starve at home."

"It is a tragic and not uncommon story: in November of that year, the *Granicus* struck on the reef off the south point of Fox Bay. The crew got her off the reef but she ran ashore on East Point. The crew pulled down the sails and built tents, taking shelter within the canvas walls and keeping themselves alive upon what supplies they saved from the wreck. In those supplies was not only the food they needed, but also rum. The rum, I believe, made them reckless and brutal. Early in March, when there were no more provisions to be had from the *Granicus*, they went in a boat to Fox Bay. They had lasted nearly five months, but they could last no longer.

"It was, of course, still winter. There were six weeks to run until the season might begin and a vessel appear. The post was not supplied, and there were no inhabitants. The survivors — seventeen men, two women and three children — found shelter, in the house of a Monsieur Godin that stood next to the harbour.

"Came a day in April when some fishermen sailed in. They saw that the building had a strange and forbidding air. There were signs of human habitation yet it was utterly silent, and, as they drew near the wooden walls, the most horrible odour rose to their nostrils, such that they were afraid to enter.

"They stood, undecided, a hundred feet away, turning their faces to the wind and muttering amongst themselves. They were decent men, accustomed to shipwreck and its horrors, who knew what must be inside. The stench of rotting human flesh is not soon forgotten, and there had been other disasters. But there was one man, braver or more decent or perhaps simply possessing less imagination than the rest, who said, We must go in.

"And so, holding his cap to his face, he opened the door of the house, and stepped across the threshold into a scene of unmatched horror. There were piles of putrid bodies on the floors and the wooden couches, dead but not entirely dissolved. It was still cold, you see. They were intact enough so that one could see not simply the ravages of death but the depredations made on the bodies by the living. It appeared that when a body passed on, the living feasted on the starveling flesh.

"This much was clear to our honourable fisherman. He was frightened almost out of his wits by the ungodly scene. He turned and ran."

Audubon is still standing away from the fire, his back a streak in the moonlight. Collins cannot be still. He makes to leave the circle and then returns. Johnny paces along a crack in a rock and back, like a cat on a chain. Only Godwin appears unmoved by the tale. No doubt he has heard — or seen — its like.

"You may have guessed, it was on this very April day that we sailed into the harbour, about to begin our surveying for the year. The fishermen, quite overwhelmed, called us to investigate."

Bayfield speaks softly but no one misses a word.

"Of all God's cruelty I had not seen anything the like of this. I entered knowing what was within but nothing could have prepared me. I kept on walking through the building only because I knew I must. Clearly, murderous violence had accompanied starvation. The walls and windows had been battered and broken and were splashed with blood. The sleeping platforms and blankets were soaked and dried with gore, and the ragged, filthy clothing was ripped, stabbed, soiled and bloodied from every possible assault. There was a pinafore that must have belonged to a girl of perhaps ten. It was on sight of this that my heart failed me; I bent over, and felt my knees begin to go."

The cough sounds again, close at hand. Bowen has risen during the tale. He walks around the fire to stand at the captain's side. He challenges Audubon with a stony gaze.

"Mr. Bowen here —" Bayfield puts a hand on his assistant's shoulder, then lifts it "— came behind to lift me and we walked together through this ghastly graveyard. I am not ashamed to say we both sobbed aloud. We saw a pot in the fireplace with a human forearm in it."

Bowen's gaze has lifted over the hills; it is as if he sees into the past and is walking still through that room.

"I did not know how to understand it. How to make my mind accept what I saw. Can you imagine? In the end I saw it this way. Life had broken the human of his civilization and the animal was all that remained. I tried to think we saw only animal corpses, that these men's spirits had fled their bodies long before breath itself had fled."

"You slander the creatures. Animals do not behave this way," protests Audubon.

Bayfield accepts with a nod. "I know you venerate the beasts. You may tell me about that another day on this coast. You may tell me we are the true savages. I say this: when I saw it, I was ashamed to be human."

"Then we can be agreed."

"But I am not finished my tale. Pointless murder of creatures is wrong. But more wrong is the murder of humans."

"What is wrong cannot be 'more wrong,'" counters Audubon.

"I think it can. Our suffering is greater than that of the beasts."

"How do you know?"

"For a simple reason which I shall give you. We are more than beasts. We hope. There was in that scene of carnage a sight even more difficult to bear. Shall I tell you?"

Bayfield fills his chest with a steadying breath and turns his blue serge back a moment, then faces the men again.

"One of these ravaged and ravaging corpses, when it had been human, had made a pattern on the wall in chalk. He or she had written the numbers one to thirty-one, in a square, seven numbers to a row, four and a half rows of numbers. It is a pattern we recognize. A calendar. This degraded, starving, cannibalized or cannibalizing half-corpse had struck out each number in sequence. Do you understand?"

Godwin pulls out a plug of tobacco. No one else moves.

"He was counting. Counting! Counting the days! Do you know what that means? It means hope.

"I saw the calendar on the wall. Its delicacy, its order, the care with which it had been maintained in the chaos all around. Numbers in straight rows. Diagonal lines through them, one after another. A drawing. A chart if you like. A man, a woman or perhaps the owner of that pinafore, a child, created it. Did she see daybreak and sunset? In her stupor of hunger and terror perhaps she only waked to strike the number; perhaps the act itself was all that kept her alive. And then even hope could not keep her alive any longer."

Bowen stands with his hands joined at the small of his back, as if he is in irons. Godwin, jaw set, glares at the horizon.

"It was by my count only ten days between the last strikeout and our arrival."

He stops. There is a respectful pause.

"It is a terrible story," says Audubon. The men can hear his unspoken "but."

"Shall I tell you more? We walked through the back door and saw another, smaller building perhaps ten feet away. And we were drawn to it. I *knew*. I am responsible for those in my command. I knew that he would be there, the monster whose creation this was. He who had commanded this disaster.

"And he was.

"He was a huge man, still muscled, with more flesh on him than any of the others: he had consumed more than his share of provisions no doubt. He had been neither wounded nor mutilated and so we assumed he was the last to die. God knows what we would have done to him had we found him alive: I expect I'd have had him shot through the head.

"He lay quite still, as if he had died in his bed at home. Around the small enclosure where they found him were hanging from the ceiling, like the four posters of a bed, the bodies of four of his fellows. He had to have killed them, or else watched them die and lived on simply because he was larger than they and no doubt more evil, and had then hung their bodies up for safe-keeping."

Bayfield's voice is lower now. Audubon strains to hear, and then realizes that the tale has ended.

The five men stand a few minutes longer. Emery steps forward, from where he has been listening, unseen, in the darkness. Bayfield heaves an enormous sigh and grips his tin mug more tightly. He drains it. He lifts it in his fist to the sky and gently lets his hand drop to his thigh, the mug upside down.

"Gentlemen?" he asks. "Is it time to retire?"

"I am puzzled as to why the calendar was the worst to you," says Audubon.

"They were marking off the days until rescue came. And it did not. We failed them."

"Ah," says Audubon bitterly. "This was your failure, is it? God had put you in charge, had he, since you are English? Could it be that, simply, life for them was set to end this way? That the monster no more commanded this disaster than did the little girl whose pinafore you saw? That man is not in charge of his own nature, or of the elements?"

But there is nothing to be said in favour of death by shipwreck, starvation and cannibalism. Bayfield has won the argument. Bowen says goodnight stiffly. Audubon watches him disappear into the tent. Godwin fades off to where he sleeps in the whaleboat.

But neither Bayfield nor Audubon moves. They stare off, Audubon, to the fire, Bayfield to the sky, where the aurora now is brilliant and huge.

"Tomorrow we part company," says Bayfield, and if he were not a captain of the Royal Navy, there would have been sadness in his voice.

"We shall turn back to the *Gulnare,* and you will go onward, north to the Straits."

"We have been fortunate to have your help and company on this journey," Audubon says.

"It is we who have been fortunate," says Bayfield, offering his hand. "Though our missions are opposed, we have had much to gain in each other's company."

AUDUBON TWISTS IN HIS TENT. It is not himself as bird that he imagines, but the bird as himself. As a man. Sometimes, too, as a woman.

He is a monk, a disciple of birds. A captive to his Work, he cannot free the truest part of himself, a man's passion to follow what he loves, to live that love throughout his whole body. He is caught in the yoke, the trap his species has devised to train, to thwart his desires — he is married, a father, a debtor, a working man who must sell his labours so that he and his family can live. There seems to him to be no solution, no flight.

He is full of awareness of his sins against the very creatures he worships. He has stalked birds. He has got them in his sights and shot them, reached for the fallen bodies in the bent grass. He has sometimes caught birds in his bare hands and squeezed the life out of them, careful not to spoil their feathers. He has killed so many. He has wired their wings and mounted them on boards; he has tamed them, which is sometimes worse. He tells himself this is part of love's labour: to know birds. Even tonight, he will truss their corpses, and store their skins in oils and alcohol to be sent abroad.

He wonders if he loves birds so much as he envies them. But why envy a bird? He knows too well their strange reptilian nature, and their immense indifference, their hard struggle to survive, which is like his own. But does he envy the bird because it is free of doubt? A bird is without shame, but he, the portrayer of birds, is filled with shame.

Birds are his passion. He is violent with the subject of his passion; it is true; love *is* violent. But he fears he has gone too far. The birds which have filled his life are deserting him.

STRAIT

At rosy dawn on July 22, Captain Bayfield and Lieutenants Bowen and Collins in the two open boats pass out between the islands and Gros Mécatina Point, which they have located, now, to the south and east of their camp. They make a sombre sight, these launches, each with seven men at oar, each with a spotter seated in the bow with his cap on. They have taken leave of Audubon and the *Ripley*'s crew: a sturdy salute from the deck suffices this early morning. They have gone as far to the northeast as Bayfield planned, and now will make their way back down the coast, to reboard the *Gulnare*.

They discover the sea to be enormous; each boat loses sight of the other in the valleys between the peaks of water, loses sight even of the tops of the inland mountains. They are in the troughs of water as much as on the surface of it. But eventually, it calms. The waves flatten out and the whole surround of hundreds and hundreds of little granite islets and outcrops is revealed. They reach the harbour of Petit Mécatina where, suddenly, they can see right to the sandy bottom.

Running up sails in the favourable wind, they pass the falls at the Étamamiou River. From its fifty-foot drop the water boils and foams in a clear, deep basin. They pull their boats up against the shore. Had this been the South Pacific, they would have stripped down and bathed. As no doubt James Cook is even now doing, remarks Bowen. They decide to dip in at the edge anyway. The water is so cold it scalds and thrills their skin and makes their bones ache.

Anaesthetized from cold, they do not feel the moschettoes bite. The captain and the lieutenants become silly. (It does not seem odd to them to continue to address one another in the formal way; the habits of years are unbreakable.) They make a war of it, themselves against the countless barbarian biting insects. The crew is cheered and works harder at the oars.

Bayfield recognizes that some note of high seriousness has gone out of his endeavour. He has left the dark vision of the *Granicus* by the dead coals of the fire he shared with Audubon. He has lightened himself by his confession. There is an atmosphere almost of celebration: he has conceived of defeat, but has not chosen it. He is now heading in the direction of the *Gulnare,* home. They will go north again in the vessel and do what they can do. He will finish, but his charts will be imperfect. He will forgive himself for that. Which shocks him and eases him. He is able to laugh when the sailors sing their rude songs.

> *Sally Brown's a bright mulatter*
> *She drinks rum and chaws terbaccer*

For a time he has accepted his limitations, which is why he will always blame himself for what happens next.

IT IS THEIR SECOND DAY OUT. They are in a small cove in which they will hide for the night from the wind, which has swung east. The best way is to pull the boats right up on the rocks. They approach too quickly a rock with a good slant on it, and Collins jumps over the bow to shore. He turns to fend off, pushing the bow out with his arms, but the boat is coming in fast on a wave and slams into his chest. His feet lose their grip on the sloping wet granite. He slides as the boat rocks back and then, as it surges forward, tries to regain his feet. The sharp edge of the bow connects with his chin with a sickening crunch, his neck snaps back, he goes limp and slips like a fish below the hull.

Bayfield, standing midway back, watches Collins's bony work-toughened hands, which have been gripping the gunwale, go limp and drop out of sight. It is a sight he will never forget.

"We've put him under the keel," a sailor shouts.

"... *the water boils and foams in a clear, deep basin.*"

Two men jump off the other side and peer down. They can't see him.

"Push us off," commands Bayfield. He takes an oar and tries to pry the boat off the rock. But they have been hoisted forward and the launch is now heavy. More sailors jump out to follow his orders, and push the launch off.

Now he is alone in the launch and can't get out. And Collins must be right underneath him. Shouting now, with ropes they pull the *Owen* sideways and up on the rocks. Bayfield jumps out. All seven men probe the water with their oars. The water is — Bayfield can estimate the temperature because he measures it daily — about thirty-nine degrees. Collins, even without a broken neck, will be in shock and not thinking clearly.

"He's got to be under the hull," Bayfield says, lying on his face on the rock and sweeping the bottom of the boat with his oar. But he encounters nothing and nor do the others, several of whom want to dive for their comrade.

Bayfield allows them, with a warning; they have only a minute or two before they will lose their reason because of the cold. The divers discover that the slope drops off quickly and that this rock is a lip. Under it the even colder water surges. The mystery disappearance must be accounted for by this; Collins has been forced under the lip of the rock and caught there by incoming waves. Bayfield sets his stopwatch. Several sailors go in for a minute or two at a time and come out to warm up: they cannot find Collins.

"It cannot be that a man is knocked in the chin by the *Owen* and simply disappears! We must find him."

The search becomes increasingly grim and frustrated.

"He can't have gone anywhere."

"We're running out of time."

Bayfield looks at his stopwatch — ten minutes thirty seconds. They are, in fact, out of time. The man is dead. Those sailors who are not in and out of the water take to calling his name, as if he'd walked away for a minute, as if he could be roused by voice. By now the other launch comes into the bay and Bowen hears the news.

"He can't be gone."

"It's as if he was snatched away."

"He was just here."

"Find him," says Bayfield.

An hour later, they do. The body is caught under the ledge a few feet out from where the *Owen* has been hauled. Collins has a broken neck and is quite dead.

———

OUAPITAGONE, *JULY 25, 13 MINUTES AFTER 5 P.M.*

Had the pleasure of completing the Survey between Ouapitagone and Mécatina, a distance of 150 nautical miles never before Surveyed. Gave the Boat's crew a glass of grog and then rowed onboard the *Gulnare* through a squall of wind and rain.

— *Surveying Journals,* Henry Wolsey Bayfield, Captain, Royal Navy

———

BAYFIELD GAZES AT THE GULNARE HERSELF. Her pretty neck and breasts brave the squall as they have braved so many others, and he feels a hot pressure in his throat at the sight of her pale full shoulders. Sometimes a figurehead will swell and split, but he is careful to keep her oiled. Sometimes a schooner will lose her figurehead in a storm; this too he is determined will never happen.

He walks from bowsprit to stern inspecting his vessel. She is in fine form, needing only a swabbing and some oil on the wood, and some splicing of ropes. He sets the men to work on her and enjoys the sight of their energetic action in all her corners and joins.

Kelly greets them with open arms but with worry creases across his plump forehead. The mainspring of chronometer 741 has broken, and another one, number 546, has ceased to work for no reason he can understand. Bayfield fixes 546, which simply suffered from a loose screw, but 741 has died of old age and is a loss to the cause.

Collins is with them, wrapped in a sail. There is no earth in which to dig a grave. He must be buried in the deep, a practice Bayfield abhors. The water is so restless, a dreadful place to be laid. Although he does not fear death, he fears burial at sea. He saw it often enough in his youth; men were lost from time to time. But it has never happened under his command.

They have the service offshore, and consign Collins's body where the water is deep. The men are angry again; it takes little to bring it out. Why did they sign on, he thinks, when they knew there would be no share of any profits? He may have to promise them a reward if they complete the portion of the survey he planned. During the dogwatch Bayfield hears the lame coxswain swearing. Although it is not Saturday he retreats to his cabin and brings out the miniature portrait of Mrs. Bayfield of Bayfield Hall. He places her on the ledge and paces back and forth before her.

"A man is often lost on a long sea voyage," he explains. "There is nothing that could have been done. It was a freak accident."

"I hope you don't consider that your excuse," says his mother.

"Never," he says. "There is no excuse."

He wants to tell her that he is lonely. But he cannot.

"You must carry on, Henry," says Mrs. Bayfield. "I gave birth to you not knowing you would venture to these hostile climes. But since you have gone there, you must prevail. I would not have a quitter as my son."

"Of course, I will carry on. It is only a question of how."

"Quickly," says Mrs. Bayfield. "And without explanations."

When dark falls Bayfield finds himself in the bow, with his arm on the neck of the Gulnare herself. She is more comforting than his mother.

BAYFIELD AND HIS SILENT CREW venture on the next leg of the survey, making their way back up to Mécatina Harbour in the *Gulnare*, testing their own work. It is all good and the schooner flies without incident along the channel they have marked. From Mécatina they continue to beat their way up the coast, passing the mouth of the St. Augustine River, the great migratory route of the Montagnais Indians. They stop to trade biscuits for moccasins. There have been bad years for game, and the men and women are gaunt, their small children listless.

Soon they enter the Strait of Belle Isle, between Newfoundland and Labrador, where so many ships have come to ruin. "Nine times out of ten," Bayfield tells Bowen, "there is thick fog in the passage, the tenth time a violent storm. The current is so strong we have no choice but to keep the speed up even though we cannot see where we are going. To drop below eleven knots is to be blown off course. So it is a game of chance. We fly blind at high speed, or go slow and are sucked onto hazard."

For the *Gulnare*, the Strait is calm and beautiful. She bravely sails in, the slave girl's carved wooden back arched above the sway of frigid green water. Whales breach all around her, one after another, as if, now that they have entered the true north, an honour guard has come to escort them.

There are other wonders to be met: icebergs like ruined castles and every night the phosphorescent gleam of the aurora. At L'Anse-au-Clair, where brigantines come in from Jersey, the locals splash on the beach with hand-held nets, catching tiny fish called capelin. Bayfield picks up ammonites that look like snakes curled around themselves. At L'Anse-Aux-Morts there is a lighthouse and a shoreside graveyard of sailors with stories of ships that have come to ruin laboriously carved in stone. Here they could have put Collins to rest, though it would not be much drier. The graves are so close to the shore the corpses must be dissolved.

Graced with easy weather, the schooner skips across the Strait between Green Island, Newfoundland, and Bras d'Or. Here Bayfield discovers a great curiosity. In mid-strait, between Newfoundland

and Labrador, there is a ripple — a ridge, permanent and standing, in the water's surface. On one side of the ripple, the water is light in colour, and forty-nine degrees Fahrenheit in temperature, with no icebergs in it. On the other side, the water is darker and icebergs stand like pyramids one hundred and fifty feet above the sea. The darker water is thirty-three degrees in temperature. Bayfield concludes that the dark current comes down from the frozen Arctic, bringing the ice castles with it. When they cross over to the dark water the sailors shudder at the change. Caught in fog where the temperature changes, the *Gulnare* fires her cannons, half a dozen times, as a warning and a signal.

Bayfield wonders if he will encounter the *Ripley* again. He feels her out there, the restless spirit of Audubon. He wonders if he is finding his birds. He would tell him, if they met again, about Collins.

He finds himself searching for the *Ripley* at each place they stop.

ON JULY 26 the *Ripley* leaves Portage Bay at dawn heading north. There is a good breeze blowing; Godwin and Emery propose to sail across the open water up to Chevalier's settlement at the mouth of the Esquimaux River. Audubon agrees, reluctantly. He knows they will miss birds on the shore along the way, but hopes that the river mouth with its estuary and klatch of islands will be fertile territory.

There is a clear passage, all the way, a distance of forty-seven miles. They are over halfway there when the wind drops, turns, and begins to roar from the south carrying the full force of the Gulf of St. Lawrence with it. The masts shake as if they might snap, and the ship flies before the wind. In only three hours they are outside of the little settlement of Chevalier's. They must wend their way through shoals and around rocky points in to shore.

Godwin balks.

"A man would be mad to ask me to do that," he says.

"A man has come to see the birds, not the sea. You promised me the estuary."

Godwin has heard it all before. "No bird is worth risking our lives."

"Any bird is worth three bad pilots," says Audubon. It is their joke now.

But Godwin is planted firmly before the wheel; only a physical struggle will displace him. Even Audubon can see that it is hazardous to head into uncharted channels in this gale. And so, they sail onward.

They fly past Chevalier's settlement and draw ever nearer to the entrance to the Strait of Belle Isle.

"Captain Emery, I am captive in this cursed schooner!" Audubon shouts.

The captain smiles, and pulls his moustaches, and says that the weather has been even worse than usual, and what can they do?

By the end of the day they have arrived at Bras d'Or, where, because the harbour is clear and open, Godwin consents to stop.

To the painter's great astonishment, the harbour is full; there are at least 150 sailing vessels, mostly fore-and-aft schooners, with a few pickaxes, all fishing for cod. Some are so loaded down with fish that the decks are awash with water. And the harbour is merry with songs of whalers from New England, codfishers from Italy and the West Indies, and from Newfoundland. Their voices ring across the night water.

He has come to the wilderness and found that throngs of people were here before him.

Audubon stands on deck and sees, again, the Arctic Tern, now with its young. It was only six weeks ago that he first spied it diving and soaring above the shores of Magdalen Island; now the bird has mated, laid, and nurtured its young.

IN THE MORNING, he walks the rim of a white sand beach. He sees eight redpolls, a harlequin drake and duck, which the locals call "Lords and Ladies" for their elaborate plumage, and a Washington eagle. In the nearby woods and ponds he finds a velvet duck, and the three-toed and downy woodpeckers. At the Hudson's Bay post, he fingers the caribou skins the Esquimaux bring across the plateau from the Arctic. He asks for certain information, which he already knows.

The fish are smaller and more scarce, he hears a captain complain. The clerk tells him that in living memory, the whales were everywhere, and the whalers could take as many as they liked; now it was rare to come upon a pod.

Walking onshore near the little settlement, Audubon and Johnny come to the log home of an Englishman called Jones. The man cordially invites them inside for tea. He has four children and an appalling wife, although Mr. Jones himself seems more than content with her, regularly slapping her bottom as she passes by in the small, fire-warmed room. Mrs. Jones has a coarse voice and is full of pretensions. She tells Audubon that her husband has ordered from over the sea a wonderful musical instrument for her to play, because she is so talented. When he questions her, Audubon discovers that it is a player piano with scrolls for tunes.

Mr. Jones takes Audubon on a walk along the shore. He talks of a shortage of fish, of the diminishing herds, which in turn starve the Indians, of the necessity to stock up for winter or die.

"You have a difficult life. I believe this place is best left to the beasts and the native people, like the Esquimaux, who can survive."

"But I love this life. I live here free of taxes, free of lawyers, free of government in all ways. I may do as I please and I owe nothing to another man. I am certain this is the best of all places to live. My neighbour — a mile away — passes no comment on what I do if I do not transgress against him."

Audubon remembers Collins, and that night around the fire, and how he imagined a happy life for himself here with his bride. Perhaps the man was not so wrong. Perhaps he will live here yet.

"Besides," says Jones, "it is not possible that God intended this majesty to go unobserved."

THE WONDERS of this country grow stranger by the day. The jelly-fish arrive. Caught on the rocks and colliding with the green-tongued kelp are shining globes like great bubbles.

Audubon is transfixed by the glowing transparent spheres just under the surface. In great masses they have collected near the rocky shores and clumps of kelp, fetching up against shallows, moving by instinct in their mass fertilization ritual. The jellyfish are stacked below into the depths like planets disappearing into space, each one luminous, the gleam of orb over orb diminishing into the deep.

Johnny meanwhile has been inquiring after the Labrador Duck, describing the bird — its pied back, the black ring around its neck and its grey and white wings.

"You don't want that one. It tastes like fish," say the Jones boys.

"Not for eating," he explains. "To draw it."

The youngest boy directs Johnny to a nest, which he claims belongs to the bird. But the nest is empty.

"If you stay awhile," Jones says to Audubon, "you'll see the curlew come. That is the bird you want to see. They call it the Esquimaux Curlew."

Audubon has seen these birds only once before. He recalls, as if from another life, the August day he and Bachman waded on an island on the coast of South Carolina, in a soft, rosy dawn. A dense flock of the northern species flew over swiftly, on their route south.

"When the curlews come, then we have a time," says Jones. His eyes and the eyes of his wife crinkle up with laughter. "In May, they pass here on their way up to their breeding grounds in the Arctic. Soon they will come down from the north. They stop here before they set off southward across the Gulf. They run so thickly underfoot that even my smallest boy can kill them with a club," says Jones. "Hunters shoot two thousand a day and deliver them to the Hudson's Bay store up the coast. They will come with the fog," says Jones. "Soon now."

IN THE EAST that evening there is a small piece of rainbow. Captain Emery calls it "the eye of the brick" and says it betokens wind from the same quarter in the morning. He is right. And the east wind brings fog.

BRAS D'OR, *JULY 29, 1833*

For more than a week we had been looking for them, as was every fisherman in the harbour, these birds being considered, there, great delicacies. The birds at length came . . . from the north . . . in such dense flocks as to remind me of the passenger pigeons. Flock after flock, passed close round our vessel, and directed their course toward the sterile mountainous tracts in the neighbourhood; and as soon as the sun's rays had dispersed the fogs that hung over the land, our whole party went off in search of them.

— *Ornithological Biography,* J. J. Audubon

THE MORNING IS STIFLED in dense mist with a wind that does nothing to clear the clouds. The waiting is over. The cry rings out, "The curlews are coming, the curlews are coming."

When the birds emerge from the cloud banks, they seem bewildered, they are so suddenly over the little settlement. Of course in the fog any arrival, even that of a man walking toward you, first invisible, then upon you, is sudden. But almost instantly the sky is dark and the rush of wings echoes up from the rocks. The birds turn and venture toward the open water but cannot attempt it in the fog. They choose instead the land because it at least is visible and because there will be food there.

Their tumultuous appearance brings pain to Audubon's chest; tears stand out from his eyes. The birds are exquisite in flight, swiftly circling around themselves and each other in groups of a dozen or more, like saucers spun by a juggler's hand. As they pass over his head he hears their sensual whistle.

But when they find the curlew berries, the birds go silent. They land, and run en masse this way and that, siphoning the berries off their tiny sprigs with their slim, curved beaks.

The birds are a wonder. When he runs after them, they cluster and squat, like partridge. Some lay their heads and necks flat on the ground until he is almost on top of them. They seem to be playing dead. But when he is in their midst, one whistles and the rest scream and fly upwards. They leap from the ground into the air as a snipe does. Overhead they turn and regroup, try to head outward but are defeated by the fog, turn and land again.

Johnny and the others chase the curlews from one berry patch to another. Each time, the birds play dead, then shriek and rise and circle out over the sea. Audubon watches the flock return, this time high over his head. He urges them to pass by, to attempt that foggy gulf and escape the certain death which his kind will mete out to them. But they come down to earth again.

It is the fated sense in this bird that moves Audubon. It is easy to shoot them; the settlers in Bras d'Or take hundreds. The birds do not fly from the guns, but continue to circle, mesmerized perhaps by the echoing of the shots over the rocks. The urgency to feed on berries and stay on their track has overcome their survival instinct.

The second day the remaining birds are much more shy, as if they know they have endangered themselves. In the fog they fly swiftly, staying closely massed together and passing low over the rocks. Whenever the fog lifts they rise high and spin in the air as if for the simple joy of it, giving that single note like a soft whistle.

For three days the flocks continue to arrive. They cross the open water in a tight mass or sometimes in a broad line, and often simply scattered together. Although no hawks or predators follow them, they fly as if to avoid capture, darting ahead, turning back, twirling around and sometimes halting completely, suspended as they face the wind.

Pacing the shore in this whirl of wings, Audubon pictures the curlews as he will paint them. Their yellow, which recalls the sun they long for. The male standing, legs apart, on a rock no taller than itself, tipped downward so that the whole of its brown and beige back, and the white stripe over its elliptical eye, are exposed. He will draw carefully each of the twelve even tail feathers and the four sharp toe-claws. It seems more important than ever before that he record, precisely, this bird.

But it is the soft white underside and throat of the female that tempts him. She is lying on the bare ground, her bed only a few sparse sprigs of yellowish moss. Her vulnerable white throat and soft rounded belly are in the centre of the picture. Her feet are folded, collapsed; her wing lies open on the rock like an empty palm. She is dead, or playing dead.

He has painted birds under attack or in throes of death from a predator. But never dead. Or playing dead. Not a bird lying on its side quite still. He never does it again. It was just that day, that bird, in Bras d'Or.

There is no visible enemy in the painting. The curlew offers herself to the painter, the viewer, her plump stomach glowing white and golden, her brown eye catching the light. The subtle marking of the feathers on the inside of the wings are so private, they speak of a terrible vulnerability.

This painted bird is docile, edible; she is a bird painted by another artist, not himself. Or by an Audubon who knows her fate, but does not want to know. Has learned but does not want to learn. Sees a future that he does not want to see.

This is not the way he paints birds. The curlew has come out of the wildness and into a man's world and has become a thing.

A BIRD IS a vessel.

A vessel for what he knows. What he has learned from a lifetime of birds. A bird is an insight. A sight into the heart of man, the core where the heart ought to be. A bird is a site. A sighting.

JOHNNY COMES down to offer him dinner on a tin plate, so that he can eat at his table, since he will not leave it. "The curlew is delicious, Father. Everything they promised."

Audubon is not hungry.

He does not want a fork and knife, but a scalpel and tweezers.

Audubon is not eating although the *Ripley*'s cook has distinguished himself with dozens and dozens of the birds. He is more interested in the purple carcass of the curlew he slaughtered, which he examines in his sombre quarters below deck. Everything of the bird is slender, the bill, the lovely neck, the body, the feet, the wings. The wing feathers are long and narrow as well, each next to the other a little shorter, making an even gradation. Only the tail, made of the twelve rounded feathers, is short. But the feathers are gone now.

There is only meat, and when the meat is pulled away, bone. The carcass is a contraption, bones without marrow, a cavity.

He is struck by the hopelessness of his measurements. He sees the pathos of his efforts to capture the bird. He begins slowly with his scalpel and tweezers to take apart the body of the bird, limb from limb, flesh from bone, organ from cavity.

This a bird: it comes apart this way.

Now he does not want a scalpel and tweezers but a pen and paper. He writes a letter to Maria, a letter he will leave with one of the ships in the harbour here, at Bras d'Or.

Dear Maria,

I have seen much on my journey and made some portraits which, God willing, you may enjoy.

This is a journey I did not wish to make. I did not wish to leave you.

I confess, I am weary. Weary of cold and wet, weary too of seeing. Seeing, for me, has always led to pleasure, but here, now, pleasure does not come, only an immense dread.

I wish I could see you. No, not see you. My eyes are protesting. Hold you. Like a blind man, against my person.

A bird is not really a bird. A bird is an elaborate costume, a disguise for a spirit. Each bird is the object of my passion, in a new disguise.

You are all my birds.

He did not write these words.

Or at least we do not know that he did. He may have done, but we do not know. If he did, the letter is gone. Saved, perhaps for years, by Maria. Collected on her death or before by Audubon's zealous, censorious granddaughter. Lost in the Civil War, or burned, or soaked in a flood of tears, or vinegar. This is what happens to letters, especially those with secrets in them.

Time is a vessel. The past is the stories we fill it with.

He did write to Maria: "Please paint a loblolly bay, and a sprig of leaf and flower of the franklinia. I have almost never seen it in the wild but I know it is in your garden on Rutledge Avenue. Please paint the sweetgum. And send your paintings to Victor in London who will know what to do with them."

He did write, and this letter did survive, somehow, the natural disasters and the protectors of reputation and of feelings.

"Dear sweetheart. You are as dear to me as my wife . . ."

HE IMAGINES he is painting Maria. He enumerates areas of desire: fingers, the tips and the inside pleat between them; collarbone, raised like a yoke from her tiny frame; shoulder, the way a sleeve or a strap can be pushed sideways off it, nudged along, giving an air of willingness, a promise; haunch with the hollow around the hip bone, top of thigh with indent of muscle (never seen but imagined). Further imagined, the ribs rising out of flesh, and the hollow beneath; the exquisite soft cloud of breasts floating over the rib cage.

THE CURLEW is difficult to paint. Its colours are within the scope of his palette, but the birds' disposition eludes him. They fly as if before a storm. They have an anxiety about them. Turn in the air, alternate between timidity and indifference, mass in numbers like an army looking for a leader. The urge to return to the south is strong in them and they have a long way to go. But human predators wait at the other end, too, in the Argentine pampas.

It is the fog that keeps the birds here. He understands this, as he walks along the shore path through the moss, worn thin where people have walked before. It surprises him to see the footprints making an impression on this seemingly impervious land. On this wilderness. Yet it does not surprise him, either, because the day seems as old as time and the watch for the coming flocks as old as man.

On the fourth day at last the fog is gone; it is clear, and sunny. The birds are off. He is glad for them.

In the garden of the house on Rutledge Avenue, Maria watched a white peacock butterfly. It rested on the branch of the trumpet-creeper.

The thorax of the white peacock butterfly was black and shaped like the long nib of a pen. Its wings were pure white, webbed with delicate red lines, and nearly transparent. There were three black dots on each side of its segmented wings; the outside edge of the wings was trimmed like a child's bonnet with a ribbon of gold.

Sometimes it raised both wings straight up. When it did this Maria drew on the figure on the right of her paper. Every few moments it flattened its wings to the horizontal, raised and flattened them several times. When its wings were flattened she worked on the figure on the left of her paper. When the butterfly flew off she waited for it to return.

"Do you see how I work?" she said to Audubon. "The butterfly is not pinned, not tacked to a corkboard. I do not kill."

"You have no need."

"What do you know about my needs?" she said. "You take everything you want."

He watched her. She was restrained, still, alert. Her fingers were quick without ever showing a need. "Bachman writes that you are unhappy with your butterflies. I am astonished, Maria. You have been so eager to help. And so clever."

"But I do not like captivity." She raised her head and spread her hands in her lap, leaving her brush beside the paper. "Can't you see?"

He looked. The garden was in full bloom. Beyond the palings of the fence was the poultry yard. The chickens pecked in the dirt; the roosters strutted amongst them. The bees buzzed around their tall papery hives. There was a bear, as well, that Bachman had got somewhere in the wild and was raising in a cage. Its rank smell did not disturb the painter; he had often used bear grease to control his hair, although the English ladies chided him for it.

Here was the terrible alligator, also penned. And here the clearing on the ground where Audubon tested his theory about the turkey buzzards, that they came to their feed by sight and not by smell. He had made a large oil painting of a sheep lying on its side, cut open with its entrails spilling out. Beside it they put a little wheelbarrow filled with offal. They laid the painting on the ground. The buzzards came quickly. They spotted the painting from the air and flew down, alighted, and pecked at it, to be disappointed. Ten or fifteen feet away sat the wheelbarrow with what they really wanted, stinking dreadfully, but the buzzards did not see it. He had proved his point.

"What do you see?"

"A garden in the nature of a laboratory. Domesticated creatures. The bears, the alligators, the bees. And myself in it."

"I cannot for the life of me think what you mean."

Yet he could see. He himself has come to hate tamed birds. On the *Ripley* they pursue him; the tamed birds of his past haunt him.

The garden creatures all belonged to the Reverend Mr. Bachman with his white starched tongues for a collar, which hung down his chest. His friend, the man with the satisfied generous smile of a life lived beyond reproach and eyes that were a fair day's blue, a blameless blue. The hives were in the vegetable garden, which was beyond the poultry yard, along the western fence. No one went near, for fear of being stung. But Bachman could roll up his sleeves, his blameless sleeves, and put his arms right inside to draw out the honey. The bees recognized something in him: authority? entitlement? godliness?

"But these creatures are not useless," said Audubon. "They are here for our assistance."

"Exactly. They are not natural. The bear and the alligator are designed to kill, not to assist. Not to be studied. The bees to sting, not to make their honey for you. Why must I be here?"

"You are a woman." In truth, he did not like to see Maria here, not any more. Yet he could not take her away.

CAPTAIN BAYFIELD spoke in Audubon's mind. Behind him was his convenient God. *Subdue. Have dominion over.* Audubon would hotly refute this presumption made on nature by gods and man. But a woman is a woman. He was hurt, as by any suggestion that Maria might find fault with him. The butterfly rose from its perch and floated nearly weightless on a current of air.

"I thought you wished to help me."

"I am angry at you, Jean Jacques." She spoke in French. The language of his childhood disturbed him then.

"But how have I offended? By teaching you? I put up the Bittern for you to paint, that dawn when I left."

"I copied the Snowy Egret as well, and you were cross."

"I did not ask you to do that."

"You want to keep me in a cage."

"Maria. What I want of you goes unspoken, always."

"It is not what I want for myself," she said.

"Then I am mistaken. And I am sorry." He walked away, to calm himself. She spoke to him then; she had taken up her brush.

"You don't understand. I am an artist."

He turned on her. All his wildness is now decorum.

TIME SLIPPED AGAIN.

"Do I disturb you?" says Captain Bayfield, descending into the hold.

"No," lies Audubon, in the way of all artists who are disturbed.

AUDUBON BECOMES all wiliness and craft. Careful, balanced, a fencer. He would not be out of place in parliament.

"An artist, are you?" he mocked. "Can this be a state of which I lack understanding? No, Maria. You are talented. But there is talent and then there is genius. There is obsession. They don't occur in your sex. Look at the birds. The female is more docile. She tends the nest."

"And the barren female?" Maria said it harshly.

"The barren females group together. They might be found with the immature males. Sometimes if a mate is lost, one of the males will —" he stopped because she was crying.

She set down her brush. Her drawing fluttered off her lap; the butterfly rose in alarm and was gone.

"Can you imagine that I am content making little insects which you will fit into the white spaces in your paintings? Can you delude yourself into thinking it is enough for me? I too wish to be out in the world. I would tramp the woodland paths and ride ponies to the frontier. I would take the revenue cutter up the rivers to the swamps."

"Maria, I repeat, with the greatest respect, you are a woman."

"Yet not fully a woman."

She came forward to him. She stretched to her full negligible height and put her arms in a soft coil around his neck. He twisted his face aside, and the warmth of her breath floated into the hollow of his neck. "Not now, Maria," he said. The back of the house loomed over them. There was a verandah on each of three floors; servants, children walked along them. Three tiers of audience. They stepped across the path, under the large leaves of the philodendron. She turned her tiny pointed face this way and that until she was nose to nose with him. He bent over her sweet breath, her downy cheek.

"Not fully an artist, not fully a woman. Is that my fate?"

He locked his hands at the small of her back and pulled her into his chest until neither of them could breathe.

"No, Maria. It is not to be your fate."

"But what, then?"

To his mind came Jeanne Rabin, the young beauty who could neither read nor write, the graceful fiery girl who bore him and died, his father's mistress. He did not repudiate her, but celebrated her. "You can be as you are, a help and a comfort to me." He had nothing else to say. He lifted his empty hands. It meant *I want you.*

Suddenly Maria was three feet away. "You fail in your imagination, Mr. Audubon."

His arms circled empty air. "How do I fail, Maria?"

"'Drawn from Nature, by J. J. Audubon.' You write it on every watercolour. But you do not draw the birds from nature. You watch them, it is true. You adore them in nature. But they are not good enough for you that way. You have to kill them. Your birds suffer to give you your art. You don't allow them life."

"They do not suffer, Maria. To suffer is to have hope. Birds do not hope."

"Is that your final word?"

He did not understand what they were talking about.

Maria collected her brushes and colours. She took up the paper between two fingers. There was half a butterfly on it.

"Can you imagine that I would be content with this?" she taunted.

Then she was gone, so slender, so quick amongst the tropical plants. She paced toward the house alongside the peacocks that strutted in their alley. He came along behind her.

"You — and my brother-in-law. There are two of you," she said. "Old men." She had changed again. It was her teasing voice. "You fight over my kisses. For you it is an amusement. You must know this. I'll have one man for a husband, not two to court me. I will be an artist of the world, not of the garden."

*"Maria set down her brush. Her drawing
fluttered off her lap; the butterfly rose in alarm and was gone."*

Wild

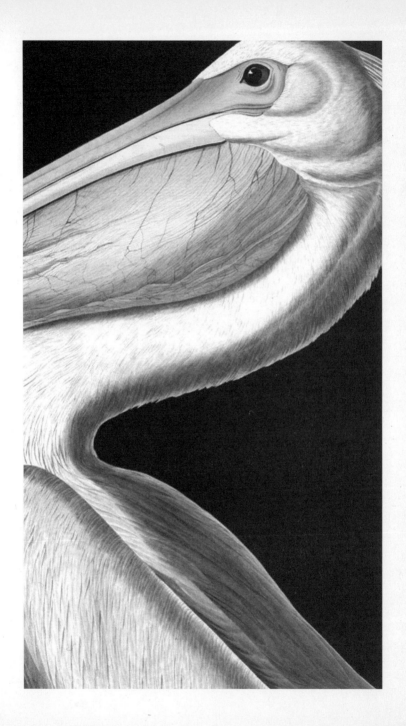

Johnny pulls his father from the cramped hold. Audubon protests. "I'm working."

"You'll work better once you've seen this."

Johnny yanks the thigh-high moccasins onto his father's feet. Audubon blinks in the unaccustomed light. There is so much sky and water, one can be blinded simply by the emptiness.

They go to the cliffs where they have seen the razorbills light, and poke sticks into the holes between the rocks. Some of these cracks or fissures are as tall as a man but not wide enough to slide into sideways. Others are the size of a fist but deeper than the sticks can probe. They find one they can crawl into. It is for this kind of adventure that the father brought the son to Labrador. Johnny is too wild, Lucy said; you must harness that energy. But now it's different — Johnny is bringing his father along.

As they make their way on hands and knees into the smooth-washed rock, birds begin to cry. Audubon would like to cover his ears but he cannot: he is using his hands for feet. The cries intensify as he crawls deeper, they echo and return; it is as if he is crawling down the throat of a bird. There is also the thrum of beating wings from farther down the wet tunnel. He makes himself as small as possible, pushing his ten-foot pole ahead of him. Birds begin to fly by his ears, trying to escape. Their panicked wings brush his face. They bash themselves into the rocky sides of the cavern. They fall and in the dark he kneels on them, squashes them under the heel of his hands. Hundreds of birds rush past him toward the air. They are crying.

"I can go no farther," he whispers to his son.

Johnny is behind. He does not hear.

"I can go no farther, son!"

"Are you tired?"

"No! I cannot breathe. You go on."

But Johnny would have to crawl over his father's body to continue. The two begin to crawl backward, still in the cloud of birds. Ahead is the laughter of the others as they scare up and spear the panicked birds. Audubon's heart beats high in his chest. Over Johnny's back he can see a bullethole of light: the opening. A dab of sky on the slick blackness. When he has gone perhaps ten more feet he looks again. The dab is slightly larger. In this way, with the crying of birds in his ears and wingtips brushing his cheeks, he gets himself out. Johnny crawls back into the crevice.

Air! Audubon crawls to the ledge, his chest heaving. He lies for a moment looking skyward, and then turns to see what they have wrought. Dazed with fear, and making their pitiful sounds, the little auks fly directly into the muskets of the sailors, who have stationed themselves just beyond the mouth of the cave and are shooting for the fun of it.

As the birds scatter and fall his heart pounds and his breath comes short with their panic. He changes places then, on that cliffside, with the birds. He imagines himself the prey and the men his pursuers.

He has done this since he was a boy. He has feared the guns, the volley of shots, the shouting, the running.

When he was nine he stood at the high windows of his father's house in Nantes. The soldiers of the Commune pointed their muskets at people in the streets and fired. The explosions ricocheted off the grey stone walls and people fled in panic. He stayed in the window and saw, through the smoke, the lucky ones escaping, running uphill.

And before that, in Santo Domingo, he ran from guns, only hip high to the dark women with their flowered skirts who dragged him through the narrow rows of sugar cane. Behind him were brandished torches, shouts, and blood-chilling screams.

But he is a man now, and no soldiers, no overseers, pursue him. He has his gun. He is furthest from being the victim when he has his gun.

He lies a minute, feeling strange, and faint. Then he kicks himself to his feet and takes up his musket. Soon they have a pile of birds on the rocks.

ON THE SHORE by the anchorage, the cook and the boy pluck the birds' feathers. Johnny has a basket of eggs. Each one is pure white, with one end dotted with blackish red spots.

"Deep in the crevice we found many eggs lying close together, deposited on heaps of stones. Do you see how clever the birds are? In this way, when the water rushes down the cavern, it flows beneath them through the rocks, and so the eggs are not ruined," says Johnny.

"How many eggs in a group?" asks Audubon.

"We know each lays only one egg and yet, deep in the crack, we found two under almost every bird."

"Because the place is more secure?" says Audubon. "Or less?"

He reaches down again to Johnny's sack and takes out a young live auk. It is tiny, its bill showing nothing of the huge thick curve which it will take on in adulthood. The chick is soft and downy. It looks blindly into his eyes and chirps, air whistling faintly through its bill. He offers his finger. The little bird snaps at it, taking it between the top and bottom of its bill as if it were a shrimp. He tries to remove his finger from the bill of the chick, but he cannot. He stands and lets the little bird dangle from his finger by its own strength.

He shakes his hand but the chick does not drop off. He puts his fingers around its little throat and presses. Still the bill does not open.

It would rather choke than let go.

Robert Havell lifts the watercolour of the White Pelican out of its wooden packing box. Audubon has outdone himself. The work gets better and better.

The White Pelican is defiant against the night sky. Behind it, a canopy of trees closes over the inlet. The pelican's big muscular body exudes strength and pride and a kind of amoral energy. It dares the onlooker to be its equal.

And Havell finally realizes that for Audubon the pelican, the bird, is not the subject of the painting. The subject is a state of being. Wild. The pelican is a creature of it, inviolate. He is crude, custodial. He is standing in the present. The future is to the left of the page, where his eyes are fixed. Statuesque, even comical in his particularity, he neither bends to it nor retreats, but challenges it to envelop him.

And when it does, the bird will rise on those contraptions he calls wings and flap awkwardly away.

Havell has never seen a White Pelican, or an Ivory-billed Woodpecker, or indeed most of the birds he engraves. They live across the Atlantic, in a land he knows only from letters, a land created as backdrop to birds, as far as he can tell.

He has never been to Labrador, or to Florida, where Audubon saw this bird, or to Charleston, where he completed this painting in the home of his friend John Bachman, aided by Lucy, Johnny, and the mysterious Maria Martin. Robert Havell spends all his days in his shop at 77 Oxford Street in grimy London. He has remained there since he began this work, which has become his life.

This has not stopped him from creating landscapes for the birds found by his employer in America. He has engraved meandering swamps, threatening thunderclouds, crescent waterfalls, ice-bound rocks and even the tiny rims of city dwellings. Audubon not only allows this but increasingly has come to rely on it as he races to finish his enormous book. Havell adds flowers and insects where these have not already been added by others. He sets stages for the birds, which, to him, are actors; he creates his own landscapes.

London is grey and ugly and dead. Increasingly Havell finds the city to be a vacancy, in contrast to the wild creatures in their dense wooded hideouts, in their mad costumes of coloured feathers. The vision of a bombastic stranger, as alternately harsh and affectionate as his father was, and not so much older than himself, has taken over his world.

Today he will engrave the plate of the White Pelican.

EARLIER IN THE MORNING he sent two boys to the coppersmith's in Shoe Lane, Holborn. They carried the plate back along the streets, between them; at thirty inches by forty inches, it is awkward and heavy. The boys then heated it over the fire, and when it was so hot that they needed gloves to touch it, they took it out of the fire and laid it on a table, where they rubbed the polished side of it with etching wax. They warmed the plate again to make the wax flow, took it off the fire again, and dabbed it all over with the dabber. Then they suspended the plate from the ceiling by four chains, one in each corner. Now, hung overhead this way, it is ready for him.

He positions himself underneath. He takes four wax tapers tied together, lights them and holds them over his head. Standing directly beneath the plate, he looks up. His tail of hair, tied at the nape of his neck, hangs down his back. He positions himself with one foot forward and one back, and one fist pressed into the base of his spine to lessen the back pain. Looking up, he begins to heat the plate, moving his torch hand back and forth so the flame blackens the wax that will be the etching ground. He never lets the flame stand still, as it would burn the wax.

When the plate is blackened, he steps away to let it grow cold, at which point it will be ready to receive the bird.

The White Pelican waits. He fills the huge page with his deep chest and a profile that strains credibility. The White Pelican is not white at all but brilliant yellow. The big yellow sac under his bill and his fierce eye are balanced, at rear, by a ducktail of soft yellow. Havell does not fail to register that this bird was painted after Audubon met Maria Martin. The artist has become more dramatic, more confident. He has been aware of the difference for some time now. In the past year Audubon's birds have ceased to be illustrations. With the pelican, the artist has managed to give the scientific information he prides himself on giving in a backhanded way; he's not looking at, but inside, this big bird. The picture is bird *qua* bird.

HAVELL WILL MAKE a new background for the pelican. He has the entry for the letter press, which Audubon has written: "Ranged along the margins of a sand-bar, in broken array, stand a hundred heavy-bodied Pelicans," he reads. These are the artist's words, or perhaps the artist's words as Lucy has rewritten them, Lucy herself never having seen the birds. "The Pelicans drive the little fishes toward the shallow shore, and then, with their enormous pouches spread like so many bag-nets, scoop them out and devour them in thousands."

He comes upon this phrase:

"Pluming themselves, the gorged Pelicans patiently await the return of hunger."

He stops over this notion: that the birds, driven only by their creature needs, should be sated, stop and stand motionless; "as if by sympathy, all in succession open their long and broad mandibles, yawning lazily and ludicrously." At dusk, Audubon has written, hunger returns to reanimate them.

He wonders if this can be true. If Audubon actually saw it, or if, in his story-telling, he has invented the scene. It is a wonderful notion, to the diligent Havell, confined to his London shop, that creatures live only to gratify their immense desires. *Await the return of hunger.* He envies the bird.

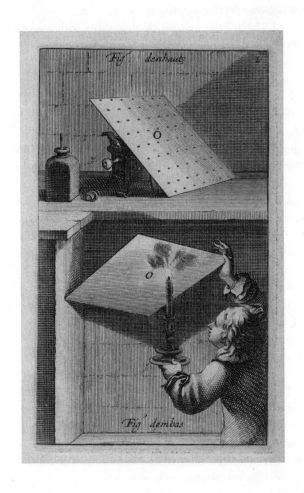

"He never lets the flame stand still, as it would burn the wax."

NOW THAT THE COPPER PLATE is ready, Havell has choices as to how he will transfer the watercolour image to it.

He could trace the original on thin paper with lead pencil, and then wet the back of the tracing paper with a sponge, putting its face to the etching ground. Then he could run the plate through his press to get an impression of the original.

Or he might trace the painting with a quill pen and India ink onto tissue paper oiled with linseed and then fix this tracing against the plate. Having done that, he would take a chalked paper, first brushing all the excess dust off it with a feather, and lay it on the plate, fold the ink version of the drawing over and trace all the lines again, leaving outlines on the plate.

But these tracing methods will leave the drawing reversed. The pelican will be looking to the viewer's right, not his left. Havell is certain this would be wrong.

He could copy the pelican by eye, using a grid. And this is what he finally does, confident he will create an exact replica of the original. If he makes a mistake he can varnish it over with a camel's hair pencil dipped in stopping varnish, wait ten minutes, and begin again. He will enjoy the process, a pleasure marred only by the fact that, since Audubon is insisting on more plates, and quicker, he will have to rush.

The etching itself is simple: he uses the needle as he would a pencil and cuts into the copper only lightly, keeping all his lines the same depth. The acid for the aquatint will make the lines deeper. When he has finished drawing, or redrawing, the bird, Havell adds the background.

He sets about to make the wall of wax. He takes an earthen pot half full of water on the fire and puts some wax into the water. He warms it over the fire until, testing it against the skin inside his wrist, he finds it is the temperature of new milk.

He likes this feeling. New milk brings good memories to his mind. When he himself was in the wild (at least the wilds of Monmouthshire), when he had run away from his father's prohibitions and expectations, he would stop by farms and ask for breakfast. The farmer would bring him a cup of milk, foaming, still fresh from the barn. He recalls his luxuriant young man's loneliness. The bolstering kindness from a stranger's hands, morning after morning, as he formed the will to prove his father wrong. He would be an artist.

And he *is* an artist.

He takes the wax into his hands and makes it into a long, flat strip. He warms one edge of this again, and presses it around the border of the plate, making a protective wall to keep the wash in, using his finger, which he wets in the water to make certain the wax sticks to the plate.

VICTOR STANDS BESIDE HIM with a leather bag full of papers pertaining to the finances, and a vertical pleat between his eyebrows.

Havell wipes his hands on his apron and comes forward.

"Good day, Victor," he says to the quiet young man. "I shall be with you in a moment." He is just ready to do the first biting: this is for the farthest point in the distance in the landscape, the high canopy of trees where the last bit of light is leaving the sky. He retrieves the aqua fortis, which he has made by mixing spirits of nitre one part to four parts water, and pours it on the plate. It will sit for three minutes. He times it on his stopwatch, a gift from his uncle, the drawing master. After he sets the watch he looks up and smiles.

"Have you good news or bad?"

"Only this: Father says we must go more quickly. The institutions which have the first numbers are threatening to cancel because the early pages are wearing out before the later ones are produced!"

"I know what he wants. But I cannot go more quickly than this. In the first six years I worked for your father, I produced twenty-five plates a year; now I am producing fifty a year — that is one every week."

"He says we must do better, faster," repeats Victor helplessly.

"If he had money to pay for an assistant, I could."

WHEN THE ALLOTTED time has passed, Havell stops out the lightest parts with varnish No. 1. He will let it dry for exactly half an hour. They go to the next room, where the colourists are working. On their easels are prints of the Yellow-crowned Night-Heron.

With Victor beside him, Havell walks down the rows. There are, at present, thirty-six colourists. They are the poor; some elderly men, a few women and boys. He does not pay them enough; he cannot. It is Audubon who has to make the payroll every week and when he is in the wilds Victor collects the dues from the wealthy subscribers. It is very simple. When Nathan Mayer Rothschild does not pay his bill, these people do not eat. When Stewart died, the former head colourist and a genius of sorts, Havell saw him buried in a pauper's grave and had only a pound to give to his wife and child. This is perhaps why his father wished him to take up the law.

Once, he had Audubon go to the slums to deliver some money owing to the ginger-haired woman behind whom he now stands. Audubon was appalled to see the barricaded alley she called her rooms, and to see her send her younger children out to work. "What do they work at?" he asked, for the children were under six years old.

"They beg," said the mother.

"I cannot bear to be in London," Audubon announced when he returned. "This is why I would live amongst the birds."

But there is no answer for it. The colourists are paid all the profession will bear. They have work in this shop only because Havell promised to produce for less than anyone else. As much as Audubon's compassion runs deep, his desire to create *The Birds* runs deeper. When the colouring is poor, the subscribers complain. When they complain, they cancel. Audubon gets angry, and someone loses her job. Now Havell himself supervises; there will be no more complaints.

He looks over the shoulder of the ginger-haired woman. Her hand trembles slightly; he feels the tension in her shoulders as she tries to control it. She is frightened; her very life depends on this.

"Let me show you what I want," Havell says gently to the woman. And he leaves the room, to return with the original. "Do you see how the male in full summer dress has such distinct lines of white and black over his eyes? We must make those lines stand out."

"The paint is thin, sir," she says. "I can do more layers but it sinks into the paper."

"You are right. So why not use gouache? The lead will keep the colour on the surface." He steps away to get a tube, passing another woman, to whom he says kindly, "That is lovely work, Clara."

At the end of the line is a child who is working on the similac vine, which is twined around the branch of the dead tree the two Herons perch in.

"Green, more green," Havell says. "You must paint five or six layers to make it truly vibrant. And stay within the lines!"

"But I gets dizzy, they winds so," the child says.

Havell laughs. He nearly became lost himself while etching the vine as it wraps the branch.

"The botanical bit has been supplied by Miss Martin," murmurs Havell to Victor. "I am told I shall receive more botanical illustrations from her. And I am to send her some paper, the Whatman Turkey, the same that he uses himself."

Neither man has never met the highly controversial Maria Martin. But Havell feels a certain kinship to her. He has copied her blossoms, her butterflies, her luna moth, her peacock butterfly. He enters her imagination when he does so, as much as he enters Audubon's imagination when he does the birds. They are very different places.

"Ah yes," Victor says politely. "She is rather good." But more importantly, there is some extraordinary sympathy between his father and the woman. Victor feels the energy and resents it. If not Maria herself, then a version of her is familiar to him as an aspect of his father's behavior; he has long been his mother's confidant.

The boy's green gets greener. "Fine, fine," Havell says.

"Miss Martin's leaves are lovely," says Victor grudgingly.

"Yes," says Havell. Her vines curl and cling. Her leaves have sumptuous waving movements. They are not as bold as the birds but they are insistent, and sensuous; they have a green life to them, which seems to him female and unstoppable and which in his mind has become equally a part of this new world, America, with its rainbow of birds.

"Tell me, in truth," says Havell to Victor, "do these creatures actually live in America?"

He is being seduced by the place.

HAVELL HURRIES back to his plate. Finding it dry, he applies the aqua fortis for the second biting. This will be the middle distance, the waters of the swamp as they wind backward. The second biting is on for seven minutes and then stopped and dried, and then he does the near distance. He leaves this on for twelve minutes. Then he stops and dries it.

Throughout this procedure, Victor speaks of some attack on his father that has been launched in a scientific journal. Another scandal threatens to erupt: it has been discovered that certain of the bird skins his father has submitted to the establishments are not genuine, but have been doctored with horsehair. He believes this hoax to have been played by an enemy, a young boy who once worked for Audubon. He seeks Havell's advice, as one who is familiar with the learned artistic circles of England.

Havell gives a sympathetic ear. Not long ago he was a young man who quarrelled with his father and went, sketchbook in hand, to the River Wye to ramble and paint the medieval ruins. He was happy then in a strange, wounded way, and the woods and the crumbling constructions of stone were a refuge against the world. He was away and had chosen to be away and a passionate hurt and attachment gave power to his watercolours. He is half tempted to tell the young man he should run away to find himself, but, mindful of the need for everyone to pull together on the massive work, he stays silent.

The etching finished, he puts the plate back on the fire. When the wax wall has softened he pulls it off and, as the etching ground melts, washes it off with turpentine. He now has to clean the plate. He does this by rubbing oil on it. Others would have the boys do it but he insists on doing it himself. The plate must not be scratched. When he is satisfied that it is clean he brushes it, then wipes off the wet with a clean cloth and dries it very carefully.

The truth is, he likes to put his hands on the warmth of it, the silky clean copper, the thick blue-black ink. He imagines himself a cook, mixing substances to the right consistency. The hard labour combines with these sensory pleasures to tire him, heat him up, leave him dirty and exhilarated by the end of the day.

Now that it is ready for grounding, he stands the plate on a slant in a tin pan and pours the ground over it so that it runs down. When the ground has all run into the pan he turns the plate end to end and pours the ground back the other way. It settles finest on the part where the sky is to be. He sets the plate nearly flat on a table and wipes off extra grains from the bottom.

This is the very difficult part, and depends much on the weather. If the day is too cold the ground will run all over the plate and show no breaks. He has to heat the workshop with a stove then, which adds to the cost. If the day is too hot, the ground will behave in the same way. Today the temperature is perfect, mild.

"He sent me another stinging letter," Victors says, apropos of nothing.

"He did? Of what did he complain?"

"That I must pursue subscriptions more avidly, that I have not sent certain guns and gifts to people he named, that I have not hurried you enough."

"You must not mind," says Havell. "He expects a great deal of you, and you are young. He is on fire to finish his book."

"But I do mind."

"Ah, fathers. I had this difficulty with my own. I tried to escape him, but I bore the name; what could I do?" They have been over this territory before.

"Exactly," cries Victor. "How much must my name determine?"

"Everything is in a name and one cannot escape it."

"I disagree. A name is entirely arbitrary," says Victor crossly. "I was never good enough for him, anyway."

"I think it may be exactly the opposite," says Havell. "A father always wants his son to be better than he, but only in what he is not."

"The name has eaten my life," says Victor. "This is not what I wanted."

"What did you want?"

"I do not know."

"That is your difficulty then," says Havell, in a matter-of-fact way. "As you did not have a passion, you were consumed by his."

Victor cannot argue. It is as if his father has taken the positive position and Victor has been forced all his life into the negative. He has had to say no. And yet he could not. Victor's words spurt from him and he paces in the workshop. "The Yoke of Man, he calls it, that he must make his way in this world and provide for us all! But it is our yoke now, for he does what he is called to do while my brother and my mother and I must do for him what need be done! And we are never good enough!"

Havell lifts up his head from his drying and polishing, wipes his hands on his smock, and stands erect to stretch his back.

"He is equally demanding of himself," he observes.

It is time to apply the resin for the aquatint ground. For this, Havell must place the huge copper plate on its edge, slanting upward in a tip pan. The foreground side of the plate with the pelican's "columnar legs," as Audubon calls them, is at his face; the sky is down.

The spirit ground is made of red wine and resin. He puts the resin in the wine when he brings the jug to the shop, so he can be sure the workers will not drink it. Now he pours on enough to cover the plate. With the smell of wine in their noses, the two men stand together watching the ground run down. When it has covered every inch of the surface, together they turn it around so that the ground runs back up the plate. It must settle finest on the sky and most thickly on the bird itself. Havell takes his dabber and touches it up, leaving Victor to hold the plate.

When he has done this they lie the plate nearly flat on the table, and wipe off the extra ground, which has gathered at the bottom. When the alcohol has evaporated so that the plate is dry, Havell strengthens the ground by heating the huge plate once more over the fire.

"I am glad to have another pair of hands to lift the plate," he says. "Now you see why we complain of the double elephant format."

"But it is the best to display my father's genius," says Victor. His anger has dissipated. The room is now warm from the charcoal brazier and the windows clouded with smoke. Havell puts him to work grinding Frankfort black on the stone to make the ink. To the ground black and the linseed oil and the treacle, Havell adds a bit of Persian blue.

He takes the ink from Victor and applies it to the warm copper plate. With the other watching, he carefully rubs the ink into each tiny crevice and burr and then cleans the surface so that only the fine lines are inked. He dampens the paper and carries it to the rolling press, where he lays it on the plate. Once it is in place Havell puts his shoulder to the wheel that moves the upper roller. He bends like an ox to his burden, using all his weight to move the roller along the length of the paper.

The two men are completely silent as they wait for the great cheeks of the press to open.

When they remove the paper they stand back to look.

And there it is, the White Pelican. In black on white.

COUNTING

———

In six weeks I have seen the eggs laid, the birds hatched, their first moult half over, their association in flocks and preparations begun for their leaving the country.

—*Journals*, J. J. Audubon

———

North is the negative of south. North is the nesting ground, the first feathers; south is full plumage. Labrador is black and white while Charleston is colour. Here, down north, the white rims along the shore are crushed shells; sea urchins dissolve underfoot. There is the occasional gleam of sun, and a white wooden cross here and there down by the water, as if a sailor had died at sea and his fellows marked the nearest place. There are hummocky dunes flocked with blue and green grasses. By the woods there is fireweed and the white plumes of Queen Anne's lace.

Labrador is the proof, the first print pulled from the press. North is the unpainted version. It is created by taking away.

THE CURLEWS ARE GONE but Audubon still walks the smooth crescent beach of Bras d'Or. As he walks, birds of all description depart in
clouds above his head.

It is only the beginning of August but the razorbills, the guillemots and the kittiwakes are going south. The young Arctic terns dart
restlessly with their parents, ready to go too. Remaining are the
immense and quarrelsome gannets, shouldering each other off their
breeding rocks. The young are a speckled grey, long-winged and
gawky. They flap their wings incessantly, letting small soft feathers —
the last of their down — drift into the air. Once they are strong enough,
they too will be off, abandoning this place to a depth of winter he cannot imagine.

Summer is so short that it might never have happened. Six weeks
only. Summer flowers are emerging even as summer birds are leaving.

In going south, the birds go to Maria. To her colours, her fra-
grance, her summer. It is a kind of exile he suffers here.

So too his youth will be gone. It has lingered; he has kept it, far
past his just desserts, far past what is natural, kept it even when he
knew in his bones in his numb fingers in his lungs that it was leaving.
Propelled as he was by the desire to cover the territory his birds covered, he could not rest.

THE SUMMER'S harvest of fish lies drying on flakes that have been
built a little way up from the water's edge, thousands upon thousands
of curling bodies. At the far end of the beach is an impromptu rendering station where the giant corpse of a whale is slung across the sand;
men climb on it, slicing away the blubber with great sickle blades.
There are firepits and copper cauldrons; blubber is boiling. There are
stacks of baleen with flesh still caught between the fibres.

Some of the whalers are black men from the Antilles; he is
warmed by their speech, their red bandanas, their tattered leggings.
Brandings on their necks mark these as the slaves among whom he
once lived. But now they are free men. He can read it in the looseness
of their step and the swing of the great knives, in their shouts of greeting. His life, he supposes, could be read as a flight from blackness. But

now the dark of their skin looks familiar. He wonders how he would greet, if he could greet, his mulatto half-sisters, one dead, one long ignored in France.

The whalers sing as they work. The voices are the same ones that rise over the harbour at night. But the day songs are different from the night songs. The night songs are rueful or lusty. The day songs are work songs, every second line shouted with a great surge of power to send the knife more quickly through the slab of whale flesh.

> *Renzo took a notion, Renzo, boys, Renzo,*
> *That he would plough the ocean,*
> *Renzo, boys, Renzo!*

Walking on, Audubon stops by a dory roped to the side of a shallop. A raggedy, garrulous group of Eggers is drinking there. The man nearest him is gaunt and weathered and toothless; he looks forty but has the voice of a young boy. He raises his cup and boasts to the stranger that they have eight hundred dozen eggs in the hold.

"Show me, then," says Audubon, hopeful disbelief in his voice.

The hold is a pit, shot through with arrows of light from the broken deckboards above. The eggs are stacked ten foot deep in baskets, old barrels, and slings of burlap. The shells are pasted with slime, gore and feathers. They are faint, faint in the dank hold. They mourn like stolen children and Audubon makes an involuntary sound of grief.

Mistaking this for awe, the Egger modestly asserts they've done well. "The birds keeps laying if you steals from them," he says. "Stupid things."

"I wish that the stupid man who says this were half as wise as the birds he despises," says Audubon.

He lurches into daylight. There is a numbness in his fingertips. He thought it was the cold but today, walking, he is quite warm and still he can feel nothing. He walks farther along the beach through the carnival atmosphere but he is not merry. They wait here to see if a guide can take them overland toward Hudson's Bay. It was his plan, but daily it seems more difficult. The tireless jabber goes on in his mind: how have Lucy's nerves survived his absence? Has Victor collected the Trash? Has Havell increased his pace and has the colouring improved?

IN THE TRADING POST, Audubon skulks amongst the goods while the faithful Captain Emery attempts to get information. "Where can we find a guide to take us overland to Hudson's Bay?" he asks the storekeeper.

"It's late in the year for that. Maybe Pamack could take you but he is gone to Torngat. Maybe Billie Parr. But I haven't seen him since spring."

"It is for my friend. He is the greatest bird artist of our time."

"That one?" says the storekeeper.

And Audubon is shocked into awareness of himself, how he must look: his beard, frizzy and untrimmed. His moccasins, stiff and muddied; his rough trousers, patched and sewn with a sailor's thick fingers and now barely hanging on his thin frame. His sore and red-rimmed eyes, which have strained themselves to see in the dark and to sleep in the long light.

The agent of the Fish and Fur Company is evasive, like a pirate not wanting anyone to know where his treasure is buried, fearful for his profits, no doubt. Amongst piles of seal skins and caribou skins Audubon comes upon the hide of a white bear. He admires it. But it is too expensive.

"The white bear is fearsome. They ride down from the top of the world on ice floes," says the agent. "We had the white whale, too, the beluga, but they're gone now."

"Gone?"

"The walrus and the bowhead, too, we don't see 'em any more. They used to come down with their calves from up north, this was their getaway. Seal, that's another matter. No shortage of seals."

Unwelcome notions knock against Audubon's heart. It is the intrusion of man here, it is the harvesting, the relentless harvesting from this land and these waters. He fears that Labrador will become, when these men are done, a worn-out, broken-down field. He fears that her native peoples will have their livelihood wrested from them, and they will fade out like the wild creatures.

He longs to speak to his friend Bayfield. He longs for his steadiness, his reassurances, his orderly way of thought.

What if, he wants to ask him, you come to the wild and discover that it is not wild at all? What if half the world is here before you? Men taking from the coast what they can, who have been doing so for as long as living memory and longer than that? And what if this taking exceeds the ability of the coast to give?

What if you begin to understand that your presence, no matter what your mission, is only the presence of a man, and nothing better? It is like that of the greedy Eggers, and can do nothing but lead to the end of this fertile wilderness? What if you can see a day when Labrador will be emptied, shorn, strained, drained of every living thing, even the original peoples?

What then? He has asked it before. Where will I go to visit the wilderness?

He hears the absent Bayfield: Am I to understand that wilderness must find its best expression as a refuge for you?

No, not just for me. In being itself. Unmolested.

Why might not this wilderness become a settled place, with commerce and trade for its inhabitants?

Because then we will lose the creatures. Lose the wild itself.

I thought you hated Labrador.

You said it would change me.

AT NIGHT, Audubon sits over his work. He hears the singing from the foredeck. The Newfoundland sailors are teaching the others "The Ghost Crew." One brave tenor rises above the flutes and fiddles.

> *Right o'er our rail came climbing, all silent, one by one,*
> *A dozen hardy sailors. Just wait 'til I am done.*
> *Their faces pale and sea-worn, all ghostly through the night,*
> *Each fellow took his station as if he had a right.*

It is Johnny, of course. So light and carefree, amongst his friends. Yet the face he turns to his father is weighed down and severe. The wildness hides in him, wanting to break out.

Audubon and the captain decide that it would be foolhardy to attempt to go overland to Hudson's Bay. And they can go no farther by water at this time of year.

He is tired tonight, and tumbles into a hammock, sleeping without dreams.

THE NEXT MORNING, as he is taking his dawn walk on deck, Audubon notices Anonyme, silent and withdrawn, in a corner behind a windlass. He realizes that he has lost interest in his pet, and has ignored him for weeks. Perhaps the raven misses his attention. He is alternately hopping toward the railings and running away. In his corner he caws, pecks himself, tries to fly and gives up. Going closer, Audubon sees what has affected the bird. A raven flies over and around the schooner calling insistently. She lands in her clumsy way on the masts, flaps amongst the ropes, flies raggedly off, and returns. She is calling to Anonyme. The tame bird is disturbed by the call, hopping toward it, climbing the masts, perching on the bowsprit to hear her. Audubon speaks to his pet but the raven is past hearing a human voice and, finally, he answers the call. He jumps off the bowsprit and falls, with his clipped wings, to the water. By the time Audubon gets the whaleboat down to him, the bird has drowned.

He is grief-stricken.

"My raven has committed suicide," Audubon writes to Maria. "It is an omen. He answered the call of another raven and jumped from the bow. But a tamed bird can neither fly nor swim. Down he sank freighted with my stories. Perhaps that will be the end of them."

THEN, LIKE A GIFT from the top of the world, it comes.

He sees the iceberg loom out of the mist. It is wet with sun melt, and gleaming in the early rays from the east. Unstable on its beam, its prisms shift and flash green. It is fugitive colour: he could not catch it if he wanted to. Before his eyes and as he ponders it, it begins to tilt and then, slowly, tumbles over itself, making a mad roar as it rips the water.

When, that afternoon, the fog clamps down on them, it is unnerving to know that the iceberg is out there drifting. But from far out comes again the sound of cannons firing. "There she is! The *Gulnare*, out in the Strait," cries Audubon jubilantly.

Godwin listens. "Aye," he says, "that's her. That's the Royal British Navy. Letting us know she's out there so she don't get hit in the fog."

EXULTANT, Bayfield has been exploring the Strait, from L'Anse-aux-Morts back to Bras d'Or. L'Anse-au-Clair has sandy beaches ruled over by outraged gulls. He dares the icebergs, the storms, the fog. Each time he sees the ripple, feels the chill of Arctic air as he crosses it, he watches the colour, the texture and speed of the water change. He has discovered a seam in the ocean.

Now he is somewhere in the middle.

He stands on deck in the fog feeling no impatience to escape it. This absence is new and puzzles him. He thinks of Collins, the crunch of his chin when the launch drove into him, his body floating white and distended in this same huge body of water. He thinks of the cargo of brilliant watercolours in the dark hold of the *Ripley*. He is proud to have seen them before the rest of the world does.

IN FLIGHT the black hawk could almost be mistaken for the Peregrine Falcon, but with broader wings and a longer tail. It flies higher, and is more majestic. It halts itself directly over the crouching, chubby bird. Then, certain of victory, it catapults down, down, lethal, screaming, the talons so large they encircle, puncture, and carry off the little bird in one savage motion. Johnny has not had time to get it in his sights.

"We must have that hawk," his father cries, furious. "How can you have let it go? It may be the Gyrfalcon."

The next day Audubon walks with Johnny and Tom Lincoln down the coast near a waterfall. High on a cliff above them they see the black hawk again. It thunders down over their heads with a nasal, begging cry: *KHYa KHYa KHYa*. A second bird dives on them following its mate, but it too is gone.

Tom and Audubon wait, lying on the rocks until they seem to have become part of the landscape. Johnny climbs the waterfall to reach the top of the cliff. The rocks beside are wet with spray. He clings here and there, becoming smaller as he zigzags to the top. Audubon watches him. He does not call to him to get down from there, it's dangerous. He wants the bird.

"He might slip," says Tom Lincoln. "I'll go after him." He does not say, *No bird is worth* . . . That has been said before, to ill effect.

Audubon lies on the rocks. He is counting. He has twenty-two drawings of birds, done or partly done. He has collected seventy-three skins, although he is worried about their condition because of the relentless damp. He has not found the Labrador Duck, only that empty nest near Mr. Jones's estate. And he has neither seen nor heard of a Great Auk.

The *Ripley* is costing $350 a month. The young gentlemen are paying three dollars week for board. He has had the vessel victualled for five months with potatoes, rice, beans, beef, pork, butter, cheese and coffee. They have been out so far forty-eight days between June 17 and August 5, the same number of days as there are years of his life. This seems to him significant. There has been rain, fog and storm on at least twenty-five of these days.

Counting, said Bayfield, is hope. Yet Audubon has never found it that way. To him, it is fidgeting, a kind of mental scratching of his sore places. He counts to reassure himself, and to keep track of his enterprise. He counts his debts and the money which is due him. Subscriptions lost and subscriptions gained. Counts his enemies and those close to him. Their deeds and misdeeds. Counts the people who are both friend and foe; Charles Bonaparte, of the royal connections and vinegar-soaked epistles; even Bachman, his dearest friend, who, although married to her sister, holds Maria in his grasp. While he, poor Audubon, similarly wived and yoked, cannot have her. Counts what he came into the world with: nothing. "*Obscene child, born of whoredom.*" And what he will leave when he goes. *The Birds of America* and all it will bring.

He thinks as he lies there of how much he has given his son. How fortunate Johnny is. His own father was selfish in siring children who had no place in life. He, Jean Rabin, has had to invent himself. His own father gave him nothing but a worthless claim on property in two countries and several bogus names. Whereas Johnny will have the *Birds*.

The young man is high now, ascending the cliff, and Tom Lincoln is underneath him. The hawk, like a sorcerer, darts into view in the sky and makes one circle, then disappears. The young gentlemen do not see it, concerned as they are with where to put their hands and feet. Audubon watches without concern. Johnny is the best of his young men, fearless and footsure.

And then, just as Audubon's scanning eyes sweep past him, Johnny slips and falls. He hits a rock some ten feet below him and slides, grasping for a ledge. His grip on the ledge fails and he falls again. Feet and feet. Forever he falls, until he is nearly at the foot of his friend Tom Lincoln.

Audubon watches this dumbshow, for no sound carries against the wind that is blowing off the water. Lincoln falls to his knees, lifts his friend's head, then one foot, then another. He appears to be wiping his hands. Johnny has not moved. Audubon is on his feet and running, he has spat what remains of his lunch to one side. He is tearing the nails off his fingers as he leaps to the cliff and up the stages of rock. His breath comes hammering into his mouth; his ears ring, he cannot see and he is pulling himself up by creviced roots, into the splash water and out of it, on the slick tarry rockface. This is the man who rode the horse Barro for three days without stopping into Kentucky, fording rivers. This is he again, the stile-jumper, barrel-leaper, he who could do anything, the man of power and grace and fire. He offers a bargain to God. If Johnny is spared he will give up Maria. (Does this count if she has already given him up, which is what he also fears?) If you spare Johnny, I will shoot no more birds than are absolutely necessary.

Please God, do not do this to me.

Johnny is groaning when he reaches the spot. There is blood around his head. But his limbs lie straight. He moves.

"He's not dead," charges his father.

"No," says gentle Tom. "He is not." And he lies down on the rock and takes his friend in his arms and sobs while Audubon kneels as in a church.

Reprieve. All life flows back to him.

Barely injured, with a cut head and bruises, Johnny walks back to the ship between his friend and his father.

THEY RETURN to the spot another day. The bird makes a fateful return circle. Johnny gets a shot and captures her. Half an hour later, he shoots the mate.

Audubon carries them, one in each hand, by the legs. They are not hawks at all, but falcons, and he is sure he has found a new species: the Labrador Falcon.

He sets the birds up in the usual way. He spreads the female's wings, showing her fine breast with the complex mottling of white and dark feathers, the way they darken in the lower body between her thick feathered legs, and the inside of her fanned tail, with the rows of white dashes horizontally. Her talons are larger than her beak, the entire foot larger than her head, which he poses in profile with beak open and crimson mouth exposed. The male he poses perched above the female, looking down on her, his black back showing its white markings at the tips of the tail feathers. She is screaming, her lethal claws spread.

He sits up all night to sketch in the outline.

He spends the day after their death painting the pair. He dutifully notes all its particulars. He believes this to be a different species from the Icelandic Gyrfalcon, which is white with a great skein of black shapes spread all over its back.

"No one can doubt it now, the Labrador Falcon," he exclaims.

He has forgotten already what it nearly cost.

AT PERROQUET ISLAND the air is filled with puffins, and the choppy waves littered with them. Audubon goes out in the skiff of a Jersey fisherman named Gilbert, who promises to land.

As Gilbert's boat approaches, the birds fly boldly over it. They have a rounded shape in the air and spurt forward with sporadic wing movements. Top-heavy and preceded by their large beak, they are comic in profile. But face on, each bird is sad, its white visage divided in two halves by the beak, which is a startling red with black and yellow outlines and a solemn white clerical collar below. Each and every one has one of the long silver fish called launce dangling from its beak. They croak as they go, but this does not make them drop their cargo.

"Do you see how greedy they are?" says Gilbert. "I suppose that's why they get so fat. They're pretty good stuffed and baked." He smiles in a reminiscent way. "The young are still in the burrows. They won't fly until September and then they will go north."

The puffins circle the boat as the men approach, flying sometimes equidistant from each other in groups of four or more, maintaining formation. They settle on the water, from which they must dive or at least duck to get their prey, but they move so suddenly Audubon rarely catches them doing it; they sit on the water, and instantly are gone, then again there they are with a loaded bill where they were not before. On the rocky ledges thousands more line up, an army, regiment on regiment. As soon as one lot flies upward it is replaced by another.

Audubon laughs at their antics. They defend the island angrily and vigorously, but at the last moment, seeing the guns, they abandon their homes. The black-backed gulls that prey on them are not so easily frightened and stand at the top of the pile of rocks protesting vociferously.

The island is made of granite blocks pushed upward to make an unruly pile, leaving cracks and holes crested with soft grass. Audubon walks up the rocks, which are like steps. Higher up, the ground cover is spongy moss with a thick crop of ferns. Underneath, in burrows like rat holes, are the nests. He bends; sometimes the head of an adult bird is there in the opening. But the nest and the young are far down the tunnels. Putting his ear to the ground, he can hear their cries from the deep underground warrens. As he walks over the island their cries penetrate the mossy tents, eerily, like voices from the grave.

Audubon is tired of sadness. Tired of the death of nature, which he can feel, prickling under his skin. Foresight is painful. He would rather be blind. Standing on the rise of the granite island with its sparse tufts of moss, he tries to forget what he has learned, that man will kill the beasts with his greed. It is too much for one man to know. This land is wide, the energy beating at it merciless. "You cannot make a dint in this plenty," Bayfield said. Andubon forgets the promise he made to God when Johnny fell, the promise to shoot no more birds than necessary. He has forgotten God, now that he has no need for him.

This is what he does. What he did. Despite what he felt, what he wrote, what he has come to understand. He did, and he does it all over again.

He raises his rifle, loads and shoots into the flock of circling, frantic puffins. One falls. He laughs. He loads and shoots again. Another. He cannot miss. Faster now he raises his gun. Shoots another. And another. He is laughing and shooting all at once. He shoots twenty-seven times and kills twenty-seven birds. Gilbert stands by, watching respectfully. They take another dozen alive.

"Not bad," says Johnny.

"How's that, Bachman?" Audubon shouts into the wind to his shooting partner. "Not bad, wouldn't you say?"

The Human
FASCINATION WITH BIRDS

It is the dog watch, and the tars are amusing themselves on deck. They have learned how to make the puffins race. They are crouched at the rope which serves as a finish line, laying bets. The little birds skid underfoot, and watch the humans, looking hard at their eyes. Audubon walks blindly through their midst.

Someone is praying. *Surely goodness and mercy shall follow me all the days of my life . . .* He hates prayer.

HE HAS THE BIRD in hand. The warmth of life still in her, though he has shot her, neatly, behind the head.

How to tell what a bird is:

A bird is constructed this way.

It comes apart this way.

It comes in two sexes differing in the following ways.

It produces young which are.

Its entrails are.

The inner cavity is.

It lays eggs of this colour, shape, size and number.

Its habitat is.

Its habits are.

What else is a bird? Something more. That animated mystery, that flying spark lives somewhere in the bird. He pins back the wings. He tears off a feather. He draws it along his cheek to feel the texture. He pulls out the guts. He tries to blow through its cavity. There is nothing there.

The time when he was one with the bird is all that ever was. And when the bird is gone it will be as if that time never happened.

THE YOUNG GENTLEMEN stand before him. They have found a whaling schooner called the *Wizard* from Boston, which is carrying letters for them all.

There are no post offices in the wilderness before us —

There are two envelopes. One, he sees, is from Lucy.

Audubon is bone weary. He has been, some days, seventeen hours at his drawing table, where the rain drips off the glass onto his watercolours. He is beyond missing Lucy. He has rehearsed his life from beginning to now, and released himself from it. Only if he, like the birds, lives in the continuous present can the hauntings of the past be put to rest. Then he can go to Maria. But if he is not like the birds, if he is an ox or a man, then he is caught in the yoke and must stay with Lucy.

He opens Lucy's letter.

The date is July 1. Such a long time ago. Five weeks. Lucy writes that she has suffered greatly from toothache and has had two more of her teeth removed. Ord has attacked him again in the Philadelphia papers; she has collected dues from six American subscribers but three others have cancelled. There are still no more than twenty subscribers in his own country. She is lonely without him and her sons, and she hopes he has suffered no further consequences of the spell he took after suffocating the golden eagle —

He is skimming, reading too fast to absorb what she says. He holds the other letter in his hand. He opens it finally, his hands not working properly.

Bachman writes:

"I have discovered a new bird — a little sparrow —"

He, down in Charleston? It seems unfair and already Audubon is angry. But there is more.

"Our sweetheart wishes me to tell you that she had made several drawings of plants for you and that the portfolio and quire of middle-sized paper you had shipped from London have arrived, much to her delight. She sends her kisses — as many as she can spare from me — not very many, I guess!

"But on a more serious note, I enclose her final letter to you. My wife took the liberty of showing me your correspondence with Maria. It is one thing for me to jest about her affectionate nature. It is improper for you to address yourself to her in the intimate manner of your last letter, sent from Boston. From now on her assistance to you, and your correspondence, shall be carried on through me."

Audubon is standing on the deck of the *Ripley* at Bras d'Or, Labrador. He had made himself a creature of the unhaunted present, in a place with a past but no history, sailing always proud and naked before the mast. Now his friend is chiding him about kisses. How easily he is called back, cut down from his heights. He is furious.

There is a paper folded inside Bachman's letter. It is from Maria.

"Non," she has written. "Impossible, no matter what you say. If you are a man who could lay aside his duties as did my father, then how could I love you? And if I loved you, which I surely do, then you cannot be such a man and I cannot allow you to betray your better instincts."

He stares at the message from Maria, there on the rocky lip of Labrador. "As did my father," he repeats. That was it. Her dreadful father, Mr. Martin with the watch chain stretched across his belly. She may not love who would do as he did, abandon his legitimate wife and children for a new lover, run away and seize a little of the world's too elusive sweetness.

Yet the man who feels the pull to do so is perhaps the only man she can love.

And *his* father? What of Jean Audubon? He too went beyond the bounds. Yet he embraced the contradictions that were his life, he did not deny himself what he wanted.

He crumples the letter. She has rejected him.

He feels her giving way under his hands, but that is not the way it is. He is in *her* hands being crushed, having the breath pushed out of his lungs. After all that he has done to the bird while asking the bird to trust him, he is now in the hands of the bird. He is helpless. He has given her the power to blow his life to bits. She has taken up her musket and it is loaded.

He has asked her for something; what, he does not exactly know. Perhaps simply to give her life to him, and to his aims. She has said no. Yet he remembers that she asked him if she could come with him, to the wild. *Impossible.* But Maria is his because of the fire he harbours for her small self. The only impossibility is that she should refuse him. He has created her with his desire, and therefore how can she escape?

Yet she attempts to. She writes these terrible words, these cool words, these words of dismissal or at least of bargaining — that she would only be his if he were free and he is not free.

But one cannot bargain with destiny and she is his destiny. As he is hers, he admonishes.

"You have a wife!" she said once.

"Of course I do. Men do have wives in this world. It is not in the nature of man to be free," he'd replied.

He regrets this remark now. Look how he tried to be.

"I am as you found me, as you discovered me, a man with a cause, a man driven forward by the need to accomplish his enormous task. Encumbered and made possible by wife and family, aided and yet struck dumb by the very existence of these others who took their name from me. It was not only reputation and ambition that drove me forward, but debt and need. Lest it be forgotten."

"I shall be an artist too," she said that day. With you or without you. Did she say that too?

"But you are an artist," he replied. "You help me. What more can you want?"

She had laughed. "My name does not appear on the prints with your name. I want what you want," she said. (*But for myself.*)

Did she want acknowledgement, was that it? It so often came down to that. With those who helped him. Bachman, his assistants, even Johnny seemed to want to put their name to the work they did for him. It would not be. The Work was his.

"To struggle," she said, "in the world, not under this arbour. Not under your name."

There it was again.

He tried to explain. To struggle is not interesting. It is not to be sought. All living things struggle. He has struggled. She is protected from that.

It is Maria's duty to be unattached, suspended in the amber of his longing. Maria is his right and his reward. It is incomprehensible that she should reject this construction and yet she does.

Audubon is as angry with Maria, brown sparrow woman in her modest dress, sewn into it so that is tight over her tiny bosom, as he is with his friend John Bachman.

He imagines in Maria a calculation, a craftiness. What ambition is hidden there, masked with duty, under the need to please? She must please, for her survival. Please her keepers, her sister, her sister's husband, even the children. She must be the one who cares for others. Or does she only pretend to be pliant? The little person he adored, whom he believed he knew better than anyone in the world, that adoring listening admiring self, turns its upright little back.

He glimpses in her a totally private being with a separate destiny, despite the helpless openness at which he marvels. Despite the fact that he has practically made her. But she is not completed. He is not finished with her and he is not ready to let her go. He will teach her, one day perhaps, to follow her passion. To forsake that which is false, that which one does not truly love. He is not ready to hear her say no to him. Will she take his teachings and apply them against him?

No. She is Maria. Winsome, tender and submissive.

He crumples the letter in his hand. Calls to the young gentlemen: "I wish to give a return letter to the *Wizard*."

"There is no point," says Johnny, reading his mood. "We'll be home before she is."

"I wish to send a reply."

"Yes, Father."

He sits at his deal table under the hatch. It is miserably cold. There is no tea at this hour of the night. He has again sworn off tobacco and grog. His clothing is damp and his hammock contains no attractions for him. What else to do but write? And as he writes, it is as if he is speaking to himself, in the habit he has developed over time. He addresses his words to John Bachman. (There are no words for Maria just now.)

"I cannot imagine," he writes, in his black spidery hand, with small ink splotches decorating the page that he can barely see, "what you have to do with my letters to Miss Martin. I think you will discover that I shall send her kisses and affection and will feel as much love for her as she will permit me to do regardless of your thoughts on the subject!"

He writes, or he does not write. He will quarrel, later, with Bachman about many things, about Maria, about his drinking, which will become an offence to the preacher, about their collaboration. He hands the letter to Johnny.

"Are you certain, Father, that this letter must go?"

Johnny tries to ward off trouble. And in doing so brings it down on himself.

"I am quite certain, young man. Who are you to question me? Do as you are told! You've given me enough trouble already, losing birds and falling off cliffs. If you are not careful I'll leave you at home on our next expedition!" On he rails as Johnny backs away, letter in hand.

Audubon watches his son row into the gloom with grim satisfaction. Now he has given Bachman an earful. Now his dearest friend the preacher has something to think about. Perhaps it will create a rift. It does not matter. All that matters is that he is on shipboard, while John Bachman is at home, pampered, surrounded by blossom and leaf, by scent and stem, attended to by the soft fingers of his women, and Audubon — equally deserving, somehow, of the attentions of the women of that family, although it is not his own family, equally deserving of all of his friend's comforts, is cold and alone and frustrated in the wilderness.

ACCIDENTAL

Sailing southward, southward at last! Never so happy to leave a coastline behind, Audubon watches from the stern. The inland plateaus vanish under their burden of cloud. To his left the iceberg weeps green water down its prismatic flanks. Its journey is southward to warmer water, which will diminish it until it heaves and disappears under the surface.

They are heading to the Dominion of Newfoundland. Godwin's land.

"And are they all like you, there?" Audubon says to the pilot, whose face is pulled sideways by a plug of tobacco.

"Aye, every last one of 'em. Cut from the same cloth."

Audubon knows the man is joking though there is no hint on his face or in his voice. It is in the way the words fall. At long last he understands the accent.

"What cloth would that be then Mr. Godwin?"

"Well, you tell me."

Called upon for a description, Audubon is at a loss. What cloth is Godwin cut from? He has seen savagery but is not a savage. Knows death and would like to avoid it as long as possible, but does not exactly fear it. He is not a slave, although born to circumstances that would enslave others. The words "acquainted with grief" form in his mind. It is a bond. But he cannot say it.

"You would be one of a kind — that's as near as I can get," says Audubon.

"You could paint me, I suppose," Godwin says. "You might get nearer."

Ah, a hint of vanity. "You are human then."

He brings his watercolours on deck and makes a likeness of the man with his walking stick made of a shark's vertebrae. He paints him weathered, squinting, with eyes that could bore holes in buffalo hide, short stubby fingers with surprising dexterity, the barrel chest, the lively bitten lips which spit out their incomprehensible vowels and turn either up or down in an instant. He finds intelligence there and good humour, the patience of one who is constantly mistaken for an idiot, and something else, peace. The man is at peace with all he has seen.

"I thank you for it, sir," says Godwin, showing scant pleasure. "You shall see me present it to my wife, so she can see my likeness when I am at sea."

"Are we going to see your wife? Is that the one port you will put in?"

"The best harbour this side of the island."

They fly before a good wind across the Strait to the west coast of Newfoundland, and Labrador disappears behind them in its vapours.

ON AUGUST 13 they sail around a rocky point and into the tickle of St. George's Bay to find a snug outport lined with houses, maybe thirty of them, and fishing dories, and grass and flowers, a settlement such as they have not seen for weeks. Well before the *Ripley* lands, the locals start down to the water in welcome. When the boat is secure, Godwin steps down to cheers and embraces from half the populace, a warmth which is soon extended to all on the *Ripley*.

Audubon is soon off for a walk over the hills. He must search to see if there are any more birds; he has only five new species, a paltry number considering the risk they've undergone. Looking out over the choppy waters from a mad network of trails through violent green moss, Audubon sees a shy shearwater and some oystercatchers with their needle-like red beaks, puffins flying with laden bill, but nothing new. Inland, there is more of the quagmire, to which he gives a wide berth, and plenty of the pitcher plant. Returning on the path, he meets a girl. She hikes with two loaves of bread under one arm and a bucket in the other hand. He steps aside to let her pass. But she stands face to him, boldly examining him head to toe.

"Are you the famous artist, then?" she says.

"I'm forced to admit to it."

She stares at him. "You are looking for more birds? I saw you go up the hill."

"I am. You did."

"You are painting our birds, then, for the people across the sea?"

"That is indeed what I am doing. Do I have your permission?" He asks, head cocked sideways to tease.

"You didn't ask it, did you, before you began? I think it's too late now," she says seriously and goes on her way.

LACK OF WIND keeps them in the harbour for a second day, which is, it so happens, the day of the Fisherman's Ball. He finds and shoots a magnificent frigatebird, knowing it by the red patch under its bill, which it blows to a fine red balloon when it is displaying. The bird has no business in these parts and he concludes it is very lost. The girl is on his heels again as he returns to the path.

"What's that bird, then? I never saw one near here," she says. "Did you bring it with you?"

"No, my dear," he says. "It is an exotic, an accidental bird driven by a hurricane into your cove."

"We gets a lot like that," she says.

He laughs. "I am one too." He points his toe as if to show a fine leg, in his hairy fisherman's trousers. A flirt. She wrinkles her nose to show that she is not impressed.

"We get the boats too, sometimes. The big storms to the south blows all manner of creatures our way." She looks at him accusingly. "Tell me what else you can see when you go out to the Labrador in your schooner."

"You can see the masts of a hundred ships and know that each hold is stuffed to the top with cod. You know that the ship will not leave these waters until it is near to sinking with fish drained from the sea."

"I have seen that," she said.

"I saw the Foolish Guillemots that you call 'murres' careen around the topsail so thickly that we heard them bounce off the canvas. I heard the laughter and the singing of Italian fishermen in the long, pale night. Men who have chased down and dragged in the giant whales, slicing their bloody carcasses on the shore. White bears riding down from the north on ice floes."

"You didn't."

He hangs his head and winks. "I didn't. But I heard tell." He lifts his head, brightening; his face glows with the thought of it. "I saw clouds of curlews arriving, it went on for days and days."

"You did," she allows.

"And a new sparrow that I named for my friend, Tom Lincoln. It is a near relation to the song sparrow but with finer markings on its breast and back. It was very shy, and had a song of great beauty and variety."

"Did it not already have its name before you come along?"

"Maybe it did, now that I think on it," he laughs. "I heard too the jingling tune of the Winter Wren. Like silver sleighbells," he said. "And also the lovestruck warble of the Purple Finch. You must know it, all trills and deep flute-like notes."

He saw the Horned Lark, its golden-speckled young on the wing, the adults sky-larking up in the sky. It pushed itself up in circles to six hundred feet until it was a tiny speck in the sky. It sang the whole while at first, but later only in bursts, stopping to flap its wings and get its breath.

"I saw the fogs reduce all to nothingness."

"I sees that all the time," she says.

"I saw the great Black-backed Gull feasting on the rotting flesh on the back of a whale's carcass," he says.

She shudders. "That's disgusting."

"Oh, and much more: the Caspian Tern, the Hudsonian Curlew, the Spotted Sandpiper that you call beachies. And I heard the guillemots streaming through the air, their voices in concert making a long-drawn wail, which might have been the baa-ing of newborn lambs."

"Ah," she says, "I have heard that too and not known how to describe it."

"What puzzles me is how each one recognizes its own egg. What do you think? By smell? I don't believe birds can smell a thing. I've been having a big fight with other men about that," he says, thinking of the Turkey Vulture and its prey. It sounds silly when he says it out loud.

"And here's a story for you. I saw, on a calm day with the sea heavy from a storm the night before, a schooner nearly smash itself to pieces on the rocks. The men, thinking she was lost, jumped ashore. No sooner were they off her deck and out of reach than a gust of wind came along and their schooner sailed off smartly all on her own!"

"I don't believe that story," she says.

"I saw it with my own eyes. I thought it was an omen, that I might die there. But then the schooner was captured by a friendly vessel and brought back to her crew."

"You're pulling my leg for sure," she said.

"On my honour I am not. It plays upon the senses, this land of yours, and over there too, the air and the water, the wild, the strange light."

"Tell me more."

"Do you know the Razor-billed Auk you call tinkers? They sit upright in solemn lines facing each other as if having a parliament, with their long tails and roman noses? When they're courting they show red feet and a scarlet lining in their mouth. Oh, and here's a thing. I wager you've never seen this — mysterious beaches hundreds of feet above the water, with beds of small round stones. What could they be?"

"I don't know," she says. "There must be some way to explain it."

"I am not so certain," says Audubon. "There may be no explanation. There are great jewels there and no one to say who owns them. The Ruby-crowned Kinglet. The Golden-eyed Ducks. The Lords and Ladies because of their fancy plumage. There is a place called La Tabatière, which means a snuff box in French but it really isn't that, for the word comes from the Montagnais Indian and means sorcerer. In Bras d'Or lives a certain Mr. Jones with forty dogs."

"Forty dogs?"

"Well, quite a few. Before you know it he'll have a player piano too, for his wife. He is happy to have no society for hundreds of miles, free, as he said, from lawyers, and from taxes. His may be the greatest riches of all."

"You're a great talker, you are," says the girl.

Then she steps aside and lets him pass.

ALL DAY THE WOMEN and children have been producing food —
berry pies and high white buns and dishes made of cod and potato.
The men stand on ladders, stringing ropes made of braided flowers
from the rooflines. They hang the doorposts of the little houses and
the posts of the fishing sheds with orange paper lanterns. The sun sets
earlier now, by seven o'clock, in contrast to the long evenings of earlier
in the summer. When darkness falls the lamps are lit and doorways
stand open, girls in ruffled dresses lining the steps.

"There's nothing but girls in St. George's," says Johnny. "The men
are all dead or fishing."

Sounds of fiddles being tuned come across the water to the *Ripley*;
it is like the warmup to a play. The young gentlemen stand on deck
with bowls of water warmed on the stove, shaving their beards. Johnny
brings his father's cleanest shirt.

"I must take myself to bed," Audubon protests.

"No, you cannot, Father. You are the guest of honour. And you are
wanted to play the tunes," says Johnny.

"But I must write my notes before sleep. You play in my place."

Johnny's face is a mask. Play in my place. Paint in my place. Calm
your mother, in my place. "Leave the notes for once," he says, turning
sharply on his heel. "We'll be having a time." He has picked up the
Labrador term for a party.

Each fisherman's salt-box house is made by himself and for himself. On the stoops the men sit tuning their fiddles while the boys tend
fires to cook the fish. In the light of the whale-oil lamps, the women
are ruddy and bold.

As Audubon walks on his stiff cold legs, carrying his flageolet
in its cloth bag tucked in his waistcoat, his mind revisits the grand
parties in England. The terrifying ladies in red turbans, the footmen
with white wigs. The ancient gleaming tapestries and the towering
silver candelabra. He remembers the Duc d'Orléans in France, himself arriving in his fur hat and smelling of bear grease to show he

was a frontiersman, only to encounter D'Orbigny's son from Coueron to prove he was not. Past lives pursue him: he doesn't know whether to laugh or to cry. The world is very large, but it has never been large enough.

It would hardly seem odd if tonight at this ball he found Charles Bonaparte, with his letters steeped in vinegar sent from plague-ridden Italy. Or Vincent Nolte himself, that imp of rebirth whose shadow has prefigured Audubon's rising and falling for the past twenty years. He must not fall again. This is the real fear.

But there are only the girls, bursting from their dresses. They take drink as strong as that of the men. He looks for the ones with the beautiful calm faces and intelligent eyes. These girls can be found everywhere; it is one of the wonders of life.

As a consequence of the brew, the party grows boisterous. While Johnny and the others fiddle, the dancers form lines and circles and tap their feet with great cleverness while musicmakers sit and make an elaborate clatter with spoons. Tom Lincoln and Ingalls and Shattuck allow themselves to be led into steps they've never seen before, the closest thing being an Irish jig or an English reel.

And Audubon dreams with his flageolet against his lips. He has survived Labrador, it seems. Soon he will see Lucy again. And soon after that, Maria.

His girl from the hillside materializes.

"What are you wanting then, Mary," someone jeers.

"This one. I want to dance with him."

Audubon has not shaved for weeks. His woollen trousers are worn threadbare, patched, and worn again. His face is windburnt, his fingers stained and rough. Several of his last remaining teeth have disappeared this summer and he thinks, although he cannot be sure, that his eyes are clouded over with grey. They certainly feel it.

"On my behalf, my son would be delighted to dance with you," he says, gesturing to Johnny.

"But it is you I am asking."

"All right then," he says. "I am charmed." And he rises.

The young gentlemen cheer.

His shoulders go back, his chest up, and air fills the space under his ribcage. He towers over these little people. Up there near the rafters his head goes blank. He has no idea how to dance, suddenly. But the dancing master's legs do not fail him and his feet find the patterns of their own accord. The muscles recall what the brain lets go. He sees Godwin prowling the edges of the party, evil spirit or guardian angel. The girl is graceful and never takes her eyes off him. "I could be your grandfather," he says to her and she smiles widely, showing a gap between her front teeth.

> *So gentle was this pretty maid, she did her duty well;*
> *Then what followed next, me boys, the song itself will tell:*
> *The captain and this pretty maid did oftimes kiss and toy,*
> *For he soon found out the secret of the handsome cabin boy.*

AFTER THE DANCING Johnny persuades him to play again. He can fiddle with either hand — a party trick — draw either way too; he is perfectly ambidextrous. There on the stoop of the house overlooking the monstrous sea he plays his tunes, one, two, three of them, until he begs to go back to the ship.

"I'll walk you back, Father."

"No, stay, Johnny. The girls will be bereft."

"I will walk with him," says young Mary with her intelligent eyes, but her mother pulls her away from him, and then Godwin is waiting to take his arm.

Am I unsteady? thinks Audubon. Surely not.

They go silently together along the shore to the gangplank of the schooner and Godwin leads him up it. Audubon squeezes his forearm.

"I trust thee," he says. He has used his oldest and most intimate form of address, the one he uses to address Lucy. "Though at first I thought ye the devil. I fancy our friend Nolte sent you to look after me."

"Are ye certain then?" says Godwin. "I've many a lie left to tell you." He says lie so that it rhymes with boy.

They laugh together as Audubon steps onto the gangplank. Then Godwin melts into the dark as is his habit and suddenly the girl is there.

"Can you show me your pictures, then," she says.

"It is too dark to see them properly."

"I can see in the dark."

"Ah. I have no doubt you can."

"It isn't truly dark. Only half so."

He lights the candles on his deal table. As he unrolls the paintings he feels an immense weariness. The terrible hours of the summer weigh on him, the darkness, the cold, the wet, his tired eyes. The weariness, and the pride. "My birds," he says simply.

There they are. Twenty-three of them, life size. Some over two feet across and three feet high. Others small and delicate and detailed. Resplendent and supremely unaware of their audience, bird by bird, they go about their business.

She stands stolid, the dampness still at her temples from the hornpipe. "Say the names," she commands.

He says the names. Red-throated Diver. Willow Ptarmigan. Black-backed gull. Eider Duck. Horned Shore Lark. Labrador Gyrfalcon.

Her eyes are huge. They seem in the candlelight to be full of tears but he is not certain. Like a blaze the paintings unfurl. Gannet. White-winged Crossbill. Arctic Tern. Puffin. Harlequin Duck.

At each name she exhales in recognition. Until there are no more. The drawings in their pile flutter in the drafts of the hold.

Her hands rise to her waist and she reaches for something, the bird, or him. "I have no clever words," she says. "They're grand, I know."

He bows.

"So like to themselves they are," she says. "Only more so."

"Ah," he says. "You need never worry. It is the right thing to say. I am so pleased that you find them so." He has always needed this. The new shore. The bird to worship. And the young woman to worship him.

He feels the strange shame that comes upon him when he is admired. It was this way in Edinburgh, when the papers printed glowing accounts. He could not show his face.

"Go back, child," he says. "It is late at night for you to be out."

She takes a last long look at the Lords and Ladies, and leaves.

THEY ARE SINGING, across the water. He wraps himself in his robe and lies on the deck. In his hand he holds not an egg but a stone, one which Bayfield gave him, a stone without a name, a green stone found on a beach. He thinks he sees a schooner, black, looking like a man-of-war, slide through the tickle where, sails slack, it comes to a standstill and drops anchor.

Captain Bayfield is up the mast in the white billows of moist air. Below him, the chains of the anchor rattle. The sailors pull the heavy iron links, which fall like hammer blows in the muffled air. Then there is a trill of these blows, a long rattling song of them as the anchor plunges through the water to find a hold on bottom.

Audubon hails his friend through the fog. Mast to mast, schooner to schooner, mooring to mooring. Sir! Well met, again! How do you fare?

But the black schooner is not there.

It is the music that undoes him. The stone is warm now from his hand; he presses it against his heart. He turns the mass of it in his palm. It is heavy and smooth, preserved in layers. Some life has been entombed in it. He feels love, strong as grief, like a slow bleed.

He thinks of those he loves.

Lucy, of course. His dearest best beloved.

Johnny, his son, the wild one who must be tamed.

Victor, the elder, the angry one.

The two baby girls, dead.

Maria, a child too, a dangerous child.

Birds.

And who has he forgotten?

The ship rocks on its anchor.

He is Monsieur Newhouse and he is handed off the ship into France, into the arms of a man he knows as his Papa and a woman who says he must call her Maman. He lets the woman lift him up. He goes still as a squirrel. His feet dangle at her knees. His empty little boy heart is all he can offer. He lets his head lean on her bosom. The heart inside his shirt taps away like a little clapper inside a bell.

Maman, he tries.

He must win her, he knows. She must love him, otherwise they may pack him off again on another ship, with another false name, and some cabin boy following him to make sure he does not fall overboard, and teasing him when he cries. The hideous and endless rocking.

When she puts him down, he takes her hand in his and holds it carefully, like a precious thing, and stands very quietly. At home, she sits with him in the garden and shows him the birds that come for the crumbs, telling him the names of the ones she knows. And when he jumps up to run after the cardinal she stands with one hand over her brow, watching after him. When it seems he will get out of sight she calls — Jean Jacques!

She calls him and he stops and turns back. But there is another call from the depths of the trees. The birds! (Even now he hears them calling, hears the rush and thunder of their wings. The birds, the mysterious birds, whose beauty has filled his days and years. In their shadow he will spend his life's allotment.) He is looking over his shoulder at her standing there looking after him from under her shading hand, in the sunlight, even as he runs from her, a delighted boy, knowing she will love him and she will wait for him.

THE SOUND OF REVELRY is loud in his ears. Nature will not die before I do, he thinks. I shall complete the Work, I shall be a famous man. My family will rest secure in my fortune and those birds shall have their monument — he thinks of his great Work now as a memorial as much as a discovery — and those who come afterward will be grateful to me. And with that, he falls into a deep sleep in which the songs and the dancing and the laughter play on until long past the dark, and when the dawn comes as usual he rouses himself, goes to the hold and sits at his table to paint as the young gentlemen come in from the ball.

"I shall complete the Work, I shall be a famous man."

The past is fantastical. Women in red turbans loiter under painted ceilings amid footmen with white wigs. A hunter in fringe strides over London hills with one hundred pounds of Art on his back. There are, wobbling in little rowboats on the breast of the deep, men in blue serge holding metal arches to the stars. A genial, nagging pastor with a sweetheart sister-in-law, and kitchen slaves named Venus and Adonis. There are double-crested cormorants in bachelor tiers; sounding machines made of chain and lead balls; iron beds set up in the middle of nowhere, with cups and saucers laid out for tea.

Fantastical. But is it imaginary?

Are the birds, *Drawn from Nature by J. J. Audubon*, a fantasy?

Is Bayfield's coast a fantasy?

Is the fecundity of the past a fantasy? Dolphins that skip across the surface of the water, a barrel of salmon in an afternoon, clouds of curlews descending to strip the berries off the bushes in a matter of minutes, a strait running with cod where the gleaming black backs of whales breach and clip the surface like so many scythes?

Does this exist anywhere outside of our imaginations? Did it ever exist? Codfish thrown on the deck by the thousands, a certain Mr. Jones who had or did not have forty dogs and lived a modest ambition, to be free from lawyers? Phalanxes of foolish guillemot greeting the European boot where it steps on the rock. Velvet moss, so deep you sink to your knees, growing in a teacupful of soil.

Say the names: Natashquan, Kégashka, La Romaine, Mutton Bay, La Tabatière, Petit Mécatina, Gros Mécatina, Bras d'Or, Blanc-Sablon.

Audubon Island. Bayfield Island. The Strait of Belle Isle, a transit to a fabled past. Giant mammals once bored through it, leaping in black arcs to the harpoon. The sky was a torrent of birds. And under it, yes, are the shadows of those adventuring men who, at the time decreed by thirteen carefully watched chronometers, came to this place. Came believing themselves agents of God and of Art.

Two men, two missions, each a vector of his time and ours. Audubon came to record the creatures and left wishing to preserve them. Bayfield tried to make the waters safe in the only part of the world where north is down and south is up, believing that the wilderness in man and in the world might be measured and brought into our ken. But the passage was fraught with peril. Men and weather have evil moods, and the future was beyond any power to chart.

Audubon's Birds still glitter 170 years later, while the creatures he watched in nature are gone. For it came to pass as Audubon predicted. The fish were drained from the sea and the clouds of birds failed to return and the native people fell prey to despair. The wild habitats were eroded and it was this as much as the destruction of eggs and the indiscriminate shooting that extinguished the wild creatures. As Audubon suspected, man could not be moved to pity the birds. He saw the future and it was terrifying; he saw the wilderness made barren, and then he went out and shot twenty-seven puffins for sport. He saved the birds in art, and that was all he could do.

What are the facts? Godwin, saturnine with his plug of tobacco, steps from the foredeck. Where is the shoreline? We can't trust these charts. They are inventions. I need to know what is there. I cannot steer the ship and read them too!

HERE ARE THE FACTS:

When Audubon reached New York in September 1833 after his return from Labrador, he found that Bachman had got there before him. He had persuaded Lucy that the family should spend the winter in Charleston, where they would all help Audubon with his birds. Audubon was only too happy to comply. He wrote Victor to buy him a new gun, put Johnny on a ship to Charleston and set out by land with Lucy for the house on Rutledge Avenue, the garden, and Maria, planning to deliver numbers and collect dues along the way.

In Philadelphia he was arrested for his old Kentucky debts, and jailed. Lucy raised bail and they proceeded on their way, stopping in Washington to see the president. In Charleston, Lucy took over Maria's task of teaching the children French while Bachman, Audubon and their sweetheart worked together in the study. For the next half-year they painted and wrote; Lucy transcribed her husband's Labrador journals for the letterpress. By July 1834 they were able to ship twenty-five completed paintings to Robert Havell.

During this time John Woodhouse fell in love with Bachman's seventeen-year-old daughter, another Maria. Victor begged for his father's presence in London, until reluctantly Audubon sailed with Lucy and John, who was unhappy to be separated from his intended bride.

Maria Martin had waited three years, often in the company of the man she loved, painting with him, laughing and teasing on garden walks, giving him an intimacy that surrendered all and demanded little.

And then she left him, as he had known she would. In doing so, she abandoned Audubon to his wife and his children, in short, to the people who loved him. It was a severe, perhaps fatal, blow to the heart. She was his last young woman, his last rapture, and his last bird. After her fecund sister Harriet died, Maria Martin married her other old man, her brother-in-law John Bachman, the Lutheran pastor. He was righteous and scolding; she had nursed him and been his scribe, and she would do so until he died.

In London, the Audubons lived briefly on Wimpole Street at the centre of a social whirl; the newspapers covered their arrivals and departures. Victor had a love affair with Adelaide Kemble, daughter of the actress Fanny who had likened his father to Byron. Lieutenant Augustus Bowen of the *Gulnare*, chastened after the Labrador journey, and without the promotion he had hoped for, brought around his godfather, the aforementioned Duke of Sussex. The duke wanted Parliament to buy a copy of the *Birds*, but Audubon did not pursue it.

He saw the duke as a flatterer, and did not forget that the British Museum had fallen behind on its subscription. Vincent Nolte, having lost his second fortune, passed through in pursuit of a third, this one to be made in the production of medallions of royalty.

On June 20, 1838, Robert Havell completed the last plate for Audubon's *Birds of America*. It featured two dippers which had been shot on the Columbia River; he invented for them a backdrop of rocks and rapids. He could hardly bear to turn the page on the land of his conjuring.

The Birds of America exists as the monument Audubon intended it to be, the monument to which he gave his life and the lives of his family. Less than two hundred copies were printed, of which 110 are known to survive. Each original subscription was accompanied by an advance payment of $220; all five folios, complete with 435 double elephant-sized prints, cost a subscriber one thousand dollars, most of which was never collected. Audubon spent more than a hundred thousand in producing the book.

WHEN THE FAMILY returned to America, Victor finally got to Charleston to meet the Bachmans. He too fell in love with one of John Bachman's daughters, Eliza. Both sons married their beloveds, but within a few years, both young brides died of tuberculosis. Johnny's wife, Maria, left two daughters for Lucy to raise, eerily replacing the girl children she had lost in their infancy. Bachman was devastated by the loss of his daughters. The friendship with Audubon, sorely tried by these losses, by the incidents with Maria Martin, and by the artist's drinking, never recovered.

Between 1840 and 1844, the Audubon family published an octavo, or miniature version, of *The Birds of America,* an endeavour which brought in profits for the first time in Audubon's publishing history. In 1842, Lucy and John James bought twenty-four rural acres overlooking the Hudson River at 155th Street in New York; they called it Minnie's Land, after his pet name for his wife. Audubon began work with Bachman on another huge project, *The Viviparous Quadrupeds of North America,* which in the end was completed by Johnny.

The great man grew old. Was astonished by the sight of his face in mirrors, unable to believe he had been forsaken by beauty, especially his own.

Beauty is unfair.

Beauty is poison.

HE TOOK HIS LAST JOURNEY in search of quadrupeds to the eastern banks of the Missouri in 1843, where he predicted the demise of the buffalo. In his famous portrait, John Woodhouse captured the white-haired man on his return to Minnie's Land, wearing his green coat with the fur-lined collar, now gentle-eyed and even distinguished.

The journey west to the Pacific was left to Johnny, who in 1849 rode out to the California gold rush as second-in-command of a contingent of one hundred men. His party was struck by cholera; the leader deserted, leaving Johnny to shepherd the thirty-eight surviving men across the Gila Desert to San Francisco, where they discovered they were too late for the gold. He returned home minus all his funds, without a gram of the precious metal, and his father did not recognize him.

Around his sixty-second birthday, Audubon had another of the little strokes that began, it seems, after he killed the golden eagle. He lost his sight, after which he became childlike, at once a great man and a relic. He asked the same questions over and over. He wanted lullabies sung to him. He took whiskey with his meals and hated the smell of rosewater. He stopped writing in his journal. He left his words to Lucy and his work to Johnny. In the end, the Holy Alliance owned him just as surely as he had owned them. And with equal parts pride and anger.

As Bayfield predicted, he returned, in what remained of his mind, to the shores of Labrador. He wanted to visit Mr. and Mrs. Jones and hear their player piano, to drink the good coffee in bowls in the cabins of the French-Canadians, and to see the Montagnais in their French liberty caps and striped leggings, the crucifixes at their necks.

Maria Martin did not find her wilderness. She continued to paint, but never with the intensity of her time with Audubon. Watercolours of the plants and of the Snowy Egret survive in the Charleston Museum, as does an embroidered reticule on which she painted flowers. There is, as well, a piano stool given her by John Audubon. She never received full credit in her lifetime for her work, although she is thought to have contributed to at least twenty of the prints in *The Birds*. Audubon named a woodpecker for her: Maria's Woodpecker. But the name did not survive. As the girl in Newfoundland had wondered, some birds, like this one, had a name already, and so even this gesture of acknowledgement was lost.

In 1839, Robert Havell closed the shop at 77 Oxford Street, which had been in the family for three generations, and emigrated to America. He fell out with Audubon over money, but found a new life in the country he had so long imagined. He settled in the Hudson River Valley, at Tarry Town, where he painted and sketched the area we know through the writings of Washington Irving. He is buried in Sleepy Hollow Cemetery.

Henry Bayfield continued to chart the coast of Labrador and the Gulf of the St. Lawrence, a task which ultimately took him fourteen years. His *Sailing Directions for the Gulf and River of St. Lawrence* was published in 1837, reprinted in 1840, and many times subsequently.

Five years after meeting Audubon, and at the age of forty-four, Bayfield married Fanny Amelia Wright. His wife was the daughter of a captain of the Royal Engineers, twenty-five years old at the time. The couple settled in Charlottetown, Prince Edward Island, and had six children. Captain, later Admiral, Bayfield was very proud that Fanny was an accomplished artist: her watercolours of wildflowers (*Trillium, Blood Root and Dog's Tooth Violet* is one plate) can be found in the Public Archives of Canada.

Bayfield lived to be ninety-three and died in his bed, having "worn himself out in the service of his country." He was renowned but not famous and had given his name to scores of towns, inlets, and waterways in the Great Lakes and Atlantic seaboard of Canada. He never ceased trying to prevent loss of life from shipwreck. In his last years, his mind, too, rambled. When met abroad on the streets, he raved about the shores of Labrador, enumerating the distinguishing features of the fogs which arose from the east, the southeast, and the north, their textures, thickness, heights and probable durations.

By the time of his death in 1851, Audubon had no control over his names. Having outlived most his enemies, he was at last more famous than reviled. But his name was given as Anderson in the death notice in New York's *Evening Post*, which may account for the small group which gathered to bury him. (The press had already announced his death in 1831, mistaking him for Alexander Wilson, who had in fact died in 1813.) The cemetery in which he was buried was moved. Some fifty years later donors raised a tall cross over his grave; on it his birth date is wrong.

His granddaughter removed from his writings many personal references, presumably to his indiscretions, and also to his origins.

THE CHART ONLY GIVES ME half the story, says Godwin. The water changes and the weather is unpredictable. The fog blankets us. I won't endanger the ship on the strength of these measurements!

Audubon asks Bayfield, You believe that human life is sacred, while animals' lives are for our use — but what if you are wrong? What if we are not better than nature? What if we are worse?

Bayfield answers, his thumbs in a perfect triangle under his chin. The wilderness is in us and in the world. It must be brought into our ken. In this way we may avoid savagery. We who are leaders have a duty to lead.

The fog swirls up, threatening to swallow the ship. Audubon speaks. You think so well of man. Can man be moved to pity the birds? To imagine their extinction?

Bayfield feels across his chest for the pocket, and pulls out his timepiece. Time will tell.

Now Bayfield asks Andubon a simpler, harder question. And you, sir, he says. Who are you?

I am a man sent from the future to catalogue the birds before they disappear. A reluctant prophet, a gate-crasher. Even when storming the doors I have to flout the rules. Even when proving myself worthy I must prove myself unworthy. I am a lie. I have stumbled into truth by watching the creatures. Perhaps only I — born out of bounds, unable to be in bounds — could do that.

A LIE IS A SPARK, a break and a reconnection. A way of dissembling, of taking things to pieces.

Audubon was a vessel. On his midlife voyage, with his hopes and his premonitions of doom, he was boarded by an unwelcome idea: the idea of the death of nature at man's hands.

The shoreline is a narrative.

The fog is fog, what we try to see through.

The wind has begun to move the ropes; both men can feel the ship nudging its anchors, ready to move. They stand.

I must get back to my birds, says Audubon.

HIS BIRDS THAT SUMMER. The Labrador Duck: last seen 1875, extinct. The Great Auk: last seen 1844, extinct. The Eskimo Curlew: observed by Audubon in Labrador arriving in dense clouds, "flock after flock increasing in number for several days," last seen in 1964, presumed extinct. The Atlantic Puffin: successfully reintroduced to Maine and Eastern Canada through nesting pairs.

ILLUSTRATION CREDITS

Every effort has been made to contact copyright holders. In the event of an omission or error, please notify the publisher.

p. 157 Audubon Prints Shipping Box. Neg. No. 325312 Photo. Rota. Courtesy Dept. of Library Services, American Museum of Natural History.

p. 173 From *Common Cormorant* by J. J. Audubon. Havell No. CCLXVI. With thanks to the Toronto Reference Library.

p. 193 Surveying Boats in Chateau Bay, Labrador, July 1833. Sketched by A. F. J. Bowen, Assistant Surveyor. Reproduced with thanks to the Champlain Society. Image held by the Controller of HM Stationery Office and the Hydrographer of the Navy.

p. 227 Photo courtesy of the author.

p. 247 Maria Martin Bachman. Permission granted by the Charleston Museum Collections.

p. 249 From *American White Pelican* by J. J. Audubon. Havell No. CCCXI. With thanks to the Toronto Reference Library.

p. 257 Illustration from *Traité des manières de graver* by Abraham Bosse. Courtesy of the Thomas Fisher Rare Books Library, University of Toronto.

p. 295 *John James Audubon.* Painted by J. Woodhouse Audubon, ca. 1843. Neg. No. 332695 Photo. Logan. Courtesy Dept. of Library Services, American Museum of Natural History.

ACKNOWLEDGEMENTS

M any, many people have helped me in the preparation of this
novel. It is a book that has truly "taken a village" to be brought
to life.

I would first like to thank David Kotin, Special Collections of the
Toronto Public Library, for showing me the library's copy of *The Birds
of America*. The power of the images, now 170 years old, set me on this
journey. The Toronto Public Library, through its friendly and helpful
staff, made available to me its extensive collection of Audubon papers,
and I passed many pleasurable hours reading in the Baldwin Room. The
scholar and collector, David Lank of Montreal, expressed enthusiasm
for the idea of a book based in Audubon's time in Labrador, and read
the final manuscript, sharing with me his broad knowledge of birds and
birds in art. Joan Winnearls helped me unearth details of the aqua-
tinting process, and John Pratt of St. John's, Newfoundland, met with
me to discuss bird facts.

I consulted a number of collections, chiefly the Memorial University
of Newfoundland Library; the New-York Historical Society; the
Charleston Museum in Charleston, South Carolina; and the Thomas
Fisher Rare Books Library at the University of Toronto. I acknowledge
my debt to the many publications on Audubon, including Shirley
Streshinsky's *Audubon: Life and Art in the American Wilderness* and
Alice Ford's *John James Audubon: A Biography*, as well as the journals
and letters left by J. J. Audubon, and his *Ornithological Biography*. It
was he who wrote, "Nature itself is perishing." The account of Egging
on the Funks in the nineteenth century comes from *The Newfoundland
Journal of Aaron Thomas*, and was brought to my attention by John

Pratt. I first read an account of the fate of the *Granicus* and its survivors in Captain Bayfield's *Journals.*

I spent an idyllic month at the Banff Centre for the Arts in July 2000,
when I was in the early stages of writing this book. I am grateful to the
Centre and to Michael Ignatieff and the members of the Cultural
Journalism program for their careful reading and responses to my work,
especially Mark Abley, whose special interest in birds was a bonus.

There are many others I want to thank: Mariama LeBlanc for
research into sea shanties; Lannie Messervey for word processing;
Kendall Anderson for picture research; Emily Honderich for her company on the trip to Labrador, and general research; Dr. George Govier
for research into hydrographical surveying and instruments; Norm
Letto of L'Anse-au-Clair, Labrador, who took us out to Île aux
Perroquets in his boat . . . the list goes on. In a class of their own are
my agent, Bruce Westwood, who has loved this novel since before it
was written, and Anne Collins, whose efforts, as always, far exceed the
call of duty. And finally, Nick Rundall, without whose happy engage-
ment in my life I would be so much the poorer.

I cannot close without saluting the legendary surveyor Admiral
Henry Bayfield, who put the waterways of eastern Canada on paper;
and John James Audubon, frontiersman and artist, who drove himself
against great odds to complete his enormous Work, and who left his
name to a cause he was one of the first to understand, that summer in
Labrador.

KATHERINE GOVIER is an acclaimed novelist and short-story writer, who was born and raised in Alberta. She has lived in Washington, D.C., and London, England, and currently lives in Toronto. She has received many honours, among them the Marian Engel Award for a woman writer in mid-career and the City of Toronto Book Award for her novel *Hearts of Flame. Creation* is her seventh novel.